THE
WANDERING
PINE

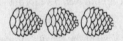

Also by P. O. Enquist in English translation

P. O. ENQUIST

THE WANDERING PINE

Life as a Novel

Translated from the Swedish by
Deborah Bragan-Turner

MACLEHOSE PRESS
QUERCUS – LONDON

First published in the Swedish language as *Ett Annat Liv* by Norstedts, Stockholm, in 2008
First published in Great Britain in 2015 by MacLehose Press
This paperback edition published in 2016 by

MacLehose Press
an imprint of Quercus Editions Limited
Carmelite House
50 Victoria Embankment
London EC4Y 0DZ

An Hachette UK Company

Published by agreement with Norstedts Agency
Copyright © P. O. Enquist, 2008
English translation copyright © 2015 by Deborah Bragan-Turner

A CIP catalogue record for this book is available
from the British Library.

ISBN (MMP) 978 1 78087 019 9
ISBN (Ebook) 978 1 78087 018 2

10 9 8 7 6 5 4 3 2 1

Designed and typeset in Cycles by Libanus Press, Marlborough
Printed and bound in Great Britain by Clays Ltd, St Ives plc

THE WANDERING PINE

STARTING POINT

December 1989, a clear Icelandic night. The stars are visible, but not the Northern Lights.

Where did they go?

At about four in the afternoon on 14 April 1998 he goes past the disused railway station in Skellefteå. He walks slowly, to avoid attention, and sees three men sitting on the steps.

He recognises him instantly. Jurma. Light rain is falling.

He feels an ache. It takes a few seconds before he realises what it is. Then, as ever, he begins to think about something else, a survival mechanism: he recalls a similar scene, from the film *Philadelphia*, or perhaps from Bruce Springsteen's music video for the film. Springsteen is walking along a street next to a factory, through a desolate landscape, maybe the factory has closed down; he is walking slowly without turning round. You have the impression that the three men sitting watching him must have been his friends when he was young, but they have remained where they were, while he has moved on.

They did not call out to him to stay around.

As a general rule, the people left behind avoid the ones who move away. So what was it like to stay there? The three men outside the disused railway station in Skellefteå were sharing a bottle of wine, definitely not their first. Jurma had lifted his head when he saw him, a gesture of recognition, but then he looked down again, as if in shame or blind rage.

It made him ache. He could not believe he was not there as well.

It was impossible to understand. A matter of chance, perhaps, or a miracle?

Is he afraid? He is afraid.

From Brighton, spring 1989, only the title of what is now certain to be a hopeless novel, and a short note.

> Now, soon, my Benefactor, Captain Nemo, will tell me to open the water tanks, so that the vessel, with the library inside it, will sink.
>
> I have been through the library, but not everything. Before, I secretly dreamed of collecting all of it together, so that it was all finished, closed. Finally to be able to say: *this is how it was, this is how it happened, and this is the whole story.*
>
> But it would be against my better judgement. Against better judgement is a good technique for not giving up. If we had better judgement, we would give up.

The following day he went out in the car and drove for several hours between Skråmträsk, Långviken, Yttervik and Ragvaldsträsk, in order to summon up his courage.

The car was an Audi he had hired at Skellefteå airport, which was located right next to Gammelstället, by the lake, Bursjön: he was convinced that it was on the land his mother's brother John had owned. You made the descent for landing, and there was the farm, 120 metres or so below; that was where he read the Bible to his maternal grandmother when she was dying.

He had, as always, looked out as they were about to land, to identify the geographical point from which his life could be viewed, and the young man in the seat next to him, in his thirties and wearing a serge suit, in other words his Fellow Traveller, had as usual also stretched forward to see and said, "So that's what it looks like now," and he had replied, "Yes, they've done a lot of building," as if that had been perfectly natural. "Uncle John has gone now," he had added, in explanation. "Really, him too?" the man, who had perhaps never flown before and never seen Gammelstället from above, had answered. "Well, there are not many left," and with that there was not much more to be said.

The man on the bench outside the central station, whose name was Jurma, must have been about seventy. It was obvious that he had been on the booze for a long time.

Strange that he was still alive. Enough of that.

He borrows a rowing boat and rows out to Granholmen.

It is called something else now, named after his mother: Majaholmen. Strange, actually, it was his father who had built the cottage. She would sit there in the summertime and look out over the water.

You really should not delve into all of this. It will only drive you mad.

Of all creatures he loved dragonflies best.

They had been gone for a long time. In autumn 1989 he saw them again. In spring 1990 they were flying around like crazy and he could hardly contain himself. It was the resurrection of the dragonflies. How did that happen?

The letters.

He was going to clear out the attic and he found the bundles of letters, seven of them, all handwritten. He had been quite sure that he was on fire.

Was it so? All this. He could scarcely breathe.

Was it really so?

She had put the Toshiba on his knee, as if it were a puppy, and the other woman, Sanne, sat on the floor and put on his shoes for him.

You always hope for a miracle. If you do not have hope, you are not human. And surely you must be some sort of human.

Is it now? No, not yet.

PART ONE

INNOCENCE

CHAPTER 1

THE SOOTHSAYER

The signs are very unclear.

Someone in the village tells the child, almost in a whisper, about the dream that Hugo Hedman had in the winter of 1935. In the dream three tall trees fell down. They were pine trees, but they had not been cut down deliberately. It was an omen. The same winter three men in the village died. The dream had been a sign. One of the dead men was apparently called Elof. Later the child understands that this man is not a "pine tree", but his "father"; however, it is very confusing.

The second sign: his mother is pregnant, carrying the only-begotten son. At the same time: one of his father's brothers is, while still very young, labelled "insane" and spends a period in solitary confinement, locked in the attic, as is the custom. He is not allowed visits from the mother, since she is with child, and moreover with *this* child, and secret rays emanating from a lunatic (*"he looks crazy"*) can damage the foetus in the womb. A few years later (possibly September 1939) he asks if that had indeed been the case; it is denied, he has not been harmed at all by anything the madman gave off. In any case it would only manifest itself later on, *but it is unlikely*. "Insanity" is, he learns, a kind of restlessness.

And so the years pass.

Suddenly he is aware that his mother is no longer crying.

He does not know what has happened, but it has stopped.

At first he assumes that she is happy now and no longer laments her widow's loneliness. Then he suspects that the tears have simply dried up. She has obviously reached a turning point and they have run dry.

She throws herself into her work, which is the school and voluntary work for Jesus. The former is a chore. Voluntary work for Jesus, she says, fills her with light.

Jesus my light.

That is her perspective. The child is filled with admiration.

The distance from the green house where they live to the school is five kilometres. No more weeping. It is as if she has given up, capitulated.

In winter, when the road through the forest cannot be kept cleared, they go on skis. Mother makes a track, he follows behind. It has to be done. She is, after all, a primary schoolteacher. A school with two classes, for infants and juniors. First a slight downhill slope from the green house, then over the stream, next a long, very windswept stretch over the fields by Hugo Renström's, before going through the forest. The school serves two villages and is therefore placed halfway between the two, which means right in the middle of the forest; so everyone has to travel the same distance, perhaps too far, but on the other hand, no-one has an advantage. It is fair, but in winter the worst bit is against the wind on the flat before the forest.

Her life really gives her nothing to complain about.

She no longer writes her diary.

When he is clearing up after her death in the autumn of 1992 he finds something that resembles diaries, from the years immediately after training college. In them, odd indications on the calendar that before her marriage she certainly lived a devout life, but, to be honest, she also enjoyed herself. "Party at Gamla Fahlmark" or "Party at Långviken". Party revelations cease with the engagement, the date is not clear.

She reiterates to her son the assertion that she is content, and that "the state's rewards are small but secure". However, she complains about women's salaries, which are lower than those of male colleagues (equal pay is introduced in 1937, but she is far-sighted), and stresses the importance of every woman having a career because one day she might become a widow.

The possibility of divorce does not cross her mind.

Her political affiliation is without a doubt within the People's Party.

She is a huge admirer of the party leader, Bertil Ohlin, who is a professor. She is deeply critical when Erlander, *who is only a Bachelor of Arts*, is insolent to Ohlin. She never suggests that the latter is handsome (the word "smart" does once escape her lips), but the child soon realises that her almost religious worship of this man Ohlin has undertones. Many years later, when pressed, she admits that his dead father had been a Social Democrat. No need to make too much of that, she implies. Before his departure from this world he was *saved, after all*. She does not elucidate. Because he was a stevedore in summer and a lumberjack in winter, she regards it as natural that he gave in to *the peer pressure of the loading gang*. She indicates that she never blamed him for his political preferences. When her son grows up and informs her that he too is a Social Democrat, she sighs heavily but says – with sarcasm or humour? he cannot make her out properly – that *Well then, your Dad would be happy*.

In every class she takes, she starts a choir. It is always three-part. This is where she is truly at home, in song. Her dedication to the People's Party is more a matter of principle, not of emotion.

Eighty-seven years old and having suffered three minor strokes, she is to be found in the dark and in a heavy snowfall, walking south on the coast road, swaying from side to side in her characteristic way and wearing only one of her Lovikka mittens. She is purposeful, as if she is going to Umeå or Sundsvall.

It is seven o'clock on Christmas morning. Someone stops her; she says irritably that she is on her way to the local branch of the People's Party in Bureå, they are having their annual meeting and she definitely does not intend to let them down. She is taken home and not castigated, because her sharp temper is well-known and no-one dares, even now, to contradict her.

It is her last, albeit abortive, political act. She considers the *Norran* to be the "liberal" local paper. That means social-liberal.

So what social class do she, the father and the boy belong to?

Sometime in 1944 school meals are introduced in Bureå parish, resulting in the children at the school being provided with a free lunch. However, it is means-tested for the first year and a financial assessment determines that all the children in Hjoggböle have the right to a free school meal apart from two, who belong to the privileged upper class. It is the school's two teachers who are affected ("the state's rewards are small but secure" and so on) – which means that he and Thorvald, the son of the junior schoolteacher, Ebba Hedman, are not given meals. Each lunchtime the pupils file up to the top floor of the school, temporarily equipped as a dining room, where his father's sister Vilma – who will later be involved in the battle over the swapped children, the Enquist changeling story – serves good and nourishing meat broth.

The two upper-class children, Thorvald and himself, have to sit on the floor in the lower corridor and eat a sandwich of rye bread and margarine, which he detests, and drink skimmed milk.

He feels singled out, ashamed, and is boiling with indignation. It is fortunate that he has a good nature. After lunch, their hunger satisfied and with bright smiling faces, the children stream past the two teachers' boys. His view of class conflict in society is now fixed. Yet he does not understand that the lower-class feeling he has is built on a misunderstanding; he is the one who is upper class.

He is not alone in trying to find out why things happened the way they did. The village too is researching into itself. There had to be some sort of coherence. Otherwise madness would ensue.

In the first half of the twentieth century Sweden is an archipelago of many thousands of small villages hidden in a sea of forests. Hjoggböle is no exception. The village preserves its history, which is long. Endless reports of people defeating poverty. At the village meeting on 1 May,

1885 it was decided that, to avoid the cost of lodgings, the widow Lovisa Andersson would go round the village with her children. Tax, one night at each household. It is a year of famine. People exchange their last possessions for flour. "A bucket, a leather sack, a metal container, a fur, four scythe handles; for this, 11 lbs of flour received." Amusing little anecdotes he can leave out of his story: the minutes of the village meeting in May 1868 disclose that farmer Erik Andersson in Hjoggböle sent two boys into the forest to fetch bark for baking bread. On the way home the boys had to pass a field of cows. The cows were hungry and when they caught sight of the boys and the bark they were carrying, they crowded around them and ate the bark. The starving boys were unable to defend themselves and did not have the strength to go back to the forest. "Support issued, 2 lbs high-quality flour, 2 lbs low-quality."

A happy outcome. They could go home without bark.

"In Sjön, Hjoggböle, a poorhouse has been built, consisting of one room; for the homeless." Evidently many of them are soldiers' widows, with children. The stone foundations of the poorhouse are still there in the mid '50s. He often visits it, situated, as it is, right next to the bunker that he as a seven-year-old plans to use for shelter against infantry attacks backed by German tanks. The foundations are behind Anselm Andersson's; when the Furuvallen football pitch was built there this memorial vanished.

Lutheran morals are already rife now, in the mid-nineteenth century. He recognises them. "Decision of the village meeting on 1 May", according to paragraph 8, is to "impose a penalty of twenty-five kronor on anyone in the village allowing use of his house as an amusement parlour; the fine will be shared out to the poor in the village."

Amusement parlour means dance hall.

One Olof Enqvist, however, is not among those who receive benefits – quite the reverse: when the house and mill in Forsen are sold at auction in May 1883 with all the contents, he buys the house for four kronor and five öre. Perhaps he pulls it down and makes use of the timber?

An uncle of a grandfather. He spells his name with qv.

*

Below the green house was the planing machine.

He cannot recall seeing the plane working when he was a child. They stopped using it sometime at the end of the '30s. He tries to remember, but he fails.

The little building, the sawmill, was still there down by the stream throughout the '40s. A very low, sagging structure. Was it open at the front, towards the road and where the milk was collected? He cannot recall a door.

Difficult to understand how the plane was operated. Had there been some sort of waterfall at the outlet to the lake, a difference in levels where the stream started, with a wheel? He finds an archive informing him that the engine driving the plane was a Säffle combustion engine, 7 horsepower, model 15, manufactured 1920.

Obviously it did not need hydropower. So why then was it in that particular place?

Was it because the timber was transported on the water?

The plane was by the outlet to the lake and only a hundred metres from the green house. As a child he was convinced that he was born at the very centre of Sweden, namely Sjön, Hjoggböle. Proof of this: the combination of the chapel and the milk churn stand and the stream and the bridge over the stream and, above all, the plane, existing as it did only as a relic and consequently deserving its own symbol on the map. Being born in the middle of the kingdom must not make you conceited; instead it carries a responsibility for *people on the periphery*. People who live south of Jörn. Or people in Skåne.

There was a great deal of sawdust left, even though the plane was no longer there, quite a large, flat, soggy heap of it. You could hunt for worms amongst the shavings.

Wasn't there a hole in the sawmill floor? Straight down into the stream? He is determined to investigate and solve the mystery of the plane once and for all. He does not recall who owned it. Perhaps it was the Sehlstedts.

One of them. *Maybe the one who carried the foot-end.*

*

The village is ancient. It has been there since the Middle Ages.

When Gustav Vasa's land register was drawn up in 1543 there were five tax-paying farmers in the village. They utilised 5.5 hectares. Unearthed finds included axes, greenstone arrowheads and a quartz dagger, which *might be evidence of* some sort of settlement from the period around 3,000 B.C.

He tries to imagine this, but fails. Nevertheless, he likes to think of himself as *indigenous*.

He returns in the summer and endeavours to create a reconstruction. In the middle of the '40s the stream had not been drained and it was still pretty; there were roach in it. People did their washing down by the plane. The bridge over the stream remained for a long time, though the plane and with it all the machinery were removed.

He makes a note: *the bridge has gone*.

The most interesting thing about the bridge was the leeches. You could lie on your stomach and observe them. When you were bathing you had to be careful about the leeches; maybe they were horse leeches, but it made no difference, they lay rolled up on the bottom and then they unfurled and swam, wriggling. You really ought to have been afraid of them, because people said they could suck your blood until you lost consciousness and passed out; but if you spent time with them every day they became friends of sorts and you coaxed them up with long sticks and laid them out on the bridge.

It made a mess if you killed them. He therefore made the decision not to kill them, but become their friend. That way there was no need to be afraid.

You could view the village in many ways, depending on where the centre was.

The obvious answer was that the milk stand and planing machine and leeches represented the centre of the village, and that made him happy, without making him *too big for his boots*.

He is at the centre, but maintains his humility.

Sometimes the villagers congregate at the milk stand for a meeting and then there will be twenty or so men down there, no women, conducting indignant discussions that almost always concern some outrage the dairy in Bureå is guilty of. It is something about the returns of skimmed milk. The bosses at the dairy have committed some indefensible infringement of their rights. Difficult to understand. He asks his mother, but she just sniffs.

Otherwise his mother is a great supporter of meetings, at least the ones held in the chapel. Those are under her control. The meetings at the milk stand irritate her, because they are worldly, and because no women attend. For her, the chapel is the centre; she would emphatically refute that the plane, milk stand and leeches were a centre.

She is of the opinion that, since it is the women in every family who make the decisions, the meetings at the milk stand are *a worldly pretence*. Pure theatre, as the real power in the village is with the women, who are not shrieking at the milking stool.

And the commotion at the milk stand, when the men were shouting that enough was enough and now there had to be a milk strike – it never actually happened. All was quiet the day after. But if all those who really took the decisions, in the home, if all those women had been there! Perhaps there would have been a result then. Because they knew what real life was. And they were used to running things.

The milk stand has gone too.

He records in August 2003 that the lake has retreated. It is almost invisible from the green house. That time in the '30s they skied all the way down to the planing machine. Once a year they gathered to clear the brushwood so that *the mirror of water, so beloved and admired by all, could shimmer clearly*. Now the brushwood is completely thick. It is as if the eye of the village has grown over, the eyelashes stuck together. Otherwise it is pretty.

Now you can make it into town in twenty minutes. Gardens are tended.

The village is ancient; he would like to imagine it as a moss-covered stump.

Yet it is breathing, very slowly, almost laboriously, like a dying woman, rather like his mother in the hours before she was taken to our Saviour in October 1991 and he sat with her, moistening her lips. When he visits the village as an adult, everything has changed; no moss, no prehistoric stump. He has to tilt his ear towards the village and hold his breath, so he can hear the distant calls.

Someone is whispering, he has to make it all connect, otherwise he will go mad.

In time he finds out that he had a brother who was born before him, a year and a half after the wedding.

She had wanted to give birth at home. The baby was the wrong way round, but on a cursory visit the midwife had taken exception to her excessive wailing and had said that the child would turn the right way of its own accord. Despite the labour pains, the infant did not come out. His mother had been lying there, groaning, for four days and nights until it was impossible to hold her down, *she had screamed so terribly*! It was a breech presentation. Then someone ordered a taxi from Gamla Fahlmark. She had been in bed on the top floor of the green house and the midwife had not come back again *because she did not have the energy*. So his mother had been carried down by his father and a neighbour, Sehlstedt. There were two of them to carry her down the stairs. Åke Sehlstedt had told him this, furtively, with one single detail: "I carried the foot-end."

Inexplicable that this sentence should lodge in his memory. He cannot be free of it.

He ponders on whether this was an image or a sign.

But it was a breech presentation. In the cottage hospital the baby eventually arrived and had the umbilical cord around his neck. It was thought that he lived for a few moments. A note about this in the diary. *Consequently he was officially born alive and not stillborn.* The swiftly departed had been baptised Per-Ola and his body photographed in the coffin. There had to be pictures of the body, that was obligatory. The corpse looked wise and he also seemed kind.

Two years later he himself was born and at the baptism was given the same name. His mother had explained that it was the *earlier* baby, with the name Per-Ola, who had died, whereas it was the later child, in other words him, with the same name, who lived. He finds it hard to know who is who. He senses something obscure, slightly suspicious. In that case, could it be that in actual fact he was the corpse photographed in the coffin, and it was his brother who lived?

Perhaps they had been exchanged.

He dare not ask, but feels uneasy. Or was it the same child all the time? In other words, he himself had died, *and nearly cost his mother her life*, in order to be resurrected. Or, and this was the most difficult: was it the case that *in his first life* he had been raised up amongst the righteous and now sat at God's right hand, whilst *afterwards* becoming the child, the one who was singled out as Per-Ola, *with the same name!!!* – and that this one, born into the world later on, was among the unrighteous sinners left to burn in hell on Judgement Day?

It becomes even more unclear when an exchange of babies actually does take place in the family.

This time it was Aunt Vilma who gave birth in Bureå cottage hospital. The nurse came in with a baby in each arm, both one day old; and in a sharp voice she had said to Aunt Vilma and Mrs Svensson, "Can't you recognise your own children!?"

But they could not, and so a mistake was made.

That was the Enquist baby mix-up. And some years later there was a big fuss about it in the press as far south as Stockholm and it even went to the Supreme Court. That was how it started. First the uncertainty about whether it was he himself who had died, or whether it was his brother. And then the story about the babies switched at birth. An affirmation of how uncertain everything was. *Just look at*

Aunt Vilma and what went wrong with the newborn babies!!!

You never knew for certain who was who. Or who you were.

It was scary. Then a rumour began to spread. It was much later, but long before he wrote *Captain Nemo's Library* about Eeva-Lisa and the changelings, and then he put the record straight about the scandal in the village by explaining it in the form of a novel. He wanted to make everything clear by presenting the objective truth about the swap, so that people would stop making things up.

The rumour was that, in actual fact, it was he who had been switched at Bureå cottage hospital. He was alarmed. What on earth could this mean? That perhaps it was his dead brother, the corpse in the coffin, who had written the books? No, that it was he who had penned them, *but in his brother's name*. He was upset that the two mix-ups were being confused.

In any event: he was someone else.

Some people said they knew for certain that Enquist had been swapped at birth. He was shaken, but he pulled himself together. However, it reinforced the feeling of insecurity he had experienced as a child. You could not be sure. He denied it, but not convincingly. He was not even sure himself. He began to agonise over whether it could be true, first as a joke, but soon it was not funny.

Sometimes you do not know yourself.

And his mother?

She would certainly be very nervous if he asked, like a skittish horse. But he would never have asked her which of the brothers had lived and which had died. And in that case what she thought of the first, dead son, or which of the two she liked better.

Perhaps the answer lay in a notebook he found after her death, in which she *makes things clear*. After the first birth she writes in it: "Despite what has happened I still know that I have at least been a mother once." Not a word more. He found it hard to make sense of this. Did she not believe she could have another baby? Or did she not want to? Had she given up, thus giving him up?

I have at least been a mother once! She must have meant for the minute the child was alive. That was the only reasonable interpretation. He understands that motherhood was important to her. Maybe it was shameful to be married and childless. Better to have been born and then perish, from croup, for example, which turned them blue. Croup had taken Grandmother Lova's six brothers and sisters. All of them had turned blue.

But the minute for which the dead boy had been alive made the difference for her. It made her a woman.

In his opinion she has an almost angelic appearance, or is, at any rate, unequivocally beautiful.

However, her beauty is distorted in a strange way when he faces a life-threatening illness and *the removal of his tonsils*. It happens at Bureå cottage hospital. He learns that the person operating on him will be Dr Hultman, the same man who attended his father when he was cut open and died.

This doctor, his father's assassin, is now leaning over him and lowering into his throat a steel pincer that will whip out his tonsils. *It must have been like this for his father! And for the ghost boy who was possibly himself who was forced out by this same doctor with his umbilical cord round his slender neck!* The doctor's grotesquely gaping face comes towards him and he rips the pieces of flesh from his shrieking mouth. He knows he is the third person exposed to the mortal danger of this face: first the ghost boy baptised Per-Ola, then his father and now him.

His life is saved, however, and he has to stay in for a week. There is the threat of an epidemic (scarlet fever?) and no patients at Bureå cottage hospital are allowed visitors. But his mother cycles into the regional centre every day and bangs on his window. Her face is contorted with worry, as if she is trying to call in to the one in distress; it has none of her normal beauty, now it is twisted with fear and confirms his anguished suspicions about Doctor Death.

She scratches on the window to attract his attention, like a bird, shut out; against the window, with its wings.

The survivor, in so far as he is this person, is regarded generally in the village as good-natured.

He hears it often and becomes accustomed to it. He is good. His gentleness radiates from childhood photographs, and his glowing kindliness. He finds it natural that he is good, but often daydreams about how things would be if he were not good. In those circumstances he would receive a beating, everyone knew that. He has not experienced anything of that sort; he knows that his mother would dispense corporal punishment only after a hard struggle with herself and only if serious sins had been committed.

He gives some thought to how it would feel. Since corporal punishment is something that is in effect completely forbidden, he begins to hanker after a taste of it, just once. It becomes an unattainable goal he is more and more obsessed with.

One day he unexpectedly achieves his objective. He has done something. What it is he has done he later suppresses, but his mother decides to punish him, by spanking his bare behind. He screams hysterically after the first blows, as this proves not to be a heavenly experience, giving him admittance to a whole new human arena, but quite simply hurts. Only that. Sniffling, he pulls up his trousers, falls to his knees in the obligatory moment of prayer before the face of Christ and feels both wronged and disappointed.

He has crossed over a boundary to a new phase and can only sum it up as *hurting*. No existential vision.

He is good. This seems to pose a problem for his mother.

Central to her religious and pedagogic instruction is to teach the child truthfulness and, pure of heart and without fear, to acknowledge his sins. If he does that, he will receive forgiveness. She thinks that the admission in itself will strengthen his standing among those who do not dare confess. That is the word she uses, standing. He understands that only those who admit *I was wrong* have the respect of the masses. The self-righteous who never admit their faults will be despised by the masses.

The problem is that he, who is always so good, never has any faults to confess. He is almost clinically sin-free. It is a dilemma for them both. Every Saturday, when he goes to bed, he is supposed to confess a sin he has committed during the week and beg forgiveness from Jesus. They have decided this jointly. It might be mostly his mother who has decided it jointly, but the decision has been taken at any rate and it causes him great anxiety. Not because it will be hard to confess. But because he cannot find anything to confess.

He is aware that he is quite simply too good.

As Saturday approaches he desperately racks his brains for something to confess. He finds nothing, possibly because there is nothing to find.

The thought occurs to him that he could consciously sin, in order to have something to confess, but his goodness is too firmly rooted, his kindness too solidly established; that would be absolutely impossible.

After chewing it over three Saturdays in a row – to his own and his mother's disappointment – without sin, he solves the dilemma by *making a sin up*. He confesses, in tears, that when he went shopping at Koppra in Forsen he stole a sweet while the shopkeeper was not looking. His mother is shaken by the confession, but commends him highly for admitting it, and after the moment of prayer, when Jesus Christ unquestionably will forgive the sinner, they both sleep peacefully.

What he has not taken into account is that the following week his mother will report the sin to the shopkeeper, whom she knows well, as they are both active leaders of the temperance society, the Blue Ribbon Association. She tells him that her son has stolen a sweet.

All hell breaks loose.

The shopkeeper takes an unsympathetic attitude: the two jars of sweets are kept behind the counter on a shelf so high that the child cannot possibly have reached it, unless borne aloft by divine powers, and the story would appear to be duplicitous. His mother returns, her face dark, says that he has disgraced her, and after a very short hearing, the child confesses that he lied. Falls to his knees and so on.

This is a Wednesday. When Saturday arrives he obviously hopes that the sin both committed and confessed during the week, in other words *the invention of the stolen sweet*, will count in his favour as the Saturday-sin; but not at all. She thinks that this sin does not fall within their joint agreement decided by her. It does not count. He will have to declare a new sin this Saturday.

It is a desperate situation.

He envies the children he has read about in the edifying books, the ones who are not good. Personally, he does not know anyone who is bad. He thinks they are all kind, apart from Maurits. But when he examines his own kindliness, the children he knows cannot compete.

They are good, but not *so awfully* good.

He bears his kindness like a cross, or rather an albatross round his neck, but he is resigned, he appreciates that this goodness has been laid on his shoulders by Jesus Christ and no-one will take the cross from him to ease his burden.

The Saturday confessions come to an abrupt halt, thanks to an event that to him is baffling. It has to do with his foster sister, Eeva-Lisa. He is not supposed to speak about her. He loves both her and his mother dearly, but is distressed by their ever more violent disagreements. He thinks that his mother, who is in principle the very essence of goodness, is not nice to Eeva-Lisa.

He cannot understand it.

On the spur of the moment in his Saturday session with Christ, and in the usual desperate hunt for his own sins to confess, he suggests that his mother should admit that she has been nasty to Eeva-Lisa. It would be fair, he implies.

There is complete silence. Her face is closed and quite unmoved. She says curtly that she does not understand what he means. She breaks off the devotions and tells him to go to sleep. He can hear that she is not asleep. Without explanation the confession hearings stop after this.

The Monday following this incident everything is normal. He cannot really understand it. During the singing lesson, with both classes together, she rehearses the song "The Lake Rests Peacefully", in three parts.

In time another primary teacher joins the school. His name is Dahlquist.

He is from Vännäs, which is situated a long way to the south, almost as far as Stockholm, and with the arrival of Dahlquist comes a new era. He is the first person in the village to use ketchup. He and his mother are invited for Sunday lunch by Dahlquist, whose salary is higher than his mother's, despite the fact that they fulfil the same *calling* (as she casually refers to it a few times to the child, *perhaps not quite so few*); so, Sunday lunch at the home of her colleague and his wife. Afterwards he and his mother ski home in the dark through the forest. He hears his mother muttering, "Ketchup, ketchup, ketchup. What's so marvellous about ketchup?" He tries to reply to the black shape of his mother's back that the ketchup tasted good, but is met with silence. It is not fitting to put on airs and graces with ketchup.

In other respects his mother likes her colleague and his wife very much. The latter was once the Swedish women's ski champion, in the four-times-ten kilometre relay, and is the only sports star in the village. At the annual skiing contest she is applauded as she sets off. She also introduces technical ski training; on a square track round the school the children can learn poling, double-poling and stride double-poling. This is quite acceptable. His mother explains that there is nothing sinful in this. Not like sport on Sundays. In situations of extreme emergency, stride double-poling can come into its own. In the south towards Stockholm no-one can stride double-pole.

Soon she seems to have forgotten her fundamental scepticism about ketchup.

*

A new world keeps on opening up thanks to Dahlquist.

In one lesson he uses the term "pickled onion" and asks the class – it is now grades five and six, as the school has been elevated to a school with three classes – what they think of pickled onions. No-one has heard of pickled onions, let alone tasted one. At break-time therefore, Mr Dahlquist arranges the pupils in a long row in the school yard and comes up with a jar of pickled onions and a spoon. He goes along the line and with the spoon pops a pickled onion into the mouth of every child. It is electrifying.

This has never happened in Hjoggböle before.

Then he goes back to the beginning of the line and gives each child a spoonful of the liquid, which runs out halfway through the class. They all think it is very good and quite extraordinary and they testify to everyone else what they have seen and experienced.

Aside from stride double-poling on skis, the only sport at school is snowball fighting.

It takes place in the morning break, if the snow is wet. Since he is, by definition, kind, he is never one of the bold fighters on the front line. He is almost always *equipment, ammunition and supplies*, and works at the back with the girls. They press the snowballs together and put them on a plywood plank that is carried forward to the ones fighting at the front. He very soon finds supply service boring and creates a new role for himself, as traitor, or, subsequently, quisling.

The *Norran* has published something about Major Quisling.

What happens is that he takes a plank of very hard snowballs, ready-made by the girls in supplies, but instead of giving them to their own soldiers at the front, he rushes straight through and gives this ammunition to the enemy, by whom he is met with jubilation, whilst his own side curses him. After a while he repeats the operation, but in the opposite direction, and meets with jubilation and curses, correspondingly.

He is now designated a traitor. The girls in the *service corps* do not want to entrust him with what they have made, but suddenly he is very

29

eloquent, promises faithfully never to betray his own side again and is forgiven, charged once more with the delivery of trays of ammunition, but soon runs over to the enemy side again. Jubilation and so on.

In this way, as traitor, he finds himself forever in the centre, never feels kind and is blissfully happy.

Apart from his kindness, he is known for his delicacy. You could even call him *frail*. When he bathes in the summer, he turns blue and shivers for hours.

And yet: on one occasion he delivers a punch. He is forced into the corner between the toilets and the woodshed by two boys in the class above; they intend to rub snow in his face. In quiet merriment they are gloating over the awful pain that lies in store for him. He is scared. Without warning his right arm shoots forward, he discovers to his amazement that his right fist is clenched, with astounding force it strikes his attacker on the left cheek and the persecutor crashes to the ground. Everyone, including himself, is enormously surprised. His opponent rises to his feet, uttering oaths and profanities and describing in minute detail the revenge he will take; but nothing happens.

Nothing happens.

Two days later his adversary, who is called Maurits, has one black eye and a heavily bruised cheek. His mother notices it during a lesson and asks what has happened. Everyone knows, everyone looks at Maurits with bated breath, but he just mutters that he fell over. Nothing more. The relief is immense. It is the only time in his life he hits someone, and after this no-one ever hits him; he tells himself he has learnt something.

At any rate he is never hit again. Perhaps the whole thing has been an anomaly.

In the winter of 1944 the Finnish children arrive.

Four hundred arrive all at once, then small batches of a few dozen; the central school in Bureå has been closed, the children are put into the classrooms on mattresses and the whole area is surrounded with security fencing, so that the youngsters cannot contaminate the parish before they have been deloused. The Finnish children have a tendency to congregate by the fence. The crowds can have a good look at them there. He implores, partly the Saviour, but mostly his mother, to let him go and see them. He is allowed to go to Bureå with his mother once, on the back of her balloon bicycle. While she carries out her errands, he stands outside the fence and watches.

A kind of trading is taking place here, an exchange. The Finnish children stand with their mouths open like baby birds and shout out incomprehensible words in their own language, pushing their hands out with Finnish coins they want to change at preferential rates that will make the Bureå children enormously rich. Some of these do make an exchange, more as an act of charity, but at least it provides them with Finnish coins to save up.

It is rather intimidating to look at the Finnish children. Every day the *Norran* has a box on Per Rim's page with common Finnish words for people to learn. The most useful words appear here; but beyond the box in the *Norran*, that is to say out of the mouths of the Finnish children themselves, come more exciting words. These other language skills are crucial, at first mainly to be able to say fuck and penis in Finnish, something none of the adults understand. Then more coherent sentences; two of the Finnish children stay and marry his cousins.

The plan is to place the children in the villages and not to keep them in the camp for longer than necessary. Around ten come to Hjoggböle. One is called Jurma; he is placed with the Bäckströms in Östra. After only six months he is already speaking excellent Skellefte dialect. Someone *of a poetic nature, who has learned the art of rhyming*, i.e. the teacher's boy, who, with the protective cloak of his mother's authority, believes himself to be proof against the Finnish immigrants, runs around at break-time shouting *Finns shit in! Finns shit in!*

It is not clear what he means, perhaps that Finns defecate inside on the floor, but more likely that inside toilets mean decay and the breakdown of civilisation; in truth he has never seen an inside toilet and therefore assumes that it is the height of squalor. *Inside toilet!* Jurma, being very strong and not at all frail, grabs him in a flash, thumps his upper arms over and over again where it hurts, shouting *So where do Finns shit???*, until finally the poet, screaming on the floor, acknowledges *They don't shit inside!!! I promise! They don't shit inside!!!*

In this way they cement the friendship that will last just one year. Jurma is his only friend during childhood, apart from Eeva-Lisa, and the forest, if you can count that. But about Eeva-Lisa he must maintain his silence.

His mother is concerned that he should not be boastful, so she seldom or never praises him.

She exhorts him to be humble; it is wearisome, but now he is more successful at assuming a modest bearing. Humility is nearly as seductive as treachery. Whether he is meek or a traitor, he likes being at the centre, though not in the role of hero. His humility is determined by her restraint.

Only once does a word of praise escape her lips.

When he asks what she really thinks about his essays, she merely answers, "I have never ever had a pupil who writes better than you." That is all. It suffices; for the rest of his life he is satisfied that he is good enough, she does not need to commend him.

Yet one time she did!

All of it – being good enough, being right to defend himself, the ketchup, learning to be humble, pickled onions, the role of traitor, stride double-poling on skis – is essential in mitigating the nightmare that he was summoned to our Saviour after the breech delivery two whole years before his alleged birth.

The village is actually several villages.

They surround a lake called Hjoggböleträsket, through which the Bureälven flows on its way from the lake Mjödvattsträsket and thence, twisting north and east, via more lakes, Falhmarksträsket, Bodaträsket and Bursjön, to the sea at Bureå. Round Hjoggböleträsket lies the village, like a snake; the parts have different names: Östra Hjoggböle, Västra Hjoggböle, Forsen and Sjön, Hjoggböle. His grandmother lives six kilometres away at Bursjön; the farm stands alone by the lake and a hundred metres further away is a smaller farm at the edge of the woods. Just the two farms: Gammelstället and Larssonsgården. In Larssonsgården, a hundred metres from his grandmother Johanna, lives the father of the young Stieg, who will go on to write crime novels. That the two farms in the wood should produce two writers is the statistical norm in these parts, everyone believes; there are more storytellers in the villages than cows' udders. Hjoggböle is larger and in time will have five authors. Each village has its writers; but Hjoggböle's fame derives from something else entirely.

It is the home of the Komet team. More of that later.

Most of them are smallholders. No-one calls himself a husbandman anymore and the word "farmer" has a note of arrogance. And yet the *Farmers' Union Weekly* is read by everyone. Mother dismisses it as "the most boring paper in the world". It was one way for her to distance herself from her upbringing on the land.

She too is on a journey of class mobility, from peasant's daughter, born at Gammelstället, to village schoolteacher in Hjoggböle. Not many can compete with that!

In the village there are between two and four cows, the men work in the forest in winter and as stevedores on the boats in summer. The child soon grows accustomed to women deciding everything; it is normal. Later in life he will, with no hint of criticism, claim that he is a product of this matriarchy. The men disappear early in the morning, return late, exhausted, asking for half a glass of water. This is how his mother describes his father's humility and the ruling structure. The men are divided into teams, who cycle the fourteen kilometres to Bureå harbour every morning.

The road is sandy, but the bicycles have balloon tyres.

The modern age dawns in around 1930.

Father, together with a brother, has bought a used Chevrolet. The stevedore team piles in and shares the cost. Where did they get the money from? One day the engine breaks down and they revert to bicycles. It may have been the hand of God.

Father and motor-driven vehicles are now a more and more enigmatic chapter, reported to him piecemeal by the dead man's friends. He also buys a motorbike with sidecar, perhaps he only borrows it; there is much that is unclear. The lightweight motorbikes the stevedores use come later, after his father's death. The lightweights are Sachs, 98c.c.; in winter, when it is below 30 degrees, a celluloid air cylinder is used to protect the face from frostbite. The cold bounces off. The child dreams of the day he can join the procession of lightweight bikes that come swerving through the darkness between the two-metre-high banks of snow, leaving or returning. He tells his mother that he is going to buy a lightweight motorbike when he is older and perhaps be a stevedore.

She does not answer. She seems to envisage his life differently. As a priest, or, a compromise, at least married to Britt-Louise, the Reverend Ollikainen's daughter. She too is delicate, but later she marries Bishop Lönnebo. It is his mother who rings and tells him when it happens.

The village is divided into two halves, godless and god-fearing.

The spiritual half is dominated by the Enquist family, to some extent under the leadership of his mother, even though she married into it. The earthly side has a community centre, where they are rumoured to organise dances from time to time, and a football team that during the 1940s has the name Komet. They play in the fourth division of the Northern Counties Coastal League and for decades are on the point of progressing into a higher division. However, northern teams are barred from the highest division. This is reserved for Stockholm teams, which fills generation after generation of northerners with hatred. The Komet team is close to promotion to division three. Being *close* fills the imagination of the young, and not just the godless children in Västra, but secretly the god-fearing ones too. The team has some impressive players, in particular the four Bäckström brothers, but also the centre half, Sven Erik Fahlman, who delivers a tremendous kick and whose character makes him a role model for the young. Almost everyone agrees on this, even his mother.

In time Fahlman will lose a leg. Perhaps diabetes. The pitch is very short, seventy metres. A trench, almost completely filled in, but dipping, crosses the pitch and causes consternation in visiting teams. The Komet team is considered hard to beat at home.

Connections between the religious and the worldly halves of the village are few. The child has never seen a match close up – naturally, because of his mother – but in the local newspaper, *Norra Västerbotten*, the football commentator reports that there are extraordinary things happening there, in the west. The reporter is a Mr Kuri, pronounced Merrkuri, and he identifies unequivocally the ones who make a sterling contribution.

It is Mr Kuri who wins hearts and minds.

The pitch is on his left when he cycles to Koppra. It is quite far off, but near enough to be within earshot. Perhaps only fourteen hundred metres from the green house.

On Sundays, after everyone has poured out from chapel service, he goes into the yard and, standing behind the rosehip bushes, he hears the faint noise of what is happening in the westerly, godless part of the village. Through the distant shouts he can visualise the tremendous game, the action. A sudden roar and he imagines a dramatic change, perhaps a leading goal for the Komet team.

He has seen photographs in the *Norran*. He can let his fantasy take over. His imagination is fed like this: partly by illustrations in the family bible, partly by pictures in the *Norran*, and partly by the sounds he seizes upon from his hiding-place behind the rosehip bushes.

The Komet team's fans are drawn from the whole parish and a derby against Bureå I.F. is seen by over one thousand spectators. Sometimes he can make out excited exhortations. "Mark the old farts!!!" Or, "Fire a low cross!" Behind the rosehip bushes the sinful temptations of sport reach his ears.

His mother anxiously calls him in; he very nearly defies her, but comes to his senses.

On one occasion Komet Hjoggböle I.F. achieves international renown.

They are very close to winning the league, which in this period is played in autumn and spring. The expression "go up" is constantly on the lips of the children in the godless faction. They decide to put all their efforts into it, following the international model. They organise a training camp in the community centre, which is in the centre of town, in the godless part, where dancing takes place, perhaps. For a week the team is locked in, sleeping on the floor, the floor where dancing has taken place, maybe, and playing snow football during the day.

It is an exceptionally cold week, minus thirty is recorded, and the snow is deep. No relatives are allowed in.

Wives are kept out; leave is cancelled, supposedly due to the risk of mystery illness. They take their pillows and quilts and closet themselves inside. The children look in through the windows and whisper about what is happening. The illustrated magazine *Se* publishes a big feature. There is great indignation in the religious portion of the village, high levels of disquiet; where will this lead?

However, it is a problem that the pitch is so small and its condition so bad, in particular the trench that irritates away teams. They need a better pitch and they apply to the authorities for support. Thus the ideological conflict between the spiritual and worldly parts of the village reaches its peak. A relation, Anselm Andersson, intervenes in the municipal council, where he represents the Farmers' Union. This is the man he calls Uncle Anselm, who once saved the life of his grandmother Lovisa, when she was newborn and about to be stabbed to death by her temporarily insane mother, thereby ensuring the continuing existence of the entire family, including the boy's.

He demands that all financial support for sporting activities should be withdrawn and that all football pitches should be dug up and planted with crops, to benefit the regional economy.

The proposal is voted down by a large majority, but generates fury amongst the godless of Västra Hjoggböle. They decide to build their new stadium in the god-fearing part, right next to Uncle Anselm's house, so that every Sunday he will be obliged to hear the sound of thudding balls and cheering crowd. And this happens. It is expensive, the pitch is excavated on a slope and Västra Hjoggböle's dazzling players are forced to cycle three kilometres to every training session. The pitch is in the wrong place, both from a religious and a secular point of view, and soon the Komet team is no longer what it was.

Uncle Anselm, who will live to be more than a hundred and will die with a clear head, unshaken values and a belief in his Saviour, has to suffer in silence. The balls resound.

The child is a part of this village. In his own way he admires Uncle Anselm, who dares to take a stand and face ridicule. He also yearns for the bewitching world of football. Because the village is divided, he does not know which village he belongs to. The village in him struggles with the village in others.

The village exists in a universe where the ground is covered in snow and the roof is made of stars that give him signs.

One day a new comic strip begins in the *Norran*. It is called "Flash Gordon". He collects the newspaper as usual from the Sehlstedts, where the postbag is left. He cannot wait, so he opens the newspaper while he is still there and then walks home to the green house through the snow, in the cold flashing light of the stars. It transpires in this very first instalment that Flash Gordon is going to make a voyage into space.

In his excitement he stands still at the edge of the forest and looks up at the starry sky. The immensity of the firmament, the theological menace that has filled him with such fear, the ice-cold grip of eternity on his heart – will be invaded by a spaceship.

Someone will venture into it.

Flash Gordon. The rulers up above are troubled, particularly God, or at least our Saviour Jesus Christ. The celestial music comes no longer from the heavenly harp alone. Flash Gordon is up there too now and from this moment he is going to follow him every day in the *Norran*. Something is happening: there is a new hero in the skies, one who offers different explanations.

And so he includes Flash Gordon as part of the answer to the question, along with his father, and the ghost boy, and to a certain extent Eeva-Lisa, and the boy who drowned in the marsh, for whose death he is in no way responsible or could possibly be prosecuted because of his age, and the receding but no longer solitary humming from the telephone wires.

Trees fall every winter, but only once as an omen. He is full of hope. It is starting so well.

CHAPTER 2

THE JOURNEY OF THE RED FOX

He never understands why. Was it in the genes?

He doubts it. There is absolutely nothing to indicate that he would be stricken by an addiction to writing. Nothing in his family. Smallholders and lumberjacks. Honest, hardworking people. Not a trace of poetry.

Almost no trace.

But what about his mother?

The notebooks from the college in Umeå are filled with ambitious texts, the longest about a Finland-Swedish nurse called Mathilda Wrede, who performed good deeds in Finnish jails and was known as the Prisoners' Friend. She serves as a model. His mother, whose name was Maria but was called Maja, was top of her class at Bureå elementary school and at the age of twelve decided that she wanted to be a teacher. She borrowed small amounts of money from the other smallholders. When she had finished after four years she owed 9,600 Swedish kronor.

After her husband died in the March, she travelled home from the cottage hospital on the bus, and the driver, Marklin, shouted back to the passengers, asking if there was not someone who would take pity on the woman. She had wept all the way, but she composed herself and trudged up to the house on her own in the dark. She paid off the loans promptly. She still had her son, an only child.

Mathilda Wrede had summoned all her strength and, with faith in her Saviour, had battled against hardship and horror throughout her life. That was the gist of the story.

Not a single spelling mistake.

His later relationship with the *memory* of his mother is strange. He reconstructs it.

In rightful reverence that she created him, he takes flight from her and so he is impelled to renounce her. Her most striking attributes – her quick intelligence, her humour and her refusal to be broken by loneliness – he covers up subsequently by asserting *how she was*: the Bible and melancholy. Look how he even denies her creativity. Just a flirtation with "women's stories", "Mathilda Wrede" and "not a single spelling mistake".

He suspects that he will find what he is seeking in his father. He believes he knows his mother. So it must be his father, not his mother, who has the answer to the ulterior but crucial question: *When everything was going so well. How could it turn out so badly?*

Moreover, his father cannot talk back.

From her there is just music.

There are the choirs at school and the Band of Hope as well as the church choir in Bureå, to which she cycles in all weathers. If the college in Umeå and the dream of becoming a teacher had not been so compelling, perhaps another dream might have been realised: singing! Singing! Maybe opera!

That is not to be.

When he is fourteen she gives him a gramophone and three records. They are Sibelius' "Finlandia", Schubert's "Unfinished Symphony" and Haydn's "Trumpet Concerto". With regard to this very fine piece by Sibelius, she provides two interpretations, perhaps obtained at college. The first is that the music evokes the national struggle, with the final hymn of thanksgiving for Finland's deliverance from the Russian empire. The second – a general observation – is that Sibelius' career as a composer was cut short while he was still a young man, because he was a drinker and so therefore he never wrote his eighth symphony. Anyone who took to drink was done for.

When, after matriculating from secondary school, he goes to Uppsala, she gives him a little cassette with a recording of a concert in the church at Bureå. She is singing the solo in – if his memory serves him well – something by Haydn. He knows she has a beautiful voice, a soprano. On countless occasions in the chapel he has heard his uncle, Birger Nordmark, read the programme for the evening and come to "Item 5: Solo by Maja Enquist".

He listens to the cassette once and is strangely moved. Then he loses the cassette. He does not know how. He cannot consciously have lost it. Or can he?

To be a missionary or a writer, you have to have a calling and be sent forth. For missionaries there is a special ceremony when they are about to go. At least when they are about to go to the Congo. He is certain that the same must apply for those who are called to write.

To consider yourself to be a writer without being called, or without having the chapel's blessing as its emissary, is arrogance. He is sure that *those who write*, like missionaries, must be called, sent forth and blessed by the congregation. Nevertheless, he tries a sample poem. It goes like this: "*Winter has left us / and spring has arrived / babbling brooks flow in a race to come first / Now we'll have fun and play marbles together / for springtime upon us has surely burst.*" He is quite pleased with the rhyme, but he does not show it to anyone, keeping it for a bound collection of poems; he has hopes of assembling several, something he does not achieve, thereby confirming his suspicion. He knows he is not called.

The suspicion lives on in him his entire life. It is like the village, which is divided. He does not understand, *somebody* inside him is called, but who is he? His dead brother or himself? And in any case, nobody inside him is *sent forth* with the congregation's approval.

*

However, he does draw maps.

First, the map of Sweden. He draws on greaseproof paper that he can place over the school map he has; it is transparent and so he can be completely accurate.

He draws on the kitchen floor in the green house. Very soon he has mastered Sweden and can do without the map underneath. It is a huge step to have mastered Sweden and he feels a kind of liberation.

His map design is based on a moral, or even military principle.

Because his mother had read aloud from the *Norran* and told him how the Västerbotten sugar-beet pickers sent to Skåne – the very ones giving assistance during the crisis for the sake of the country – had been badly treated by the mean and horrible Skåne people, he makes the southernmost counties quite small, little fleshy growths, rather like cows' udders. He also has a problem with Jämtland's border with Norway. It could, and should, be extended, seeing that Sweden's northerly border does not reach as far as the Arctic Ocean; Norway and Finland are sitting there like two potato dumplings. He is worried that the Norrlanders will be cut off now that convoys up there are being shelled. After numerous gradual extensions, he finally lets the Jämtland border go right out to the ocean. Obviously that means that Norway is sliced in half, like a sausage, but that will improve the prospects of the Norwegian resistance movement. In this way Sweden has direct access from Norrland to the Atlantic and he locates a marine base there with four frigates and the Gotland cruiser.

It is fun to draw, and each time he is very careful about putting the village, Hjoggböle, in the correct place to be sure where the centre is and so that he can feel secure. He places Stockholm at the southerly end, the name clearly marked, but at the edge, so that its distance can be appreciated.

That is at the beginning. He draws several hundred maps of Sweden, *inwardly* much more faithful than the school map. Next, he starts sketching orienteering maps.

The symbols are not difficult. There is deciduous woodland and sand dunes and coniferous forest and streams and contour lines and churches, which have the same symbol as the chapel. It is all easy to draw.

Only at this stage does he produce maps of the village.

In a way he has lifted the centre out of the map of Sweden so that he can make a map of the middle itself, Hjoggböle. He knows the village after all. It is just a question of documenting it. The western section, the godless part, is the hardest, but sometimes he has to guess. Up to the co-op there is no problem. After that uncertainty creeps in. For example, he is unwilling to draw a map of Långviken; he went by it once on the bus, but that was just passing. It is a sin to lie or make things up and he is in two minds. Fabrication is permitted only for a spiritual purpose, in order to explain Christ's deeds and miracles; making things up about Jesus in the form of parables is allowed.

But making maps is something else. No-one is inspecting what he does either. No-one is looking over his shoulder to criticise his carelessness; the symbols are abstract and the maps apparently similar. He finds it tempting to indulge in this clandestine redesigning. He therefore begins to record invented landscapes.

At first they are relatively simple maps. He incorporates that with which he is familiar.

To begin with it resembles the terrain around Bensberget, but he very soon changes the contours so that the deceptively low height of this mountain (112 metres above sea level) is changed into a more plausible 246 metres above sea level. Strangely, the Dead Cats' Grotto, which he does not discover until the age of eleven, is shown on one of his early maps. He draws the grotto on the map *before he discovers it*! It is located at the point where the contour lines thicken, indicating a near-vertical drop; however, if you look very carefully, you will see in the middle of the scarp a tiny gap between the lines, leaving room for a path passing through a cave, which, he realises later, is vaguely reminiscent of the Dead Cats' Grotto, a place where a person can stay hidden from his pursuers for a very long time.

Thus the map has foretold what will actually happen, and he takes this as a lesson.

To begin with he records landscapes that are beautiful and accurate, then later as they ought to be. First he draws the village exactly as it is, later he will add something else. He is scared by what he records and *what he will add*, but at the same time it makes him unaccountably excited. He correctly locates Hjoggböle I.F.'s football ground on the road to the co-op, to the left, but he makes it somewhat larger than it actually is. He knows the pitch dimensions required for international matches, for example between the Komet team and the Lapland team Lycksele; now he sketches in these new dimensions, theoretically making it possible for the Komet team to make its entry into Europe. In addition, in the field to the side of the new stadium, on the east side towards Sjön, he draws in a huge hillock (86 metres above sea level), covered in trees, where a person can easily hide, unseen by everyone in Sjön. This is where he will be able to watch the matches, concealed from the true believers.

In all of this he is alone with his secrets. He cannot be exposed. The maps ostensibly resemble the village, but it is not the village. Now that he has breached its boundaries, anything is possible. Wordlessly the greaseproof paper's coded messages reveal a foreign landscape private to him; a landscape without people, but with houses and crofts and dotted paths and escarpments and, finally, the grotto that is the viewpoint from which his invented landscape can be observed.

There is one problem: he lacks people on the map. There are no symbols for people, other than indirectly – crofts or things like that. Where a crowd of people gathers, such as at the football pitch, there are no symbols for the assembled body. Above all no symbols for their movements or their feelings for one another. In his father's *Soldier in the Field* handbook, from the time of the Home Guard, all the movements of the troops were recorded, the tanks too, and on the geographical map of Europe there was a red dot for every million inhabitants. England was red all over, as if someone had poured a bucket of pig's blood on top of the island. But the platoon in *Soldier in the Field* was never an individual, and the English dots do not move.

He contemplates whether he should add symbols for people, but he is not sure.

He is not at this stage afraid. He manages physical objects and natural phenomena calmly. Without hesitation he draws in *marsh* in front of the steep hill, so that the German tanks attacking from the east will get stuck. Fearlessly he draws a church on a little mound, low altitude for the sake of the old people *who have bad legs*; he puts it next to his grandfather's tar kiln, marked with a round circle and a wreath of smoke. It is the only time he breaks with the designated symbols and invents one, but he does so with a clear conscience for the sake of his grandfather and because he was always allowed to be there when it was emptied. He confidently creates a lagoon at Ryssholmen, at the precise spot where the six Russian soldiers are buried.

But what about the people?

That is the next step, and he does not take it.

Only once does he reveal the secret of the maps. The class is given an essay to write on the subject of "A Walk in the Forest" and he draws an orienteering map with a dotted line for the path to follow. It is an almost fictitious landscape with some features of the village, but disguised and essentially false, and in his essay he describes the walk in words. What you can see if you follow the path.

Still, the landscape lacks people. It is completely empty. No people, full of peace. You could imagine other beings. Birds, that is all, and dragonflies.

Dragonflies are the only airborne creatures he can identify with. Later on they disappear for many years, like the Northern Lights. Then he is almost in despair.

In the end, in the spring of 1990, they come back. Talk about the miracles of Jesus.

His father left a notepad in which he had written some poems; his mother burns them after his death, she never explains why.

He does not bemoan this fact. Not even when he is an adult. It is her right.

In the junior section of the Blue Ribbon Association, the Band of Hope, which is led by his mother and where for decades he is to all intents and purposes the deputy book-keeper, they are taught about alcohol dependency. An addiction that is beyond his comprehension.

There are other puzzling addictions. His own relentless cartography, with its distortion of reality, makes him suspect that even inventing things like this is addictive behaviour. Misrepresentation and make-believe are essentially sins. Apart from our Saviour's parables, naturally.

But if he managed to eliminate addiction, for example to the fake maps, would it be an end to perversion? Something that had to be concealed. Like *going to the sandpit so that he could chew dry sand*?

He never discloses these potential sins at the Saturday confessions, and in any case the sessions have stopped.

In time the village of Hjoggböle, situated deep in the forest, twenty kilometres from the coast and a thousand kilometres north of Stockholm, will gain a kind of national fame because the 150 inhabitants produced no less than five writers, defined as members of the Swedish Society of Authors.

He is asked many times, why this striking concentration of storytellers?

He usually answers humorously, the result of inbreeding: everyone married within a radius of twenty kilometres. Inbreeding resulted in a large number of village idiots or authors, difficult to determine which was which. This was before the boom in bicycles at the turn of the century, when the range of action for young men extended from walking to cycling and inbreeding largely came to an end. You could joke about it to avoid thinking about it seriously. Or perhaps you conjured up a picture of perpetual discourse round the fire or in dark kitchens; a storytelling tradition more than a thousand years old, from which written accounts, not oral, now suddenly emerged.

He knows that neither of these is true.

He has never heard a fable or a story. He just sits quietly on the snuff-coloured linoleum mat in the kitchen and draws maps on sheets of greaseproof paper. No fire. No old women telling secrets. The gory tales of the Old Testament are interesting up to a point, but he soon knows them by heart. Otherwise mostly silence. He has no friends, but he does not miss them. He has the forest and *Soldier in the Field* with anti-tank barriers marked. In the forest he builds bunkers against future attacks, but these are not something to record. Not even voices, just silence tucked up in the snow. Winter with snow and Northern Lights and birds in the rowan trees and humming telephone wires resonating against the gable roofs. But this is not a story.

Or is it?

During his childhood, rules are established about what questions he must answer and how. The questions are the intractable ones about sin and guilt and heaven and hell and life and eternity and the unchangeable and ice-cold silence of the starry sky, the answers shaken only by Flash Gordon's daily travels into space in the *Norran*. But this is not much of a story either. Perhaps just a warble or a low wail. These uncompromising existential questions to the child may not be bad questions, but the answers are razor-sharp and inexorable and fundamentalist.

Everything is beyond his comprehension. Yet he still has the forest. The forest is the best of playmates, but it does not tell much of a story! At any rate not one he can repeat.

Why him?

There is no-one else in his family who has become addicted to writing. Land workers for centuries and not an intellectual of any kind in sight. No peasant student. Not even a preacher.

If only he did not think in a different way.

He makes careful enquiries.

None of his relations has been before the district judge or convicted of a crime, there is no sign of alcohol abuse or loose morals or godlessness or adultery. They all have a reputation for being religious, often deeply religious. His father's brother – who for a short time was regarded as mad, but soon regained his sanity and in the autumn of his years worked

47

as a volunteer in the ice-hockey section of Skellefteå A.I.K. – he was just a digression.

Was there really no-one in his family before him who had this calling?

It is denied. But the mother of his paternal grandmother is mentioned.

His grandmother's name was Maria Lovisa Hällgren, she was known as Lova and she was born on 20 September 1873. In the middle of October that year her neighbour Anselm Andersson observed Lova's mother, Brita Margareta Hällgren, crossing the field west of the house, scantily clad and apparently on her way to the forest or Bensberget beyond.

He stood watching her movements, suspecting something was amiss. She had a bundle under her arm and when Anselm drew nearer he could see that it was the child, Lovisa, who was scarcely a month old.

He approached her, but he could not engage Brita Margaret in conversation. She just stared into the forest and did not stop walking, despite Anselm Andersson's friendly but increasingly insistent questions. At that moment he noticed that not only was she carrying the baby under her arm, she was also holding a knife in her hand. She would not reply to him, but steadfastly carried on towards the forest, even though Anselm was now anxiously pulling at her arm. Then she dropped the child on the floor and tried to pick her up; Anselm twisted the knife out of her hand, whereupon she sobbed and wailed, but did not offer any defence or explanation.

Anselm Andersson had understood what was happening and he took her into the house. He had saved the life of the child, Lovisa, who for ever after that would be called Lova. Anselm Andersson had realised that Brita Margareta Hällgren had gone mad and was going to kill the baby girl, and he also knew why.

Lova's mother, his father's maternal grandmother, had had seven children, of whom Lova was the youngest. In 1873 an epidemic of croup occurred. Croup caused a swelling inside the throat that led to blueness and suffocation, quite simply by preventing intake of breath. Mostly it affected young children. It was probably due to diphtheria. Six of the children contracted it within a month and died. All six. One after the other they had turned blue and died. Presumably Brita Margareta grieved at first, then grew silent and finally became deranged, making up her mind to kill the baby and herself so that no-one should be left behind.

She might have thought that now *nothing matters*.

There could be a more positive interpretation, in the biblical sense, and later this was widely accepted. People thought that she had probably heard God's voice, like Abraham did when God ordered him to *take now your son, your only son, whom you love, Isaac, and go to the land of Moriah, and offer him there as a burnt offering on one of the mountains of which I shall tell you*. God had Bensberget in mind. And that was where she was going with Lovisa, but perhaps hoping that God would restrain the hand holding the knife at the last moment, as he did when he said to Isaac, *Do not lay your hand on the boy*.

That is how people made sense of it. She never did explain.

The fact that one-month-old Lova had survived the croup was judged to have something to do with her mother's milk. It had saved her. But after the death of her six children his great-grandmother Brita Margareta had become very nervous, or by common consent, mad; the episode when Anselm Andersson prevented her going into the forest to kill her baby daughter had confirmed this. However, the family did not want to send her to the lunatic asylum in Umedalen, as that would bring shame on them all, so instead they took personal responsibility for her and locked her in the attic.

There she stayed until her death twenty-seven years later.

The only thing she did for those twenty-seven years was scribble. Sometimes she wrote on sheets of paper, or pieces of plank, or at worst, on the walls. In the end, after they had taken the carpenter's pencil away from her, she used a six-inch nail to scratch her words on to the walls. Nothing of what she wrote was kept and after her death everything was burned and scrubbed and repainted.

She never saw her daughter Lova again. It was only natural – they did not know what she might have done in her state. There was also a suspicion that a nervous condition might be contagious. The baby girl was the only member of the family who could carry the legacy. According to a family story, what the madwoman wrote on the pieces of paper, bits of plank and walls was some sort of poetry. People had heard that poems and insanity were often connected. The writer Fröding whom everyone talked about was crazy, for example.

So that was what happened to his grandmother, Lovisa. Saved like Isaac, the son of Abraham. The knife-wielding mother imprisoned with her eternal poetry. The question never answered was whether the scribbler's verse had contaminated the only surviving child, little Lova.

She wrote on the walls. The meaning was very unclear and then it was painted over. She took great pains, you have to admit, whatever it was she was trying to write.

The madwoman had scribbled things down. That was a clear response to the question about whether there was anyone else in the family who was prone to addiction and writing.

His mother let slip that his father had written verses in a note-pad, before his premature death. They had been "poems" of various kinds. Verses, one might say. He had always done this. Moreover, a month before he died, he had bought a violin. After his mother died, the child inherited it. It had almost never been played and yet one could imagine that, were it to have been played for a while, it would actually have sounded quite well played. At least that was what his father had believed. Generally speaking, the fiddle was considered a gypsy instrument. This was confirmed in the books of Sigge Stark, and therefore by the readers of Sigge Stark. It was not everyone who read them, they were not very edifying, but they were believable; many felt that much could be learned from Sigge Stark, about gypsies and fiddle-players, for example. When a gypsy came to the village and played the fiddle, some rivalry would always emerge over a pretty daughter still at home. That is not to say that the fiddle in itself was an instrument of sin.

Enough of that: his father had bought a violin, that much could be established, and in addition, he died with the violin unplayed; there was not necessarily a connection.

And the poems that went up in flames? Just prattle, his mother declared. She explained that she had discovered the notepad containing the verses after his death, read them and *devoured them with such ferocity that the paper was set alight, like a pyre of love*. That is what the child understood her to say. She had read the notepad and the verses were so good, so intense, that they burst into flames while she read them, fired by her grief and love. Like pointing a burning glass at the *Norran*. Another explanation, one that she had given him before, could be eliminated: that poetry was a sin and that was why she burned the notepad.

What actually happened remained unclear.

At any event the notepad was burned and the violin unplayed.

That was his father. Burned notepad and unplayed violin. There was not much information to be gathered about the roots of his writing obsession. Surely there was something else like poetry in his family background? He couldn't be alone in his addiction? What about his grandmother, little Lovisa, the survivor?

He had many memories of his father's father, P.W.

He could recount innumerable stories about foxes, because he had a fox farm. It stank of foxes, but you got used to it. He was a blacksmith too. And he had a tar kiln.

But his grandmother Lovisa was strangely silent and faceless.

When he went to her house, she always gave him a slice of bun and a treat, in the form of a sugar lump, but that does not give him any particular insight into her character. She had borne ten children, of whom four died, a case of natural wastage, nothing to make a fuss about; though she did burst into tears when one of them was mentioned.

He remembered Knut, who died of something at the age of one.

That time it was not croup, but something else, Spanish flu perhaps. If anyone was ill and had to stay at home, it was almost certain to be Spanish flu, or the stomach. There was an expression for that, *the Enquist belly*, something to do with *being delicate*. Small children could not be said to die of the Enquist belly. But they did often die.

In the face of death people were expected to be courageous and not show their emotions. The right way to behave was to take a deep breath and remember the child for a moment, to shed a tear and look forward to the great reunion on the other side. But not everyone could assume this mantel of quiet patience: Lova's mother had undeniably given in to her feelings of sorrow when she went up to the forest to sacrifice her lastborn child.

Lova was the village correspondent, he had discovered. She was the one who submitted pieces to the *Norran*.

Where had she learnt to write? All her relatives worked on the land and no-one wrote. The question was, what did they read? There was one single library in the village, a black box containing some fifty books belonging to the Blue Ribbon Association and looked after by Mimmi Sehlstedt. There was Runa and Sven-Edvin Salje and Bernhard Nordh and all the instructive books about alcohol avoidance. Bernhard Nordh especially was good; not even Stockholm authors could compete, that was common knowledge. He had read all the books himself. But he had never seen Lova come over to the Sehlstedts' kitchen and ask to look inside the box.

And writing? He could only recall one sentence she had written to him: "*I hope you will not spurn my little gift.*" She had sent him a birthday present, a small tin of sugar tablets. For his fifth birthday. He did not understand the word "spurn", but his mother explained. He was upset: was she suggesting that he was ungrateful?

His grandmother was a tiny old countrywoman, almost shrivelled, whose husband, Per Walfrid, had a shape and a face and told stories about foxes and built tar kilns; the boy was allowed to go along when they changed the barrels and the black tar poured out. Then his grand-father told him about the fox that had to be shot for its fur. He loved foxes.

But his grandmother had no face; she was only very small and silent. In his eyes her smallness was her chief characteristic.

Yet Lova was the only person in the village who wrote *things that were published*. In the newspaper.

She was known for that. No-one else could do it apart from her. She wrote short articles about chapel auctions and holidays with the preacher, Bryggman, and above all obituaries. Every time someone died, an obituary needed to be written. Lova did it. It was an important piece, it had to be right, and Lova was best at it. Lova could write in such a way that what was good was fixed for eternity, like a bright memory; the sting of death had struck, yet it had lost its sting, for the deceased had been taken up to heaven. However, when her favourite son Elof died, she did not write. That was the exception.

Best of all was when Lova wrote verses about the deceased. She signed them with L. or L.E. She wrote a long poem about Beda Renström that was generally described as good. Beda had been only thirty-six years old when she died. "*When the peal of bells drifts away on the air / and dust melds with earth again here in this place / then we will return in our thoughts to your presence / and deep in our hearts will remember your face.*" "Your" was written with a small letter to denote that it meant Beda, not God. He had inherited a bundle of newspaper cuttings of her articles, given to him when it was announced in the *Norran* that he was about to make his literary debut.

It made him happy to think that the person who sent them to him had a message for him.

Lova wrote her verses, but his grandfather wrote nothing.

It was debatable whether he could write at all. Yet it was not as simple as that. You could still be a bearer of tidings, or want to sketch out a story, or make something lasting that would be there after your death.

He was the village blacksmith, he burned tar kilns and he built a rowing boat for his daughter-in-law and grandchild when his son Elof died, a heavy and unwieldy thing. In due course he set up his fox farm behind the hut where he built the rowing boats. He loved his foxes, but he usually held his nerve and shot them and sold the furs. He bred a few. One became so beautiful and unusual, he sat and watched it and would not shoot it. It was a variety of red fox, known as a cross fox. No-one knew how he bred it; it was generally thought that red foxes were only found in Norway. The fox derived its name from the mark of a cross on its back. Many people came to look at his red fox, which gradually became so attached to Per Walfrid that it was almost human and consequently even more difficult to shoot.

In 1930 he undertook his long journey to Stockholm with the red fox, an expedition that by chance would be documented in a Stockholm newspaper.

It happened that an exhibition of animal furs had been organised in Stockholm. Since his grandfather thought that the red fox he had created, or bred, whatever word you want to use, was so remarkable, something that would be considered almost a work of art in the capital city, he decided to make the trip. He wanted to show the people of Stockholm his fox. It is possible that he misunderstood the rules of the exhibition: that he should have attended with the skin only. But he assumed that the fox should be exhibited alive and should accompany him. And thus it transpired.

He built a wooden cage into which the fox, despite a certain degree of resistance, could be placed. There was a feeling of alarm and anxiety amongst the villagers and a crowd of them gathered down at the milk collection table to see him off on the bus, which on this special day was driven as usual by Marklin. Many of them genuinely wished him and the fox every success, even though a journey to Stockholm must be regarded implicitly as foolish: no-one in the village had been further south than Umeå, and in any case not in the company of a fox. But his grandfather had often been described in the village as rather *contrary*, though this said with respect, and he could be pig-headed when he chose. He was known for being proud of his foxes, but no-one could have predicted that he should go so far as to drag the poor fox to Stockholm with him and present the creature *as a work of art*.

He had taken the bus to Skellefteå and then transferred himself and his travel companion on to the train to Bastuträsk, where he changed to the southbound Nordpilen to Stockholm. To begin with he sat with the cage in front of him on the floor of the compartment, but after a while he came to his senses and put it up on the seat opposite so that the fox could view the passing landscape or at least the lights from the cottages in the foreign land that lay south of Jörn. P.W. had plenty of water and food in his rucksack and they divided it into reasonably equal shares; they both appeared quite calm and unconcerned, despite the amazement of some of their fellow passengers. In those days it took some time to reach Stockholm, a day and a night, but the two travellers from Sjön, Hjoggböle, managed to sleep for a short while and once they were in Stockholm they would undoubtedly stay awake, overwhelmed as they would be by impressions of the capital city.

No-one knows how P. W. Enquist took care of the transport arrangements for the fox in Stockholm, although other details of the expedition were well-known in the village as late as the 1990s. At any rate he arrived at the exhibition. And there they were immortalised by a newspaper photographer. What happened was recorded in the caption. "*P.W. Enquist of Hjoggböle was the worthy winner of the first prize trophy for the most beautiful fur displayed by this red fox.*"

The picture is fantastic in its own right. His grandfather is wearing a leather hat pulled down over his ears – so it must have been winter – and is holding the fox in his arms. The fox is gigantic; P.W. is staring wide-eyed with fear or pride straight into the camera and has the fox in a firm grip. It looks heavy and it is not struggling to be free, but pressing closer to him, as if seeking protection against the hostile surroundings.

The fox has turned his head towards the photographer. He is watching this Stockholm man with a worried expression. Grandfather and the fox seem as one. They know what they have done. They have travelled a long distance, embarked on an expedition together. They have taken the risk of leaving Hjoggböle, the first in the entire family to do so, in order to achieve something. This is it. They turn to each other in a terrified and determined embrace. United, they have overcome the dangers of this foreign, unfriendly land.

P.W. did not write verses or obituaries and certainly not a novel. But he made this red fox, broke loose and took first prize.

Then they made their slow way home. It was the only long journey he ever undertook. He would never leave the village again.

CHAPTER 3

THE FELLOW TRAVELLER

One of the three tall trees to fall was not a pine tree, it was Elof.

Over time he understood the difference.

He needed to interpret this figure now and make sense of the sign.

He sleeps in the bedroom on the first floor of the green house with his mother.

The bed was acquired before his birth, actually for the ghost boy, but now he lies in it himself, in this coffin for the living. There he has his repose, safe in the arms of God. The bed is extendable to accommodate his growth. In this way he remains for ever the child in the coffin. In essence he spends his entire childhood as a newborn infant, growing taller only by stealth, and he is therefore always dependent.

His mother alone in her narrow bed. The marriage bed, a double, is now sold. A chest of drawers on the left, a glass of water for her false teeth; she lost her own when she was seventeen. She never discusses it, does not want to share her humiliation, but when she laughs it is restrained, almost afraid, as if she still feels the shame.

The child will inherit her smile as well: faint, embarrassed, seemingly shy.

A staircase descends from the bedroom. It was down this that his mother was carried when his dead brother was lying the wrong way round and she was in labour. When, much later, Åke Sehlstedt relates this to the now grown-up child, he puts it succinctly: "*I carried the foot-end.*"

So there should be no misunderstanding.

Surrounding the bedroom is the village, then the country and after that the world; but over everything hangs his dead father.

There is not a great deal to know about him.

He had died. Something to do with his stomach. Without warning he stopped breathing in the hospital. Perhaps it was his appendix, as Dr Hultman supposed, or possibly porphyria, a rare inherited disorder he would pass on to his son, like so many other things. A Dutchman had introduced porphyria to Upper Norrland in the eighteenth century; it caused blood in the urine and 30 per cent of sufferers died before it was obvious what it was. It occurred in Holland, South Africa and Arvidsjaur in Norrbotten County. There was a joke among doctors in Uppsala that if you flew over northern Norrland in the winter, you could see which villages had cases of porphyria. The snow was stained with red where the men urinated. Later in life he sees it as a streak of internationalism in the provinces and himself as a citizen of the world. Not even people in Stockholm had this. He feels powerful; porphyria is a secret order, it is different, almost superior, like the Knights Templar – though some did die.

Better this than the appendix. Practically everyone died of appendicitis. Much better to die of an international disease. Medical records are kept at the municipal offices in Bureå; some time in the 1980s he asked to see them and it pleases him to think that it definitely was porphyria.

His battle with death had lasted three days.

As he lay dying in his bed at Bureå cottage hospital he appealed to the Saviour and entrusted his son to him. According to his mother. His father's last words were about the child, his heir. And that carried a responsibility.

Later the son almost reproaches her for this. Driven by her zeal for salvation, she did not leave her husband in peace, even on his deathbed! She wanted to have him save the child *there too*! *Undoubtedly at her request*, the father had sent two written messages to the boy, who was only six months old at the time. One was: "*Per-Ola, become a Christian.*"

He was in pain and then lost consciousness and yet he had managed to write, albeit shakily, inside the cover of the hymn book. The trembling hand made it all the more momentous.

He had been taken up to heaven and that was where he was.

It was difficult to find out much about who he was. Only that he was up there. His brothers spoke mostly about how funny he had been: he told stories, was the most popular in the team of stevedores, good-looking and nice to women, *but in a respectful way* that everyone liked. However, this was not in accordance with the facts, in the eyes of his mother.

Not wrong exactly, but it was *unnecessary to dwell on it*.

She believed that the real features of his personality were written up in the Book of Life, the good and pious qualities. He had many friends and displayed loyalty and humility. By dint of her earnest prayers during his lifetime, he had obtained complete salvation, that much was beyond doubt – even as early as the start of their engagement. In effect she had managed it all herself and now he was dead and in heaven.

All that business about telling stories and being nice was definitely exaggerated. Beside the point.

All the child knew about his father was this: in the end he was saved, not actually on his deathbed, but shortly before they were married. It was not clear exactly when he allied himself with the Saviour.

But he was saved. It had made her so happy.

When questioned as an adult he repeatedly insists that he does not miss his father.

"Absence of a father *is a strength*." No weighty burden of expecta-tions. In a good-natured way he pities the many people who have had a father and therefore never known freedom. This is the position he adopts. All that the child knows about "his father" is that he did exist and he was a good man. He has gone up to heaven and as such is untouchable.

For obscure, possibly purely documentary, reasons, in this village a photograph of the corpse is always taken: the camera captures the image of the body in the coffin. This record is not kept on the mantelpiece. *Special care* is taken of it. The boy is allowed the privilege – particularly at holiday times – of studying his father's photograph. It makes him seem omnipotent. When was it taken, he asks in a tremulous voice, was it while he was alive? You have to die first before the photograph can be taken, his mother replies, can you see – there's the coffin! But when does he go up to heaven? After he is dead, but before the photograph is taken?

She finds it a strange question.

So many things are unclear. His mother is easily irritated, but the child does not understand the chronology: first you died, then the picture was taken, then you went up to heaven? But then he had to *lie there in the coffin while they went to fetch the camera*? For some reason his mother does not reply, but just turns to leave. The child perseveres. *First you died, then the photograph in the coffin was taken, then you went up to heaven*. In that order? Wrong. *First you died, then you went to heaven, then the photograph in the coffin was taken*. Perplexed, the child studies every detail of the photograph that reveals, if that is the case, only the *outer casing of someone who has already gone to heaven*!

He is, as it were, not there.

With growing suspicion the child examines this photograph, entirely documentary, of the empty shell that no longer contains his father.

Apart from this, his mother talks very little about her dead husband.

The child is now hers alone. When she does speak of him it is with kindliness, but it is very brief. He was wonderful. She does not use that word. She mentions him perhaps once a year, always with affection, almost love, at any rate with respect. In the end he had come through and been saved. But it had been hard.

To begin with the child does not know who she is talking about in such a reverential way. The absent person bears some sort of relationship to the child, but not a significant one. Not one that might disturb her own obvious ownership of the child. He is still *somehow related to the pine tree*.

He has gone. The child contemplates the invisible one painlessly. The child bears no blame, nor does the mother; he exists in eternity and must not be mourned. His memory is not swathed in sorrow, but the title "Elof" endures. The child does not know where he is, but he does exist. He may be nearby, as well as up above. Above the clouds.

Does he have a name? He speculates for a long time. Then he finds out. Elof. Per Elof. All the men in the family are called Per. It passes down through the generations, like porphyria.

The signs fade and everything begins to clarify. His father is in heaven. He is quite close, but above and apart. Much later in his life he reproduces parrot-fashion his mother's view that he *does not miss his father*.

First there was the bedroom, on the first floor. Beyond that the village. Followed by the country, which could be drawn on greaseproof paper. And then the world.

But above it all, and quite close, is his father.

He has a collection of pictures of angels, mostly the decapitated heads of children on beds of rose-petals. It was something you could collect. One or two of these angels were different, depictions of men, but with wings. They look like Jesus. The child – who is now four – understands these to be guardian angels. He is convinced that his father is such a guardian angel. Thus there is an explanation: his father is a guardian angel, he is in heaven, that is to say higher than the roof, but not as high at the summit of Bensberget, the local alp, at 112 metres. Now he has the outward appearance of a man, like the living uncles. He is dressed in a black serge suit with white shirt and tie, he is wearing a hat, a dark-coloured bowler-type – the boy has seen this in several photographs – and he has wings.

The wings are white and he looks very nifty when he flaps them.

Sometimes, sitting at the bedroom window by the rowan tree, the snow-clad valley spreading below him, the boy feels an involuntary fear and loneliness.

It is possible to be alone even when his mother is in the house.

At these times he concentrates his thoughts on his father, who almost invariably appears. He is dressed in the black suit, with the wings. He does not say a word to the child as he deftly flutters the wings, as if in encouragement, great or small. This means the child, who is still four or maybe already as old as six, can contemplate his father's situation and what advice he can give. And he always comes, summoned by the child's silent cry for help!

It behoves him to have trust.

It happens especially in the winter, when the hum of the telephone wires resonates against the roof of the green house, like a *celestial harp*, the phrase he was commended for. The praise that was so rare, because she trained him in humility. His mother was almost rapturous the first time he uttered these words and she said to him *Per-Ola, you're becoming a real orator!*

This is before his implicit faith and openness is shaken by Flash Gordon's journey through the heavens.

Since his father always comes, and since he can rely on his father in times of extreme misery and self-deception, the child very soon begins to regard him as not simply a guardian angel, properly dressed in a serge suit and small wings, but something of a benefactor.

When, a little while later – he has now reached the age of eight – he reads a book entitled *The Mysterious Island*, he discovers that the men shipwrecked on the island are helped by a similar benefactor, Captain Nemo. He is the only survivor on the submarine *Nautilus*. Hidden deep in the dormant volcano, he intervenes on behalf of the castaways in moments of crisis, but without making himself known.

At first the child is confused: how can his father be there, at the centre of the volcano, beside the castaways on the mysterious island,

and at the same time be swishing his wings upstairs on the first floor? Is he in the body of Captain Nemo? Or perhaps his father is only one of many guardian angels. Who protect other children as well.

He is irritated. He had thought he was the only one with a guardian angel.

He quickly dismisses these thoughts, secure in the knowledge that his father, in spite of everything, is the only one who directs his beneficence *just to him*. This bestows upon the two of them a closeness that bodes well for the times of *crisis and immense vulnerability* to come. Since his mother sometimes reads aloud from religious tracts, which abound in big words, he soon learns these expressions about *crisis and vulnerability and great danger*.

It gives it colour. He is quite pleased if he can feel a modicum of *crisis*.

Nemo changes everything. The image of the besuited wing-flapper fades away.

A different picture of his father appears.

It is the impression of his father as a secret friend, a well-wisher who has remained the age he died, thirty-one years old.

The Benefactor is dead.

He died when the child was six months old. He repeats this like a mantra to anyone who is sympathetic. *He died when I was six months old*. This often makes him the object of pity, which he likes. He notes that most people feel sorry for a person who has no father. Tragic, or lonely. He enjoys the sympathy and is happy to say again: *My father died when I was six months old*. Sometimes it is rather tedious. Actually those six months were *a load of old bullshit*, he might think to himself – now he is an adult and has learned how to abuse language with profanities – but he keeps on repeating it.

He does not suffer particularly. Nothing to feel sorry for.

It all hinges on *how* a father disappears.

A child might think that it is his fault if his father disappears. The child has done something to be punished in this way.

Some people do feel like this. But in his case: no guilt whatsoever. His father died of a burst appendix! Who can help that? He did not die in an inappropriate manner. The proper way is to die of a burst appendix at the age of thirty-one, *when the child is only six months old*. There it is again! His mother always assures him that Elof was a fantastic father, for as long as it lasted, in other words half a year, so it was all blameless and unsullied. The child knows that his father has gone up to heaven and sits at God's right hand, looking down with a benevolent but exacting smile.

This makes it rather different. Much better. This way he is not guilty. And not nearly so lonely. Quite the reverse. This way his father is a benefactor, nearly always a very good thing to have. The surviving parent, his mother, bestows upon him a protector and he should give thanks, *to her*. For her goodness. Though he is not completely sure that he is right about "goodness".

The child often entreats her to talk about him, the departed. At those times she tells him that the true believer and good father was taken up to heaven and sits up there, dressed in a full-length white gown, and so on. And that is that. It takes about a minute. Then full stop, and on with something else. No details! No special paternal quality! Nothing to give him a face. He is *briefly mentioned*, but is given neither character nor humanity. Dead, taken up to heaven, at God's right hand. Not escorted off to the side, but aloft, to be swallowed up by eternity.

This is how she means to kill him, after his death. The boy suspects that she harbours a fear that someone, the father, will assume part-ownership of the child. The child whom now she shares with no-one and whom she will always possess, she alone, for ever and ever.

If he does not run away from her.

The child adores his mother and admires her.

He knows that she has created him, but he is restless in the loving hands of the sculptress. He starts to hatch a plan of escape. But it must happen in absolute secrecy. She must not find out that she is no longer the sole proprietor of the child. He will never tell.

He is sure that she would burst into tears if he did.

In *The Mysterious Island* Nemo was the castaways' Benefactor *in secret and without making himself known.*

He starts to think of the word with a capital B. It is *secret*. Benefaction must take place secretly. His mother must not know about it. To have a father who is a Benefactor is the best of things, almost a security. You knew that he was sitting up there at God's right hand and *cared*; and that you could consult with the Benefactor in difficult and awkward situations. Particularly when Jesus and God did not have time, as they seldom did, barely ever. It was strange, but you must not criticise them for it; if you did, his mother's face would darken and she would fall silent. It did not help to beg for forgiveness. It was almost a mortal sin, like going to Holy Communion and not being true to your faith.

But this was later, when the child was about to fall apart.

Obviously you should not in any way suggest that God or Jesus did not have time or could not be bothered. *Not one sparrow is forgotten in the sight of . . .* ! And so on. She has biblical proof of everything. The child has the definite impression that God and Jesus are always rushed off their feet. You were surprised that they did have the time, but you had to wait, it was as if they were always busy making hay in heaven.

But a father was a different matter. In Christ's silence you could almost hear the Benefactor breathing. Then you could sit quietly in a corner and report all your concerns to your dead father – Elof, that is, not a pine tree.

And in return he gave you *wordless counsel*.

This was something no other child had. It was wonderful to have him there, a privilege. He was chosen. Not advice in the form of words.

It was his presence and above all the soothing motion of his hand that penetrated the awful darkness.

If he woke up at night, shaking with fear at the realisation of *eternity* – a word he had heard so many times during the otherwise incomprehensible and therefore not even slightly frightening sermons in the chapel – *that eternity actually was never-ending*, mercilessly stretching out into infinity, punishment eternal, holding an everlasting horror; if he woke up and recognised that even his mother's peaceful breathing in the darkness did not mean salvation, since she too was wrapped in this ruthless eternity, far, far beyond the starry darkness: at times such as these, the child could call on his Benefactor and ask for advice and guidance in his anguish.

If the punishment for sin was eternity, which was endless, was there any mercy in this timelessness?

He had been forced to listen to the tale about the nature of eternity, written by one of the most feared authors of the Catholic inquisition, called Mia Hallesby. Called! There had to be an explanation for who was hiding behind this apparently innocent woman's name. In her parable on eternity, *the word that measured the extent of punishment*, there was a mountain in the sea and a bird. The mountain was a mile long, a mile wide and a mile high. Once every thousand years a bird came and sharpened his beak on the mountain. When the whole mountain had been worn away by the bird sharpening his beak, *only a second of eternity had passed*.

His mother had read the story to him as if it were a parable of Jesus, and it was drummed into him that *this was eternity*.

At night, when he awoke, engulfed in eternity, the Benefactor was there as his salvation. There he was, emerging through the darkness, a Fellow Traveller *raising his hand in a gesture of calm*. There were no words to accompany a movement so inspiring and mighty. His father seemed to be master of eternity, exercising power over everything. Even time. Yes, he was in fact *all time*; the sign his arm made denoted calm. Dread of eternity stretching out disappeared and time was restored to the child. Because eternity was so terrifying, filled with threats and torments at the very least, in almost every case the Benefactor's presence was essential. He was *inside* eternity.

He gave a sign with his hand and his gentle movement; and that was enough. He did not hear his father's voice.

Once he tried to imagine his father's voice.

It would be like the deep male voice he had heard on the radio programme "If War Comes", telling people not to trust spies and to stick black paper up at the windows. Was this Elof's voice? A fleeting moment, then he knew better. Signs were more reliable, the right hand indicating that he should not worry.

Signs had to be interpreted.

It said in the Acts of the Apostles that it was perfectly natural to interpret signs, so that the people could understand. First, tongues of fire on the day of Pentecost, sent down from on high, but not burning. Then the crowd, all speaking different languages, understanding everything, whatever their native tongue. He was only a child, but he had a special responsibility in the family. An interpreter of signs, in a way the head of the family, meaning something special.

You had to step up yourself and accept this role, not because you were arrogant, but unique.

He had once heard the word "utterance" explained: it meant that people spoke to each other without words, but with guiding gestures and tongues of fire.

That was what the word meant.

The conversations between himself and Elof were like this. Gestures and interpretation and questions. In this way the child could deliberate over difficult and testing situations. If he had a problem and needed some advice, he could mull it over for a while and come up with an utterance. Then the father mulled it over up in heaven and gave an utterance to the child, like sending down a tongue of fire. They sat like this, uttering utterances, until the point at issue was allayed and diminished. Quite simply.

You could do this because he was dead and the Benefactor.

That was in the beginning. He gained *a loyal friend*. Almost like a dog, for those people whose blessing it is to have one. This was not the case for him, as his mother had no wish for a puppy, or a cat, after the one she used to have left a pile of excrement on the iron stove. It was only that cat, he argued, *all kittens are not the same, it is probably not inherited*; but his mother just laughed, and still no cat.

The Benefactor had a name. Not Nemo. He was called Elof.

Later on, when he is older, he feels a sense of grief for his father.

He was quite young when he died and what could he really have experienced? Everything the child read in the local paper, *Norra Västerbotten*, maybe the football results in the Northern Counties Coastal League, or how things were going in the war, about the armoured battle on the Eastern Front, *the tank battle at Kursk!* – about all these elementary things the dead man had no information.

It might not always be much fun, just being dead. Sitting at God's right hand. The streets were paved with gold in heaven, his mother had assured him, and perhaps it was quite pleasant to take an afternoon walk along those streets; like being in Skellefteå, but in *the golden city!* Strolling along the golden streets. Exciting the first time. But wouldn't it become a bit humdrum in the end? Was there a forest in heaven? Or trenches? Just sauntering around in the golden city and in-between, only being able to look down on the child, still down there amongst all the excitement of the Northern Counties Coastal League or Kursk.

Is it not his duty to keep Elof informed and let him join in? Take part in all the fun. Report things. No false accounts. Tell his father the whole truth.

He can see what he needs to do. Bring his father down to earth and make him more than a Benefactor – make him a Fellow Traveller.

Things had been happening since he died. Things he had not been told about. The new bus route between Skellefteå and Hjoggböle. The invention of wood gas generators, so that buses did not need to run on petrol. And more besides! His father would be completely left behind by progress, if his son did not step in as adviser and informant, he tries on one occasion to tell his mother. Looking at him in silence, she pats him on the top of his head, his hair newly cut, without responding. An hour later she asks: "Do you talk to Pappa?"

He confirms that he does. Then, just like that, no more questions. Presumably she does not want to know more.

The same evening she spends a long time sitting alone with her Bible, tears in her eyes, rises after the evening meal and goes to bed early. During the night he can hear from her breathing that she is sleeping badly or not at all. The following morning he tries to explain, that *it is my responsibility to include Pappa now that he is dead*. Her expression withdrawn, almost despairing, she does not reply and he does not bring it up again.

At Christmas his mother does not want the two of them to be alone together.

It is a time for joyous celebration – sitting at home deep in the forest commemorating the birth of Christ is very devout, but lonely. Jesus was an only child as well, she used to say, and Joseph was not his father. Maria was *a single mother with Jesus*. To a certain extent she wants this almost biblical comparison to sink deep into his consciousness. It does not help. It will be lonely anyway. No three wise men will pay a visit to the snowbound green house.

Besides, they have a very big family on his mother's side. She was born at Gammelstället, a farm with cousins, animals and his grandmother.

Every year at Christmas-time they set out on an expedition there.

His uncle is called John. He has four children, who are therefore his cousins, a wife, six cows, two horses, Tindra and Stella, eight nameless pigs, and, living in the attic, a farmhand they feel sorry for because he has never married. He is an old bachelor who scratches the eczema on his scalp while he eats his porridge, *which means he puts the eczema into his mouth*. No-one likes it, but he will not mend his ways. It is worst at mealtimes because there is not enough room. It is a squeeze to fit everyone round the table, but the alternative is the two of them alone in the green house. It is actually much better there, apart from the old man's eczema while they are eating.

Gammelstället is the only house by the lake other than Larssons-gården. There was no proper road to it, so first you had to take the bus, which ran on gas and was driven by Marklin, and get off at Harrsjömyren. This was a marsh that his mother had helped to drain in her younger days, she used to say, a fact undisputed by her brother. He would be waiting there with a sledge. It was a sleigh on runners, with skins to sit on and sides, pulled by Stella. She was nicer than Tindra, who used to bite, especially in summer, when the child was there helping.

He was supposed to be gaining experience in haymaking for his future life as *a well-to-do freeholder* – his mother was aiming high for her only son: freeholder or priest. Preferably priest.

At Gammelstället they were not quite so devout; they were not heathens, but they had not found salvation, though he did not bother to discuss this with his mother.

Christmas was more fun amongst those who had not found salvation.

His grandmother was called Johanna and in summer he used to sleep outside with her, under sheepskins. He would read to her. Sometimes she admonished him, especially that time she was dying. It was only ever when he was reading that her warnings were issued.

When she was dying she had told him about Pappa and alcohol.

The child views the trips to Gammelstället as expeditions. The difficulty involved is not to be underestimated, he confides in Elof.

The expedition is not without danger, he usually says to him. He explains, *without causing unnecessary alarm*, what will happen. To begin with they wait down by the milk stand at about six in the evening, long after darkness has fallen at around two, dreading that something has happened to the bus and they will not be able to set off. Finally they see the lights of the bus in the distance, almost as far away as Forsen; they grow larger and larger and the bus stops, as if by command. They are down below the green house, built by his father with the help of *his* father, the village blacksmith, something that obviously happened before he died and was snatched away. *This really is information his father does not need.* They climb aboard and pay. Then Marklin puts a piece of firewood into the gas generator attached at the back. The gas generator is, he explains for the benefit of the puzzled Friend, who has not been party to this particular piece of technological progress, like a steam engine fired with logs, because this is wartime and Hitler has forbidden petrol motors.

The moment arrives when Marklin puts it into forward gear.

The bus begins its cautious ascent up the slight incline towards Sehlstedts, but usually all is well. It drives along for miles in the pitch-black night until, in the distance, they see an enormous black horse with a sleigh: it is his uncle's and almost certainly his cousin Ivan, who is the same age as him, will be there too; the bus stops and it is time to set off through the forest.

All year long the child can look forward to this really quite daring adventure. Often he is afraid that something *will be found wanting*, an expression his grandmother uses when she wants to sound grand: for example, the horse and sleigh might not be waiting in the darkness by Harrsjömyren, where his mother says she used to go wading in long boots as a child, cutting marsh hay, before it was all drained, that is. And if the sleigh was not there, what would the poor widow-woman and her small child do in the blackness – freeze or starve to death or maybe vainly try to defend themselves against a wolf attack? He could imagine the scene. He did not want to scare Elof, but he had to tell him.

He used to conjure up this dangerous adventure in his mind several weeks before it happened. First he asked Jesus for help and advice. But the Saviour was rarely at home. Not that it mattered, his Fellow Traveller was always around. He had never accompanied them on this expedition, there was not time before he died, but now *he came with them*.

That was how it should be. For those who had been taken up to heaven. *You had to take them back*.

It was desperate. Elof must have had some qualities his mother chose to conceal.

People in the village said he was practical; he was certainly not some-one with two left hands. He would be able to accompany them on the Christmas expedition and help out. In the bus. For instance, he would be able to help Marklin deal with the gas, assist with the sack of firewood and then, sitting under the sheepskins in the sleigh, suggest how to find their way through the forest with no lights at all, the howls of the wolves echoing around them. Afterwards he would be there for the whole Christmas holiday, possibly outside at night under grandmother's sheepskin. She wanted to be on her own with the child. But even under his grandmother's sheepskin, the child would not explain the reason for his strangely calm and almost cheerful silence.

The Fellow Traveller was present, unseen, a little to one side, but benevolent, silent, his eyes wide in amazement. Because Aunt Lilly went out onto the bridge and blew into the whistle for Santa. Because Santa came from the byre where Uncle John had just gone to pacify Tindra and Stella, or so he said to the children, but everyone knew.

He gave all this information to the Fellow Traveller in silence, so that he could marvel at it but not be awkward. The boy sat on the kitchen bench and counted his Christmas presents, silently moving his lips as if in conversation with someone invisible. And no-one could see that he had placed his father, the Fellow Traveller and Guide, on the bench beside him and all was bliss and joy.

No grief or loss. The one who died, the Fellow Traveller, is present with him on this bid for escape.

As he grew up his thoughts were no longer those of a child. But his Fellow Traveller stayed with him. His presence had become a prerequisite, impossible to alter. The child became a father and Elof a child. He took his father along on all his new experiences. In all that his father *had never lived through*.

He does not understand that he is on the run.

When the now grown man sits on a plane as it takes off, he is sitting by the Fellow Traveller's side, silently moving his lips and saying that *it is not dangerous and look how small the cars appear to be and that house over there!* Elof never had the chance to fly in his lifetime and now the world is being pointed out to him from the window of the plane.

You can show things to dead people. Like a father does to his son.

He can sit on a high-speed train between Paris and Lyon and his young father, the Fellow Traveller on the run, is next to him. No longer wearing the thirties-style ill-fitting serge suit, but a leather suit from Åhléns department store, quite pricey. But still a 31-year-old child with no experience.

This train is from another planet. It is Elof's first taste of the new world and he needs guidance and instruction. *But in a friendly way! With love!* Because the now ageing boy loves his 31-year-old father. The train, gliding through the countryside without the slightest shake; and the dizzy speed of more than 320 k.p.h.: this is being shared by the Fellow Traveller. Never before has he travelled by train, but now it is absolutely crucial that he shares the experience that was denied him by the sudden stomach pains and loss of consciousness at Bureå cottage hospital in the skilled but helpless hands of Dr Hultman.

He explains gently, *but without boasting*, how the train was built and that his father does not need to be afraid. *Don't be frightened, Pappa*, the now seasoned seventy-year-old boy might say to his 31-year-old father on the high-speed train.

When he goes to the theatre he arrives in good time and tells his father about Strindberg or about the main stage at the Royal Dramatic Theatre; and that *it will be starting soon*. And in a whisper he summarises pieces of information, *without a doubt this counts as one of the greatest theatres in the world and one that Swedes have good reason to be proud of*. Then his father might ask: *Have they staged your plays here too?* And without being boastful, he would silently nod. If he watches a film, he thinks that now Pappa is seeing it for the first time. He is going to find this very entertaining and quite amazing. In this way everything is twice as much fun.

The Fellow Traveller is a child and he is a father. If he turns his head he can see his father watching intently, with curiosity, joy and surprise, open and uninhibited. He can see how his father's brief life slowly and painlessly slides into his own.

Does he really need to escape?

He knows that his mother is the person who has influenced his life most, the person who created him. In his flight he takes his father with him. Someone has to care for Elof, after all. He thinks of it as his task. Not like a father forcing knowledge on his boy or placing expectations on him that weigh like a sack of stones upon the shoulders of the not-so-young child, but as if they had changed places, and now, reunited, they are both fleeing.

Yet the Fellow Traveller does not have the answer to the simplest question: why it began so well and turned out so badly.

CHAPTER 4

THE CALVING COW

In the summer of 1991 his mother moves from her flat to the Torparen old people's home in Bureå, where she will die the following year. He comes up to clear it out.

The basement area does not contain much, but the move takes a few days. He rediscovers old notebooks, letters, Baby Jesus' crib and round hats. A class reunion is taking place at the same time; it is forty years since they passed their school certificate.

The school was a higher elementary school with no final examination and they were the first class in the parish to take the school certificate. This they did as private students during a week of exams at the secondary school in Umeå. He gains his grey student cap and life can begin. Faithfully following in his mother's footsteps on her journey of class mobility – from peasant's daughter to schoolteacher – he applies to the teacher training college in Umeå. Like her, he would *train to be a primary schoolteacher*.

It is 1951.

That summer he works at the Bureå sawmill, mostly carting bark from the drum. There is a constant thundering noise from the surging water and he hates it. He secretly lays the foundations for a lifelong appreciation of the necessity for technology in the workplace.

He is still delicate, but not to the same extent.

In August he is notified that he has not been accepted by the college, but is eighth on the waiting list. He sees the bark drum looming ahead of him. Was this what was supposed to happen? He has also applied to the high school in Skellefteå and he is offered a place there. The first day at high school there is a telephone call from Umeå, informing him that a number of applicants have withdrawn and he has reached the top of the waiting list. He hesitates for a few hours and then decides to continue at the high school.

While the high school offers an uncertain future, the college offers security. After four years there he would be an elementary schoolteacher and perhaps, like his mother, gain a position in Hjoggböle. Instead he will matriculate and Uppsala, Copenhagen, Berlin, Los Angeles and Paris will follow.

Which would have been better? He does not know. He remembers every detail of the four years at the higher elementary school in Bureå, as clear as the air after a heavy fall of rain. The three years at high school are a blank. After the gigantic leap he took in the first four years, he seems to be inching laboriously forward for the following three.

It might have something to do with the rector, Nilsson.

He often muses on life's crossroads. It had all hinged on one day.

A few decades later, in 1975, he had written a play he called *The Night of the Tribades*. An incredibly beautiful female journalist from the Danish Broadcasting Corporation wants to come up and do an interview. He declines, but having lost his way in the corridors of the Royal Dramatic Theatre, he accidentally bumps into her. He cannot give his excuses now; the interview takes place and changes his life. She is walking cautiously towards him along the corridor, almost shy; he is completely spellbound, leaves his marriage, marries her and lives with her in Denmark for fifteen years.

If he had gone down another corridor, his life would have been quite different. He does not know where crossroads will lead him.

Among his mother's notebooks and papers he finds an obituary notice, cut out of the *Norran*.

As is the custom, it gives a glowing appreciation. "*Elof Enquist's sudden death has caused consternation in the neighbourhood. The enormous sorrow of the family he leaves is shared by the people of the village, who had* come to know him as an honourable and good person." So far so good. But further down towards the end of the obituary, he reads the following sentence: "*Elof Enquist was a philanthropic man and a member of the Knights Templar.*"

He stares at the sentence, cannot believe his eyes. And right at the bottom: "*His last and dearest wish was to leave this earthly life and meet his comforter.*"

Who wrote that!? Was his dearest wish really to leave this earthly life? Who wrote it?

Knights Templar!

He thinks he knows, more or less, what this secret, closed and exclusive order stands for and what sector of society it recruits from. What a thirty-year-old stevedore from Hjoggböle is doing as a member of the Skellefteå chapter of the Knights Templar is a mystery. Recommended by whom? And why? How did he gain entry? He recalls that every Christmas after his death, his mother receives a flower arrangement from a "society" his father belonged to. She cannot explain. "*It was all so secret.*"

There is a great deal about his parents he does not know. Things do not add up, for them, or for himself. A Knight Templar! Almost a Freemason! Something is wrong. The map of his parents' life, which is also the map of his own, remains full of empty white fields. The countless photographs of the stevedore gang, pinned up in front of the pulp boat in Bureå harbour, are safer. The labourers are lined up like a football team, his father in the middle, often smiling. Sons of the workers, the stevedore gang. It is a fact. He likes the pictures. This is what he wants to see.

But Knights Templar? That is not right.

He decides to seek out the truth about his father's secret order. It takes some time, but finally he discovers that this father was initiated on 24 September 1931, *proposed by factory owner Frans Eriksson and freeholder Per Johan Lundström*. He is placed in the lowest rank. The inner workings are secret and women are not allowed; despite normal progression of one rank a year, so that the level of grand master can be reached in seven years, his activities appear to be non-existent. He stands still. Not even the second tier. It is unclear whether he attends more than one meeting. And yet the tribute on 19 September 1935 and, as mentioned above, the flower arrangement every Christmas.

The chief requirements for members are temperance and restraint. Acceptance into this order is seen as proof that someone is *of significance*.

If he perceived this as success, why did he give up?

The order operates on a series of different levels. "*A higher level is a new experience, providing the person attaining this level with new knowledge.*" "*Each Brother knows only those levels he has already attained.*"

Under normal circumstances he would have reached the fourth or fifth level before he died. But it is blank. Was he striving upwards, forwards, or inwards? It is not clear from the document. Only that he gave up.

Was he restless?

Since he is an only child – the only-begotten son! – his mother has certain expectations. *If everything goes according to plan he will finish up as a priest.*

It is clear very early on. He is going to be a preacher.

Holding back her tears, his mother gives him the hymn book, with the messages from his father inscribed on one of the endpapers. His eyes glistening with devotion, he obediently tries to read. It is written in letters of fire throughout his childhood. *Follow the message! Do not let your father down!* The haunting words inside the hymn book, written with a trembling hand, in pencil, when his father knew he was dying. At his mother's request he reads them over and over again and a familiar uneasiness sweeps over him. The first line is crystal clear. "*Per-Ola, become a Christian.*"

How do you shake off a legacy? And is it the legacy of the lumberjack, the stevedore, or the secret Knight Templar?

Why the uneasiness? Why is he against his mother? The first signs of recalcitrance! He sees himself through her and begins to wonder.

Isn't there something ambiguous about her ties to the revivalist movement? A touch of the high church seems to be lurking there. If she thinks the child is destined to be a preacher, she must envisage a future for him like the local minister, Forsell. This man cycles between villages and chapels and supports his swarm of children by working as a grave digger. Perhaps she has Bishop Giertz in mind. She has a copy of his book, *The Hammer of God*, and reads it often, despite the theological abyss it must reveal. The Oxford Group! Will the child be Forsell the minister or Giertz the bishop?

He does not know what she might envisage.

Yet imperceptibly he slips into the role of preacher; it is like an existential drug. The parables! *How Jesus meets us wherever we are*! Every trivial event can be interpreted as a poignant Christian message, even proof! That is the preacher's function: to see Christ everywhere around us.

The Saviour is to be found in the most unlikely places, like the photograph of Christ at a depth of 485 metres in the Kristineberg mine: an image of Christ created by devout miners in an explosion and documented in a photograph in the *Norran*. And eventually on a 25-cent postcard. The sharp-sighted *preacher* is the one who can immediately see *the reality* behind *the apparent* and blasts Jesus forth from the rock face. In contrast to the writer of fiction, who makes things up: an act of profanity. That is the difference.

His role model is a great master-preacher, like Dahlberg, the mission director, active at the summer meetings of the Women Teachers' Mission League's summer meetings. That is what he wants to become. When Dahlberg gives the blessing, he always leaves a slight pause before the last word in "*and give us . . . peace*". Without the pause he would be someone else entirely, or perhaps no-one at all. Dahlberg is a magical figure to emulate.

He decides that he too will start using a pause and make himself a magician.

*

He is in the habit of sometimes conjuring up this Jesus, blown out of the rock like this. It carries on well into his adolescence.

He is about to enter his first serious competition, a regional championship in junior athletics. High jump. It is in the morning. He has been jogging in the forest, because he has learned that this is what you do before all-important competitions. This one is at Örjansvall in Skelleftehamn. It is where he meets Christ.

Christ is disguised as an unassuming, elderly primary schoolteacher, or, as his mother sometimes says in jest, a teacher of both infants *and* juniors, thus emphasising the distinction. The female figure stops on the forest path and asks: "But, is it you Per-Ola?" He comes to a halt and answers: "Yes, it is, what do you want of me?" Perhaps he does not say *what do you want of me* in so many words, but he would like to think so. Something of the tone of the Old Testament, *God addresses Abraham*, as he is about to sacrifice his child with the knife.

But it is obvious it is Jesus Christ on account of the beam of light.

This Jesus asks him how he is and he says, "I'm nervous, I'm jumping in the regional finals today," and Jesus Christ says, "Don't you recognise me?" He hardly knows what to say, for Christ has an uncanny resemblance to one of his old teachers, Ebba Hedman from Sjönom, telephone number 6. But he is confused by the mysterious light radiating from her. The whole thing is like the road to Damascus, like Saul becoming Paul! Though what this encounter has to do with his competition training is unclear; and that Jesus speaks with a distinct Västerbotten accent is alarming, because it is inconceivable that Jesus could come from round here. And so they stand there: and the light shining from the figure before him grows stronger and stronger; and Jesus Christ, who has assumed human form in the body of an ageing village school mistress and appears to him in his warm-up session while he is doing a little cautious stretching and leg-swinging, at that moment Jesus says, cool as a cucumber, "*Per-Ola, I will pray for you tonight.*"

And he feels a great calm. Throughout the entire competition he jumps confidently, as the bar is raised higher and higher: and beats his personal best! And to everyone's surprise takes third place on the podium. If that is not a miracle, then what is?

This is how a just God meets us, in disguise.

The point was: should he choose the academic path and *study his faith away*? Or become a preacher and tell the spellbound youngsters how Christ helped him up on to the podium in the junior regional championship in Skelleftehamn?

What was that if not preaching?

His mother's insistence that he should become a priest did not mean that he was bound by this. He told himself. But he could become a preacher! *Those who can see Jesus Christ disguised as a primary school mistress are very few.*

He realised that this was how his life ought to be. It was at any rate better than the awfulness of working under the bark drum, with the dreadful thundering noise. The Saviour would never venture in there. Imagine preaching in all that noise.

His future was to see greatness in small events; and simply dressed mistresses from village primary schools would always turn out to be Jesus Christ in disguise.

The words *God in disguise* had been etched on his mind.

It was thanks to Rector Nilsson.

He had recited Gullberg's poem in Bureå Church to the music of Lars-Erik Larsson and ordered the whole class to attend.

It was breathtaking.

Rector Nilsson was the one who opened the door. He had established a higher elementary school in Bureå and he was the first and only teacher; he taught all subjects the first year, but was called Rector. From Linköping and aged twenty-six, he gained instant fame over the whole parish.

No-one was as well-known and acclaimed as he.

He bore no comparison to anyone else in the parish. There was something unsafe about him, but he was never spoken about in a derogatory way, though perhaps with some hesitancy. He was impossible to gauge, his background was obscure; he had served in the Red Cross in Budapest after the end of the war and had knowledge that was not to be found in books. He had absolute authority and was dangerous, people could not fathom him, and teaching was his passion. He was married with no children and he said at the outset that he drank alcohol, but no-one had ever seen him drunk. So it was assumed that he only said this to annoy the vicar, Ollikainen, chairman of the school board.

He played Stravinsky at morning prayers and explained what they were listening to.

For four years he ruled the hearts and minds of this first class to take the school certificate in Bureå parish.

It is here that, for the first time, a door is opened for the young innocent from Sjön, Hjoggböle. He is shown no favouritism and his marks are average, but the extraordinary teacher from Linköping makes a habit of reading out his essays; he thinks they are interesting, that they are seeking to say something unusual or unexpected. It is not perfection that is being encouraged; it is always someone else who is awarded the highest mark. But his essays are read aloud. And this makes him try all the harder.

Ultimately, it becomes natural for him to feel no fear when he writes. But only when he writes.

He rails ever more furiously against his awareness of sin, like a calving heifer; he cannot fight his way through.

He keeps going round and round.

Was this piety really so necessary? Was it not sufficient that he was good? Did he have to be so incredibly devout as well? All this holiness. The calf will not come out; he is in pain and often bad-tempered.

His mother understands nothing.

He is obsessed with *this deathbed business*. He must reluctantly accept that his father appears, with one foot in the kingdom of the dead, as very pious – it is undeniable. But as time goes by, he begins to wonder. His mother had been sitting beside the deathbed and perhaps she had encouraged the dying man to send one last greeting. In actual fact there were two greetings. Both in pencil. First: "*Per-Ola, become a Christian.*" He could manage that. But the second: "*Per-Ola, become a priest, a true priest, don't just do it for the money.*"

He was not to enter the priesthood in order to earn money.

Why did the prospective widow now, in these final hours, need to meddle in her child's career plans? He was after all only six months old, as he later tells everyone, *all too often*. The message given by the trembling hand was clearly from his mother. She was obviously sitting there at the deathbed in Bureå cottage hospital, beside herself and at her wits' end, the great darkness surrounding the green house in the forest being all that remained, and her tears were falling; but then she controls herself, puts the pencil in Elof's hand and directs it, practically with force, in the right pedagogical direction. That must be what happened.

He defends himself.

When Elof, despite his charming character, his great popularity, especially with the women of the village, and his humorous personality, when he against all the odds and *despite everything, had been saved*, in effect through the sheer willpower of the beautiful schoolmistress! – wasn't that so? – didn't she think so? – he could at least, even if he was half dead, drag his only son with him to join the redeemed.

The child plans a compromise. He is not going to be a priest, but will opt for preaching about miracles. On a smaller scale, to smaller congregations, for example the parable about Jesus putting him on the podium in Skelleftehamn. A preacher's work is greater than a priest's. It is about seeing the truth in Christ beyond the mundane, in other words the village schoolteacher.

These are his thoughts. It is like a poison.

*

Absence of fatherly advice brings other problems.

In the spring of 1948, just before the Austerity Games, in other words the Olympic Games in London when Swedish champions won so many gold medals against their rather war-weary competitors, he succeeded in masturbating for the first time.

He experiences a short and startling moment of bliss and watches with amazement and uncertainty the very small, clear bubble coming out of his penis. He has taken a step towards love, with no guidance at all, and does not know what blessing has been bestowed upon him.

He learns very soon, however, that this is a sin. To be punished. Not so that his spine rots, as it does in the young boys *down south towards Stockholm*, who are reported to be bent double by their twenties, their spinal cord gone. No, for the people of Västerbotten masturbation is more of a mortal sin to be punished *later*. After death. Indeed, during your lifetime you remained healthy in body and spine; he could see that for himself in all the muscular and onanistic lumberjacks around him. Thoroughly healthy sinners! Which was a kind of proof.

But, when you died and went down to hell, you were boiled in oil for eternity.

No-one in the village establishes in words, either clear or unclear, that this is a sin; no-one would be able to *utter* the dirty words, clear or unclear, *but it is in the air*. His unease is not lessened by having read, the autumn before, Ivar Lo-Johansson's *The Genius*, in which the perpetually masturbating hero finally castrates himself with garden shears, a horrific book that haunts him at night.

To begin with he suppresses his consciousness of sin, because it is, quite simply, so nice to wank. But he soon realises that this is the worst of sins, boiling oil and so on. Not a word from his mother. Nothing about hands on top of the blankets or unchaste thoughts. Nothing whatsoever about sexuality throughout his entire childhood. Not a word.

Perhaps she is merely too shy.

In the autumn of 1946, when he is twelve, he and his mother leave the first village for ever, and the green house.

She sells his father's work!

Without asking him. The cottage on Granholmen as well. He is told about it in the summer. His mother is going to take up a post in a neighbouring village. It is called Sjöbotten. Sjön means the lake and Sjöbotten means the furthest end of the bay, as well as being the bottom of the lake.

It is common to joke about the journey from Sjön to Sjöbotten. He does not.

Now they live in a small upstairs flat in a house next to the school. He has his own room and the flat has an inside toilet as well, even though in summer it is more pleasant to do as usual. He asks her constantly why she wanted to move. She does not give him an answer. He asks why they have to leave the summer cottage on Granholmen as well. It is too far, she says. He implores her – they can easily cycle to his little childhood island, with lookouts high up in the giant conifers and grandfather's unwieldy boat. She says that she does not want to spend every summer there on her own with him. He is offended. To sit there staring, she makes plain.

Perhaps she means: I am still young.

In the second village he does not have as many cousins, almost none, only seven in fact, and it is in the new village he begins to masturbate. He will soon be fourteen. It is like a compulsion, to be dependent.

It is his first obsession.

Now he knows that he has a compulsive nature and hell is drawing nearer. Time after time he falls into the trap of sin. At least once every day, preferably twice, he visits the outside lavatory, and the small clear bubble gradually gets bigger, with time turns white, streaming, a kind of fountain, and each time gives pleasure and guilt.

The objects of his fantasy vary initially.

To begin with it is the image of a small fat woman who is working temporarily at the co-op supermarket; she is the first one he pours himself into. Then, strangely enough, more and more often it is Queen Sibylla – or is she a princess? he decides on queen – whose stern and dismissive face is in a peculiar way at odds with the ample bosom hinted at in the photographs. Later in life he is accused of *undigested Freud*; is this where it started? The queen occupies his fantasy world more and more; he can walk around with a distant look, as if contemplating the edge of a mysterious inner precipice: in actual fact he is thinking only of Queen Sibylla's wantonly voluptuous body, which he quietly but relentlessly penetrates. He is inside her, and away from this world.

His mother, seeing the child's pure and far-seeing gaze and mis-interpreting it, says mischievously, "You're a true poet!" He jumps guiltily then and leaves the lascivious queen's nakedly quivering and willing buttocks, which offer themselves to him so greedily, and which are so excitingly out of keeping with her ice-cold, haughty countenance.

Rescue ultimately comes in the form of Åhlén & Holm's catalogue.

Although all types of lewd pictures are off-limits in the villages, and this in itself creates a sexual fantasy world of unthinkable proportions, it is nevertheless possible for a few erotic pictures to slip through when they are least expected; blameless and yet striking with the full dynamic force of sin. Every year Åhlén & Holm's mail-order catalogue arrives, with its glorious array of practical and unnecessary items, most of which are far out of reach for economic reasons, but as reading material, fascinating and tempting.

And advertisements for brassieres.

They can, staggeringly enough, pass the watchful eye of the revivalist movement, because pictures of the seemingly rigid female breasts, like marble, covered up, absolutely chaste, are thought to be without danger; all the heads are cut off, and likewise the lower body. What remains is some sort of torso on which the breasts are concealed in armour-like bras. Yet he can nonetheless sense the contours of the breasts. There is no doubt: these are women's breasts.

In some way undressed. Perhaps actually Queen Sibylla's. Difficult to prove otherwise.

Now he could look, and fantasise, and use all the swelling volcano of his true poetic nature. The outside lavatory is perhaps not a natural place for Åhlén & Holm's extensive catalogue, but why not? He tells his mother he needs to find out more about screwdrivers and household tools. He insists that is natural for the catalogue to be in the lavatory. It provides reading for everyone. Especially at Christmas. He can even suggest that the old catalogue, placed in the lavatory, can be used as toilet paper. Better than the *Norran*, or wood shavings.

The revivalist movement left its underbelly exposed through these adverts in Åhlén & Holm's catalogue. They needed eyes everywhere. The deep-ocean current of forbidden sexuality was where you least expected it. Even in the Bible! The Old Testament in the large family bible contained not only a lavish abundance of archaeological pictures, Egyptian frescoes and Aramaic warriors, this rich history of ideas that surpassed all later culture, but also Doré's fantastic and *almost bulging* illustrations of the human body, often undressed.

The prophets of the Old Testament as well! Those licentious texts!

In Ezekiel chapter 23 he read about the condemnation of the sinful kingdoms, given the names Ohola and Oholiba. The second of these was actually Jerusalem. *She did not give up the prostitution she began in Egypt, when during her youth men slept with her, caressed her virgin bosom and poured out their lust upon her.*

You had to use your imagination. And interpretation. The most forbidden of all, the female body, pounded and throbbed under the forbidden armour. Youngsters learned very early that the only essential thing, the meaning of life, was a woman's vagina.

It was there, under protective covering.

The armoured breasts in Åhlén & Holm's catalogue were certainly not as sensual as the naked pictures in the family bible, Doré's remarkable illustrations of the Deluge depicting naked women twisting themselves round snakes and tigers with the ark in the background; but the family bible had its place in the best room and was the stronghold of belief itself, irrefutable, flanked by two candlesticks. And to masturbate before the Lord's Holy Scripture would be the most horrifying mortal sin.

He did not even try. It was the most prohibited thing of all. But in the catalogue in the lavatory, with the brassiere advertisements: there he found Woman. Boiling oil or no: the female body conquered all.

In the end it was essential, and also in fact fully possible, to learn to live with sin. The preoccupation with onanism seemed to wear down the nagging anxiety of sin-consciousness. You could not be fearful of sin the whole time. You had to eat and sleep as well, and go to school, and wank, and sleep, and school, and homework, and wank. It was hard graft. Consciousness of sin became more and more diluted. It intensified, obviously, during sermons in the chapel and the Band of Hope and individual moments of prayer with our Saviour, but then it was back to worldly matters. Hell faded a touch, like the awareness of eternal torments: so wank again, and homework, and wank, and forgive me dear God, and food and sleep.

It was possible to live with masturbation.

Only every now and again things seemed to be balanced on a knife edge. The worst time was when his maternal grandmother died.

He had been very fond of her. She was queen of Gammelstället. She was harsh with everyone in the family and was in charge, like all the womenfolk, but she was *strangely sweet-tempered* with him. When he shared the sheepskin rug with her at Christmas, he was allowed to lie with his head on her arm. Now she was extremely weak, and the cousins stayed on the ground floor, weeping, but Johannes asked if Per-Ola could come up and read something from the Bible.

While he read, she fell asleep. Minutes before she was taken up to heaven, he had been reading.

During her last days she had been lying quite still up in her room in Gammelstället's attic, and when he entered she had mostly just looked at him, unable to say anything special. She had once been a very beautiful woman and, in contrast to everyone else in his family, had come from somewhere that was not within a ten-kilometre radius.

She came from a place far away.

There had been conflict when she married into the family. It was said that she had served as a maid for the Lindgrens at Gammelstället and bewitched the son. He, that is to say the child's grandfather, who died so early that he only lived on in his grandson's memory as the person who carved a weathervane for him, had taken up the fight with the family in general, who regarded Johanna as a – though no-one used the word – misalliance. She was born in Byberget in southern Västerbotten, next to Vindeln; it was near to the Västerbotten Deger-fors that was overrun by Belgian Walloons towards the end of the eighteenth century, *the foreigners in Degerfors*. It had something to do with operation of ironworks. Dark Walloons bringing their process with them.

There was something mysterious about Johanna's parents; her father was recorded as a "tenant". He became a father, to Johanna, when he was nearly forty, almost an old man, a Walloon farmhand placed for the rest of his life on a pull-out sofa in the attic. And so the tenant had an exquisitely beautiful daughter who almost cast a spell on Grandfather and made him defy the family ban. *She came from Byberget and there was something odd about her family, but Albert didn't care.* Perhaps there was something dark-skinned, exotically Walloon, in the very idea of having a wife from so far away.

From the south, round Vindeln! It was so deeply seated within them all, even in him. A fear of the foreign and the unknown, and the self-assurance! *Never mind the Atlantic – you should see Hornavan Lake in Lap-land!* The foreigner roaming into the village! The threat!

If a gypsy came travelling along the road, his mother always locked the door and they went upstairs and sat in silence until the danger had passed; it would take him nearly seventy years to realise where the fear came from. Immigrants! But his grandmother, who was the family's own foreigner from the frightening and far-flung Byberget – *south of Umeå!* – she was the one he loved. And now she was lying silent, her gaze fixed on her grandchild, taking slow and painful breaths, and he knew that she was dying.

He knew nothing about her life. Other than that she was, right up to the last wheezing breath, a tremendously beautiful woman, who – regardless of the conflicts and resistance in the family she married into – had immediately taken the helm and calmly controlled everything and everyone. And no-one, no-one! dared to contradict her.

Much later he would write a novel about her called *The March of the Musicians*. But now she was lying there, her breath rattling, watching him, as if she wanted to repeat one more time what she had said the day before: "My dearest Per-Ola, now I'm going to die and I don't want you doing anything silly or taking to drink like Pappa."

Like Pappa? What did she mean? The "tenant"? Had he taken to drink?

At the moment she died he was sitting by the bed, reading from the Book of Ruth, the one he liked. There were just the two of them there. The others were downstairs in the kitchen crying. He had her to himself. He felt almost happy, she had moved one hand on the blanket like a sign, then tilted her head upwards and *then she took so long to breath he knew her life could not continue*, and she was dead.

Don't take to drink like Pappa? Was it the mysterious "tenant" father she meant, the Walloon blood, or what did she mean exactly?

He wept at the funeral, and when he came home he felt he had to *do something important* for her sake, now she had departed this life. She had given him a yardstick. It meant something.

He went up into the forest to think it over. Then he fell to his knees and prayed to our Saviour, who did not reply, but he was used to this silence. So he directed his appeal to his grandmother Johanna Lindgren. It was a perfect, fresh evening in the forest, as if intended for prayer. He was kneeling. He was praying. It was more a promise than a prayer. *Dearest Grandmother, in your memory and as thanks for the love and care you have always shown me, I promise and swear not to wank one single time for a month, calculated from tomorrow morning at seven o'clock or from when I wake up.*

After rising from his knees with tears in his eyes, he made a beeline for the lavatory to masturbate, which was not breaking his promise, but was one last time before the month of abstinence began, according to his holy promise, early the following morning at seven o'clock.

For the first few days his grief for his grandmother is still strong and all is calm. He remembers what he promised her memory and has no problems keeping his promise. But by the fifth day it is as if the Åhlén & Holm's catalogue, lying in the box in the outside lavatory where the wood shavings used to be, has been *activated*. It is as if a radioactive sexual beam is radiating from the catalogue, especially the bra section. He thinks about it more and more; each time he visits the toilet it becomes more and more difficult.

And finally, on the eighth day, he breaks the holy promise he has given his dead grandmother Johanna Lindgren.

He does not know where his consciousness of sin came from.

One thing is sure: it was not his mother. From her never a word about sexuality, about the harmfulness of self-abuse, about hands over the blanket, nothing. In actual fact absolute silence about everything to do with sex. Neither good nor bad, only silence. The question did not arise. No sex education, no scare campaign, no bright euphemistic picture of how children come into the world. Silence.

Some things were obvious in a farming village like Hjoggböle: cows were put to the bulls, rabbits copulated (the innumerable rabbits that would save the economic crisis during the Second World War, these small balls of fluff constantly copulating! So much could be learned from them!); perhaps it was assumed that the sexuality of animals was an observational study that made words unnecessary.

But then where did the sin begin? The guilt? If it was not with his mother?

He does not know. But it came from somewhere, rolling in like a grey mist over the pious revivalist movement, and it never lifted, and it had no words.

Why did she not tell him? And what relationship did his father and mother themselves have, in the short time they lived together in the green house?

But not a line. Not a note. And of course not a word of confession.

He learns that the world is full of sin and that putting a foot wrong mucks things up, like the cattle being let out for the first time in spring.

So he defends himself against sin through abstinence.

It is a test, but he is largely blessed with success. It is the miraculous road of faith through the minefield of sin. A fine image. This is how he thinks of it after he finds his father's copy of *Soldier in the Field* in the attic and studies manoeuvres and landmine clearance. *Soldier in the Field* and *Robinson Crusoe* are the two works that accompany him throughout his life.

Most things are forbidden, he learns, but there are minor prohibitions and major. Amongst the minor is the lure of phenomena that are basically unknown to him, because they are purely theoretical concepts, far beyond the horizon of the village. They include a ban on seeing anything at the theatre or cinema. The first time he sees a theatrical performance, apart from Bullen Berglund's guest appearance in Bureå, is much later in Uppsala. He only sees one film before the age of sixteen. It is *Can the Doctor Visit?* based on the memoirs of the Lapp doctor Einar Wallquist. The evil force in the film is a gypsy-like figure, who illicitly shoots an elk. He is punished. Alcohol possibly also counts as one of the small and negligible proscriptions and sins, because alcohol is practically impossible to get hold of. Just does not exist.

Once, however, it had been disastrously close; someone had seen some bottles of punch essence on a shelf in the I.C.A. store in Sjöbotten, the village to which his mother had transferred.

The leadership of the Blue Ribbon Association, of which his mother was vice-chairwoman and his uncle, Birger Nordmark, chairman, had been mobilised and they had intervened and dealt sharply with the supervisor. His pathetic squirming and agitated assurances that it contained no alcohol had been futile in the face of the Blue Ribbon leaders' clear and forceful admonishments.

An example of a major taboo, in other words one concerning a practical reality, was card-playing. Even Old Maid, which might well pave the way for habitual, entirely sinful card games and the associated lure of alcohol. Another was all forms of dance. Serious prohibitions also included football or sport of any kind on Sundays, as well as all forms of sex. These were critical, because they were all in some way within reach. Sex was no problem until the year before his grand-mother's death. That was when he began to think, wank, fantasise, and know the anguish of sin.

The problem with sex within the revivalist movement in the Väster-botten coastal area was its strong Moravian aspect. Belief had a sexual subtext that was hard to dispel with prayer, even if you made an effort. It was stamped like a brand on to the belly of the spiritual life of Västerbotten, as it was on the whole coastal landscape. Some time in the first half of the eighteenth century a number of captured Västerbotten Caroleans had been held in prison camps in Siberia after Charles XII's war and there they met some German Moravians. When they came home they were firmly entrenched in the Brotherhood's way of thinking.

They had come walking round Bottenviken.

For once the great European influences seemed to come from the north, in a huge arc practically from the North Pole! And Zinzendorf was part of it, a branding iron on the mindset of the pious farmers. It was devotion and mystical blood, with a strangely enticing sexual undertone.

The inconsistencies were very noticeable. Gloomy horniness, not that it was ever acknowledged afterwards.

The psalms were sung with slow, plaintive despair: earthly life was a misery, sin a sack of stones. The tempo was drawn out unbearably in order to serve as a reminder of Christ's suffering on the cross, and yet at the same time the joyous finale signified his wounds. The wounds were not painful; no, they opened up like vaginal crevices to penetrate, or in which at least to rest, clasped in their moist membranes. Here, above all, was the source itself of the Moravians' lust-filled, life-giving drink: the blood of Christ.

He found this natural and proper and slightly exciting, but he did not associate it with Queen Sibylla's breasts; the bar of sin-consciousness came crashing down before these tantalising and sensual mounds. Along with the others in the chapel and in the junior association he mumbled the prayers that almost dripped with the warm blood of Christ, he lay down in the desirable crevices of His wounds, finished his prayers with the obligatory words *For Thy blood's sake, Amen*, mournfully sang the joyful songs, *We are the brothers and sisters of Jesus, who dance in His wounds, His blood is warm, His love is filled with the sweet taste of His blood*. Or the really rousing one from the *New Songs of Zion*, song number 58: *Oh heavenly Immanuel / Pour on my wretched soul with blood / Let me drink this blessed nectar / And behold your godly might. / Embrace me with a bridegroom's arm / To enter Paradise in calm / And let your blood-red heart restore / That I might live there ever more.*

Swimming like this in the blood of the sacrificial lamb – which in no way implied death or pain or suffering, but on the contrary was tender and healing – was actually rather pleasant. It was the closest he could come to the greatest of life's secrets.

God's gift: woman's warm, pulsing vagina. The meaning of everything.

Old Zinzendorf, founder of the Moravian Unity of Brethren and mild religious revolutionary, was, here in the Västerbotten coastlands, actually the right man in the wrong place. He practised polygamy himself and by the middle of the 1740s had decreed ritual defloration upon marriage, with the couple *in the blue room*, observed by the elders; and organised macabre and homoerotic naked dancing on the moonlit Bohemian meadows.

Maybe the child did not understand much of this, but the teenager was hit right in the scrotum, and the adult would look back with an interested smile, as if this might explain part of what happened.

There was, he realised later, so much about Zinzendorf that attracted him. That the text of the Bible *should be constantly reconsidered!* And *Christocentrism!* And that the Moravians largely did away with a punishing God and let everyone mingle in Christ, who was mild and slightly sensual and who opened his forgiving vagina to everyone in need: basically to all the doubled-up, sex-starved young men like himself. What women saw in Christ did not concern him much, but perhaps the beautiful young man on the cross held something for them too. At any rate it was good that in the Moravian church God was removed to a dark cupboard, a kind of angry and resentful punisher whom Jesus with any luck could mollify.

And the Holy Spirit? Something incomprehensible but basically harmless. There might be so much to it, and difficult to interpret, that the problem was put aside for the future.

In any case the equation did not balance.

The lavatory sins: Queen Sibylla's enticing buttocks, or was it her bosom?; Åhlén & Holm's bra adverts; the blood of Jesus; consciousness of sin; the *cartes blanches* of the Moravians as opposed to the angry, absent, punitive God – all this baffled him. His father, the Fellow Traveller, might have had the same problems in his youth, but his mother would not have had time to discuss his bewilderment during their short marriage. He could not imagine them engaging in a candid conversation about sex.

He has to enter religious confusion alone.

Much later he visits Christiansfeld.

It was the Danish Moravian colony created by one of the last decrees of Johann Friedrich Struensee, physician to Christian VII, before his execution. Early one morning he had stood in the churchyard, God's Field, as it was known, and found the flat gravestone marking the resting place of Efraim Markström.

Born in Bureå, baptised Nicanor.

And he knew at once that if he really had joined this sect in his youth, he would most certainly have been a different person. Not have travelled so far. Not have felt this restless unease. He may have found an oddly narrow, but lasting happiness in association with this remarkable Christ, who here invited all to the final warm crevice of God's Field. Could he think so? Yes, he could.

The hot, blood-filled vulva of God's Field.

He would have been brought back to God's Field, somewhere in the world. There were so many places where an abandoned Moravian colony could be found. And he had no need to be so fearful. How else could they be understood? This ritual emotion. This unprecedented attack on the inert fundamentalism of the revivalist movement.

You had to bow your head in the anguish of sin, and only in silence feel the irresistible draw of the warm, the forbidden. But *Moravians were also heretics*; salvation, grace and redress were not given by one God, from above, like divine mercy.

The reprobate had to stand by himself, on his own feet, and walk. Though it would take almost fifty years before he understood.

How many shared his reaction to the Swedish Evangelical Mission's Moravian heritage?

He did not know. It was not mentioned. Not by the children who sat at his side in the collective readings of Rosenius, Skelleftebygden's own Luther and great religious revolutionary. During those sessions with the postil, each two hours of unspeakable boredom, there was no trace of the alluring subtext for a young person at his sexual awakening.

The connection between ritual and sexuality. Whose existence was never suggested. The connection between the obedience of faith and the most forbidden. He knew it was his own problem. Where everyone else found warmth and security, he found only guilt and anxiety.

Who was the Jesus Christ who towered above him with his bene-dictory tentacles?

He is confirmed and thus gains entry to communion rites. He finds himself caught in a nightmare.

It is an act of confession. He is seen to be a professing Christian, resolute; when the class at the higher elementary school in Bureå organises a party there is a rumour that there will be dancing. His mother, whose attitude to dance is well known, contacts the chairman, Reverend Ollikainen. He issues a ban on dancing, presumably he dare not do otherwise; the word soon spreads that it is his mother who intervened.

Silence greets him in the school yard, but he is used to that.

Despite the ban, the class party goes ahead. His mother says categorically that he cannot go. However he wanders off to the bus stop where his other classmates from the village are waiting to leave for the orgy and hands over a 78 r.p.m. gramophone record of his, with "Saint Louis Blues" on the A-side and "Do You Know What it Means to Miss New Orleans" on the B-side. The three female classmates who board the bus feel sorry for him, and one of them almost has tears in her eyes; she is the prettiest and therefore out of reach, but he has had his dreams. He says a few almost hateful things about his mother at the door to the bus, but then he defends her with staunch silence and a wan smile.

The tears of the unattainably beautiful girl strengthen him and he walks home tall and erect. He cannot dance anyway. It's all bunkum.

Earlier in the day he tried a last desperate attempt at persuasion, and his mother, in tears, said that she alone had responsibility for his salvation, whereupon he promptly replied that, "If Pappa was alive, I think he'd let me go," but no.

Rebellion is close, but he steels himself. The calf is not yet out of its mother's womb. He falls asleep that night still believing in the Saviour.

Communion is the deciding factor.

It takes place in a church, not in the chapel. To go to communion without believing is a mortal sin, he is informed. His mother is in despair when he refuses to accompany her to the most important confession rite of the year, Maundy Thursday Holy Communion. It is raining heavily as she walks to the bus that will take her, but not him, to the body and blood of Jesus.

He assumes she is weeping.

He is now fifteen and either terrified or furious, he does not know which. He considers whether to fall to his knees and beg for the Saviour's advice and instructions, but at once spurns the idea. His dead father, the Benefactor, seems strangely unmoved by his situation. In actual fact it is increasingly rare for his father to be relied upon in these matters. In truth, has he really been redeemed, even though he is sitting up there? He seems to be slipping away, in a kind of sorrowful silence, no longer consulted or useful.

Minutes pass, he despises himself. Is he afraid? He is not afraid. But he knows he has hurt her.

Suddenly he puts on his raincoat, fetches his bicycle and sets off.

He knows the way very well. He has cycled it many times. He always times himself, sometimes in the forest, sometimes on the main road; he gauges his performance. If his mother can dream about a life of song – perhaps opera! – he can dream about life as a cycling star. It is only fair. Even now, on the way to communion, he has carefully plotted times. At key points he knows how well he is doing. Each bike ride a Tour de France. Even on the way to communion. A time trial to the sacramental wafer and wine.

He checks his pace this time as well.

It is natural for him to think of his action as a sporting performance. What is the alternative? The suffering of Jesus on the cross, which anyway has not started yet because right now it is time for the Last Supper. The torment of Christ will not start until tomorrow.

Why is belief so closely related to anguish?

He takes cover in a measurable sporting feat. It is cold and raining heavily, he pushes himself on and feels a kind of happiness. 19.25 at the bend after Harrsjömyren – only half a minute below his personal best. This is the first time he has said no to her. He does not weep. Only the rain whips his face; like the great cyclists, his head is down against *the merciless storm*. He has refused to accompany her on the bus; he is a free man and is riding to the communion now with *brilliant times*, despite the weather conditions. He has said no, now he is free; so is he is giving in? If so, it is with passion.

When he turns on to the flat ground in front of the church he records his next best time *ever* for that stretch.

He receives Christ's blessing at communion.

When he tells his mother about the enormous struggle on the cycle ride, he does not mention his time, *almost a personal record*.

She would have been heartbroken.

During this period of his life it is often like this. He can never feel warmth in the community of faith; when he enters the almost forbidden world of sport, it is like coming in from the cold. And yet he has given in now and ridden his bike to the Lord's Table, and for her this will appear to be an acknowledgement. It is a step backwards. He does not know why he made the cycle ride. It might be for the sake of her tremendous loneliness, a feeling of solidarity in her isolation. Perhaps he does not want to give her the love of Christ, but only his own compassion; it may be small, but for her not totally insignificant. How much longer?

Maybe they both know that everything is essentially lost, that this is the last time.

The thundering sound of the organ reverberates as he, the last one, enters God's temple for the great act of confession. He glances round for his mother. As he takes his seat by her side he thinks he hears a sound, like a helpless whimper, but he is not sure.

PART TWO

A BRIGHTLY LIT PLACE

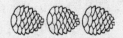

CHAPTER 5

ON THE THRESHOLD

He finishes his fifteen-month-long military service in Regiment I:20 in Umeå the month before alcohol rationing is abolished; his mother's brother John takes out a litre of his allowance and sends it on the bus the 150 kilometres from Bureå to Umeå, an act of solidarity that contributes to the success of the demob party.

In essence he keeps the promise to his mother never to start *boozing* – that is the word: the dream of becoming an athletics champion has been slowly kindled and that involves asceticism, *months of abstinence on principle*.

In the military he learns nothing new, other than endurance. When, as an eight-year-old, he carefully studied his father's copy of *Soldier in the Field* from the 1920s, he did not suspect that ten years later he would be replaying the offensive strategies, ideas and knowledge from the same book, on real terrain. He discovers to his pleasure and surprise that before the age of nine he had already covered an officer's basic training, everything from firing angles and battle group command to building anti-tank barriers.

Now it is just a question of running through it all again.

He tries to view his military time as ridding himself of puerility. Afterwards he will exaggerate the immense hardships of his military service; he suggests that platoon commander training in I:20 means that he is specially trained for the Norrland Field Troopers. He refers to severe adversity, for example two months in a tent in January in the forest outside Hällnäs, in the unbearable cold, and winter manoeuvres in the Tärnaby mountains. Certainly true, but hardly the whole truth. He has difficulty keeping poetic excesses in check.

It is not hardship. He makes reference to his lumberjack genes, enabling his body to tolerate most things. Snow, forest and cold were part of his childhood, he implies. He recounts gripping tales, well into old age, to his trembling, wide-eyed grandchildren, about the daily battle to strip bark from the conifers to make bread. It's no big deal, he assures them. Fundamentally nothing was a big deal. That was the right attitude.

Military service comes to an end after fifteen months. He sees himself as a poet on field-trooper training, having lumberjack genes, and being kind-hearted – but the future is hazy.

He does not apply for officer training, despite prompting.

He is not a natural leader within his platoon.

There is conflict. He thinks of military service as *one of life's tests of personal character*, and discovers sinister weaknesses in his own. He falls asleep one night at his post in the snow during a manoeuvre and gathers that his carelessness has cost his platoon their lives. That is what his company commander bellows at him.

He is still a kind person.

A long-term relationship lasting from high-school days comes to an end. Unsuspecting, he opens the Dear John letter in the barracks during boot-cleaning, and reacts badly. His horizon darkens. Umeå is no fun. He thinks he has been dragged into a military prison by mistake, and the few female guards eye him with contempt through the bars: there are two regiments in the town, K:4 and I:20, with three thousand conscripts, who, on the very infrequent dance evenings in Umeå, desperately chase after all possible quarry, around thirty women – that is his impression – all of whom despise the uniformed squaddies.

Still no university in Umeå.

He sobers up after the farewell parties and takes the train down to Uppsala. He sits up throughout the night watching Norrland roll past and feels confused. He convinces himself that a new phase in his life is beginning. He is not sure what the outcome of the previous phase has been.

He has a kitbag, with a change of clothes and a typewriter.

He has not yet written anything on this, but according to hearsay all students in Uppsala have a typewriter. He is thinking about writing poems himself. During military service his character and endurance under extreme conditions have been tested, with unclear or questionable results. He is sceptical about himself, for good reason, but harbours a faint hope that he might have a poetic nature. His mother has bought the typewriter, confident that he will write his sermons on it, and advanced him 600 kronor.

He has never been to Uppsala.

He puts his kitbag down on the platform and considers himself. He tells himself he is *a peasant student newly arrived in the city of learning*. He likes the term *peasant student*, even though his father was a stevedore and had no cows and *in the opinion of the village* he had been or had become the *teacher's man*. He suddenly perceives the words as denigrating, or contemptuous.

Had his father seen it this way? No-one left to ask.

Bunkum, he says to himself, thinking of a quotation from Verner von Heidenstam's novel *The Charles Men*, which he has read on the strongest recommendation from his mother, and for which he is now full of admiration.

He is not afraid of anything and he has no plans.

He starts studying chemistry, changes to art history after the first few months, then changes again to literature. The compass spins round and round, as it does at the North Pole.

Within seven hours he has managed to find a room and a friend.

It is in the centre of Uppsala, number 7 Bredgränd, where a couple of sisters, the Rothviks, rent out two rooms. The sisters are in their eighties and say they are very particular about good character; he speaks convincingly about himself (*religious, conscientious, no drinking or smoking*) and obtains the room. In the other room a student from Västerås, or more accurately Västervåla, has already moved in; he is called Lars Gustafsson and in their first conversation he says that he intends to study philosophy, maintains that he has composed at least one, possibly several, string quartets, and paints watercolours in his spare time.

He does not explain what he means by "spare time", but he is hugely impressive and plays the flute.

Gustafsson is short in stature and does not have a particularly sporty demeanour. He is already a student at the age of seventeen and therefore probably a genius, or perhaps merely diligent, but in every way he gives the impression of being an intellectual. He is friendly towards his new-found friend from Upper Norrland, who by the second night can hear the rattle of a typewriter coming from the room belonging to the man from Västervåla. On the third evening Gustafsson is visited by a friend who says he is called Lars Lönnroth. As the three of them drink tea together, Lönnroth makes it clear that his father, who is a member of the Swedish Academy, became a professor at the age of twenty-seven and that this should not be impossible. Lönnroth is also short.

He finds that in general intellectuals are rather short and bony; he is almost six foot six himself and when he describes to them his sporting career and his dreams for international competition, they regard him in silence. *They are silent on the subject of sport*, and are difficult to read. He wonders about this: perhaps it was wrong to mention sport, it might have been the *wrong tone*. The following day he goes to see Gustafsson and shows him some of the poems he wrote at high school, *handwritten*. Gustafsson reads them thoughtfully and advises him to type them up.

Even that assessment is hard to interpret.

During the coming months he studies several of Gustafsson's poems and shows him some more of his own, now typewritten. One of Gustafsson's poems is about a Mr Pullen, an Englishman, clearly mentally retarded, maybe stupid, but a genius at building model boats of almost full size. One of the models takes a very long time, perhaps twenty years, but he does not give up. Mr Pullen is generally reviled, but one day he opens the door to the shed containing the model and lets everyone come in. Then they all see that he was not just the village idiot, but could make a work of art unlike anything ever made before. It is understood that this is the meaning of life, that idiots can be geniuses, and what is important is to be able to produce a work of art one single time.

He reads the poem, thinks it is brilliant, becomes strangely distressed and remembers his grandfather and the journey with the fox and understands completely. You can create art in many ways, like the fox farmer P.W. or Mr Pullen. But he also suspects that the poem about Mr Pullen is a *purely documentary* self-portrait of the student from Västervåla. He asks Gustafsson if it is a self-portrait and is upset when Gustafsson takes offence.

It wasn't meant like that, he says in his defence; he's sorry if his analysis has been taken the wrong way. It was very positive criticism, he explains.

At this time Gustafsson is a bit peculiar, but considerate, and says during one of their many tea-times that he appreciates his new friend, but would like to give the incomer some advice. He thinks that all these high-jump ambitions and his limited experience of life, coming from the primeval forest of deepest Norrland, may make him appear eccentric here, perhaps an outsider, deviating from the norm in Uppsala. Regarded as slightly strange.

As if he were *odd*? he asks, paraphrasing. Exactly! replies Gustafsson. He has to take care, says Gustafsson, because Uppsala is a very intellectual world. A possible feeder team for a rookie like Enquist is, he affirms, the Literature Society. He does not use those words, but that seems to be what he is thinking. Gustafsson has a concerned way of tilting his head and uttering a rueful *Hmmmmmmmmmm*, indicating deliberation and sympathy, possibly brilliance as well. Gustafsson is rather special too, like himself, but the antithesis.

When he shows Gustafsson the draft of a novel from high-school days, preserved for posterity in a co-op plastic bag, his friend nods with an appreciative but quizzical look.

After a few months they get on very well, have identified each other as *different*, but with respect for one another: a good-natured sports lunatic with poetic ambitions, and the archetype for Mr Pullen. They look on each other with friendly indulgence. Much later in their, to be honest, successful lives, they will maintain this mutual and tolerant sympathy, despite political tensions. Yet neither of them will abandon their original definition of who the other really is: *decent sports lunatic from the wilderness* and *model builder on temporary release from the care home*.

The Rothvik sisters become increasingly fond of their strange lodgers, and draw them into their lives.

The sisters have not had a good time. That is because of *the other one*. She – the abnormally fat one or the abnormally thin one in turn – has been conniving, mean, underhand, deceitful, a danger to public safety. Conversations take place in whispers. The one currently speaking – it alternates – is concerned that the other one will distort the truth with lies, giving the innocent lodgers a false impression. A bad impression. Perhaps even exposure to life-threatening injury, not just spiritual damage.

The sisters, one exceptionally overweight, the other almost emaciated, are united only in their mutual hate, each for the other. They have lived their entire lives together, never disturbed by men, and therefore have naturally come to hate one another. At regular intervals he is dragged into the kitchen as confessor and confidant, and the absent sister's dirty schemes are ruthlessly analysed. Tears flow. He is always on the side of the one who is speaking, and understands completely. He is kind-hearted, *even wears a winter hat in midsummer*. The kitchen confessions are a welcome break from the increasing intensity of student life; he is also well on the way with his first, and ultimately rejected, novel to which he has given the title *Report on Fleeing to the Islands*. The manuscript will eventually extend to four hundred pages, but the best of it, he thinks, is unfortunately the title.

It is disappointing in its way.

One morning in May as he sits with his novel, he hears a violent crash from the kitchen: a thud, a sort of gurgling sound. He hears the thin Rothvik sister hurry into the kitchen and then a wild scream that brings him and Gustafsson dashing from their rooms.

Miss Rothvik, the exceptionally fat one, has fallen and hit her head on the corner of the metal draining board; she has cracked her skull, her brains have streamed out, and the kitchen is full of blood and something that looks like yellow brain matter. She is without a doubt dead as a doornail. They make a desperate attempt to lift her, but she is limp and exceedingly heavy, and is still losing blood. The surviving sister is screaming hysterically, Gustafsson grunts in sympathy and quite rightly puts his arms around her; he himself rings for the ambulance which duly arrives.

She is still stone dead and is carried away.

The two lodgers try in vain to calm thin Miss Rothvik, but she weeps inconsolably and repeats again and again, "How am I going to manage now she's dead?" Nothing in her conduct suggests that she has in any way been critical of or, more accurately, hated her sister. Neither of them has ever witnessed such naked despair; moaning and wailing, she sobs that her beloved sister has abandoned her. *We loved each other so much*, and now she is alone. How could she, how could she?

An hour later the door bell rings and there are two police officers standing outside. He opens the door and one policeman says, "We understand there's been a death here?" and he hears himself reply, *You're too late, we've already cleaned up the evidence*. Gustafsson laughs nervously behind him, and he realises that with this memorable response he has for the very first time managed to make a deep impression on his friend in the next room.

Perhaps a punchline, maybe the first truly effective theatrical line he has achieved, to be followed by many more, possibly not quite so memorable; and after this Gustafsson will look at him with greater respect, maybe, for all he knows, even admiration. But the policemen do not laugh; they glance at him with disgust and without asking they walk into the kitchen, where, unsurprised, they look at the bloody mess that is now all that remains of nice Miss Rothvik.

This is how his first year at Uppsala ends. The next week they move out and away from each other; they do not see much of one other after that, in fact not at all. Three years later Gustafsson makes his debut. Five years later he does so himself.

He likes Uppsala at once. Nothing proves to be as he has imagined.

The day after he takes the Rothvik sisters' little room, he visits the legendary bookshop LundeQ, where he purchases a copy of *Manners and Customs of Polite Society*, a classic of 385 densely printed pages.

If he is going to be beaten in this new environment, it will not be through ignorance. He is going to know it all, then what will be will be.

He reads this manual quickly, but with great care, to gain admittance into the real world; he reads it twice, so he knows all there is to know about how cutlery should be laid out and used, in what order you take your seats in a theatre, from both right and left, with or without a lady, and the historic reasons why you should not (or in certain circumstances should) toast the hostess.

After only two days, armed with this, the new-world equivalent of *Soldier in the Field*, just as informative, and just as essential in the face of unexpected emergencies and threatening attacks from the Enemy, he is ready to make his entrance into the world of Stockholmers. He is, of course, in Uppsala, but the concept of *Stockholmers* is firmly rooted in him: hostile, supercilious, *the people who live down south, in the direction of Jörn*.

But Uppsala is not like that. To his surprise he discovers that he is living in an ostensibly classless society.

No-one has any particular affiliation; he himself is neither worker's son nor teacher's boy. He is possibly someone from Västerbotten, which is an asset in Uppsala's world of nations, where the Norrland nation is the biggest club, with countless parties and national teams in both handball and football. But not even after a year, and in fact never during his time in Uppsala, does he have an idea who, among his growing number of friends, is upper-class or lower-class.

Parents are erased. There are no rich or poor, or rather, this is hidden in a subtext no-one recognises. Shameful to live on inherited wealth. Don't talk about it. Embarrassing. From a class point of view everyone is seen to be free of history, to have only their own talent or stupidity or peculiarities.

And his own peculiarities are suddenly not so unusual.

He does not know whether to rejoice or lament. Young Gustafsson's concern that young Enquist will seem *odd* is irrelevant. Most people appear to be interested in sport or film or music charts or T. S. Eliot or sex.

Fumbling and floundering, he begins to seek contact with female students.

In this area he has been rather slow. Practically backward.

He kisses a girl for the first time *in his second year* and is shocked to find he has saliva in his mouth. Loses his virginity at nineteen. He knows that his shyness or backwardness is shameful, but steels himself and acts like a man who is calm about it all, an expression he has stolen from Tranströmer. He breathes in all the new impressions and does not know what to do with them, books and women in equal measure. Newly set free, he is terrified of being imprisoned, he believes that feelings have to be *for life* and avoids them in panic.

Feelings are like eternity, a mountain in the ocean, a *commitment* for the kind-hearted. It scares him out of his wits.

A new sports friend studying theology turns out to be a wholesaler in condoms, a surprising sideline for a would-be priest. His friend has carried out a market survey among the future theologians and established poverty plus a high demand for French letters, a term he endeavours to drop into conversations. The first condom he himself saw was demonstrated to him immediately after the end of the war, that is the Second World War, by Hasse Svensson, or possibly it was Maurits Renström. The rubber had been buried behind a woodshed next to the schoolhouse. They all stood in a circle and shuddered, but the impression given by this muddy bit of rubber was that condoms somehow grew out of the earth, maybe planted with skewers like pine seedlings.

Now he is in another world.

The theologian makes a breakthrough in this profitable niche and arranges large deliveries very cheaply. For a relatively tiny sum, he orders a wholesale packet of three hundred condoms and puts them in a drawer so they are readily available, hoping that *some time very soon* they will run out.

One day his mother comes to visit and while she is cleaning his student room she discovers to her consternation the entire stock casually arranged in the top drawer. He comes back from the kitchen, sees her sitting on the bed, pointing in silent horror at the open drawer – a shock, not over the existence of condoms, perhaps, but over the dissolute and debauched bordello suggested by the number – and he says "Yes?" in a normal voice that he will later remember and marvel at. She says, "What is this??! What is this??!" And in the same neutral voice he replies, "Well, if you buy a large quantity it's really cheap and Erling sorted it out," and he shuts the drawer.

And not a word of explanation. She falls silent and does not raise the matter again.

Suddenly he feels like an adult. He has been carried away in a space-ship to another planet and has been freed; it was easy and completely natural. That is what he tells himself. Later he will realise that he is not free.

He wants to be free and is afraid of being caught. Suddenly his good nature snaps shut like a mousetrap and proves to be only cowardice.

In the autumn of 1957 he is on his way to Greifswald; it is the first time he has left Sweden. The university in Greifswald is celebrating its quincentennial and a Swedish universities' sports team has been invited.

He is doing the high jump. This is his entry to the G.D.R., a state with which in time he will have a certain involvement. The political situation is charged after events in Budapest, but he is still a political virgin. Yet surprisingly he visits a bookshop in Greifswald and purchases three books on the history of the G.D.R., which he then consumes in amazement. It is the old history reinterpreted by the new regime; he dutifully perceives it as comical, but is nevertheless attracted to it.

Everything is different from what he has learned; everything basically has a Soviet explanation.

Wide-eyed, he reads politicised history. In 1769 the Englishman James Watt is granted a patent on the steam engine he designed, but this school textbook adds, *"The Russian Ivan Polzunov had already designed a steam engine of a different type, which fell into oblivion."* Ridiculous. Another example of a Soviet scientist inventing the wheel. Isn't it? After a while he finds the quotation thought-provoking. What's there to say that this man Polzunov really didn't exist? And invented the steam engine?

Imagine if we have been misled.

Before his decision to change to literature and work on his thesis, he had planned to become an historian.

There is history and there is political science. He is introduced by his senior lecturer, Hans Villius, to critical evaluation of sources according to Weibull, and the topic of his undergraduate dissertation is Hitler's orders between 12 noon and 5.00 p.m. on 25 August 1939.

It is a delight to immerse himself in the minutiae of that afternoon in the German headquarters. He lives these five hours; he is literally absorbed, reads diaries and assimilates. General Halder's diary is a goldmine, he discovers, almost on a par with *Soldier in the Field* and

Manners and Customs of Polite Society. At 4.30 p.m. Hitler changed an order for an offensive on the Eastern Front. What happened?

Villius is a brilliant investigator. Everything becomes almost a criminologist's task. Suspicion is a virtue, truth always a dubious concept. His students soon regard all historical texts as manipulated. It is necessary to believe one has been misled. The investigator's task is to reveal this by critically evaluating the sources. After a while he begins to see history as a crime novel in the English style, where in the last chapter the suspects are gathered in the library and the murderer – that is to say, established historical truths, or rather the conquerors who produce history's lies – is revealed to the astonished reader.

There is something dubious about statements of fact. The question is whether anything at all can be believed. The image of the compass at the North Pole, spinning round and round, does not yet enter his mind in this crisis of fundamentalism.

The G.D.R is a foreign planet.

The Greifswald jubilee is a memorable event in many ways. They all appear to be dissenters against the oppressive regime, but history is not as simple as that. He treasures the East German school books, returns to them many times, laughing at first, and then crazily obsessed by the thought: *What if we have been misled? Perhaps history needs to be rewritten.* The East German view of how everything fits together, clearly controlled by the central committee, is both absurd and irritating.

It is not simply the astute senior lecturer Villius and his Weibullian scrutiny of historical texts that haunt him. It is as if the familiar questions of his childhood return – about good and evil, sin and innocence, heaven and hell, right and wrong. *How does it all fit together?* Splendid existential questions. And then the fundamentalist answers, taken from the Bible or the devout sermons of Rosenius.

There was nothing wrong with the questions, only the answers. *What if we have been misled?* What is everything is the other way round?

The children of fundamentalism can easily go wrong for good reason.

He appreciates that, but his strength of character – like a legacy, a cross between the Evangelical Mission and the Knights Templar! – makes his receptivity to change enormous.

He has been brought up with the right questions. He was given the wrong answers. But he should be grateful for the questions.

He stands here, at the threshold of his first life, wide open for anything at all, even historiography of the G.D.R. With fascination he reads the chapter "The Penetration of Opportunistic and Imperialistic Ideas into the Labour Movement", which establishes the deception of social democracy and the responsibility of National Socialism, and he thinks, *They want to convince us that this is absurd*. Isn't it absurd? Yes, it is absurd.

But the idea that he could be misled persists. Might history need to be rewritten?

Perhaps the monuments are hollow. Nothing was cast in one piece.

Greifswald is a week of forging contacts.

He gives thanks to Rector Nilsson at the higher elementary school in Bureå who, counter to the spirit of the age, schooled the young postwar generation in Bureå parish, at least the first pioneer class, in the German language. The nights are spent in bacchanalian parties. A group of students watch a night-time cabaret, the star of which is a young female student he meets after the show, called Gisela. With the force of a tornado she sweeps the shy Swede, who is perhaps not quite so awkward now, off his feet. They enter into a relationship that will be painful and that he will not be able to deal with. It carries on; they write to each other. She wants to fly to Sweden, but he cannot face taking responsibility for her, does not dare to take the step. Her letters become increasingly desperate.

On his return to Uppsala he starts to write a love story set in

Greifswald; it is trash, a cop-out. He is afraid. This does not conform to his image of himself as good-hearted rather than cowardly; it shakes him. Many years later he writes a novel about sport and politics, but actually he believes he is writing a novel about Greifswald.

The celebrations in Greifswald become more and more chaotic; the *resistance to oppression* is warming up, if that is indeed what he is witnessing. The anaemic yet nevertheless liberal social democracy of the friendly state in the north seems to be viewed with benevolence. The East German students are filled with optimism. There will soon be an uprising! Against the Soviet occupiers!!!

He and Gisela trail through each night as drunken, shadowy figures.

On the day of the competition he pulls himself together, but makes a pitiful jump and comes second. He does not care, he is infatuated and terrified. He has been cast out into a Europe where later he will spend such a large part of his life.

His visits to Europe become more frequent. Sometimes they are sports-related.

He is considered to have a great talent, judged to be enormously flexible, with rigid hips. That is the psychological definition given of him.

What is he? *Flexible but rigid*.

He seems to be within striking distance of real success. At the World University Championships in Turin in 1959 he is fifth in the 1.96, *despite lousy tracks that were far too loose*, as he puts it to himself, and he notes that his form is slowly improving. The world's elite high jumpers are there and he feels he is *right beside them*. In the Swedish Championships he comes fourth, so *not on the podium! Not on the podium! And no nomination for the Sweden–Finland International!* The national sports magazine *Idrottsbladet* states, in a phrase that makes an indelible impression, that he is the *best of the rest*.

Is that where he will remain?

Later an invitation from the Israeli Athletics Association, so now things are *on the up, on the up!* He is there for six weeks. He travels round the country competing and lives at the university in Jerusalem.

The times are still innocent and he thinks he loves this courageous little country.

That is the expression: he loves this courageous little country. He keeps repeating it. The conflict with Palestine does not exist. Sometimes he cautiously raises the question in conversation, but he is assured that the refugees in the camps do not *want* to leave. The cloudy picture he gains is like the classic image of the municipal worker lazily leaning on his shovel. The half-million Palestinian refugees *actually want to stay in the camps*, that is the theory. For six weeks in Israel he devotes only a fraction of his possibly not insignificant talent to political thinking. He hitchhikes up and down Israel, stays for a week in a kibbutz north of Gennesaret, and spends five nights sleeping on the beach in Eilat.

In political terms, he is still staggeringly naive, considering how much he has read. But there is something else. Isn't it Kerouac's *On the Road*? Suddenly he sees, like a shadow in front of him, the Fellow Traveller, his father, though no longer as the Benefactor, but as an irresponsible, anarchic Kerouac, on the road, on the run from all that is expected of him.

He is convinced that his father hated his kindliness. That was definitely why he went into hiding in a Secret Order.

If that was what he did.

He could have stayed in Israel.

Isn't this what he has always dreamed of, to go with the flow, alone and free of responsibility? The sports commitment is not onerous, he takes part in five competitions, wins them all, and lives in a flat in Jerusalem with a crowd of basketball players. He will see one of them again when he writes a book about the Munich Olympics in 1972. He meets him in Augsburg; it is the Olympic qualifying heats in basketball. That time in Israel they all wore white shirts with the sleeves rolled up and life was easy. The Israeli basketball team lost their qualifying round and were sent back to Israel. The stars of the Israeli squad stayed and were mown down at Fürstenfeldbruck, the military airbase outside Munich.

But that is later, in 1972. Now it is 1963 in Israel and he is a sportsman, still an innocent of sorts, but he has written two novels. Everything in Israel is still free and full of fun, and that is exactly how he wants to live his life.

He has read about a life of freedom, and now it has been affirmed.

His relationship with sport is complicated.

One summer he is working at Nyman's workshops in Uppsala, assembling engines for boats. He is forced to stand, which ruins his suppleness, and he becomes embroiled in a furious union battle to be allowed to work sitting down.

Thus his political awareness develops.

He tours Sweden with the high-jump mafia, Richard Dahl, Benke Nilsson and Stickan Pettersson, and in the occasional competition manages to receive monetary compensation, that is to say, more than is permitted in the amateur rules. He is seized with misgiving, but also with pride – he is in one way Gunder Hägg's equal: Hägg was disqualified many years earlier and is *therefore his brother in misfortune*. However, no-one reports him, nothing happens, he gives up.

It is not so remarkable that he has chosen an individual sport. A jumper is essentially a misfit, a Peer Gynt character. He is not reliant on anyone else, everything depends upon him, and he is not in any collective group. His only relationship is with a measurable quantity, *the result*, and he determines that himself. In outrage he listens to the sport-haters, the intelligentsia who claim that competition entails the defeat of another human being. That sport is an exercise of power. His own single obsession is to improve his result, not to win. Better to be seventh with a personal best than to win with a bad result. That is what he tells himself.

To all intents and purposes it is true. In primary school the high point of every term is when he receives his marks; that is, after the first terrifying term in infants' with no marks at all. Some marks are raised from B+ to Ba-. There are thirteen levels. He adores them all; he could envisage fifty of them. He is obsessed with improvement. He is not interested in what the others in the class get. In the 1940s Västerbotten sport is struck by tragedy: a cheating hammer-thrower, a Västerbotten hero by the name of Eric Umedalen, who confounds all the enraged moralists by not just hollowing out his hammer, and almost setting a new world record, but also by lending the hammer to his competitors.

There are two reasons. *Great competitions require great results*. And above all: *It doesn't matter who throws the hammer, the important thing is that the record is improved*. He finds Eric Umedalen fascinating, and credible.

When he looks at himself he thinks he is the same.

Alone, absolutely alone, and not related to anything in the world around him, with improved results. At any price. And because he is aware, he thinks of himself as the odd one out; he hides his passion for sport from his intellectual friends, and his writing from his sports friends. Gradually, very gradually, his results improve. Then they level out, at just less than two metres.

But what is he doing?

He has a sudden revelation. As he hitchhikes with a lorry through the Negev Desert, it feels as if everything has finished, as if he has made a mistake. *Like Dante I am in the middle of the journey of my life*, he thinks, but it does not help. It is no longer fun. Life is not fun, nor is studying, or love, or sport. The only thing to enjoy is writing. That is where he finds refuge.

He once came from the loneliness of belief into the warmth and community of sport. Now sport too has become cold. He finds himself infinitely far from the childhood where it all began, on the small fields around the villages where they played football and where the light dipped so slowly and never disappeared, even at midnight. Was that where he was captured?

It was so perfect, so simple and pure then. When they cycled to Långviken together. Why couldn't life always be like that? Why should sport just be loneliness, why should a continuous improvement in results be your only lover?

It was not meant to be like that.

He writes tirelessly.

True to his habit as a teenager, he loads himself with a dozen books every week from the library and ploughs through them. Plough is the right word. He ploughs impatiently and then suddenly is caught up in a book that affects him. Then he closes his jaws round his prey, and he reads and rereads. He did this as a child, the only difference then was that he did not have many options. But *Robinson Crusoe* at least fifty times. The salvage lists! The cave! The counting of objects! The security in the carefully established number of muskets! And the gunpowder kegs! Or Kipling's *Kim*, parts one and two, which for some obscure reason found its way on to his mother's bookshelf; the bookshelf that would eventually be two metres long. He loved *Kim*. He read it over and over again. Like a truffle pig on the Siberian tundra, if such a thing exists, he carries on rooting around, in despair, without hope, only to stop, paralysed with pleasure. There! A truffle!

He consumes Eliot and Tranströmer like truffles.

At night he writes like a maniac, without caring whose voices echo in his own. In 1958, after the football World Cup, but with no connection to the Swedish silver medal, he sends a collection of poems to Bonniers.

After much hesitation he gives the collection the controversial title *Images*. Rejection is swift.

He notes that, nevertheless, the publishing house stresses in its written reply that it is most grateful for the submission. But unfortunately they have no opportunity to publish it. Possibly the fundamentally ascetic title was too short. A reader may not have had time to appreciate the almost ironic coldness. He should have called it *Report on Flight to the Islands*.

*

In the second village there had been a very gifted classmate, Åke Jonsson. When the higher elementary school in Bureå was set up, his mother had suggested that this young pupil should also be allowed to continue his studies.

It was undoubtedly the right thing to do, she told the parents. They had deliberated and one evening visited his mother, accepted the offer of a cup of coffee, but said they wanted to discuss a very serious problem.

It was a matter of principle, they had said. In tears they had prayed to God for advice and guidance about their son's future. They had finally decided that he should not carry on studying. There had been more tears. Surprised and upset, his mother had asked why, and they had said that they feared *their child would study his faith away*.

So it was not to be. He would thereafter remain in the godliness of his parents.

He does not think about this event much nowadays, but in his own life he finds confirmation that these ardent believers, in their concern for their son's continued belief in our Saviour Jesus Christ, made the right assessment.

He can see it in himself. In Uppsala his faith is watered down.

His firm conviction, anguish, trust, consciousness of sin, it all slides very slowly and inexorably downwards and mingles into worldliness and poetry and almost disappears. What had once been so vital now seems so remote. No dramatic rift, it just slips away. *He studies his faith away*. It is strange that it happens painlessly, especially considering how painful it had been before.

It just slips away.

At very long intervals he rings his mother.

Her voice so far away, she thinks about him often, wonders how things are in the city of learning, how his exams are going; he pacifies her. When he replaces the receiver he feels ashamed, but does not know why. When he visits her in summer she does not look as strong as she did, almost gentle, no insistent questions about *how you are with Jesus*, the phrase Reverend Stjärne used to terrorise him with. She only asks him once, on 12 August 1959, before his return to Uppsala, asks him almost shyly how he feels towards his Saviour.

And he gives a conciliatory answer.

He notices how she, who once governed a whole village with an iron hand – yet he was never struck by the iron hand, of course, he was so good-natured – how she has mellowed. She demonstrates an astounding and completely new tolerance at the dawn of the modern age. She even says she wants to follow the radio broadcast of Ingemar Johansson's fight to be heavyweight world champion in June 1959, but she falls asleep by eleven in the evening and snores loudly. When he wakes her in his early-morning euphoria and recounts the Swedish knockout, she says sleepily, "Praise be and thank the Lord for this miracle," and goes back to sleep.

Her concern for him is so much more uncertain, or helpless.

One midsummer, when a sudden sweep of high pressure over the Västerbotten coast brings temperatures of thirty-five degrees, he says he wants to visit friends and unfortunately cannot be with her on Midsummer Eve. She bows her head in resignation and does not ask, but tells him to put on his woollen cap in case it gets cold. He agrees, puts on his cap and disappears, but of course takes it off as soon as the glorious summer heat hits him at the door. After a while his obedience, or hidden disobedience, over the cap takes on an almost symbolic significance. He has found a way to live with her solitude and demands and fundamentalism, if indeed the latter still exists.

Perhaps the word is compassion.

He has learned to say yes to every detail of her instructions, and then do as he wants. He knows deep down that she can see through him. He is, after all, her only child.

Apart from him she has no-one, except the Saviour.

Oddly enough she accepts the fact that he writes – passages he claims might become novels. There is no longer any trace in her of everything he imagined as a child, of the *sinfulness of making things up to write*. He begins to wonder whether he misunderstood her. Weren't those ideas hers? Or were they his? When he has submitted his second collection of poems to Bonniers, to another swift rejection, he tells her on the phone about his disappointment. She seems to be genuinely sorry and tries to comfort him, as if she were a friend and not a mother.

Once he asks her on the phone why she never remarried; there is a moment's silence and then she answers in a very low voice, "Well, I didn't think you liked him."

Only after he has rung off does he understand what she means, and who she means. Who *he* was. He was a supply teacher, there for less than a year. Could something have come of it? His impression then was that his mother and the supply teacher *got on well*. That was all. But for the sake of the child nothing came of it. The child wouldn't like him. He must have shown some sign.

He is struck by guilt. She had been considering him.

He pulls himself together, *Bunkum!* he thinks, but he cannot sleep that night.

Despite his apparently magnificent physique, there is something wrong with him. It is *the Enquist stomach*.

At regular intervals he has gastric bleeding, he is taken into the University Hospital, is diagnosed, and no-one really understands why it happens. Finally the haemorrhaging is so bad he has to have an operation, is informed that the operation is called a Billroth II, in which a large section of the stomach is removed. The surgeon talks about acute gastric mucosal bleeding.

Together they piece together the cause.

At the age of fifteen he had discovered that an aspirin tablet placed under the upper lip, like a ball of snuff, produced a strange euphoric lift. He uses up all his mother's boxes of aspirin, sometimes up to fifteen tablets a day. Suddenly his almost non-existent blood count comes to light, he can hardly walk, aspirin abuse is revealed, slowly he regains his strength, but the gastric mucosa will never be what it should have been. Ten years later he is operated on.

Aspirin dependency! The warning bells should have sounded!

Increasingly he is living in two quite different worlds.

When he once revealed to his friend Gustafsson that he wrote, during that first year in Uppsala, it was in a burst of inner confidence. It is never repeated in front of any other friend. He is terrified of appearing arrogant in saying that he writes. Arrogance! The peasant student thinks something of himself! He therefore keeps quiet about the only thing that now has meaning. He lives a life that is outwardly normal, he takes his exams, plays handball, does the high jump, and goes to dances: unparalleled normality. At night he writes, but shows no-one, apart from the publishers, on whom his efforts are regularly inflicted. When he has switched entirely to writing novels, it is a different publishing house, Norstedts, which is subjected to them. The first two novels receive cautious, but for all that, very long and well reasoned rejections.

After having submitted the third manuscript, he is invited by a young publisher at Norstedts, Lasse Bergström, to come to talk to him in Stockholm.

He takes the train.

Coincidentally, on this same day in November, straight after the meeting, he will travel on to Bosön, and there he will stay at a training camp called "Tomorrow's Men", for the sporting stars of the future. Thus he has a stopover at Norstedts on his way to do the high jump at training camp; he walks over the bridge to Riddarholmen, and sees the fantastic light blue of the publisher's sign radiating towards him.

There it is. He is almost giddy. If only he could enter art's open embrace! If only he could make his debut! Then everything else would be – well, *bunkum* maybe.

The corridor is endless, and then it turns a corner, leading to rooms where all the doors are open. He sees extremely pretty young women walking around with a literary or poetic look in their eyes; he knows that they are observing him closely. Ogling him. Is this very tall young man the publisher's new Stig Dagerman, who so famously took his own life when he could no longer write? He acts like someone who views the world calmly, a phrase he has borrowed, as already mentioned, from Tranströmer, and smiles back.

Dagerman is said to have received very large advances.

Furthest away is the young publisher Bergström, who will go on to become the director. Bergström is very friendly and takes his time, and it turns out he is interested in sport – he seems to fully appreciate the psychological tragedy in always ending up *just under the point you dream of*: 1.97 in the high jump, but never 2 metres; 16 seconds flat on the short hurdles, but never 15.9; 13.98 in the triple jump, but never 14 metres. *But it is a driving force as well*, the publisher says, with more sensitivity than irony.

How did they end up here? He is convinced that this development does not bode well for *a job interview*. The wrong tone.

Somewhat laboriously they arrive at his latest novel, now submitted, and whilst the publishing house cannot accept it, it does have qualities. He specifically mentions *qualities*. Bergström has a letter in his hand from the reader, who happens to be one of their greatest authors, Olle Hedberg, and reads out parts of his report. Hedberg thinks he can discern a fine talent, but it is uneven.

Well, yes, uneven. "Read it all," he pleads, when Bergström pauses thoughtfully at a passage and skips over something: he has an uneasy feeling that the grain of criticism is concealed therein. Bergström hesitates, and then he says, "He also writes something about 'undigested Freud'."

Undigested Freud?! An icy chill spreads through him. Just about the worst comment anyone could make. Did it really say *undigested Freud*? He is seized by irrational fury at the thought that he is about to spend a week at the Bosön Institute of Sport, in an effort to improve his results in a field he knows deep down he has given up, when instead he could have devoted the whole of that week to burning away with a blowlamp all the *undigested Freud* in his manuscript. He can guess where it is. Mostly at the end. Psychologising and undigested Freud. He suddenly feels grateful. *The dross in this otherwise excellent novel is "undigested Freud"!* He has suspected it all along. The thought of having his name on a book whose purity is sullied by undigested Freud makes his blood run cold. Perhaps he has always been contaminated by undigested Freud.

Still a virgin until he was nineteen! Obsessed with Queen Sibylla! What does that mean?

The image of Queen Sibylla's hypothetical bra flashes before him, but he tries to pull himself together and gain intellectual clarity, as an aspiring writer should, without any residue of undigested Freud. As he mumbles his thanks to the publisher for this important observation by Olle Hedberg, whom he very much admires, he realises that a young writer, who perhaps shortly will be making his literary breakthrough, ought not to grovel. Stand up straight when the wind is against you, and then you can stand up straight when it's in your favour.

A dilemma for the future, but he foresees the problem.

At the same time he has to deal with his learned humility. After a few moments' silence he asks in a perfectly neutral tone: "What do you think I should do?" To which he receives the answer: "What do you think you should do?"

An extremely good-looking secretary enters with some papers and smiles softly at him, as if he certainly were the new Dagerman. He knows instantly that here in this publishing house he feels at home, a haven he has long been seeking. He wants to stay here. For ever. In this warm crevice. He suddenly has an almost vaginal experience of the glorious royal publishing house on Riddarholmen. This was what Zinzendorf meant about Christ's wounds! The warm blood! The vagina!

It was P.A. Norstedt & Sons he meant!

He pauses in his increasingly exultant inner monologue, suddenly alarmed: might it have been this, and not Queen Sibylla, that was meant by undigested Freud? That now must be burned away with the ruthless torch of his intellect? Like taking the old wax off your skis with a blowlamp? But both the secretary and Bergström are looking at him expectantly; he has to say something.

And in a thick voice he says: "I'll never give up. I'll be back in six months."

He marries – it is the relationship that began at school in Skellefteå, was broken off and started again – and has a child, a boy who is immediately named Per Mats Olov.

He is present at the birth, which was unusual in those days, and cries uncontrollably.

He welcomes the sudden boom in manufactured baby milk, as it leaves the *feeding* largely in his hands; his wife is a teacher and for the first year her salary alone supports the family. He takes pleasure in making up the formula, and the baby sucks; he weighs the child every day, *every day*, before and after the many mealtimes. The boy soon gets used to the procedure and seems quite happy to find himself on the scales all the time, like being in another cradle. He puts the results of the ceaseless checks into tables, with graphs, not because he is concerned the infant will not have enough food, but *to improve the results*.

He recognises himself in the boy, who is good-natured. He begins to appreciate that the child is good and he does not reproach him or wish he had a less kind-hearted child.

The boy lies in a basket under his desk. At this desk he types with the rattle of machine guns on his far from silent Facit typewriter, and the child sleeps trustingly at his feet. If the boy wakes and cries, he takes the sock off his right foot and sticks his bare foot into the basket. The baby grabs hold of his big toe, chews on the toe from time to time, and falls back to sleep. In this way he can continue, with the same unbearable clatter, to write his novel up there at his desk.

The whole time he feels the hand round his toe. It feels peaceful and safe; it is as if the calming heat of the baby's little hand goes up through his toe to him as he writes, and from there up to Elof, his Fellow Traveller, and finally right up to Per Walfrid, the creator of the red fox, in a quiet, warm, unbroken line of love.

*

He had said to the publisher *I'll never give up; I'll be back in six months*, and he does go back.

He goes back and he is accepted; the company will publish the novel *The Crystal Eye* in the autumn of 1961, in accordance with a contract signed by both parties, and said Enquist on his part is entitled to draw a non-repayable advance of 1,000 (one thousand) Swedish kronor.

He receives the contract through the post. He holds it in his hand.

CHAPTER 6

EXIT *HOMO LUDENS*

Now a door has opened. Nothing is the same as it was.

However, he feels beyond any doubt that he is full of holes. It is knowledge, names, insights he lacks, the sorts of things that he as *a writer under contract* ought to possess. He might be able to boast that his laboriously learned humility is *the greatest in the land*, a joke practically borrowed from Strindberg, but what use is that? He tells himself that none of the others have faults. This fills him with determination. He believes he knows what his substance is; he has something to tell, but around this there are – holes!

Not until much later does the feeling let go. He understands that almost everyone has nearly as many flaws as he does, and finds solace in this.

He reads, but now in a different way.

Before it was American social realists, such as Dos Passos and Steinbeck, or Swedish clinical stylists like Söderberg and Dagerman. Now he prefers Nabokov's *Pale Fire* or Burroughs' *The Naked Lunch*. He loses himself in the novel's form. A winter with *Finnegan's Wake*, the novel's equivalent to the blind alley of Western folk music, does not make him any the wiser. But the compass is still spinning. One day on a visit to his mother he finds by chance the essay he wrote before his school certificate examination. It has the significant title "A Sports Ground and Life There". He reads it and discovers to his horror that he wrote in the same way as a fifteen-year-old as now. He fears that his essays from the first classes in elementary school might even be better.

What was it his mother had said? *That he wrote well* – or wasn't it something about unique qualities? But which way is the curve on the graph pointing now? Downwards? He fears that sometimes it is not he who writes, *he is an echo*. What is he himself?

He starts reading the Icelandic sagas, again.

Asceticism as well. Afflicted by his stomach ulcer, or to be more precise, by aspirin abuse, and having undergone surgery, he is forced to be teetotal. Not a drop until the mid '60s. He finds asceticism natural.

Later he will recall these years and be surprised. It was so easy. How could something become so difficult that was once so simple?

He finds himself right in the thick of the '60s' onset, a decade of amusement that would later become political. *Homo ludens* becomes *Homo politicus*. Though behind them both is the same person.

Most of the people he associates with now are scarcely aesthetes; they are basically vulgar, they love cartoons and pop music, all with a sophistication that demands brilliance. The spirit of the age will grow breathless with vulgarity. "Depraved" is the word on everyone's lips. Since it chimes with something depraved within his own mind, he is quite delighted. Why do they all gather here in Uppsala? Is it really the major literary *feeder team*? Some names, such as Sara Lidman or Folke Isaksson, he recognises. But where do they come from? Missenträsk and Luleå. And where does his own generation come from?

The contract for his debut novel, the gilt on 1,000 kronor securing him a minor fortune, was his entrance ticket to a new world.

He takes his Masters degree in 1960 and proceeds immediately to his postgraduate thesis in literature, which will take him six years. It is not an academic career that beckons, not a tempting future as a lecturer in Skövde, but the grant of 900 kronor a month allows him to write novels. Thus he becomes a cheerful scholarly parasite and drags out his studies; when this lifeline comes to an end he will have published four novels and the research world will charitably keep quiet. His circle of friends is now completely new. Björn Håkanson, Torsten Ekbom and

Leif Nylén start up a journal with the title *Rondo*. He submits a few articles he calls essays and thinks of himself as part of the subversive guerrilla movement that will bring down the ruling cultural class, which is in Stockholm.

Without understanding it, he is in search of the secret codes of cultural life, more mysterious even than the rites of the Knights Templar.

He plays tennis with Leif Nylén, before the latter becomes the legendary drummer of the progressive rock band Blå Tåget, which will emerge, in the light of history, as the only lasting product of the era's fascination with concretism, pop art and situationist theatre. Both are new parents, to a certain extent supported by their wives and therefore on a short leash. He knocks on his friend's door and asks his wife *if Leif can come out and play tennis*. She cannot easily say no. Since as a child he had no friend to whose home he could go and ask if he could *come out and play*, this is a novel experience.

He is happy to regress. The early '60s are an auspicious time for a sheltered child who is let out to play for the first time.

It is five kilometres to the tennis court and the liberated duo have only one bicycle between them, but by virtue of mathematical problem-solving – he passed his school certificate, after all – they devise a method. One of them cycles two hundred metres, puts the bike down, covers the next section fast on foot, is overtaken by his friend who is now on the bike, and so on. He works out mathematically, to the minute, the time gained.

No contradiction between childishness and an essay on Burroughs.

The underground, soon to be above-ground, resistance group in Uppsala has offshoots in Gothenburg, the country's second young literary centre, and to a certain extent also in Lund, but only marginally in Stockholm. However, the capital city possesses the deadliest weapon in the form of the national newspapers' culture pages, arming the walls of the stronghold. The image is a familiar one to him. The same battle against the Stockholmers, now just as then.

All the greatest talents positioned outside, ready to mount their attack, keeping the entry points clear.

In Uppsala at the beginning of the '60s there is a succession of very young intellectuals, or to use a sports term, *dozens of rookies*.

Lars Gustafsson, Madeleine Gustafsson, Leif Zern, Torsten Ekbom, Björn Håkanson, Tore Frängsmyr, Jan Stenkvist, Lars Bäckström, Kerstin Ekman, they are all there. Maybe all busy with their studies, but all nevertheless with their attention on *something else*.

In practice the culture section of the *Upsala Nya Tidning* can be used as a source of support. There is a head of culture called Hugo Wortselius, an excellent and of course completely overlooked film critic (*a provincial newspaper!*) and hard-working idealist who is said to fall asleep at night over his typewriter, so the keys are imprinted on his forehead. It is an urban legend. "Vårtan", as he is called, looks after his tender plants with love and generosity. Short article 60 kronor, long article 120 kronor.

They are, by today's standards, staggering sums.

His debut book opens the doors to Vårtan's treasury. He writes reviews, deadly serious ones. He strives in vain to avoid the hallmark of the literary jungle's struggle for power. Perhaps he does pursue the power game, but in his imagination it is a tantalising life that unfolds.

In fact, he is completely happy.

The Crystal Eye is a quite sweet, well written, but fundamentally uninteresting novel that is not awarded a single review in the Stockholm press, a depressing fact since this comprises quite a number of papers. However, the book does receive a short and very positive review in the *Smålandsposten*. One of his friends tells him that the review in *Svensk Kennel*, the magazine of the Swedish Kennel Club, is also clearly positive; he looks for the publication, but cannot find it, so it might have been a joke.

Finally, after two months, there is a review in the *Upsala Nya Tidning*, firmly stating that this book really is not bad. That is how the article must be interpreted. The reviewer is Lars Gustafsson, the flute virtuoso and companion at Miss Rothvik's demise, but the article can *in no way* be dismissed as a review written by a friend.

Everything has gone well. In time the novel will sell a total of 164 copies, but that does not mean very much, he maintains. Nothing at all, in fact. He is not a slave to commercialism.

His son Mats, no longer comforted by his father's big toe, but in all ways a replica of himself as a young child, not least in his kindness, is growing up. He is now so tall he cannot fit on to the scales and thus cannot be measured. He is still an essential part of his life, almost as important as his debut novel. He is not sure how a father figure should be; he consults the Fellow Traveller but receives no help.

All of a sudden he realises that his father, the theoretically extraneous, truncated father figure at Bureå cottage hospital, has created through his absence the problem of *how to be a father*. The main character in his first novel is quite rightly a young woman. He conceals himself in her. It would have been far too revealing to write about a young man. He lays the foundations here for an escape strategy that culminates later in many of his female portraits in the theatre. His own child grows, but if he looks back he sees nothing of value to share with this child. As a father he is completely blank, though devoted, and certain that everything he does is wrong.

He is happy that the time they live in gives him the chance to be man, the player, and feels only the faintest anxiety that this is permitted.

Not the slightest hint of what is to come later in life.

In November 1969 he experiences his first official baptism of fire.

The Literature Society at Uppsala University organises regular evening readings in something called Slottskällaren. There is a vaulted cellar and red wine; there has to be a vaulted ceiling and red wine these days.

Only once is the pattern broken: a young poet, Urban Torhamn, has come up from Stockholm to read from his latest collection of poetry, which has received great critical acclaim everywhere, *in all the Stockholm papers* – typical – and doubtless in *Svensk Kennel* too. He brings an unusual drink with him, the only Swedish champagne in existence, Knutstorps Sparkling, which he keeps under the table. He drinks out of a teacup he has also brought with him.

Everyone makes a note of this. It is in these small details that the important characteristics of different tribes can be distinguished: a successful intellectual from the Stockholm tribe *drinks Knutstorps Sparkling out of a teacup*.

He does not offer it to anyone else.

During the debate after the reading, the Stockholm guest enters a verbal skirmish with the rising local writer Enquist. The home tribe is loyal and ousts the stranger with some astute points in support of their man.

At the evening reading (with red wine under the vaulted ceiling) where he has been invited to read, two other young prose writers are the main feature. For his part he thinks that he has been invited only as an act of friendship by the organisers, but that is strongly denied. The two others are Göran Tunström and Lars Görling.

They are, he soon discovers, a killer combination.

Göran Tunström, also a debut writer, is about to publish the novel *The Dandelion Head* and become one of the country's greatest and best-loved storytellers. It manifests itself in this, his first public reading. He remorselessly spreads his Värmland charm around him, *and not unwittingly!* thinks the jealous colleague who is to follow him a few minutes later.

He notices, in the primarily young, attractive and female audience, how the erotic haze surrounding Tunström thickens, and he realises with growing alarm that this is not going to be easy. He listens in horror. Tunström is innocent and pure, he thinks, full of hatred, *but it is the innocence of a professional assassin!* Peals of laughter as well. There is an awful, childish attraction around Tunström, who is in no way academic and for that reason a victor from the very first line.

His inflection is from Värmland. As far as dialects are concerned, this is still a non-political time; the Värmland dialect has a high rating, whereas Norrland dialects will have to wait until after the miners' strike of 1969 to have, from a political point of view, high status, and force native young Stockholmers to make desperate attempts at Väster-botten intonation.

Tunström has everything, including genuine non-political Värm-land diction, and his reading is phenomenal.

All the young female students listen bewitched under the vaulted ceiling. They still have their clothes on, but mentally they are halfway there; some are sitting on the floor at his feet. Tunström is quiet and shy and reads for half an hour from the short novel that will soon be a classic. The girls have their mouths open, breathing so hard their breasts are heaving.

After Tunström comes Lars Görling.

Görling will come to have another distinction. He has written an ice-cold and brilliant first novel, his second is called *Triptych*, the third will be called *491*; and after that he will kill himself. Every decade has a suicide victim, in the '40s it was Dagerman, the '50s Gösta Oswald, the '60s Lars Görling. No, Oswald just drowned, maybe.

Lars Görling has been in jail, no-one knows what for.

He reads calmly and terrifyingly and there is a deadly hush in the audience. He comes from nowhere and writes better than all of them, and there is something quite black in his voice. The movements of his mouth are slight, but the text is as heavy as lead, and no female students flock at his feet. He is so young and gaunt it hurts.

Next it is his turn to read.

From the very first sentence he can hear his voice shaking and he knows that at any moment it could break. If it did he would sound ridicu-lous. He speeds up. A nightmarish twenty minutes. He is perspiring, profusely, and knows suddenly that what he is reading would not even have made the grade for a publication like *Svensk Kennel*. It is a disgrace;

the faster he reads, the more and more violent is the tremor in his voice. He is thinking that there has to be a first time, and this may well be the last, but *even if all fails, he has at least tried*. He recalls his mother's words in her diary after the death of her first son: *I have at least been a mother once*. Little chance of another novel or a reading after this, but *he has, nevertheless, been a writer once*. His voice grows all the more inaudible. He imagines the girls still hanging on Göran Tunström's lips, even though they are now motionless.

He perseveres for twenty minutes and is met with *genuine applause*. The three young writers smile at each in relief: it is over. It is, in its way, a perfect example of the sociology of young Swedish narrative art in the '60s, where the provinces are everything and the centre nothing at all.

Tunström from Sunne, Görling from jail and Enquist from Hjoggböle.

What sort of world is it that they will now depict?

Since he works with language he is tempted, like so many others in the early '60s, to assume that it is all a surface structure. The surface is contaminated, and this is beguiling. In the impurity there is a hint of reality, and if you play with language, perhaps reality will be uncovered. Wherever he turns he comes across the word "knead". Language has to be pressed and stretched. Pop art is welling up like rising dough. Out there, obscured by language that is moulded and shaped, the welfare state has come to fruition, but the word "politics" is rarely used. If it is, it is as though twisted surface structures are engaged in a class struggle, one against another. A novel of social realism must consist of ranks of manipulating text in a battle for the letters.

It is appealing and fun, but in a way he feels as though he is duping himself.

In 1964, in the midst of peptic ulcer operations and literary research and a high-jump tour in Israel, he unexpectedly writes an historical novel set in the eighteenth century, *The Magnetist's Fifth Winter*, which is absolutely pure, almost scrubbed clean, as if his inner torch has burnt away all his aesthetic knowledge and wide reading and underneath has found complete anachronistic simplicity.

Perhaps he is only "a *storyteller*".

Consistency is not his forte. Two years afterwards he publishes *Hess*. It is a monstrous novel; he seems to be in a railway siding with countless tracks. There are hints of almost everything he will later write; nothing has really found its mark in him, apart from a few old-fashioned yet astounding chapters about a boy in the shadow of the chapel. In a gigantic language game his own shadow is discernible for the first time.

He feels embarrassed, as if he has given himself away.

More and more he wants to understand who he is.

The playful manipulator of language and the teller of Icelandic sagas are pulling in opposite directions. Meanwhile, with his intellectual friends in the underworld he reels off the Swedish pop charts by heart, carefully follows every detail of the sports results and presents nocturnal analyses of the ideological difference between the true, raw Rolling Stones and the altogether too lovable Beatles.

Presentation is a much-used word. It is the age of situational theatre, pop art, installations, everything an echo of experiments made in the '20s; on the other hand, they will be reproduced in the '90s with a total lack of concern, so it will all even out. A whole generation ideologises Brecht's maxim, "Bad writers borrow, good writers steal." One month in the winter of 1964 he writes a pop novel with two of his friends, Leif Nylén and Torsten Ekbom, under the pseudonym Peter Husberg. It is called *The Casey Brothers* and is shaped like one of Alexander Calder's mobiles with texts transcribed from a *threatening world of language*; that is to say, the magazine *Idun Vecko-journalen*, the sports paper *Idrotts-bladet* and the Official Reports of the Swedish Government. The book takes three weeks to pen. A number of critics write about it at length, demonstrating their wisdom.

At the same time, in a move of self-critical perspicacity, the Three produce a criticism toolkit, a guide to *contemporary critical language*, an instrument that takes unstructured letters and words and slowly, laboriously hones them, finally achieving perfection. The consummate language of the perfect critic.

There is an expression: *It is at the crossroads between language and morality that our new freedom is visible.*

The tone, and the enigma, is taken from the much admired and trend-setting Gothenburg critic, Göran O. Eriksson. The criticism toolkit is published in an essay in the literary journal *Ord och Bild* and receives a great deal of attention; it is regarded in the reviews as a clinical expression of the premise that if language is manipulated, a surface structure will emerge, and it is only here at the crossroads between language and morality that our new freedom is visible. The three developers of the toolkit have been right inside language, their eyes averted, to keep the worst stupidity at bay.

Something like that; there is broad agreement about it.

This criticism toolkit, however, is only put to practical use one single time, several years later. During a telephone conversation with his friend Ingmar Bergman on Fårö, he listens to Bergman's customary cry of anguish about how terribly difficult it is to talk to journalists, and how he hates them, and he doesn't know what answers to give to the questions. Bergman does not start to like interviews until later in his life, when he has got bored on Fårö.

Enquist, who collaborated with Bergman on a couple of plays for the theatre and was familiar with his black humour, then recalls the criticism toolkit Nylén, Ekbom and he had created in the mid '60s and what this toolkit had forced out when it was finally completed. He tells Bergman that his problem with the journalists is easily solved. "Whatever they ask about," he says, "just pause for a moment of reflection and then answer, 'Yes, it is at the crossroads between language and morality that our new freedom is visible.'"

Bergman, both bemused and elated, asks if he really can use that to answer *everything*, whatever the question, and is firmly reassured that he can. The interviewers are going to be *confounded*. Bergman is delighted, goes to find a pen, and carefully notes it down. "It is at the crossroads...between...language and morality...hee-hee-hee...that our new freedom...hee-hee-hee...is visible."

In this way the criticism toolkit finally has a practical application.

If you are in the middle of an age, you never know when it is going to turn. It turns now, in the middle of the '60s.

Everything is fun, he is *Homo ludens*, he has written a novel, *The Magnetist's Fifth Winter*, which is *his own* in the sense that he wrote in accordance with his own wishes and not the spirit of the age. Suddenly he receives literary prizes and in time the book is translated into twenty-six languages, but he does not really know how it has happened. Before this novel, and after it, he writes something else, but does it stem from himself or the spirit of the age?

He does not know what is *himself*.

At the same time he is having such a good time. Perhaps play is not completely irresponsible? Maybe it contains a curiosity that will suddenly turn in an unexpected direction, to politics, a world that is not just play? When the pop novel *The Casey Brothers*, compiled and assembled by the three friends, is published, they are invited to a reading and discussion at the Academic Society in Lund.

It is very prestigious. Prime Minister Tage Erlander speaks there once every year, to a full house.

Astonishingly the three young writers from Uppsala also attract a full house. From the podium they take it in turns to read from their linguistic entertainment. Their youthful solemnity is declared both *touching and funny*. Uninterrupted laughter. It is undoubtedly a great success, the incomprehensible has strong powers of attraction, and the young female students he once saw flocking round Göran Tunström, like iron filings to a magnet, here in Lund obviously regard *the three young men* as pop stars, albeit intellectual.

The party afterwards is wild.

He signs his autograph on women's bare arms, once on a half-naked breast. It feels natural under the circumstances. There is red wine here too. The ground begins to sway. He is more and more intoxicated, not just from the wine; the night is spinning. Later he goes home with a pretty student who is studying law. They agree that they are going to listen to the latest Beatles record; it turns into a long night and he finds himself in a wonderful new world. He is married. This is his first digression. He feels no remorse, not for a second, but there is apprehension; she is very pretty and six months later she dies in a car crash.

In some way this event at the Academic Society in Lund, and the long night that followed, signals the end of something. The age suddenly changes, to the tune of "Sergeant Pepper's Lonely Hearts Club Band". Pale light from the street in the student room. The first time like this, but not the last.

The playing starts, reaches its peak, ends, and something else takes over.

It came so suddenly. He does not really know what happened. But he would miss the playfulness, curious experimenting, and childishness, the spontaneous theatre of life perhaps, irresponsible and fun. It was so good while it lasted during the first half of the '60s, later to be forgotten by all and denied.

But he had played, and not alone, and not just in the forest.

Writing literary criticism is not a bad training-ground.

He leaves *Upsala Nya Tidning*, and Vårtan's tender care, with regret and in 1963 starts at *Svenska Dagbladet*.

The conservative mouthpiece of the right. Nothing remarkable about that.

Ten years later it would have been remarkable, but not now. He does not think about the political colour of *Svenska Dagbladet*, such is the spirit of the age. The newspaper is prestigious, that is enough. The head of culture is Åke Janzon, a brilliant theatre critic who spreads his fatherly wings over the young Norrland writer from Uppsala and gives him completely free rein. A sighing frown might cross his friendly face if the feature article is too esoteric, but he lets it through, and gives his support. The three years he spends as writer on the culture section of *Svenska Dagbladet* are wonderfully calm and free from conflict.

It comes to an end for a strange reason. He writes an article with the headline "The Safe Stars' World". And leaves *Svenska Dagbladet* for the *Expressen*.

Not because there is anything wrong with the article, apparently the reverse.

It is an attack on the conservative debater, a professor of medicine called Björk, who complains about the new left and new social democracy. He responds to Björk with a contribution that *arouses general admiration*, thanks to the sorrowful liberal tone of his subtext, his efforts never to see things purely in black or white, his desire to listen, and his explosive anger in the face of all forms of fundamentalism: in short a liberal masterpiece that makes him both loved (even by the culturally conservative professor in question) and, in time, distrusted by the intellectual left who rightly suspect that inside the splendid Social Democratic sheep that is Enquist, lurks a liberal wolf.

If only they knew.

He keeps quiet about the long, hard indoctrination in the *Norran*'s social liberalism and his mother's love for handsome Professor Ohlin, and is surprised when the head of culture for the *Expressen*, Bo Strömstedt, rings and invites him to lunch, in the style of the times, at the Operakällaren.

Strömstedt has read the article and a review in the theatre journal *Dialog*, in which he summarised his impressions of the three shows he has seen – that is to say performances two to four in his life hitherto – number one was Bullen Berglund's shooting drama at Bureå Folkets Hus – and Strömstedt wants him to move over to *Expressen*'s culture section as literary and theatre critic.

With opinion pieces in political areas and others.

He agrees almost immediately. Not because he has been unhappy at *Svenska Dagbladet*, on the contrary, he takes his leave with sadness and believes it to be mutual. Neither is it for financial reasons. If God makes sure that even the little sparrows do not fall to the ground, he will surely look after him. Forecasts might be dismal, but, with God's help, the outcome should be brilliant. He will not need to work selling hotdogs in the street.

Nor is it because a move to the *Expressen* is a step up; not at all. But from the start he likes the paper's tone. It is bold, often raw, devotes a disproportionate amount of space to vulgarities he would never dream of admitting he was interested in, which he is; the culture pages have a tenor quite unlike the lofty cathedral-feeling of *Dagens Nyheter*.

In addition it is, politically, a schizophrenic newspaper in the good spirit of liberalism. The editor-in-chief is Per Wrigstad, who leads the newspaper with weighty authority towards the dream of a People's Party victory, which is some way off because of difficulties with recalcitrance in the Social Democratic, *almost Albanian, single-party state*. That is the tone of the editorial.

The head of culture, Bo Strömstedt, who in time will become one of his best friends, rules over another part of this media empire. Empire is the right word. The paper has a circulation of nearly 600,000 and is very profitable. But the culture section runs itself. To be more precise, it is run by Strömstedt, who will eventually become editor-in-chief, and the last of the great Swedish newspaper journalists. As a result, a significant and, as already said, schizophrenic liberal freedom develops between the newspaper's editorial and culture section.

The editorial is party-faithful, and unyielding in that respect, with the confidence almost of a Soviet central committee. The culture section on the other hand, under Strömstedt, unleashes a debate during the '60s and '70s that often directly opposes the editorial. Many of the most important speeches from the new left are printed on the culture pages of the *Expressen*, often followed by an ill-tempered polemic in the editorial.

It is regarded as quite normal to take a pounding in the editorial for articles in the culture section. More of an honour. The newspaper's image is one of disunity, as if the self-image of internal argument and the raw tone of the evening paper create a safety net beneath the official dialogue. In-house enmity is natural, almost an argument for the soul, something unconscionable in virtually all other newspapers.

At any rate, all attempts at political uniformity drown in the tone of forbearance emanating from Strömstedt's office. He has an organ in there and *even in working hours* plays spiritual songs he learned in his Pentecostalist childhood. It is all part of what passes for normal on this newspaper.

Soothing notes in an environment full of tension played by a nonconformist. And Strömstedt writes the best prose of all the contributors into the bargain.

Revivalist people are everywhere. On the editorial pages and the cultural pages and among the freelance writers, all over the paper there are nonconformists enduring great discord to the sound of Lewi Pethrus' "Promises Cannot Fail".

He finds the atmosphere on the *Expressen* deeply sympathetic, its split personality perfectly aligned with his own values, both uncertain and noble.

It is a new age. Something has happened.

As a writer on the culture pages he can sense it in the first few months of the winter of 1965. It starts with a very insignificant episode; the new leader of the People's Party, Sven Wedén, has rather carelessly suggested in a televised debate that those who support the Vietnamese National Liberation Front are not true democrats and do not belong in the People's Party.

The repressed liberal within him acts swiftly and he orders the transcript. It is correct, Wedén really did say this. He writes a sorrowful article informing the new liberal leader that many people are now leaving the party and he appends the transcript of the debate. It evidently causes quite a stir inside the party, where many young liberals have one foot amongst Liberation Front sympathisers, and there are murmurings. Telephone calls are made to Strömstedt. Letters of complaint are sent to Strömstedt.

He reads one of them with greater interest than the rest. It is from Bertil Ohlin. "*In my opinion Eneqvist's article was so lacking in objectivity it is not worthy of serious discussion. Enekvist is not the only young writer who, with not the slightest hesitation, thinks he can enter public debate without familiarising himself with the views being criticised. I sometimes wonder how this trend has taken such a hold. Clearly a number of our young writers regard themselves as experts in all manner of problems in society.*"

His mother must not find out what Ohlin thinks. She would be very unhappy.

But his ideological roots, during the years at the crossroads between language and morality, are strangely tangled.

There is something in Ohlin's irritated comments on the sudden incursion of amateurs, *this trend* in public political debate, that is a sign of a shift in the times.

He would certainly have forgotten this little skirmish, which was partially played out within his own half-concealed liberal allegiance, had it not been an omen. The preface to a couple of decades of increasingly active political engagement on his part.

The row also brings about his first contact with Olof Palme, who writes to thank him. He had been a participant in the same live televised debate, immediately registered Wedén's indiscreet exclusion of the party's young liberals, and when he tried to discuss it on air, was stopped. Now that it had been made public he was pleased, unsurprisingly.

Palme encloses the transcript of the speech he made at the Christian Social Democrats of Sweden Congress in Gävle in July 1965. It is a speech about Vietnam; perhaps he, who is also irritated, wants to demonstrate that his thoughts on this question are both advanced and clear. Palme's Gävle speech is the most important speech to be delivered in postwar Sweden.

In July 1965 Palme takes an almost brutally unequivocal stand on the Vietnam liberation struggle. It is only four years before he will become the Social Democrat party leader and prime minister; he is formulating now the ideological divisions that will dominate the next decade.

In other words, the speech marks the entry of the Third World into Swedish domestic politics.

Who is "this man Enekvist"?

Cultural radicalism in public discourse changes political allegiance in the middle of the '60s in Sweden. *This man Enekvist* is a part of this, but hardly realises. Olof Palme robs the hitherto commendably active and successful young liberals (Nestius, Tham, Tarschys, Wästberg, Eva Moberg and many more) of their cultural radical agenda. Cultural radicalism, so dominant in Danish politics, and something he will understand so much better during his fifteen years in Denmark, was in theory almost absent in Sweden, but in practice very much alive. And consequently so was debate on the Third World, Africa, Vietnam, cultural politics, sexual politics, feminism and more.

Olof Palme stole it all.

Oddly enough the *liberal* cultural radicals withdraw, disconcerted, and lie down quietly on the rubbish heap of history without protest, because their ideas have prevailed. But not within liberalism.

These things happen.

The letter of thanks from Palme was the first in a correspondence that would last sporadically for many years and cover many subjects.

Some years later Palme rings to invite him to join a committee, called the Swedish Arts Council, which will carry out a fundamental review of Swedish cultural politics and will in fact lay the foundation for the great radical reform of 1974 that will dominate far into the next millennium.

He is flattered and accepts. Perhaps a little puzzled too. Why such trust in him in the area of cultural policy?

Late one night several years later after a few glasses of wine, he asks Olof Palme why he picked him for the committee. Palme looks at him coldly and replies: "I read an article of yours in *Ord och Bild* where you were writing about sport, and when I realised you were involved yourself I knew you were not as bloody narrow-minded as the rest of Swedish writers."

So was *the lunatic's passion for sport* suddenly a quality? And he had been so embarrassed.

He soon detects a problem with relations between social democracy and the intelligentsia. He would find himself right at the crossroads.

Actually not so strange, but at the same time quite remarkable. If you viewed Sweden as a Social Democratic single-party state, governed by apathetic diehards with no vision, it was distressing for the intellectual's self-image to identify with this apparatus of power. Downright embarrassing, in fact. Better to be a communist than an arse-licker.

Readily confused with disloyalty, self-criticism was not one of social democracy's strengths. And as for the question of party membership – unthinkable! A free intellectual could not be a party member. You had to be free! Besides, it was an established fact that social democracy *lacked vision*. A fact established over and over again.

What did it mean? It was unclear. But not only could it be said, it *had* to be said. All the time. No piece about social democracy complete without noting the lack of vision.

In this period in the '60s, in the leap from revivalism to cultural radicalism to social democracy, analysis of social democracy's lack of vision is demanded of him too.

Desperately incapable of providing an answer he draws on a parable, only slightly more mysterious than that of our Saviour Jesus Christ. *"Social Democracy, he said to His disciples, is like Yeast and Dough. The Yeast is Socialism, the Dough is the Market. Those who want to eat bread know that Yeast on its own is impossible to eat, just look at how the people of the Soviet Union are cursed under the unpalatable Yeast of Communism. It is not possible to consume Dough on its own either. Isn't American Capitalism an example of this? These poor people only have Dough to eat. Just the right amount of Yeast in the mixture makes the Dough rise and become good edible bread. And so it is with Social Democracy."*

The comparison is actually not bad.

Not because it provides a definitive image of social democracy, but because it interprets intellectual concepts about the movement. Ideologies really ought to have a clearer profile! *Yeast and dough and rising! Unclear! Illogical!* It was hard to understand how social democracy was such an incredibly successful social experiment, perhaps the only practical, functioning one.

But theoretically flawed. It collapsed under all discerning intellectual analysis. Doughy. Something ambiguous and obscure somewhere in the middle.

So the undeniable clarity of communism would be better. The dramatic images, the inexorable consequence, the eggs broken for the omelette and the awareness that this is not a tea party. Altogether tremendously alluring, it rubbed the intellectuals' erogenous zones and at least appeared to be not just doughy.

It was not funny being an avowed socialist. Besides, the social democratic community was suspicious of people with a poetic temperament. Within social democracy there was a fundamental suspicion of writers and artists: you can never trust them. When you embraced them, they gave you a kick in the groin. It hurt! And was hard to forget. They seemed fickle, said they espoused radical values, but lacked reliability, and were to be found mostly in professions that seemed alien: *fiddler at the rapids, water sprite, gypsy violinist!*

All this could be viewed as curious. But writers, if one's observations were correct, also had a tendency to want to rise quickly above their class, abandon their affiliations, and look on those who are left behind with disdain and condescension. The dream of radical clarity, in other words *no slowly rising dough*, often drove them to the left, where they sulked about the usual: socialists' lack of vision.

In the party they always talked about solidarity. And a failure of loyalty to the party was definitely not a good career move. Those who did not leave were excluded.

There were not many officially accepted writers left. Most of them were on the left, but were regarded with unease by the party. At party congresses the same poem by Svante Foerster was always read out, of which the final line was: "*Voting is requested and will be enforced.*" It was a kind of safeguard.

He does not really know how it happened.

But gradually he became one of the very small unofficial group accepted by the party as "Social Democrat writers".

In part he only had himself to blame, or thank. In the heyday of the '60s' new left he petulantly declares himself to be a Social Democrat. In moments of awareness about *undigested Freud* he does not know if this is directed at his mother or his father, but it is certainly *petulant*. He accepts the appointments the party gives him, always within the cultural realm, but nevertheless markedly political. Such as the Broadcasting Commission and the Arts Council. He carries out a one-man commission on film policy. In his articles he talks about "my party", even in the midst of a temper tantrum about it.

He has made his decision and finds it reasonable to maintain it. Being a socialist is about as intellectually obscene as being a high jumper, he thinks; I need to accept my limitations. He takes a deep breath and resolves to face the consequences, but after a while sees that it is not so bad. It is turbulent from time to time, but not very. Contempt for him, because he is a Social Democrat lackey, drifts away. At least he is clear and unmistakable.

That is just it. How clear and unmistakable is he?

"That man Enekvist." What are his values, and where do they come from?

On moral issues they vacillate. He knows, but he covers it up. He is essentially much more conservative in his values than he wants to appear. He seems to share some of the conservative moral values of the Swedish working class, thinly disguised for the general public. *Personal responsibility! More nuclear power! Wind power stations are noisy! Immigrants should have to learn Swedish and work and pay tax! You should pay your way! Benefit scroungers are a burden! The Work Strategy! The Work Strategy! No soft approach in criminal policy! Better administration and stricter requirements in schools! Discipline! More school exams and earlier! Every month!* And so on, and so on. Not necessarily all of this, but in this general direction.

Easy to explain, but not always attractive.

He has taken a step into the political arena and learned tact and tone and manners. But he is not a proper cultural radical either. Aren't his ideological roots in a culturally conservative revivalist movement instead? Rather than in social democracy? Or, what came first?

Once Erlander tells him that, in a speech he gave in Värmland about revivalism's relation to the labour movement, he quoted from Enquist's novel *The Coach* to illustrate what the labour movement had learned from revivalism: *belief in personal responsibility*. There was a connection between the revivalist, temperance and labour movements, and that connection was *personal responsibility*. And that could be deduced from his novel. But did he himself understand it?

How about clarity? In which ideologist do his values originate? Marx, Bernstein, or the teacher at Hjoggböle primary school, Maja Enquist and the Swedish Evangelical Mission?

He makes up his mind not to bother about it. *It is as it is.*

Sometimes the Social Democrat compass, now firmly fixed where previously it was spinning, indicates curious deviations. It is *the Social Democrat diehard's* secret longing for something wilder and more dangerous.

He is now working on the *Expressen*'s ferocious culture pages in an almost permanent state of war, but he does not complain. It is essentially stimulating. He becomes used to taking a pounding and making new enemies. On one occasion it is rather special. He is on a trip to Germany and the Balkans and is following in the papers the dramatic evacuation of Phnom Penh. A city of three million now inhabited by five million, no food, raging epidemics, and suddenly a complete evacuation is ordered. He finds it drastic, but maybe reasonable: *everyone needs to be cultivating the land and seeking food*.

A sound peasant reaction. Concrete does not feed anyone, nor do streets of gold, and in any event not in Phnom Penh.

However, he will learn that completely correct viewpoints can be totally wrong when time is running out. The western press is outraged at the evacuation, while he is shocked at their hypocrisy in not asking who created this hell in the aftermath of Vietnam, in other words the U.S.A. He writes a short article about the media's crocodile tears, containing the sentences, *"Then they cleared the house and began cleaning up. They scrubbed the floor and walls, because people mustn't live in humiliation here, but in peace and dignity. Crocodile tears are flooding the West. The whorehouse has been cleared, and it is being cleaned up. Only pimps can feel sorry about that."*

This accurate analysis, possibly with the exception of the word "only", is followed in the next few years by the horrific reality of The Killing Fields, a million dead, unimaginable suffering for those driven out, and the existence of one of history's worst mass murderers, Pol Pot. For over a decade he is known as a *Pol Pot-sympathiser* with a *sentimental attachment to genocide*. The former, about Pol Pot, is particularly embarrassing: he conceals the fact that at the time the article was written he did not know that Pol Pot existed or who he was.

He is ashamed about his ignorance of this, but otherwise he feels no shame, believing he was absolutely right in what he wrote.

Doesn't he feel a little exhilarated by the mudslinging? His Social Democrat dreariness suddenly gains if not a golden edge at least a little tinge of blood, a red thread in the greyness. Perhaps he is not made entirely of concrete? *Sentimental attachment to genocide* – it has taken decades to shake off *the yoke of goodness* – wasn't it *like an albatross round his neck?* Only now it emerges, like frivolous vomit.

Yet he is rather shaken when it persists year after year. This hatred. That he suddenly has so many enemies. *So many!* Didn't they know he was the most good-natured person in the village?

There must be something else as well. Some of them genuinely despise him. It cannot just have been the evacuation of Phnom Penh. Something else.

But his value system contains worse vestiges of ambiguity than this. And then everything fights back, almost to the death.

Some years later, when he is going through a divorce and his private life is turbulent, he buys a work apartment on the black market. Not a nice thing to do, in view of the play about financial crime he and Anders Ehnmark have just written that has been staged at the Royal Dramatic Theatre to enormous media excitement. But that is not the main problem; he was not alone in making a purchase on the black.

The problem is his relationship with his conscience.

The Tenants' Association, inspired by their play *Chez Nous*, start a big campaign against black-market apartments, and his block is dragged into the storm that ensues. The estate agent he contacted, and who had provided him with a contract for 38,000 kronor, is being prosecuted and he is forced to appear as a witness with other black-market purchasers. *Forced* is a debatable word. He does it. That is where it all begins.

He hired the agent himself, on his own initiative. Buying an apartment on the black market is not a crime, but easy selling; he gives his testimony to help bring down the agent. It is all very newsworthy. He appears both as a law-abiding, upright witness and as suspicious, because he bought the flat. But that is not where the problem lies for him.

He suddenly realises that *everything* is wrong. He was the one who contacted the agent.

He should have refused to be a witness. Then again there is definitely the issue of contempt of court. Probably carries a sentence. But if he had listened to his conscience, he would have taken responsibility, *personal responsibility*.

Now he is committing an act of treachery.

He has broken the most fundamental rule he learned as a child: you must place your conscience above the law. If you contravene the law, you take your punishment, because civilised society is built on this principle, an agreement between people that must be observed. But human conscience prevails over all these principles. If you choose your conscience, you can take your punishment calmly.

But what he has done is the worst of all possible alternatives. And betrayed all the principles he was raised with. He does not know for certain where his morals came from, the Bible or sport. But he has done wrong, and it hurts.

Those around him do not understand what has happened to him, find his violent reaction bewildering, but his conscience is very bad. In many years of debate he has become used to taking knocks. It is easy to take a knock for something you believe in, however hard the blow. But when it is for something you cannot stand for or believe in: then you fall at the slightest nudge. In fact it will take years before he is rid of this gnawing pain inside him that he can only call *shame*.

It slowly fades, but never disappears entirely.

For the first few months he locks himself away, does not want to see anyone.

All he can do is write, perhaps about shame. One long night he completes the final chapter of *The March of the Musicians*, the description of Uncle Aron's suicide: how, after raping Eeva-Lisa, he walks resolutely out over the ice on Burefjärden one stormy night, breaks a hole in the ice with a metal spike, loses the spike, returns home to fetch another, makes the hole wider, gets caught by the rucksack full of heavy potatoes meant to pull him down, and finally, after many hours in the snowstorm on the ice, succeeds in sinking down into the dark abyss, the deepest blackness of the ocean.

Almost an act of bravery.

Shame was the driving force for Uncle Aron. But it was nevertheless a feat, a sporting achievement, to commit suicide with such tremendous determination and physical difficulty; it was admirable, indeed, truly admirable.

But right now, as the '60s draw to a close, the time of innocence is over. He is in a place that is very brightly lit.

It is to do with a novel he has written.

What has happened?

A few months after the Soviet Union's invasion of Prague in August 1968, his documentary novel *The Legionnaires* is due to be published. No abstract discussion of morals now, this is serious.

The book focuses on the extradition of 146 Baltic military refugees to the Soviet Union, undeniably offering an alternative view of this Swedish ordeal. There is a certain nervousness at his publishing house: will the book be seen as sympathising with the Soviet agenda in some way? In view of the current situation that would be disastrous.

An emergency meeting is called.

The publishing director, Ragnar Svanström, gravely proposes that the book should not have a specific publication day, as all titles do, but should just *sneak out*, as it were.

He is furious, and Lasse Bergström, who is still subordinate to Ragnar Svanström, has what is for him a most unusual, but controlled, fit of temper, and demands that *The Legionnaires* be treated like all other books.

So it is. *The Legionnaires* does not sneak out.

CHAPTER 7

AN EXPEDITION

Everything has happened in a very short time.

He finishes his thesis on literature and knows that something is over. He will not continue his studies into Freud's influence on Strindberg's *A Dream Play*. He has been playing, and reality has caught up with him. He has been happy prolonging his stay in childhood's room; everything has gone according to plan. The instant he opens the door he comes out into the stark light of a place where he feels unprotected, and right at the centre.

In drama it is called the *pivot*, he has learned. That means the crucial point. In this case a novel he is writing. He is in a little house in Graneberg, in Uppsala. He moves a table and chair into the boiler room down in the cellar; it is very cramped but entirely safe. No-one looks over his shoulder at what he is writing. In the seclusion of the boiler room he can reassemble, piece by piece, the dreadful reality. Is he good enough? Was Rector Nilsson right? What he writes is unlike anything he has read or done before. He is moving into unknown territory. What does he have to lose?

He is not afraid.

Looking back he does not really know how it happened.

In the spring of 1966 he went to New York for the PEN Congress, went on to the southern states, and followed the solitary "freedom march" started by James Meredith on 5 June. Meredith had been denied entry to Mississippi University because of the colour of his skin; on the protest march he was shot by a sniper. Martin Luther King, Stokely

Carmichael and thousands of others took up the baton.

Bus across the southern states. Why does he want to catch up with the demonstrators? He does not know. That is the problem.

History tips over at this point, in 1966, from the fight against segregation in the southern states, to Vietnam and the Third World. Meredith is shot but recovers; others continue the march. It grows. When the march reaches Greenwood, Mississippi, Stokely Carmichael makes the famous speech that will mark the beginning of the Black Panther movement.

He reaches the march. It is terribly hot.

A truck with heavily armed Black Panthers glides threateningly past him and other protesters; he feels unsure. Is he a participant or an observer? Whatever is he doing here, for the last three days of the march?

He is – it would be repeated later many times – right at the centre of an historic event, and he does not understand it. June 1966.

A resolution is forming.

He has made a break in his journey.

During a lunch at Oak Ridge, and in a discussion about the Vietnam War, an American who has lived in Sweden suddenly and with unexpected hostility says that *Swedes have the only transportable conscience in the world, they travel round like professional moralists, and they never talk about their own moral conflicts. Transportation. The extradition of the Baltic soldiers.*

The extradition of the Balts? He recalls reading about it as a child. It was in the *Norran*.

It had sounded awful. People who had fled to Sweden were handed over to the Russians, to be executed. He knew who Russians were, because he knew the island of Ryssholmen in Hjoggböleträsket. Six Russian soldiers were said to be buried there. During some war in the eighteenth century they had been murdered by the courageous villagers. There were supposed to be adders on the island, in large numbers. He had never dared to set foot there, even though he had rowed round it many times in his grandfather's heavy boat. There was reason to fear Russians. And then innocent soldiers were handed over to them.

Several hundred. In fact there were even more; three thousand German soldiers were extradited as well, but no-one cared about them.

He understood very little of it, but the phrase *the extradition of the Balts* stayed with him. Now, in the middle of the '60s, everyone is talking about the Vietnam War, but something stops him. You cannot confess the sins of others. You need to scrutinise your own, and not only for Saturday prayers. Not, as a repentant Swede, beg for forgiveness for American imperialism. As if at arm's length. Where it does not hurt so much. With no Swedish ordeal. The shorter the distance, the greater the pain.

He makes a decision.

There would be a Swedish ordeal then. He makes up his mind to set off on an expedition. He can finally imagine setting foot on Ryssholmen.

That is how it begins, in Oak Ridge. Can it have been 12 June 1966?

Much later, when he has entered *the subsequent darkness* and desperately wonders how it could have gone so badly, he seems to cling to this memory of a bus journey to Oak Ridge, as if it were possible to resume his life. He had taken a bus south, made a stop in Oak Ridge, met an old school friend from secondary school who was living there; she is married too now. Does he have something in mind?

Certainly, he has travelled a long way; otherwise he would not have come so far.

She cries at the bus stop the dark night he leaves. They kiss each other, as if it would have been possible. It is not. But in the autumn of 1989, engulfed in the subsequent darkness, he calls her in desperation, making plans for the resumption of a different life. As if he could have begun again, and made things right, and started out, *On the Road*, from the southern states. Resumed his life, and been saved.

Ten or more conversations in November 1989. The voice on the telephone distant, in every way, sounding perplexed.

What does he remember in the autumn of 1989 of the march in

1966? That he did not belong there. That it was hot. That he wanted to write a novel about the extradition of the Baltic soldiers.

Everything had been written about the extradition of the Baltic soldiers, and nothing.

It concerned the extradition in January 1946 of – in the end, when some had escaped and one had mutilated himself by sticking a pencil into his eye and another had cut his own throat – 146 Baltic legionnaires enlisted in the Waffen-SS who had been detained in Sweden. They had come to Sweden as refugees at the end of the war and were now being extradited, despite the tremendous strength of opinion in their favour. The extradition divided Sweden, and also marked the beginning of the Cold War for its part. Before the extradition *Soviet comrades saved us from the German hordes*; after the extradition the Soviet Union was *a lawless killer state*.

The Swedish government was considered to have sent the legionnaires to certain death.

A disgrace, which lived on, and a Swedish ordeal. But what actually happened during the political process in Sweden, and afterwards in the Soviet Union, no-one knew.

He decides to find out.

In retrospect it appears obvious that the book had to be written.

But he is the one who does it.

The form is not evident, hence the uproar when it comes out, the seismic commotion when it is published. The novel has the title *The Legionnaires*. In future he is judged as if this novel were a lens: viewed through it, he is either the creator of a documentary masterpiece, or a swine.

An extremely controversial book and a dreadful novel.

He comes across the word *dreadful* in a long letter written by the former Finance Minister Ernst Wigforss when he had read the book. *The Investigator* – that was the term for the book's narrator, who could easily have been called Per Olov Enquist – had spent a long day in the summer of 1967 down in Vejbystrand in conversation about the extradition with the now eighty-year-old Wigforss, an intellectual Social Democrat icon he greatly admired.

Wigforss is very thin, friendly, unmistakably clear, and holds the cracked coffee cup with a steady hand; he has the reputation of being *very frugal* and does not throw away broken china. He is worried at the prospect of the meeting, eager to explain why he did what he did back then, and how he thought about it, and how he continued to think, agonising and unable to sleep at night, until finally he was able to repress it; how it came about that he, with Foreign Minister Östen Undén and Prime Minister Per Albin Hansson, supported the political decision for extradition so unequivocally and resolutely.

In a letter of September 1968 – they were later to exchange many letters and became penfriends of sorts – he describes his impression of the novel. *"P.O. – this is a dreadful book you have written. The Baltic soldiers and the extradition and the individuals who had a part in these events are examples of how human beings and their societies tear one another apart. One is forced to experience it again, for reading destroys all ability to forget. The fates of these living and once living people have opened up the vista of devastation underlying that time, that time of war and of Nazism, everything that makes me call your book dreadful."*

It was not possible for anyone who had been involved in the extradition of the Balts to be free of the affair.

A decision is taken and dominoes topple forward into history. Training college in Umeå, or flung out into the world? Curious on a personal level, but in this case it was other people's lives falling.

Wigforss, this mild and moderate humanist, whose *Memoirs* he had read and admired, was tormented. The responsibility, in the decision year of 1945 when he was in government, had been partly his. Sweden was morally weighed down by the war years' concessions to Hitler's Germany, and Wigforss, like so many Social Democrats, believed that the Soviet Union, which had been hit hard and lost forty million people in the war, had borne *the heaviest burden of victory*. It should not now be singled out as a lawless state and treated differently from other allies.

Wigforss was hurled into history, and did not emerge, just as the young Investigator would be hurled in and history would change his life. It was an unsettled Swedish debt that caused the pain. If indeed it was a debt. A Swedish dilemma, at any rate.

It remained to be investigated. The unusual thing was that the project had in tow an investigator who quite openly described himself as a source of errors. His long series of interviews included not only those extradited, those in exile in the west or those now living in the Soviet Union, but also officers and camp guards, opinion-formers and leader writers, priests and soldiers, and all political decision-makers still living. The latter appeared to be united in their anxiety over the question. It would stir things up; some things should not be spoken of. And who is this young author who wants them to *relive* their nightmares?

He finds himself tossed into other people's lives. Not historical figures, but living people, to whom harm can still be done. He tries to expose the mechanisms of a political crisis, but the truthfulness of this is constantly obscured by people's lives.

Caution is needed.

He does not try to cover up the project. He says that he intends to write about the extradition of the Baltic soldiers, and very soon realises that he is stepping into a minefield.

The issues about domestic policy are sensitive. Although the decision was taken by the coalition government, it was the Social Democrat government who carried it out nine months later, despite public opinion. And despite increasing awareness of the special conditions that would certainly apply to Soviet citizens from the Baltic who had enlisted on the wrong side, the Waffen-SS, in the Great Patriotic War.

In short: execution as a traitor.

The extradition was an embarrassment for social democracy and always would be. He also senses immediately a growing suspicion that actually concerns his honour. Should he, whose allegiance is clearly on the left, and who is also a Social Democrat, now produce a Social Democratic white paper excusing the scandal, wiping out the debt, and *licking the arses of the Soviet executioners*? The suspicion is already there.

The novelist's sheltered solitude, agreeable narcissism and peaceful darkness in his private room are all now a distant memory. No more safety in the historical novel, the eighteenth century and the magnetists. This material is a venomous jellyfish.

He is not untalented, and not insensitive, and for him his honour is important. But how will he reach *truthfulness*? He knows the risks, not simply that he is suspected of engineering a vindication for social democracy and the Soviet Union, thereby losing his honour, but also the antithesis: that, in order to enhance his own integrity, he will assure the murder of the murderers, whatever the testimony of reality.

This is also his first encounter with exile, not his own, but theirs.

Baltic civilians had also had their villages, which they had left. He should have been able to understand. Was it the village that concealed his own deep-seated sense of exile? Or the other way round?

An expedition into the heart of a Swedish ordeal. It is painfully obvious from the first moment that he has been adrift in an exiled Baltic world, filled with contradictions.

The exiles' world is mysterious, bursting with emotion; he does not know if he is mature enough for this passion. It was not just soldiers who came over the sea in the last year of the war. Above all there were civilian refugees. The three Baltic states, occupied in turn by the Soviet Union and Hitler's Germany, had lived through most things. Not least ethnic cleansing, genocide, and, during the German occupation, the most effective Holocaust any European country had ever suffered, partly with the involvement of the occupied people themselves, with an eradication of Jews exceeding 98 per cent.

When the Red Army rolled westwards in the autumn of 1944 the exodus began. They came over the Baltic Sea in small boats, and in large numbers. He learned a rule of thumb: 40,000 Estonian civilians, 4,000 Latvians, 400 Lithuanians.

And now they were in Sweden, what would happen to them?

No-one really knew. Among Swedish politicians in the summer of 1945 circulated the unspoken idea that they should be *sent back* to the Soviet Union. There was "no reason" to let them stay; they were just waiting for a Soviet proposal, and it had to be treated with understanding, even if not with enthusiasm. Sweden had a debt to pay to the victor. The U.S.S.R. had saved Sweden from the German hordes, despite Swedish transportation, iron ore and ball-bearings in support of the German war effort. Does the Soviet Union want to have its civilian refugees back? Absolutely.

Then the storm blew up over the Baltic soldiers. A small group, initially 167, and, what's more, Waffen-SS! The storm raged. If SS-soldiers could arouse this level of compassion, how would it be for the civilians?

The extradition of the Baltic soldiers made the Swedish government appreciate the nature of the minefield.

That probably also applied to the Soviet side. The debate over the 167 men gave the Soviets a strategic insight. It would be disastrous if civilian refugees were also extradited, an awful lot of political blood would be spilled, relations between the U.S.S.R. and Sweden severely damaged for a long time to come. It is a fact that the threat of civilian extradition was real: it was not just Sweden who extradited to the Soviet Union the first year after the war. Many horrendous tragedies unfolded across Europe; the British government, for example, with Churchill and Eden bearing chief responsibility, and with the legendary Eighth Army executing operations, extradited seventy thousand Cossacks and

Yugoslavs who served in the German army. Not just the soldiers: women and children were sent too.

Thousands of suicides were systematically covered up by the victors in their writing of history.

Or the tragedies when Vlasov's Russian Liberation Army was forcibly repatriated: those who had enlisted on the German side, the deserters and the prisoners from the Red Army. Over a million. The civilians accompanying them were extradited too.

In all respects the storm surrounding the 146 was a lesson.

A request for the civilian refugees was never made. The extradition of the Baltic soldiers intervened.

Afterwards *those who were allowed to stay* would really know about it. They would acknowledge that the extradition had actually saved them, that they all had a debt of gratitude to the 146. As the years passed the acknowledgement lingered on, like the guilt felt by survivors from the concentration camps: why was I saved? It was a comparison never made, *Waffen-SS and concentration camps!*, but people remembered this guilt. And that Sweden had guilt. To a certain extent the guilt was a political power they hoped would legitimate their existence in the new country. And in any case history could not be rewritten.

For twenty years this was laid in stone. What happened to the people who were handed over? *All executed.*

It might be true, or it might not. But deep down in the civilian refugees' consciousness was sorrow for the homelands they had lost, *the grief of the people driven from their village*, during an occupation that no-one in the new country, Sweden, challenged. In actual fact no-one seemed to remember the names of the three small states, Estonia, Latvia and Lithuania. So close, almost visible from the coast of Gotland. Yet absolutely non-existent. Bitterness surfaced now and then, but also the sense of debt to those who were extradited.

Extradited, so that others could go free.

The myth about the forced repatriation of the Baltic soldiers was intensely present and completely true, regardless of what had happened in reality. The debt was established, and was not determined by the outcome of their fates. And then a naive young writer comes along and claims he wants to write a book about *what actually happened*.

Actually? It was a minefield. Lucky for him that he had never been burdened with expectations. He moved lightly and surely over the minefield, a cynical glint in his eye.

The eyes of the displaced looked at him with sadness, suspicion, hope that he would understand, and sometimes with hatred. Pivot means crucial point.

"We will have blood on our hands!"

That was what one of the ministers responsible for the extradition, Nils Quensel, had said in a government meeting. The Investigator – he is soon identified by this label – naturally investigates Quensel, as one of a number.

Not without a certain curiosity.

Quensel is a novel in himself, he is later mixed up in both the Haijby and Kejne affairs, and is surrounded by rumour. As a lawyer and minister without portfolio, it was alleged he had been too intimately involved in the care of young boys on the road to crime; he had called them up to his office, where he spoke to them severely and urged the thin ones to eat properly. He was said to have checked that they maintained their weight and ordered them to take their clothes off so that he could make sure they were looking after themselves, and if they had not filled out nicely he was forced to give them a smack on the bare backside. It was not just rumours that surrounded him, there was substance and slander by turns. Homosexuality was a punishable offence, and in this area those in power were said to *keep each others' private lives secret*.

He was an almost mythical figure in the '50s debates about legal corruption.

Quensel had come out of it badly, but now, in his gigantic apartment in Östermalm, alone and frail and about to die, he wants to talk about the extradition of the Baltic soldiers.

He was one of those who plainly opposed it.

And yet the interview goes badly from the very start. Quensel sits bolt upright, on his guard, stares at him with hostility, as if they were still in the turbulent times of the Kejne affair and one more piranha is about to bite through his throat; and after only a few minutes the visitor makes a dreadful mistake.

He uses the Swedish *ni*, the polite form of the word "you" to address Quensel.

Quensel leans forward and hisses through tight lips: "Don't call me '*ni*'!" It happens so suddenly the Investigator completely loses his composure. "I'm sorry, I don't understand . . ." Followed by the same enraged rasping voice. "Don't call me '*ni*'!!!" And again the helpless reply: "I'm sorry, what should I . . . ?" Once more the same hissing. "My title is President, I am President of the Court of Appeal." And for several seconds his confusion is total. President?

In panic he racks his brains. How will he remember this title? It is not common, not in Sweden. *President Quensel?* How will he remember? But then he thinks of President de Gaulle.

He's got it. Relieved, he carries on.

It is a remarkable conversation.

The heavy leather-clad atmosphere is almost soporific, but so too is history, stories from the '50s, like the man before him who a few decades ago *steadily lost his reputation* in a situation that would later be called *media-driven*. Now the mythical Quensel sits in front of him, no longer on his guard, more slumped, the hateful hissing slowly dying away, and he softens. He no longer tries to defend the lost reputation he desperately tried to cover up with the title President. The young author in front of him does not look intimidated, by the title or by the fear of a beating, but he is not malicious either, is not *out to get* Quensel; in the end they converse for over three hours, with calm objectivity, never calling each other *ni*, and never *President*.

"And in the end I requested the floor and I said: We'll have blood on our hands! Blood on our hands!"

There was a psychological resistance to investigating all of this, everywhere.

In the autumn of 1968, a few months after the book's publication, Tage Erlander writes to him: "Perhaps you will recall that when you came to see me and we discussed your plans, I warned you against writing a novel about the extradition of the Baltic soldiers. It was one episode in the course of a war in which millions of tragedies unfolded, and I imagined that there was nothing more of any weight to be gained from going through it again." Adding in the next breath that now he has "completely changed [his] mind".

Erlander is sceptical, but in the end he comes forward. From Bertil Ohlin, who is not directly involved, but would certainly have valuable comments, there is a firm *No!*, on the grounds that he has no faith at all in *that man Enekvist*. In view of what has happened in the past he can understand this, but amazingly the only reason all collaboration with him is refused is that *in a review of* Alcestis *at the Royal Dramatic Theatre* he gave a mildly political interpretation of the classic.

He rereads his review, is perplexed, but pleased that a politician is interested in the theatre, and ponders yet again his mother's love for Bertil Ohlin.

Erlander, this legendary Swedish prime minister, makes a comment a few years later that he does not really understand.

In *The Legionnaires* there is a long chapter about Swedish refugee policy from the '30s to the mid-'40s; it is not a pretty story. Erlander says, almost in passing: "I'm grateful that you've been considerate in the book and not mentioned that I was Möller's state secretary."

Considerate?

He is puzzled. He has certainly not been consciously considerate. That Gustav Möller as Minister of Social Affairs was in many ways chiefly responsible for the refugee policy is one thing. But State Secretary

Erlander? He is not enlightened until many years later, when he understands what Erlander meant with his little remark. His third wife, Gunilla, has been state secretary in the Department of Culture for six years; he has learned the conditions of this outwardly sheltered, but inwardly central position of power.

The state secretary in the Department of Social Affairs had obviously had a greater responsibility for immigration policy than he had realised.

On the whole he learns a great deal, not just about the political game, but also about the mechanisms of a political crisis. But as the months pass he has a feeling that it is all now happening *at the last minute*. The archives will always be there, they will not die, and he has learned how to handle them from his life in the Uppsala university library, Carolina Rediviva. But the people?

He is aware that death is breathing down his neck. Most of those who were part of it are now growing old. They will soon die, he knows, or their senses will dim, or they will become indifferent, or quite simply forget. Around him the debate about Vietnam rumbles more and more vehemently, but he is held captive in his expedition. Ohlin's sharp analysis that *Enekvist is not the only young writer who with not the slightest hesitation thinks he can enter public debate without familiarising himself with the views being criticised*, he finds undoubtedly thought-provoking.

But is it *a trend*?

He learns that political novels, like democracy, cause friction. They take time, and work. But he also learns that so much in the political decision-making process is down to chance. Perhaps carelessness too. Foreign Minister Christian Günther should have been the speaker when the final decision was taken; he was on holiday in Dalarna. The case was badly prepared. Per Albin Hansson, as revealed in the classified Foreign Ministry documents he went through when they were released in the '80s, was personally responsible for the extradition decision to a much greater extent than had been known: he not only forced through the positive response to the U.S.S.R. (to their vague enquiry about how Sweden intended to handle the military refugees) – he also personally dictated the passage that came far closer to them than their enquiry had warranted. In a sweeping gesture he included not only *the refugees from the front after the signing of the German instrument of surrender on 8 May 1945*, but also the ones who had fled previously.

Without this addition, the tragedy of the Baltic extradition would never have existed, because they had all arrived earlier.

Not surprising that they regarded him with suspicion, perhaps fear. What was this? A trial for a crime barred under the statute of limitations. His innocent recklessness did not make it less disquieting.

Some of the witnesses faded away while he was writing. The one who bore the burden of guilt in public was strangely enough neither Ernst Wigforss nor Per Albin Hansson, but Östen Undén. At their meeting he is very old, very tired, but absolutely clear on his position. He had inherited a dilemma, since he had not been a member of the coalition government who made the original decision, and had long fought against the extradition, but he gave in.

In the judgement of history he became the architect of the extradition.

In a dark apartment high up in the so-called Erlanderhuset in Marieberg – strangely the Investigator remembers all the politicians as if they were always in very dark rooms, and were very close to death – the former Foreign Minister had spoken quite openly, but with no hope of being understood by history. At the door, the conversation over, Undén had hesitantly said, "I have quite a detailed diary entry about the extradition, it would clarify . . ." And then he had asked, "May I read it?" But the old man waited, looking beyond the Investigator, his eyes not yet totally blind, thinking, and then he murmured, "I'll think about it, I don't know, I'll ring if . . ." And then he said no more and the conversation was over.

That was how it began. A learning process for him, but for the people involved a torture that revisited them before they died, just when they had managed to forget this Swedish dilemma that had finally become an abscess. And still the people who were questioned did not know what this strange author would produce as a result; another indictment, or an acquittal?

He understood if they said no. But they almost never said no. Not even the quiet legionnaire who had poked a pencil into his eye the week before the extradition. He had been exempt from transportation on the steamer *Beloostrov*. Now he was living in a small apartment outside London, had a daughter who was a National Liberation Front activist, and with wrinkled brow he listened to the horrific tale of how fear of Soviet communism made him poke the pencil into his eye.

But they all wanted to explain themselves. In the end it became an almighty chorus.

They died, one after the other.

He did not hear from Undén again, did not manage to make contact with him. He must have wanted to die in peace and quiet, now that he had completed his life's work and said what he wanted to say, and had become increasingly blind so that he could not see out over Riddarfjärden, or read his old diaries or the newspapers that reviled him for the extradition of the Baltic soldiers.

In a letter from Wigforss there is a short passage about him. "Undén is in quite a bad way now, and nearly blind. But I know that someone is reading the book to him."

He is now thirty-one years old. He has bought a house in Graneberg, outside Uppsala. He believes he can do anything.

Everyone advises him against the project. He does not hesitate for a second. He wants to set out upon *terra incognita*: the east, where there is only the empire of evil, and the recently occupied small Baltic countries that in Sweden are shrouded in total silence. He is entirely alone in his enthusiasm. Even well-informed, sensible intellectuals can only with difficulty pick out the Baltic states on a map, such is the mood. It angers him. He seeks his way in an exiled world he finds not only mystifying, but gradually also both moving and desperate. They have fled from a country that Sweden *for reasons of principle* has forgotten.

The unknown world of exile opens up to him.

It is not homogenous. The political range within Baltic exile is enormous, from social democracy to fascism. They are astonished that someone, a young writer, is interested, and in surprised and distrustful bewilderment they embrace the only Swede who is concerned with their tragedies. They speak ill of each other in front of him, like the Rothvik sisters did. He notes it calmly and tries to probe further. He likes the expression *probe further*.

He knows he is exposed to misinformation, but defines the word as *fragments of truth brought together in a mendacious way*. This creates a problem, as well as a possibility, if the liars' grains of truth can be identified and used. Between journeys he lays out the pieces of the jigsaw on his desk in the boiler room.

The definition covers Soviet misinformation too, he discovers later.

He has forgotten the anguish of belief, forgotten the warmth of sport, and he has found the excitement of political mystery. Most people advise him against travelling to the Baltic to search for the repatriated. With a sigh they suggest he is naive and does not understand that the Soviet authorities will mislead him; he sighs too and agrees. The twentieth time this is repeated, he sighs just as sympathetically. He will not allow himself to be *exhausted* by his now quite openly established political naivety. Now that he has realised, with the help of a host of witnesses, that he is going to be misinformed, he begins to puzzle eagerly over the mechanisms, the mechanisms which will remorselessly destroy his childlike clarity.

He is suddenly aware of his own ironic subtext, and it scares him. He sees that he is being driven in a certain direction, as a reaction. That is not where he wanted to be.

*

As time goes on he has many contacts. Some of them he can even trust.

An old Latvian Social Democrat Party leader, Bruno Kalnins, is living in exile out in Hässelby Strand. He is elderly now, but still vice president of Socialist International, and has connections at the highest level in Swedish Social Democratic circles. Kalnins calmly tells him that he knows very well what happened to the people extradited: no-one was executed, but a large number were sent to camps in Siberia. Kalnins is curious about *how many*. He thinks it would be a good idea to go over and find out. Asked why no-one has told the truth about their fate before, in other words, told him or the public that there were no executions, Kalnins asserts that everyone in exile knows, but keeps quiet for political reasons.

For political reasons. They both reflect on this in silence.

Kalnins thinks he should go. But on one condition: he should not do it in secret. He must clearly explain the aim of the visit to the Soviet embassy and apply for authorisation. He is puzzled by this, in view of his *political naivety*, and so on, and thinks he certainly will be hoodwinked now. Kalnins points out that the risks for people he sees in secret are great, while he, as a *prominent* Swedish author with connections within the Social Democrat Party, risks nothing. He must not play with their destinies.

He must not play with their destinies. That is the point.

He is given authorisation by the Soviet embassy.

And he goes searching. Ninety per cent of the book is already complete, the Swedish part; now it is about the Soviet part, which he starts to call "The Homecoming". He searches in harshly lit places and places shrouded in darkness. Everywhere conversations, authorised and clandestine. He has addresses. The first journey he undertakes is on an almost empty ferry travelling from Stockholm to Riga and named after Lenin's wife, Nadezhda Krupskaya. The exiles from across the world who have gathered on the boat, only about thirty of them, seem ashamed.

They are visiting an occupied homeland. Some people hate them for it. Contacts, or boycott? It is a fundamental question to which there is no answer.

Once he travels in disguise. This disguise, a camouflage that makes him to a certain extent invisible, or at least he imagines he is, is the week he spends in Riga as part of the delegation of the Sweden–Soviet Latvia Friendship Society.

He is disguised as the person he is accused of being, a helpful idiot.

He no longer minds. He is obsessed with his task, not with his good name. He likes his colleagues in the delegation; they possess an integrity and gravity he recognises from a previous life. They gradually find out that he is on an expedition, which explains his mysterious absences from time to time. In most cases his interviews are completely open and he gives an almost confident impression, but *on certain evenings he spends a lot of time in Riga's parks*. He believes that following someone is done in the form of zonal marking, rather than marking a specific opponent, to borrow football terms, as he explains to his friends in the delegation. He thinks he can detect man-marking and he has fortunately never identified anyone on his tail. On the other hand, he is directly exposed to zonal marking and bugging.

But one must not play with the lives of the extradited.

During his trips and after the book's publication he did not only speak to people who had been repatriated.

Bruno Kalnins had given him an address; it was for Kalnins' old friend Fricis Menders, a Social Democrat veteran now eighty-five years old, a professor of economy, a dissident and regarded with some fear by the regime.

Menders lived on the outskirts of Riga. He had been given detailed directions, not to take a taxi, to stop if he thought he was being watched, but if the opportunity presented itself, to hand over a letter from Kalnins. What happened next is described very inadequately in *The Legionnaires*.

Followed? Watched? At eight in the evening he made contact

with the man, who was old and a Social Democrat and lived on the outskirts of Riga. "Were you followed?" he asked. During the conversation he brought a tea caddy from the pantry, and under the tea were some handwritten sheets of paper. A letter. "One can never be too careful." What experiences did he have? "One learned a great deal in Stalin's time." Had anything changed? "One can never be too careful. If you stayed here for a year you would know. Control, suspicion, censorship. You're too young to understand."

That is all, in the novel. But it is actually only the beginning of the story.

The apartment where Menders and his wife Lidija lived was perhaps thirty-five metres square.

Outside the room, where they clearly slept on a pull-out sofa surrounded by piles of books, was a tiny kitchen, where an ancient woman sat on a chair. She was certainly not a relative. She did not say hello, she sat bent and wizened, her malevolent eye on the guest, a sort of witch with knitting and, as he soon gathered with the help of smiles and gestures from the Menders, the *observer* the authorities had placed there. Her iron bed was also in the kitchen.

Throughout the entire visit she does not say a word, but rarely does her glance drop to the knitting. Menders makes a quick sign indicating danger, they shut the door to the kitchen, but she instantly rises and opens it again. They are now speaking in German. The conversation is partly overt, partly conducted in an imperfect coded language. He has learned, in conversations with the ones who had been banished to camps in Siberia, that those who experienced the Gulag are remarkably expansive, and appear to have no fear.

They seem to have nothing to lose, as they have already lost almost everything. Menders is frank and yet at the same time holds back, as if he is undecided. His wife offers tea.

The situation is extraordinary.

When, after an hour, his wife shuts the door to the kitchen again, the witch with her knitting gives up and does not open it. "Are you an old friend of Bruno's?" Menders asked very quietly; he confirms that he is.

Menders reaches for a pot tucked in between the piles of books. Its size is astonishing, but it apparently contains tea, and he digs out some papers hidden under the leaves.

The rest of the story is more painful.

Menders says softly: "I have a few letters I'd like to send to Bruno Kalnins. Can you take them?" He answers: "Yes, of course."

Menders turns round, holding the letters in his hand, is silent for a moment and then asks, with solemnity, as if wishing to mark a very great and perhaps dangerous mission, his distinctive German becoming even more formal: "Are you quite sure, with the utmost discretion, you are prepared to deliver these letters? Think carefully! Are you sure?"

He replies: "Yes, I'm sure."

The letters – the bundle of paper is surprisingly bulky and obviously contains very many letters – are typewritten on greaseproof paper. How many pages? An amazing number. Countless closely typed lines. He takes the bundle quickly and pushes it under his clothing; Menders' wife opens the door to the kitchen and they drink tea and talk about nothing in particular. Later he walks through the dark street of Riga back to the hotel. No-one follows him, presumably.

Three days later he goes through passport control with the bundle of papers tucked into his underpants, lodged like a jockstrap between his legs. No problems. The president and secretary of the Writers' Union bid official farewell at the airport. On the plane a glass of champagne and an apple, as usual.

The following day he hands the documents over to Bruno Kalnins, who seems elated.

A year later, after the book's publication, he is spending an evening with Bruno K. and suddenly remembers the letters. He asks what Menders had written about and whether it was something interesting.

Kalnins looks at him with a strange smile and says: "It was of the utmost interest. It was a dozen articles for my Social Democrat newspaper *Briviba*. About the economic situation in Latvia, with some exceedingly valuable information." At first he does not properly understand what Kalnins is saying. "Articles about what? Not personal letters then?" And Kalnins replies: "They have aroused a great deal of attention. Of course we're publishing them without naming Fricis as the author." And no more is said, because they both understand.

In other words it was something other than letters between friends he smuggled through. Contraband, in a manner of speaking, more dangerous. And yet he still does not know what will follow.

Had he felt like a secret agent? At any rate what happens next is less pleasant.

After the publication of the book and in the midst of the storm of opinion surrounding it, there is an announcement in an emigrant Latvian newspaper in Germany, *Latvija*, that Fricis Menders has been arrested.

The paragraph in *The Legionnaires* is quoted and the anonymous Social Democrat is named as Fricis Menders. He is indignant over this betrayal, but it means nothing, because reality has already fitted the pieces of the puzzle together. Official information in Latvia is also cited, giving the reason for his arrest as his handover of state secrets to "an American journalist". It is puzzling, but maybe quite obvious; the German newspaper assumes that the Soviet authorities had not wanted to damage Soviet–Swedish relations by identifying the person who did the smuggling as Enquist, now under fire from the Baltic emigrant right, and therefore perhaps in future useful as a helpful idiot.

So what is the truth?

It is made clear in a letter he receives from Bruno Kalnins, who, due to the publication in *Briviba*, is also involved in the tragedy. He says:

> Brother! One of my friends was in Riga a week ago and spoke to Lidija Menders. He was able to read four letters from Menders from the place of deportation and the court.
> It is apparent that Dr F. Menders has not just been expelled

from Riga, but has been sentenced to deportation (according to the penal code "*sylka*" in Russian, "*nometinajums*" in Latvian), a punishment different from expatriation. This means that Menders himself did not have a choice in where he would be sent, but it had to be determined by the authorities, that is to say the K.G.B. The K.G.B. decided that he had to live in the old people's home in Kapini, in the Kraslava region. Menders is not permitted to leave this place for five years. He is allowed visitors only by permission of the K.G.B. So far no-one has been given permission.

Very informative. Utterly dreadful.

The rest of the letter is a report on a consignment he had sent to Menders with Kalnins' help: a package consisting of a pair of boots and some medicine for Menders, who has heart disease. All sent via official channels, obviously, in this case a person with the name of Z. Zakenfelds, Pasta kaste 261, Galvenaja pasta, Riga, Soviet Socialist Republic of Latvia. He reports directly to the First Secretary of the Communist Party of Latvia, A. Voss.

The parcel disappears en route and never reaches Fricis Menders or his wife, Lidija. He is not surprised, as he works on the principle that members of the K.G.B. steal like magpies. This is not least because the money he sends to the widow of the legionnaires' leader, Elmars Eichfuss-Atvars, the first time – in a test case – reaches her, whilst subsequent amounts are absorbed into the mysterious Soviet–Latvian administration.

He gives up then.

It was a pity about the heart medicine for Menders. Menders dies in deportation, in the year 1971. In January 2007 the letters, photographs and notes of "this legendary Latvian resistance fighter" are deposited in the Museum of the Occupation of Latvia.

They are written on greaseproof paper.

Were his actions wrong?

Perhaps. Not wrong to smuggle out the manuscript. But he should have realised that it was volatile material. On the other hand Fricis Menders himself was the best judge.

But the combination of the articles published in *Briviba* following his visit and the ten lines in *The Legionnaires* was disastrous for Fricis Menders and his heart condition. It could be expressed very simply, with no embellishment.

He had sent Fricis Menders for deportation.

Is he naive? Hardly.

Does he not understand? He understands.

Is he reckless?

He does not yet want to answer this question. One must not play with people's lives. During the time of his conversations in Riga, he treads carefully in the Soviet undergrowth, but around him he hears the tiptoeing. He does not intend to give up, and in that way he is reckless. Yet he learns more, every day. The Menders case teaches him something too. The other cases are distinctive, but still similar. He knows that he is about to write a novel that will be unlike any other. Therefore he is going to be reckless. Going to be? But will he stop before then?

He is a long way from the village. He knows the questions.

As time went on, ventures into the Soviet undergrowth produced interesting experiences.

In 1984 he makes a long journey through the Baltic states and writes a series of articles for the *Expressen*. The year is a turning point for communism, he can see that, but he does not yet understand it. In Riga he visits the family of a Baptist who by reason of *his insanely and obstinately held faith* lives in wretched conditions and has been downgraded to park cleaner despite his university education; there is something about the intractable refusal of Baptists and Pentecostalists to enter religious organisations controlled by the state that causes the authorities great anxiety. Only an hour – a record – after his return to the hotel, an anonymous person from "the Foreign Office", in other words the K.G.B., rings to say that he is the target of provocation and must immediately cease these contacts. Evidently zonal marking, and therewith microphones.

All unsurprising.

More remarkable is the reaction to his articles, from the same trip, on economic decay in the Baltic states. A downturn, lamentable conditions in the food sector, in Riga there has been no meat for sale in the shops for a year. And so on.

On his return home the Soviet ambassador makes a furious telephone call to editor-in-chief Bo Strömstedt, criticising this denigration of the Soviet economy. He says the writer travelled to the Baltic under false colours, that he had actually been a journalist, that in future every visa application will be refused, and that this mouthpiece for Radio Free Europe, where, what's more, he has been quoted, is a fraud.

In retrospect he finds the reaction interesting. He notes that it is possible to write about Soviet oppression of opinion, that is normal. Everyone writes about it. People are used to it. But under no circumstances may one question the holiest of communist cows: the idea of relentless growth. That under communism, *development*, despite problems with dissidents and Baptists and their like, points steadily upwards. Even if only at 2.3 per cent a year. It goes *inexorably* forwards.

He has actually observed – in the prosperous Baltic of 1984, made up of the Soviet republics who have discovered they are in the desirable western neighbourhood – the economic implosion that will cause communism to collapse six years later. He has seen, but not understood. Like everyone else he assumes the irreversibility of the communist system. It is simply *inexorable*.

He sees, notes, but draws no conclusions. The thought of the collapse to come is – unthinkable.

But no more visas, until the Wall falls.

The Menders case was a chilling lesson in what the conditions were. It happened in parallel with the investigation into the extradition of the Baltic soldiers, but at the same time was right at the centre of it.

The outlook for the 146 repatriated men was determined by which ones they were. What background they had.

And what these members of the Latvian Waffen-SS had done.

In the opinion of the exile group, they were an elite unit that should in no way be mistaken for the SS. They were recruited in the *liberated*, in other words occupied, countries; they could be Latvian or French or Swedish or Norwegian. For example, Knut Hamsun's son Arild Hamsun served in the Norwegian Waffen-SS. And, if they could not be regarded as patriots and freedom fighters, they should at least be viewed as forcibly conscripted. Much later a German debate about a seventeen-year-old future author and Nobel Prize winner from Danzig serving in the Waffen-SS for only a few months, would strike a more unforgiving note.

The truth was far more complicated.

The majority of the extradited men were innocent and young – the youngest of them would eventually become his friend for life. Enlisting for them was a means to safeguard the cause of a future free Latvia. But before and during the life of the Latvian legion there was also a Baltic police battalion in all the Baltic states; units whose appalling history is well known, complete with cleansing operations, systematic murder of Jews and civilians, raids against partisans and full-scale war crimes. What blurred the identity of the Latvian Waffen-SS during the last years of the war, when resolution was close and the end seemed unavoidable, was that individual members of the police battalion infiltrated the legion.

In many cases it was obviously to conceal a past.

So the group who arrived in Sweden consisted of many completely disparate human destinies, on whom it was impossible to pass general judgement. Around forty of them were given long sentences in the Gulag. But it was not primarily for their spell in the legion that they were judged.

Over time he would unravel the initially controversial question of *what happened to them after extradition*. It was complicated, but the picture he presented proved to be correct. And he would not have wanted to write his book any other way.

There would be a time, after the fall of the Wall, when the archive was opened and the Baltic states became free.

It did not lessen the controversy surrounding the history of the war years and the representation of the legionnaires. Much later, in an afterword to a new edition of the novel published in free Latvia, he wrote that the story of the history of the legion, and who they were, and what happened, must become a task for Latvian historians, in a free Latvia, with free access to all the archives. It was not the business of a Swedish author.

He waits for many years, but nothing happens. He is surprised. Why, even in a free country, delve into this story, now unpleasant *in a different way*?

The Second World War continues to be dangerous territory. To probe deeper into the past is, *on reflection*, inappropriate. This investigation is still charged. Much later he notices, without surprise, how this traumatic event regularly causes violent political conflict.

Baltic participation in the Holocaust, for example. The occupying forces who were suddenly transformed into a Russian minority. Disputes about passports. Disagreements about citizenship. Or surrounding an Estonian statue that was moved. Or about marches of remembrance by the surviving veteran legionnaires.

He would continue to have contact with the people who were extradited.

On one occasion, in the middle of the '90s, the Conservative Swedish government invites them to Sweden. There are forty still living who can manage the journey. They visit camps such as Ränneslätt and are invited to a grand dinner at the Ministry for Foreign Affairs. He receives an invitation too, from the obliging minister, Margaretha af Ugglas, who gives a speech on behalf of the Swedish government and makes an official apology for Sweden's actions. It is a fine dinner, he knows most people there, and the atmosphere is calm, with no sense of pathos or antagonism, but it is all slightly unreal.

Towards the end of the meal one of the former legionnaires stands and gives an elegant and simple vote of thanks.

The Investigator is much older now, thirty years have passed since he set out on his expedition. He listens with slightly mixed feelings. He knows the speaker. This man told him a funny story once, when the Investigator was invited as a guest to an old comrades' dinner in Riga a few years after the liberation of Latvia.

At that dinner in Riga there had been seventeen legionnaires and him, and they had spoken calmly and candidly about the past. In comparison to them he was young, but they had shared a feeling of warmth and friendship, as if they were all involved in something that was part of history, and yet that was also part of life, and that had changed all their lives, his as well. They had stayed late into the night and it had all been very good.

The story told by the man, who would later make the vote of thanks at the Ministry of Foreign Affairs, was about his services in the German police headquarters in Riga during the German period. He had a desk job, picking out from lists the names of people who were communists or Jews and were to be interned, *or whatever else was going to happen to them*. Anyway, his German superior had said to him: "You're just sitting there with all your papers. But you need to learn how to handle a weapon too. This is war." And he had laughed and said, "No, I can't handle a weapon, I'm lousy at shooting." But his German boss had said: "You can learn! But you must learn to shoot moving targets. Not just stationary targets."

"I can rustle up a few Jews," his boss had said, "and then you can practice at shooting running Jews."

And the speaker, who just now had thanked the Swedish Foreign Minister for the dinner and the apology, had protested and said, "No, I can't, I'm useless with guns," and there had been no shooting at running Jews; but he was laughing when he said, "that's what the Germans were like," and it was somehow a funny story.

And what more was there to say?

They are sitting at small round tables in the Swedish Ministry of Foreign Affairs.

He is listening to the minister, and the vote of thanks, and to the friends he now knows better and likes more than he did when he began the expedition. It could not be simpler, including the joke about running Jews.

He knows that the expedition has changed him. He is not the same as he was.

This dinner is *a metaphor for the expedition*. It is as if he is, in some way, right up there at the centre of European history, and *it is the way it is*, the clarity of history obscured by people's faces. No excitement, no joy, just a kind of calm. Guilty or innocent, people's faces are in the end just human, like his own perhaps. This is how he feels.

European history is the way it is.

The book comes out; it is not *sneaked* out after all.

Six months later he is awarded a number of prizes for it, including the biggest Scandinavian literature prize, the Nordic Council's Literature Prize. The ceremony takes place in Stockholm City Hall, in the Blue Hall, which is crowded because the Council is convening. In front of almost one thousand people he gives a speech and expresses his gratitude for the prize.

Afterwards there is a dinner in the Golden Hall.

As guest of honour he is placed at the same table as all the Nordic prime ministers. They speak to him with caution and expectation, as if he has now become an expert in political crises and the mechanisms that drive them and is therefore deserving of respect and admiration. He finds now, as he will again, that he can very rarely speak to politicians about anything important; there is a mutual reticence, the important things are somehow *reserved for the book.*

He can only speak through a book and they only listen through it. Face to face there is only a blank.

But why this cautious regard for him, almost fear? Do they all dream of one day becoming writers? Or are they quite simply sceptical? He decides that they are expressing *admiration and respect.* He is not an expert on the mechanisms of political crises, but they think he is. He does not disabuse them, but knows the ice is thin; it has all happened so quickly. He feels as though he is in a brightly lit place, at the very centre, only eight years after he held the contract for his debut novel *The Crystal Eye* in his hand. Wasn't it for 1,000 kronor? The five prime ministers look at him with wonder. It is only three years since that night in Oak Ridge. Has it gone full circle? If it has, what does a circle look like?

What will they say to him?

What will he say to them?

In the evening the conversation grows more intense. The Danish prime minister Jens Otto Krag confides in him that he prefers bourbon to whisky. He agrees, seemingly discerning. It is at that level. He does not know what direction it will go in now.

CHAPTER 8

BERLIN AFTER THE RAIN

He went to Berlin for what should have been a year. It was the first journey in the fox farmer's footsteps.

The German identity was not self-evident. In the mental aftermath of the war Berlin and Germany were still for Swedes almost non-existent. Like the Baltic states, he sometimes thought.

Sweden seemed to be surrounded by non-existent cultures.

He took the step without hesitation.

At first short, tentative test-visits at the end of the '60s to the Literarisches Colloquium Berlin in Dahlem, the beautiful palace on the shores of Lake Wannsee, with a view of the equally beautiful villa on the opposite side of the water, the setting for the preparation of the Final Solution. Already Walter Höllerer steers him through the Berlin literary jungle. L.C.B. publishes a series of pamphlets: on each cover is a photograph of a guest of the Berliner Künstlerprogramm, seated on a wooden chair, taken by Höllerer's wife Renate von Mangold; the body language of the author sitting on the simple chair presents the embodiment of inner truth.

Enquist is on one cover, bearing his soul, icily calm, steely, wearing dark glasses, looking almost fascist-like, and staring straight ahead. His posture is thoroughly and *wilfully* Swedish and he looks in good shape; in his countenance his eyes, he hopes, convey age-old wisdom and say clearly "*I have traversed continents.*" His face is, however, framed by quite long sideburns, the fashion of the time.

Berlin will endure as a journey of self-realisation. Perhaps the sideburns will disappear.

He gradually gets to know some German authors.

The Gruppe 47 meeting in Sigtuna in 1965, which he witnessed in terror as an invited Swede, without daring to say anything at all, was dominated by monumental Germans: Enzensberger, Grass, Uwe Johnson and Helmut Heissenbüttel. He had anxiously observed these *living legends*, whose response in their fluent and supremely distinctive German language, with the verb placed desperately far away, at the end of highly complex sentences, *almost certainly* concerned existential and political questions far beyond any comments he could have made. At least in his faltering schoolboy German.

But German identity somehow becomes a real possibility for him.

Wasn't it the case that the gateway to Europe lay directly south of here? And wasn't this the very gateway he should go through?

It was through this southerly portal into Europe that over the centuries Swedish writers had *squeezed themselves out*. Greifswald, Berlin, Prague, Munich. The great heart of central Europe, especially Germany. The entry to this was in the south. The German culture that had very briefly – *was it just thirteen years?* – collapsed, but now would rise again, inexorably, and occupy its rightful place at the centre of the Europe he knew would soon be his.

That was about the size of it.

The door to Berlin had also been slightly ajar a few times.

Late in the autumn of 1969 he had passed through Berlin as the last stage of an extraordinary journey from Minsk; *The Legionnaires* was going to be made into a film, half documentary. Interviews had taken place in Latvia, a kind of repeat of what he had done for the book.

All went well. The Swedish team, led by the former Investigator, moved freely, at the same time conscious of the *tiptoeing* all around them. The director Johan Bergenstråhle, the cameraman Staffan Lamm and he had finally realised there might be a problem taking the tapes through customs. They did not have authorisation to export filmed material. So they decided to make a detour, eastwards; it was to be his first flight to Minsk.

It was a strange journey into the heart of Soviet darkness, now full of futility. They had stayed for a week of freezing cold at a hotel on the outskirts of Minsk, weighing up their options. Strangely enough he had met some friends from Greifswald there. Gisela was one of them. She was now an administrator for a boxing squad from the G.D.R. He therefore spent one night in a sports hall, witnessing a Soviet boxing tournament; it was a short and intense reunion with the young student he had met many years before in Greifswald.

It is over.

He knows he cannot return to 1957. He travels back on the boxers' bus, gets off at the hotel, and never sees her again.

The three men stranded in Minsk are drinking with increasing desperation, but late on the fifth evening they decide to take a gamble and to leave the hotel with their film cameras and tapes and catch the Moscow–Berlin train that passes through Minsk at five minutes past midnight.

The floor of the ticket hall is full of sleeping people.

In theory the journey home is doomed to failure, but thanks to their inebriation they think everything is possible. *Our comrades at the border are sure to temper justice with clemency!* And besides, news of the Swedish working-class revolutionary uprising in the ore-field, the miners' strike, had reached them in Riga, though in such a confused way they thought it had already sparked a conflagration.

Now that the world was in the grip of insanity and the unthinkable had already almost happened, namely that safe and dependable Sweden had been thrown into the blaze of revolution, why bother with frontier problems? Bunkum.

They drink themselves into a resolute stupor.

At Brest-Litovsk inspectors enter the compartment where up to now they have been alone. There are not many people travelling west in the Soviet Union, at least not in this rather primitive cattle truck. The three Swedes present a logistical problem for the inspectors owing to their intoxication, which makes them *difficult to get through to*. The alcohol conceals the contraband. The photographer Staffan Lamm is in a deep sleep, his head resting on the suspect metal tins, Bergenstråhle is apparently unconscious, and he keeps upright with great difficulty; not one of them can be checked and time at the border is short. *The three men* are sent off by the resigned border guards, who regard their decadence with distaste, on their way west.

It is all so easy.

Still influenced by his exiled Latvian friends and enemies and their thinking, he wonders whether the film expedition has been under surveillance the whole time. That, like useful idiots in fact, in their drunken, irrational flight, they have been both monitored and protected; but in view of the chaos and ruin, he doubts it.

Over the plains of Poland in a snowstorm. Into East Berlin, then West Berlin. The world seems to be empty of controls.

Perhaps this is the case. Perhaps everything about *the Wall* was quite simply an exaggeration. Forced from behind, maybe the Wall was hollow! Over his desk in the boiler room he has a print of Max Ernst's "Europe After the Rain", the one with the ravaged city overgrown by jungle.

That may be where he is heading.

He has been awarded a scholarship for a year and takes his family with him to West Berlin. This is when the permanent move will happen.

At the beginning of January 1970 he drives with his wife Margareta and their son Mats, who is now nine, in a car packed with all the things he will need for work, directly south through the G.D.R. to West Berlin. The gloominess of the grey East German countryside is almost numbing, but he steels himself, thinking that socialism is not built in a day and it always ends up in social democracy.

The baby of the family, Jenny, is now two.

She is blonde and constantly smiling, and they decide to send her by plane with Marianne, the nanny. The itinerary sounds crazy, but is based on *in-depth research*. Since the occupying forces still control permission for air travel, and there are no direct flights from Stockholm to West Berlin, and the nanny is only sixteen and cannot manage a change in Hamburg, they find a simple, practical solution: a direct flight from Stockholm to Schönefeld in East Berlin. Buses go from there to West Berlin.

You have to trust East German comrades! He says it in jest, but with a touch of gravity that alarms everyone.

They wait patiently, a snowstorm closing in around them, at the designated bus stop in West Berlin where the transit bus from Schönefeld should arrive. No bus and no child.

And they finally realise that something has happened.

They should have arrived at four o'clock in the afternoon.

No-one comes. At about eight, after having returned to the apartment in West Berlin, he manages to contact the East German airline and is informed that the plane was forced to turn round because of the snowstorm over Berlin and go down to Prague, where the passengers must wait for better weather.

Now it is time for more than deep concern. They know that the only language the nanny can speak is Swedish. By eleven o'clock there has been no further news, but an hour later it is reported from Schönefeld, where contact has now been established via Stockholm, that the plane has taken off from Prague and the estimated time of arrival is 00.45. However, fifteen minutes later there is another bulletin: a worsening snowstorm over Berlin has forced the plane to change course and go down to Budapest.

Then the information suddenly stops. He decides to go to Schönefeld to follow events on the spot. He takes the car and drives to Checkpoint Charlie, where he is told he does not have an entry permit for the airport.

He goes into the East German guardhouse to talk to the East German comrades.

They are drinking coffee and do not look as easy-going as he had expected. He steels himself, endeavouring to appear calm and friendly, and briefly sets out the Swedish government's favourable attitude to the G.D.R., whilst declaring that official recognition is not far off; the men in uniform share his anxiety about the child, but seem to be powerless, which surprises him. This is the G.D.R.! He shows them a photo of the child, golden-haired and smiling shyly; they look at the picture in silence. He asks them to ring. They shake their heads. At least the chief guard does, but he assumes the others share his view. However, the chief does finally make a telephone call, to be told that the snow over Schönefeld has thickened. He uses the German word *Dickichkeit*, which is reminiscent of something from Brecht.

He returns to the apartment at 6 Meinekestrasse, where he finds his wife weeping in despair. He manages to get a call through to Stockholm and discovers that the plane took off from Budapest, but was forced to abort its landing in Berlin because of the worsening storm and is now heading for Warsaw, the only East European airport within reach that remains unaffected by the blizzard.

Hamburg would have been closer, but politically impossible. He has the sharp feeling that Europe is divided.

He makes one more trip to Checkpoint Charlie.

He struggles through the deep snow to reach the East German side and speak to the comrades, who recognise him.

The situation is now intolerable.

He is at the centre of Europe, but the borders are real. The chaos in Minsk and Brest-Litovsk was apparent, but there is no confusion now, the Wall is not hollow, and the ravaged city certainly is overgrown by jungle, but he can no longer see any beauty in it. The comrades in the guardhouse are tired and are weary of him. Their remit does not include being *travel agents*. He stays with them for half an hour, but now they are all shaking their heads. They say that the storm will eventually ease. It is inevitable, like the victory of communism; perhaps that is not how they express it, but it is hard for him to concentrate on what they are saying.

He drives back to 6 Meinekestrasse.

At 4.45 in the morning they hear a taxi, and there, at last, is a nanny crying with relief and a two-year-old girl, resiliently beaming; this little girl who has already been across the whole of central Europe, and visited the five cities of Prague, Budapest, Warsaw, East Berlin and West Berlin.

This is how the door to Berlin opens.

He made the decision much earlier. He is going to write a novel about sport and politics.

The new-found authority attributed to him after *The Legionnaires*, alternating between hatred and respect, baffles him. In what does he *really* excel? He has written about politics and ethics and the Second World War, but what did he do during the war? *Soldier in the Field* and anti-tank barriers and on one occasion blackout paper in the windows in Hjoggböle. While millions were exiled and slaughtered. When the *Norran* reports that Hitler's Wehrmacht has launched an offensive in the Ardennes his ten-year-old self is excited; he thinks purely in terms of military strategy and will not let any moral qualms spoil *his experience of war manoeuvres*; only his mother's tears curb his enthusiasm.

This authority does not relate *to his actual ability*. He is regarded as a *white elephant*, appears constantly on television, leads debates, and participates as an expert himself in politics and ethics, but this esteem perversely skirts round the one area in which he believes he has complete mastery.

That is sport. What he reads about sport he finds amateurish. The doubters understand nothing, the believers cannot write. But the problem is: does he now view sport only as something full of emotion and innocence, and as an escape?

He understands the innocence. When he travels up to Västerbotten now he often hires a car and spends the light summer nights driving around alone. In village after village he searches for what remains of the fields where they played football or for the pitches that have survived. Very light summer nights. Not another person. Just the *guilt-free geography* of the playing fields.

He believes he can shape something out of this. He needs to build the surround now, the frame.

He will create a frame, like a picture maker.

Unresisting, he slides into the underworld of Berlin sport.

He sees all there is to see of boxing. He finds East German amateur boxing technically brilliant, but *morally rigid*, far too sedate compared to the professional galas in West Berlin. He still has the idea that the brutality of professional boxing presents the only respectable image of capitalist society.

Later he changes his mind and considers brutality to be brutality *per se*.

Six-day cycle racing is an experience, since it takes place in the Sports Palace. History seeps out of the walls; it is the film recordings he remembers, Goebbels' last horrendous rallies, when catastrophe and collapse are already a fact and yet everyone roars their loyalty.

It is in the walls.

The track is made of engineered wood and he is full of admiration for the workmanship in the surface. He is sitting at the front of the E section; the cyclists bank up and down past him in rhythmic waves, taking it in turns to push for three or four laps and drop back. The spectators of West Berlin's working class sit in the infield drinking. Sport is frothing with beer.

He joins them.

Prostitutes hang round the edges, pulling up their blouses, letting their breasts hang out for the passing cyclists, in encouragement or in contempt. He recognises the isolation in a cyclist's world, recalling his childhood race to the Lord's Table, but beer consumption among the spectators is now colossal and he does not really know where he is. In a bad dream perhaps, that he is trying to stifle.

He finds a variety of beer called Kulminator; it is very strong, thick, like diluted syrup, and can knock a person out.

Is he sinking? Not yet.

And football?

The night the door to Berlin opened and his two-year-old daughter Jenny undertook her twenty-four-hour journey of discovery through Central Europe, the snow had arrived and it stayed for a long time. Snow football was something new, it characterised matches at the Olympic stadium.

What was the Komet team compared to this? Before his athletics career he had played football in the fourth division himself. He was in goal. He described himself as fantastic on the line, quick to react, spectacular, but as timid as a mouse two metres outside. He could never clear or catch a cross. He hesitated, continually let in unnecessary goals between the dazzling saves. He started to believe it was in his psyche, that it revealed an inner weakness, a flaw in his character; eventually he was not alone in this assessment, it spread to the team and the management and he switched to the loneliness of the high jumper facing the bar.

If only he could have been a different person!

Hertha B.S.C. was nothing like Komet Hjoggböle or Bureå I.F.

Football in West Berlin really was something utterly different.

It was cold that winter in West Berlin. The abnormally low temperatures gave Saturday afternoons in the Bundesliga a special and almost unreal mood. The heavy, harsh *breathing* he experienced the first time he came to the Olympic stadium would typify everything that year in Berlin. Like a branding iron it left a mark on his innocence. He had emerged from the bowels of the underground railway, up from the underworld towards the light, as part of a swarming black mass; he could see heads, breath and backs form a huge, purposeful, steaming creature that moved slowly and yet feverishly through turnstiles and gates and spread out into sections that were still obstinately covered in snow. It stank of currywurst, and cold; the gathering grey dusk and the dirty slush bestowed on the matches a frightening atmosphere. Hitler's old Olympic stadium opened out, cheerless and brutal in the piercing ice-cold wind.

The arena always seemed more overwhelming from the inside than from the outside, and the bitter, windswept passion of these winter matches contained a striking beauty. The first time he could scarcely make out the opposite stand; all he saw was the driving snow, the barely cleared rectangle of muddy green, the ice-blue beam of the floodlights penetrating the blanket of darkness; and the atmosphere that held not just the fundamental tone of acrimony and partisanship usual in the Bundesliga, but an overtone defined by the cold, the boredom, the rage, the damp and the pressure of the grey concrete sides. Scaling the murky walls of the giant cave the crowd looked like a threatening outspread grizzly beast; clinging fast and roaring in fury or mortification, its response impetuous and savage and heartless, from the presentation of the visiting team's players (*Na und? Na und? Na und?*) to the contemptuous chanting at every mistake they make, *Üben! Üben! Üben!*

This is where they brought their emotions.

Hertha B.S.C.'s home crowd, a not inconsiderable proportion of them from West Berlin's working class, seemed to be transformed under the force of the cold, the damp and the driving snow from the jovial, beer-swigging, humorous and sentimental spectators of summer evenings into something else: more callous and also more thrilling. They were lashed by the snow and they yelled. They yelled at the game and at the opposition and perhaps also at themselves. *Schweinehund! Schweinehund!* At half-time he saw them spill out of the fortress to seek out the 1936 statues that surrounded the Olympic stadium, whose purpose was to create the classical art of a great civilisation for Hitler's Olympiad. He saw them pouring out in search of *art as urinal*, saw hundreds and hundreds of sports lovers stand and relieve themselves in the fellowship of statues.

How, he wondered, could the roaring, pissing sports lovers in Hitler's Olympic stadium be in harmony with the *guiltless geography* of his own playing fields, that made him go back on light summer nights to the old meadows on the Västerbotten coast and that once had freed him from the imprisonment of faith and the merciful tentacles of our Saviour Jesus Christ?

For the first time in his life he is in exile, meaning, upon closer analysis, *beyond Sweden's borders*.

This is his first year of exile. In time he will spend twenty years in exile: in Berlin, Los Angeles, Paris and Copenhagen.

At the same time he realises that in this instance the concept of *exile* is nonsense. He has his family with him, he is free, he has chosen this exile, and he can return home whenever he wants. He is in an economically privileged position, he draws a monthly stipend from the Berliner Künstlerprogramm and he lives in a large, rent-free apartment seventy metres from Ku'damm; it is owned by a count domiciled in Frankfurt, who has, judging by the pink decoration, an interesting sexual profile. His desk is a four-metre-long marble slab. The apartment is available to scholars; the previous occupant was Peter Handke. They meet briefly at the handover; Handke looks at him, nonplussed, saying, "I've read *The Legionnaires*, was it you who wrote it?" He says it was. Handke says, "I thought you were older!" What more is there to be said? Handke, an Austrian, is also in exile, an exile that fits as comfortably as his own. *I thought you were older!* Is there a hint of criticism in this?

They do not say much more than that to each other.

Thus he is transferred into the System.

Its official name is the Berliner Künstlerprogramm, set up in 1963 at a time when Berlin was thought to be a dying city, inhabited by pensioners and dogs. He is taken aback by the catalogue of illustrious scholars: Auden, Bachmann, Butor, Gombrowicz, Handke, Jandl, Sanguineti, Tabori. It is a breathing space too for Eastern European writers, who by some miracle have been given permission, or fled.

For them it is true exile.

The System is fantastic and takes care of him; he feels he is in exile, and yet at the same time he is not. However, in some of his new friends he can observe the conditions of exile. He becomes friendly with Zbigniew Herbert, the Polish poet who strangely never won the Nobel Prize; exile wears him and his family down, and he drinks too much. He notes that alcoholism goes hand in hand with exile, like a free gift, almost impossible to decline. Exile is *a wasteland*, if no alternative exists. Exile is short moments of heroism and drama and admiration and in between long cold mornings of abstinence and silence, staring at the ceiling and waiting for nothing.

He likes Zbigniew very much; in his quiet despair the Cold War and the Wall can be seen so much more clearly than at Checkpoint Charlie.

He is aware that all the visitors, who are giving a year of their life to the dying city, are children of the Cold War. Were it not for West Berlin's isolation, these enormous sums would not be available to break that isolation, or, in concrete terms: the splendid apartment at 6 Meinekestrasse, the monthly stipend, the constant invitations to *Veranstaltungen*, an advantaged life in a city that is not allowed to die a cultural death, all this is possible thanks to the Wall.

What is his own aim?

To work. He reads Witold Gombrowicz's diary of his time in Berlin, published in 1965, reflecting that it is the same scholarship, the same dying city, another apartment, but something has happened. Five years earlier, in 1965, Berlin was a quiet enclave, remote from the rest of the world. Gombrowicz feels provincial too, as he did when he passed through this gateway to Europe, but it is more of a Polish–Argentinean rusticity, as he tries in vain to understand German and attempts to forge contacts with German intellectuals such as Grass and Uwe Johnson.

They speak shyly to one another. About what? About pipes.

No, there is nothing dying in this city now.

But there is death, and there is conflict.

In a way that is puzzling even to him, he finds himself *in the midst of '68*, the year of revolt, student protest and the new left. He does not really understand how it happened; he has been immersed in his work or in the Soviet Union or in conflict or *somewhere else*. As a bystander he watches the occupation of the Students' Union in Stockholm for about half an hour, before the Uppsala train leaves. The riot starts somewhere on a street called Holländergatan; he is standing fifty metres from the speaker, who he sees to his surprise is Olof Palme.

Physically that is as close as he comes to the youth revolt in Sweden.

Here he is hurled straight into the youth riot of West Berlin, and its afterbirth, the Red Army Faction, or the Baader-Meinhof Group.

No, in 1970 this city is not dead.

He feels as though he is living at the political centre of the world. But by grotesque coincidence he has chosen to write about sport, which is not exactly high on the current agenda in West Berlin.

He carries around with him a burden of shame vis-à-vis sport. He is convinced that writing about sport is considered an anathema. Intellectually. And so it is essential to be critical, preferably contemptuous. Or alternatively, *discerningly furious*. Ivar Lo-Johansson had set a norm when he wrote *I Have Doubts about Sport* in the 1930s, a terrible tale about the awfulness of sport, in which the sports lunatic dies, justly, from an infected foot chafed through needless training. One of the most pretentious pieces of trash in the genre. He hated the book, with the intensity of someone listening to calumny against his lover.

But sport for him had meant an end to solitude, so why not write about it?

Why not in Berlin?

The week after their arrival he begins to trawl through West Berlin's antiquarian bookshops in search of the story.

In the roaring blaze of youth riots he undertakes an archaeological investigation of the history of sport, to help him understand what is happening around him. The antiquarian bookshops are a goldmine, particularly for literature about the German workers' sports movement of the 1920s. From time to time unexpected predecessors turn up. He finds that a sports lunatic called Bertolt Brecht made the film *Kuhle Wampe* about the movement, and he manages to see it.

Someone had been there before him.

Why not Berlin? Perhaps there he would be able to discover the point from which the story should be told, the tale that would be the most Swedish of his novels. Something akin to a revolution was exploding around him; contained within a wall, West Berlin was alive, not dying a slow death, inhabited only by old ladies with dogs, but the pulsing heart of a rebellion against hierarchies. And it too would eventually take the road to terror and the Red Army Faction. This conflagration was, like him, enclosed in a city behind walls. The Wall created strange effects on him too; *the energy* in this city was indeed confined, but it seemed to bounce off the surrounding wall, back in again, making West Berlin an echo chamber that in the end thundered with a strength that multiplied. In contrast to the West Germans he was privileged; he had a Swedish passport and could move freely onthe other side of this Wall. Outside, the Wall was surrounded by a mysterious kingdom, with different names according to one's ideological position. Maybe the Evil Empire, or *Die Sogenannte Zone*. Perhaps the splendidly iridescent communist paradise of the G.D.R.

Inside the walls a riot, probably. He was not -sure at first.

If he was going to write about sport from the vantage point of West Berlin, however, it was impossible to ignore the surrounding state that built the Wall, the G.D.R.

So, the Evil Empire or the Antifascist Bulwark. Furthermore, it was the G.D.R., more than any other state structure in history, that used sport as a political instrument. The hated, secretive G.D.R. had decided that sport and politics belonged together, as the world would soon discover. It was the Central Committee's intention that a towering mountain of medals would force recognition, first of the G.D.R., and then of the superiority of communism. For that reason too there were doping laboratories, at first highly secret, later exposed. At the beginning of the 1970s very little was known about this. But it was what the book would be about: not just a father and his son, but sport and politics. And a cheat.

He made many friends within the German new left and for all of them the G.D.R. was something of a *containment problem*. Though hardly because of its instrumental exploitation of sport for political ends. As an example of fossilised real socialism, the G.D.R. was a confirmed object of hatred for the new left. Another was obviously world imperialism in its American or West German forms. A third was just as clearly social democracy.

Class traitors.

Much later there would be many ideological interpretations of *The Coach*, as the novel was called. One that recurred was: the hollowed-out hammer was a metaphor for the *class treachery of Social Democrats*.

He detests that type of metaphor; *metaphor is the equivalent of touch phobia*. He does not want to write a book about Social Democrat betrayal. Not even metaphorically. Besides, he is obsessed with the actual event, after twenty-five years still boyishly sad that his Västerbotten hero, the cheating hammer-thrower Eric Umedalen, had been brought down, not even slightly metaphorically.

But there is an undertone in the book of a defence plea! Of what is he accused by his new friends in Berlin?

To a certain extent he is an exotic phenomenon in this new environment.

An intellectual Social Democrat. The word "intellectual" was in itself a term of abuse: an intellectual was someone who talked but did not act. That would become the central point in the Red Army Faction ideology. But, what is worse, he is a Social Democrat and admits it *without coercion!* On the other hand, and this redeems him: he comes from the far north. To all intents and purposes, from the depths of the forest, and from the Swedish working class. Might he be a worker at heart? He does not correct this misunderstanding. There is a shortage of proletarian children among his leading comrades, and a *Swedish Social Democrat* of this sort might differ from what they have become used to thinking of as their *main enemy*.

A Social Democrat obviously beguiled by his deceitful leaders, but from northern Sweden. He is spoken to in friendly fashion, like a very intelligent young man from another planet called Sweden who has been led astray. A Swedish Social Democrat. Needs further analysis. Definitely interesting.

Perhaps a worker, albeit in disguise?

Viewed from the outside, it is an odd disguise for a young lumberjack, as he sits at his almost regal marble desk at 6 Meinekestrasse.

A worker or not a worker: the energy in this city is incredible and he writes with greater and greater intensity. He also writes with a tone of desperate or defensive irony, as if he is apologising for something embarrassing that he has done, or with passion *stands for*, constantly in an aggressive position of defence, yet still the popular village idiot from Hjoggböle. He finds himself bombarded by impressions, and criticism, and has to consider how to defend himself. Old childhood memories creep in. *The anti-tank barriers he built in the forest against German attack!* Yet he is among friends, they speak to him with the voice of affectionate reprimand, and in the fortress of West Berlin they are all surrounded by the G.D.R., the state for whom – just like for him! – sport is deadly serious.

Deep down he seems to love this deadly seriousness. Lowered like a litmus paper into the Berlin brew, he changes colour.

One day he might be in the notoriously well-bugged dissidents' apartment on Chausseestrasse with Biermann and his friend Robert

Havemann, and the following day breathlessly and with total identification watch Wolfgang Nordwig's attempt at the world record in the service of the G.D.R. regime. On one occasion he is eating lunch in East Berlin with his Swedish publisher, Thomas von Vegesack, and the chairman of the East German Writers' Union, Hermann Kant, *later on to lose his reputation* and be described as a Stasi agent; he has read Kant's novel *Die Aula* and liked it.

Kant relates a story.

He had done a book tour with readings, including one for a group of border guards at the Wall, whose job it was to shoot down anyone trying to cross it. The young soldiers listened with rapt attention. After the reading Kant was thanked and the chief of the border police presented him with a memento of his visit, a miniature model of a watchtower with tiny soldier-dolls equipped with submachine guns. He thanked them politely for the gift.

The three men shake their heads, give a little sigh, a sorrowful laugh. Hermann Kant has given a very simple and fine account. The ironic caption could have been *"The Author is acclaimed"*. Instantly there is a moment of mutual understanding of the almost pleading subtext: *This system is irreversible, what can one do?* The silence of the three men at the lunch table and their reluctance to comment, apart from a murmuring of *"dreadful!"*; the message implicit in the guards' thoughtless gift to the esteemed writer, who will later be reviled; all of this is almost tacit criticism of the System and all of it constitutes a *typical* conversation in the spring of 1970 in East Berlin.

He has plunged into the core of European madness and hence it is fitting for him to write about sport.

He has to defend himself from all directions. It is the way the situation is. Then return to the marble desk on Meinekestrasse.

All of a sudden he is writing – for the first time in his life as an author and almost against his will – about himself. The cycle ride to the Lord's Table, the Celestial Harp, Greifswald. About a mother, and an absent father. It is well disguised, but for the first time it is there.

Perhaps it is the distance and the Berlin setting that makes it possible.

The West Berlin intellectual left he meets is extremely articulate. He supposes that for Swedes the year 1968 is associated largely with Paris. But a year later the revolution has taken a firmer hold and it has done so here in Berlin: where people express themselves more clearly, act more desperately, draw extreme conclusions more quickly, and expose divisions more dramatically.

His task now is to write about a cheating hammer-thrower from Upper Norrland. It is as if the story is slowly seeping into Sweden, thanks to this vantage point inside the Wall.

He gets to know the smell of tear gas.

The demonstrations always gather a long way down by Olivaer Platz and rumble up along Ku'damm. He learns the chants quickly: *Ein Finger kann man brechen, fünf Finger sind ein' Faust, Mao-Tze-Tung!* Or sports slogans, taken and adapted from Hertha B.S.C.'s home matches: *HA-HO-HE-Springer in die Spree!!!* For a while at the start it was friendly and pure-hearted, he filed between the rows of heavily armed policemen and *it was in a good cause*. Later the situation worsened, tear gas and violence and counter-violence, and in the end he could go out early on a sunny morning in the remarkable heavy Berlin air that he would never forget, and see the evidence of the Red Army Faction's actions during the night: bank windows smashed, the pavements a sea of glass. Indeed not just bank windows; the enemy's extent seemed to have increased and included not only car dealers but sweet shops, furniture stores and hairdressers.

There was glass all along Ku'damm. The time of restraint and idealism was over. It happened quickly. From the murder of Benno Ohnesorg, via the Vietnam demonstrations, to the break-out of Andreas Baader and the shooting of the librarian with the symbolic name Linke. In retrospect the Berlin left would be mythologised, whilst at the same time the Red Army Faction would rightly be demonised; leaving several hundred people, if not thousands – *sympathisers* – in a quandary.

Ulrike Meinhof contributed to the undercurrent of what was almost Greek tragedy.

The basic tenet of youth rebellion was disobedience. Was he really the right person to appreciate this?

He had been brought up to be good!

Certain tragedies create saints. To go so awfully wrong for such good reasons! Ulrike Meinhof became for him a personification of the problem of West Berlin's enclosed trauma. Maybe not just West Berlin's. To see an intellectual such as Ulrike M., who was constantly berated by self-righteous comrades about *intellectuals as prattling, cowardly swine* – such was the language – who do not dare to face the consequences through action: it was an almost bewitching tragedy. From a distance it was easy to be wise after the event, and yet it still cut to the heart. Don't talk! Do something!

It was a blow to the solar plexus of the extreme intellectual Berlin milieu. *Die Tat*! And that was why the eloquent and idealistic Ulrike M. moved from theory to action.

The same winter that he was busy at his almost regal marble desk on Meinekestrasse, she wrote an outstanding TV play, *Bambule*, about young women in a reform school. *She who gives in will be crushed*. And then she goes from working as a journalist on the magazine *Konkret* to robbing banks, terror and a life of lawlessness.

He always read Ulrike Meinhof's columns in the left-wing mouthpiece *Konkret*, and had listened to her in a couple of debates. He normally liked to sit at the back, but not when she was speaking.

When he hears her she is still within the law.

Brilliant and *plump*. Superficially, and in terms of brilliance, not unlike some of his Swedish friends on the left, such as Agneta Pleijel or Maria Bergom-Larsson; the latter would eventually *decide*, mercilessly, in three full-page articles in *Dagens Nyheter*, that he was certainly in some obscure way brilliant, for example in the novel he had written in West Berlin, but really just *scheissliberal*.

He measures Ulrike Meinhof as if she were one of them.

Brilliant, quite sweet. She has not yet taken the step from bourgeois intellectualising, i.e. writing, to action. Maybe she is ashamed of *making things up*.

How can he not understand her?

In all probability tormented by the *shame* of the very gifted *about not acting*. Her dilemma is illustrated by the story of the foreign minister in the Weimar Republic who arranges for a telegraph office to be set up in the imperial toilet and sends *counsel* to the world's leaders without noticing that connections were lost long ago. The cables cut. His counsel does not reach beyond the walls of the toilet.

It is the role of the intellectual, they doubtless say to her.

She has a plump charm he remembers from somewhere. Isn't it someone from the village? As if he *transforms* her, in a salvation experience, sitting in front of her on his West Berlin chapel pew, into the girl from the village. Vilified now, but she could be saved from sin! Yes, wasn't there someone from Hjoggböle she resembled? Or might it be Eeva-Lisa, about whom he must not speak?

Definitely. Fascinated, he watches her from a distance of a few metres. Ulrike was from the village! Somehow. If only he could get in touch with her! And could say the right thing! So that misfortune does not strike her!

Later, when she turns to murder and bank robbery and crime, he often reflects on what might have happened if he had been able to save her. He could have gone up to her – after the meeting! When the chapel coffee had been drunk and the congregation had gone home. If only there had not been *so many people* round her!

She might have listened.

A Swedish writer from Sjön, Hjoggböle, with several renowned novels behind him, and translated into a number of languages, might have been able to open her eyes, so that she could *survive*. He would have been able to tell her about *the Swedish model*. Not the Saltsjöbaden Agreement directly – it was too mediocre – but something about popular movements and so on. Free collective action. The work-first principle. A little about the Workers' Educational Association. She really seemed to be so clever. From her mouth, it is true, came harsh allegations against the oppressor state, and certainly, to begin with, she too would have called him *scheissliberal*.

But all the same, wasn't she the girl from the village?

There was something deeply disturbing about *the girls in the uprising* and their pietist background, which made him, the disaffected revivalist preacher in exile, worry.

Everywhere these dropouts from chapel meetings! In the spring of 1971 he followed the trial of the famous leftist lawyer Horst Mahler for several weeks. Among the intensely committed spectators, only controlled by the police with some difficulty, he was almost the only man. The tough core of onlookers was female. There was something – wasn't it pietism? – that reminded him of something else, and it both scared and enticed him.

There was always someone with a connection to the Red Army Faction in this city. Sometimes these contacts were made through school. His nine-year-old son Mats played every day with a girl called Jette, whose father was the well-known cabaret artist Wolfgang Neuss, to be found at that time in a drug haze in Mexico, but whose mother Margareta was born in Kalix, Norrbotten, and therefore reliable; and Wolfgang was a friend of Horst Mahler's. He had not met Mahler personally, only heard him constantly spoken of in these Kafkaesque relationships.

And so to the trial. Mahler had moved from theorising to doing. Not like Feltrinelli in Italy, whose own explosives detonated in his stomach, but almost. An action was suddenly brought against Mahler for involvement in a robbery. It was inconceivable, Horst Mahler was a very well regarded lawyer and it was all surely provocation, right up to the moment he was sentenced to six years on grounds of *irrefutable evidence*. Later, a free man, he began the long, but very speedy, march through the ideologies to finish up, quite naturally, on the extreme right. Didn't he become a banker? Or, as people said: still slightly to the left of Genghis Khan.

The weeks spent in the courtroom in Berlin's Moabit district were exciting. He particularly admired the razor-sharp young Red Army lawyer for Mahler's defence, who ruthlessly dissected the role of social oppression in this *act of provocation against innocent Mahler*. The lawyer was called Otto Schily. He would meet him again much later, in 2006, at the inauguration (he is by now a member himself) of the Akademie der Künste on Pariser Platz; Schily has become a little rounder, grey-haired, but is still razor-sharp and ruthless in his fight *against* terrorism and is now in a manner of speaking the highest chief of police, as Interior Minister in the German government.

There was so much talent in West Berlin's left. Some of them burned themselves out, destroyed their lives and the lives of others. Others rose and finally took their *rightful places*, at the very top.

There was not much room for art while the prairie was burning.

With Peter Weiss and Gunilla Palmstierna he attends the premiere in Düsseldorf of *Trotsky in Exile*. Peter, who was once regarded as the G.D.R.'s most valued sympathiser and was called a useful idiot, found himself under constant attack after the huge world success of *Marat/Sade*, and is now hated by the militant left; there are violent disputes over orthodoxy.

Peter Weiss is not orthodox.

The question is whether, in their opinion, he should write for the theatre at all, and if he does, he certainly should not have an exclusive premiere in Düsseldorf's new theatre, *among the mink stoles*. At the final dress rehearsal the performance is disturbed by action groups shouting and laughing derisively and at the interval they invade the stage and destroy the public address system, making it impossible to continue.

On the day of the premiere a meeting is hastily arranged between the action groups and Peter Weiss in a cramped room at the university.

Enquist takes the minutes. The mood is hostile. Peter Weiss describes the protestors' action as non-political and believes it will lead to a reactionary backlash, and Gunilla Palmstierna – a friend who has been with him on the Arts Council for several years and who has drawn up the guidelines for the new cultural policy, spoken about Free Collective Creativity and support for Free Groups and how cultural policy will counteract Commercialism's Damaging Effects (this is how the two of them write, this is how they think) – has designed the set and talks about the theatre workers' reaction to the previous day's disruption.

At this theatre, perhaps Germany's most authoritarian, where the stagehands and actors have no rights and are underpaid, have long working hours and are completely without influence, there is a strong feeling of discontent that has gradually taken the form of increasing political awareness. In contrast, the demonstration has made the theatre workers furious, made them stand with cudgels at the ready behind the stage. In a split second it has brought an end to left-wing trends of recent years in the theatre. They saw the demonstration as an affront.

They sit for three hours, almost no air left in the room. One of the women activists – the majority are women and they do not appear to him to be pietists – snatches his notebook to read what he has written. It is in Swedish. He asks for it back. In an icy voice she asks why. He says it is his. She looks at him scornfully, says coldly *"Schwein!"* and throws it back at him. He finds himself identified with artists who are bought by the bourgeoisie; they stare at each other for several minutes. He refrains from his warm, boyish smile.

No, unlike Ulrike Meinhof she is not the girl from the village, and he cannot dream about her.

That evening the premiere takes place in astounding calm. A fantastic array of mink soles and long sequined dresses is on display. Thus far the action groups' premise is sound. The actors receive rapturous applause, but Peter Weiss is met with loud booing when he goes up on to the stage.

The latter is almost a relief.

*

There was not much room for art.

Socialist plays on glittering stages were an anomaly. Poetry after Auschwitz was an impossibility. Authors sitting bent over typewriters were like the comical foreign minister during the Weimar Republic, enthroned on the toilet with the wires cut; their counsel is never delivered.

Action was all that remained. And with it the risk of burning in the prairie's flames.

He tentatively investigates what the alternatives are. He makes contact with a theatre group in Kreuzberg; they are warm and funny and no-one calls him a *Schwein*. One of them is also playing the role of Mother Aase in Peter Stein's production at the Schaubühne am Halleschen Ufer; he follows the rehearsals. It is an exceptional production; he learns more about the theatre than in many years of reviewing. He reflects on what it is to write drama. What was the remarkable secret? Could he do it himself?

That is how it is in Berlin. He is learning.

He started to write *The Coach* the day after the Soviet invasion of Prague in 1968, a week before his novel about the extradition of the Baltic soldiers was published.

It was August 1968, the year that shook world. He started to write the book in a garden in Uppsala. After that he wrote most of this novel about sport and politics in West Berlin, where he first lived from December 1969 to July 1970 and for a second six months in the spring of 1971.

In this way the geographical and temporal genesis of the book could be pinpointed precisely; that is to say, the point from which the story of the cheating hammer thrower and his era was viewed.

West Berlin became that point.

A very Swedish story that actually began in the 1940s in the Väster-botten sports world, but was now observed from West Berlin and the youth revolution. Another vantage point was that of the hammer throw-er's boy, Christian, the one who tells the story; he was both harder and easier to identify.

What did he think about Berlin? How did he relate to the spark that would ignite a conflagration? Did he ever understand the enormous power *disobedience* had among these young people in this hierarchical world of West Berlin?

Or had goodness taken such a hold of him, like a cancer, that he would never understand the grime of life?

Reluctantly he begins to identify with the thought itself. *Provocations will call forth the harsh and rightful face of the oppressor state.* But he notes that the people, for example the German working class, did not keep up. They have stayed in the sleet at the Olympic stadium. Whilst he is still with the Swedish Evangelical Mission, Rosenius, the starry heavens and the celestial harp.

He believes himself to be at the centre.

At the centre one seldom sees clearly. But it can still be useful to find oneself there. Even if Berlin was not the centre of the story, it felt as though it was: he may be the wrong man, but he was in the right place. The province implanted into the centre; the feeling of uncertainty and anxiety about his presence in an enclosed city he did not understand, and where he would write a book about a cheating Västerbotten hammer thrower from the 1940s.

When he has finished he almost lacks the courage to read through the book.

In the novel he discovers a wounded, wronged aggression, a novel written by a young provincial author dropped into the middle of the European revolution. In the novel he has been given the name Christian Lindner. He finds him ideologically ambiguous, ruthlessly honest, often intellectually ingratiating, sometimes cynical and sometimes resolutely naive, *one must tell it as it is*, a young person with many countenances, who has not yet made up his mind.

Yet he likes him, *as he was*, a litmus paper dipped into the European insanity, and knows that he would have been unthinkable without Berlin.

In a part of the land so far away from the centre as Västerbotten, sport meant a great deal.

The importance of local sports heroes increased when real life appeared to be played out down there in Sweden. And the unfairness of the centre towards the provinces – in other words *us* – produced rage and lifelong hatred.

Hatred? He exaggerates, but not much.

Niggling small injustices. The fact, for example, that the top of the football league system was not open to Norrland – the Norrland clubs could only reach division two, never the All-Swedish – created a nagging sense of being wronged. An organisational inequity, most obvious in the area of greatest importance, sport. The so-called *Norrland window* did not open until the 1950s, allowing for at least one Norrland team to play in the top division. It was an outrage, hard to forgive.

Even greater credit is due to those who succeeded despite the malevolence of the centre. The skiers! The Nordahls! But not only them.

Regional team level in athletics or football was the highest one could aspire to, but some people managed to go further. *The Cheating Hammer-Thrower* – an honourable working chap competing *for us* – was an idol. He made the regional team, competed in the European championship, set a *national* record. He proved it was possible to succeed, in spite of the chicanery and devilry of Stockholmers.

And then the idol fell. It was painful; he would always remember the day the *Norra Västerbotten*, the liberal local paper, printed an article that said *it could not be explained away*.

It was the same with the deepest root fibres of this novel: they inter-twined with the shallowest. In the end it was impossible to disentangle them. After the huge excitement surrounding the publication of *The Coach*, someone wrote in, curious; it was Artur Lundkvist, who had no doubt seen something more in it than just sport. How was it, he wondered, that this sensitive portrayal of a cheating father and his son was written by an author who was reported to have lost his own father at the age of six months? How could this young writer know how a father ought to be?

Well, maybe that was why it happened the way it did.

It said in the book's foreword that "for the informed it is easy to see, in one of the book's central episodes, a parallel with a famous case in the history of Swedish sport", but that the person involved "in no way served as a model for Mattias Jonsson-Engnestam-Lindner". And that "the only model for him and his life is society, and progress".

And you can always say that.

However, he had met the hammer-thrower himself, "the model". Not because he wanted or was able to confine the character in the novel to this man, but because he wanted to meet him. He was living outside Östersund. He was looking after horses, he was good at talking to them; they were like dogs, rubbed their noses against his cheek and told him not to be sad. It was hard for him to remember. He died a year or two later. He was exactly the same fine, unassuming sports companion and hero he had imagined, as a child, twenty-five years earlier.

He had been right. It was basically Stockholmers' fault.

The book came out in 1971.

The Coach is about cheating. Real cheating, by a real person. Not institutionalised cheating in the service of the state. Not doping.

In this novel about cheating there is *not a single word* about doping.

He assumed that facts existed somewhere. But that was some years later. In 1972 he was to write a book of reportage on the Munich Olympics, the Olympic Games in which the G.D.R. all but crushed the competition, and this comparatively small nation (not yet recognised as a state, but well on the way, partly thanks to its sporting prowess) could match the greatest. But not a word about doping then either. He knew that in the G.D.R. muscle fibre tests were carried out on seven-year-olds to identify who should be trained for shot-putting (short fibres) or jumping (long ones); but that was all.

In the autumn of 1972 there is sudden frenzied publicity about a special new field, blood-doping. He is taking part in a televised debate when a doctor and professor at the Swedish School of Sport and Health Sciences reports that legal medical experiments have been done with students, involving altitude training, storing blood and injecting, and that this has improved results by between 5 and 8 per cent. He calculates rapidly in his head, working out that the result over the 3,000 metre hurdles can be improved by thirty seconds, which is the difference between a regional champion in Västerbotten and an Olympic medallist. The doctor confirms this.

It is earth-shattering. *So what is measurable then?*

He recalls that in this debate he regarded it as a victory for medical research.

During the year in Berlin he is still ignorant about doping, as are most people.

Later everyone would know all about systematic doping in the Eastern Bloc. *There was even doping at the time of* The Coach, he thinks nostalgically. It is state doping, for political ends. State doping would later be replaced by market doping, for those sportsmen who could afford to pay private companies, that is to say, secret laboratories. And thereby harvest the commercial fruits of the sports market.

In this book, however, he writes more, and with emotion, about the lost opportunities of the workers' sports movement. He dreams standard dreams. He does not know that he is at a turning point. A novel about cheating, without knowing how sports history is changing at that particular time. *The main thing is to set a record*, as the hammer-thrower says, or *Great competitions demand great results*. But the records produced by the doping scam were later seen to be almost impossible to break; *progress* tied itself in a knot. It was nearly impossible to set records after that.

Maybe Mattias Jonsson-Engnestam-Lindner foresaw a problem, but just not this one.

He leaves West Berlin.

On the last day he takes his leave of the cleaning lady they had, Frau Meckel, "inherited" from Peter Handke.

They have been very fond of each other.

Frau Meckel lived in Kreuzberg, was a refuge from the German-Polish territory, and a sincere believer. He knows what the expression "sincere believer" means. She is worried about him, fearful that he will be corrupted by *politics*. They often discuss religious questions. With sadness she has looked at the posters he has put up in his study, the gigantic room with the four-metre-long desk. She tells him that she prays for him every night, that he will not let political sin contaminate his soul.

On the last day she gives him a handwritten diary with memories from her life; she grew up in Breslau. It is a brown notebook of about eighty pages. He thanks her and says he is looking forward to reading it, which he later does. Then she asks him if he would object to them praying together, on their knees. He drops to his knees beside her. She prays for him, that *politics* – she repeats this word, *politics* – shall not infect him and destroy his life. She has tears in her eyes, as he does too, though he hides them, almost shameful.

And afterwards they say farewell to each other. It is the end of his year in West Berlin.

CHAPTER 9

A THEATRE IN MUNICH

Storm?

He really should not complain about the storm, other people say; first *The Legionnaires*, now this one surrounding *The Coach*. A simultaneous headwind and tailwind ought to help you stand up straight.

The reaction in the sports pages to *The Coach* swings between rapture and rage. He has stepped over the boundary into someone else's preserve: theirs. He is an intruder from the world of culture. Or a renegade, like the traitor who ran over to the enemy in the school playground with snowballs. But at the same time *The Coach* is a sensation on the culture pages, because the novel gives shape to a love that intellectuals have had, shamefully and deep down, and never dared to admit. A love of sport. And does that make it acceptable?

"*An elaborate, multi-layered book, which can be read at any level. How anyone could eschew so much insight into our own life and time, I do not understand*", writes Karl Venneberg in the *Aftonbladet*. *Dagens Nyheter* sends send a reporter – he has moved before review day – and devotes five columns on page one to him. A large photo of him and his wife sitting in the stand at National Stadium in Copenhagen. *Second at the National Stadium*. Editor-in-chief Olof Lagerkrantz writes in his full-page review that "every step he takes offers sensationally fresh observations of society and the individual. It is written by a man who now in his thirty-seventh year has achieved mastery of his craft."

That is just it. If he is thirty-seven years old and at the pinnacle of his career, what is the future? Is it empty?

*

Is it now that it starts?

He daydreams about novels he has written and what he might, almost certainly will write; but *just at the moment* it is a void. *Before* is fine, and *soon* everything will definitely be fine too. But *just at the moment* everything is at a standstill. The fantastic wave of success weighs on his shoulders like a sack of potatoes, and something does not feel right, something is wrong.

His diary, 13 January 1972:

Acedia? Don't even know what it means. Bloody miserable, at any rate. Talked (too long!) with Bo S. on the phone about sports politics. What's frightening – but this doesn't apply to Bo – is how every debate about sport has to start from zero. Every argument has to be so elementary, before you can get to anything exciting and constructive.

I don't know if I've got the energy. For anything. I'm so horribly over-sensitive, take everything to heart, dig myself in deeper, want to be liked but couldn't give a damn at the same time, and take every criticism as a sign that everyone hates me, paranoid. Two storms, one after the other, The Legionnaires *and* The Coach, *was a bit much.*

Occupational diseases of the writing profession. Lethargy, paranoia and alcohol. Drank, per head, one bottle of red wine yesterday. The question is: if you allow yourself one bottle of red wine a day, can you keep to this, or are you just laying the foundations for more profound alcoholism that will explode sooner or later?

I don't know if I can be bothered with anything at all. Where has it gone, the bloody engine that drove me on through the '60s, through The Legionnaires *and* The Coach? *(Wasn't it running low even then?) Concentrated fury, desire for revenge, power – there was something there in any event. And now there is just this grinding, empty, meaningless neurosis.*

I really need to do something about it.

Watched television last night. Again. Read a bit of manuscript

for Norstedts. Must remember to pay the insurance before Friday.
(Can I really manage 15,000 a year in future?) Slept badly and woke
early. M. in a deep depression, doesn't want to wake up, just wants
to sleep, sleep, doesn't really want to live. I wonder if it is just the job
– the feeling of absolute emptiness, a grey wall, alienation. She thinks
she means nothing to anyone. And I can't do anything, though I
ought to help her.

Came into my study late, ten o'clock. I'll write the report for
Norstedts. Need to keep the discipline of work. Only have myself to
blame. I have a bloody lot to say, I tell myself. There's only one person
at fault, and that's me. Tomorrow the Broadcasting Commission in
Stockholm.

The days pass.

Diary entries much the same. Meetings at the Broadcasting Commission, the body who will judge whether radio and television programmes comply with the agreement on objectivity and impartiality:
during this period in the '70s the Broadcasting Commission is a central
arena for conflict, and he is now a member, which means arduous ideological battles. Every ruling is examined in the media, especially the children's programmes, whose whispering left-wing subtext throws many
into a rage. He does what is expected of him to safeguard diversity. It
is deemed insufficient. He loses some friends.

Entries about conflicts at home, red wine, the boy suffering. 15 January:

It's heartbreaking to see his attempts to hold us together. He rose
early, set the table for breakfast, tried to mediate, was kind. We
don't deserve the lad.

He is bereft of ideas. What does he want success for? He starts to
write a novel about Swedish emigration to Argentina. It is predictable
and lousy. He decides to travel to Misiones in northern Argentina. He
cannot write. What can he do in fact?

In the spring a new decision: he will definitely not make a six-month research trip to Argentina, not yet. On the contrary: he will go to Munich and write a reportage book about the 1972 Munich Olympics.

He is not without guilt.

He knows he is setting out for a territory that is well-known but nevertheless hostile, entering the field as an offside player from the culture section, to be tested *in real work* now, and on turf well trodden by others. He takes his time, arrives in Munich a few weeks in advance, prepares carefully. He will also write regular columns for *Expressen*, the paper on which he normally contributes to the culture pages; suddenly it feels exciting, with no responsibilities, like a boyhood dream. In 1959, thirteen years earlier, he had entered the high jump at the Universiade in Turin, a dress rehearsal for the 1960 Rome Olympics. He had hoped to qualify for Rome. If only he had made 2.03! But it was not to be.

On that occasion he could never have imagined what the Olympic Games were like.

Now he has a pass, can move around at will, has a free hand, has credentials with *The Coach*, and knows personally many of those in the Swedish team.

He has a free hand.

For the first day he wanders, unconcerned, around something that *really does not interest him*; this is the *innocence* he has envisaged as the working hypothesis for his book about the modern Olympic Games. Take, for example, the fifty-metre free pistol. At the entrance to the shooting range he meets Grace Kelly for between three and five seconds. She possesses a grey-toned, almost enthralling beauty, wears no make-up, pure, and he is still unsteady some time later when he is met by the surprising Swedish gold medallist Skanåker, whose political analyses ("Anyone who has learned to withstand the Swedish tax system under Sträng has no problem with Olympic nerves!") arouse general admiration.

And so it begins.

The boxing tournament is fantastic. Filled with blood, bravery and losers.

He seeks out the losers, especially in the weightlifting; that they *have only three attempts* reminds him of his almost paralysing fear after having missed twice at the high jump. Among these elite people the losers were the easiest ones to love, almost human. When the Soviet favourite for gold in the middleweight, David Rigert, started with an arrogantly heavy weight, he missed once, and then a second time, and then he became visibly scared. At the third attempt his face was white with fear, he missed and fell backwards; howling like a wounded animal, he staggered down into the warm-up room and dropped to the floor, full-length. The crippling fear! He recognisèd it.

Half an hour later he discovered Rigert in the park outside. Sitting in a grubby dressing gown, he had stopped crying; his trainer was sitting just a few metres from him. He had not put his arms around his shoulders, as *such is not the sporting custom* towards people who have trained for four years and thrown everything away in a few moments. The trainer will loyally sit a few metres away, and respectfully be there.

And say nothing.

He notes that Rigert has a cigarette, is sitting cross-legged on the grass, smoking, but without inhaling. He blows the smoke out like a beginner. It is clearly his first cigarette.

He writes in his notebook: "*smokes his first cigarette, a beginner*".

Some people once played a leading role on this Olympic stage. Now they are extras.

Once in a while his resolve to remain silent and only see is broken. He spends a long time talking to John Carlos, the Black Panther on the podium in the Mexico Olympics, who is now a salesman for the sports footwear company Puma; a panther metamorphosed into a puma.

A fine human being, but *demeaned*.

Later he notices that the free theatre group and rock band National-teatern steals his article and makes it into one of their best battle songs; he is flattered. It is not often he is appreciated by the Gothenburg left.

Everything seems easy and entertaining; colleagues in the paper's Munich editorial office quickly accept him. He is moving in a sphere unfamiliar to him, a long way from the author's isolation at his typewriter. A world stage. Huge dreams, 95 per cent destroyed by the dreamers themselves. A line can be a destiny, if you listen carefully.

He writes without concern for expectations.

The technician employed to key in everyone's articles is called Kråkan; an odd person, very solitary, he sits in silence at his special machine no-one else can operate. It is still long before the emergence of information technology. He is good-natured and different and dutifully keys in for the editors in Stockholm the countless pages produced in Munich. He only complains about one writer. He is critical of the articles written by Enquist, the author imported from outside.

"It's hard for my fingers," he mutters, "my hands won't fly." He will not be specific, but keeps saying *the way you write, my hands won't fly*. Nobody else complains but he feels guilty and puzzles over it: *why is it that only when faced with his articles, Kråkan's hands won't fly?* Towards the end of their time in Munich Kråkan suddenly suffers a nervous breakdown and is on sick leave. All very mysterious. The editors assure him it is not his fault, that Kråkan has very particular and unusual problems, that his articles are excellent, and it is not because of them and the fact that Kråkan's hands did not fly when they were keyed in that the breakdown occurred. Enquist's articles are perhaps rather out of the ordinary, but widely esteemed in Stockholm. They say that no-one understands *Kråkan's hands not flying*.

He thinks he is writing without premeditation and without *acedia*. Apathy gone. No more questions about *what to do*. The monstrous sack of stones has vanished.

It is as it should be, right up until the moment early one morning when the unthinkable comes to pass.

He remembers the moment.

It is early in the morning in the press centre and the incomparable Mark Spitz is about to show the world his seven gold medals, but he is delayed and the press officer, Klein, announces instead, in his extremely correct and distinctive way, that something has happened *dieser frühe Morgen* that has turned the world upside down; though he uses different words: a group of terrorists, assumed to be Arab, has broken into the Olympic village, shot one of the Israeli team and taken the others hostage. The group is later named as the Black September organisation and demands the release of Palestinian prisoners.

Half an hour later Mark Spitz is led in, ashen-faced and preoccupied. He only just manages to answer the questions directed to him.

Thus the thirty-hour chase is taken up.

He has always dreamt of being at the centre of things when a turning point in history is reached. But at the centre, if you do by some chance really find yourself there, it is difficult to see. At any rate to see into the future: that the Munich Olympics would mark the beginning of a new form of warfare, where armies no longer confront and destroy each other, that the fight would be between invincible yet impotent military forces and terrorists in unreachable hideouts – no-one could see that then.

But that is what happened.

The centre is an overrated place. Seventeen years later, in November 1989, he is in Prague the night the Wall falls and a hundred thousand people flock into Wenceslas Square, but he does not understand, he is so close to the centre that the crowd of people obscures history and he would rather be asleep. He does not understand it this time either, he can only feel sorrow. Everything was so enjoyable. He was writing so well. He was full of energy, no feeling of fatigue; he had dreamt of witnessing these Games for the whole of his life, of watching and writing. Now only sorrow.

He realises that the main theme in *The Coach*, the role of politics within sport, is now cruelly affirmed.

*

He, of all people, should have known.

A fantastic stage is built in Munich. The whole world admires this theatre, everyone is there. The stage is lit, television cameras are directed towards it, the world's press in the stands. A play is announced, a play about sport. For two weeks reality will be kept at bay.

They are wrong. The lighting of this theatre and stage is too bright, the attention too intense and temptation too great. Many others want to take the stage, as the whole world looks on, callous actors with their own objectives. And they do just that. They leap onto the stage, wearing black masks, and enact a play about the world outside, a performance we can call the Palestine Conflict.

In retrospect it was so easy to understand. *Politics* would swallow these Games in one gulp and they would be over. What was it Frau Meckel had said? Hadn't she prayed to the Saviour Jesus Christ that he might be spared the *poison of politics*?

He wonders what she is thinking now.

The press centre in the Munich Olympics, known as the Pit, becomes the focus of the world.

For the reporters the press centre was the very heart: the Pit was a huge, padded hollow in the middle, filled with leather armchairs and low tables and hundreds of television monitors replaying every second of the entire medley in all its arenas. You could hide in there, never set foot in any other part, but this *frühe Morgen* the Pit looks shabby, almost dirty. It was normally occupied not just by the reporters, but also by the incredibly attractive hostesses, dressed in blue, whose job it was to assist, guide, smile and answer questions; there were said to be 5,000 of them. He noticed at the opening of the Games, here in this press centre, they appeared to be not only beautiful and friendly, but also in essence clinically unreachable, coated with plastic, almost godlike.

Later they looked somehow down at heel.

The ones he speaks to on the first day are different two weeks later: worn out. By the end the Bluebells, as they are called, are all exhausted, craving contact; no longer *distant*, they are drained. Conscious at first of their good looks, as the days and weeks pass they tire of the Olympic Games and of drinking too much beer, they are weary of the Pit and the television monitors, almost imperceptibly they put on weight and grow flabby, they strike up conversations about anything other than sport, anything at all, and finally, desperately smoking and wearily seeking companionship, they hope the Games will soon be over so they can be released from the media prison to resume their normal roles.

Whatever those roles were. A lecturer in Enköping. Or a Swedish queen.

There is something about the *way the Bluebells wilt* that haunts him. Is he thinking of Oscar Wilde's novel *The Picture of Dorian Grey*, about a portrait that grows old, while the human subject of the painting remains forever young?

Does he discern his own portrait?

And then the 1972 Munich Olympics erupt.

The weeks before the eruption are wonderful. He is going to write a book of reportage about an Olympiad, but is aware of his weaknesses.

He is a *timid* observer. Tall and silent, he wanders around *watching*. It is his method of working.

A wandering pine tree.

A few hours after the news of the hostage-taking, he visits some of his friends in the Swedish team. It is still possible to have free access nearly everywhere. No barriers yet around the Olympic village and the hostages, if indeed it is possible to cordon off the village. It is like an anthill, with innumerable passages and subways, unattended. These Olympic Games were to be characterised by rejoicing, *Heiterkeit*, not by Teutonic discipline and military surveillance. The Munich Olympic Games were to wipe the German slate clean.

Twelve years under Hitler would be washed away.

He was aware of this and he approved of it, right up to the moment when he, like all other lovers of *Homo ludens*, was appalled by its brutal consequence, death. All the security measures had been tailored to this *ideology of enjoyment*; it was possible to move freely and unhindered, as the terrorists had also noted, and they had consequently gained easy access to the Israeli camp.

Where is the central point in history?

He is given a tip-off on how the Israeli camp can be entered via a basement passageway. He goes down, like an accredited Dante into the underworld, where corridors will lead him to the cellar under the Israeli team, which happens also to be the Canadian squad's parking area.

Does he intend to set them free? No, he just wants to have the accuracy of his working method, *innocently watching*, confirmed.

When he writes about sport he does not really know what his role is. Is it that of the Investigator, from his work on *The Legionnaires*, or is it that of the child, who hears the noise of the Komet team from his refuge behind the rosehip bushes?

Fourteen years later in 1986 he will find himself in Mexico for the football World Cup; he is still playing the role of a *very tall but silent wandering pine tree*, except that in the course of his awkward sauntering, he plainly sees some things that no-one else sees.

Everything at Mexico '86 is extremely well protected by thousands of soldiers. No *Heiterkeit* at all. He is expecting to go to the press box and watch the showdown between Uruguay and Germany. Well outside the stadium he sees, between the rows of heavily armed security forces, whose presence is intended to prevent any demonstrations, how a German television crew lugging cameras and leads is allowed in amidst the serried ranks. A long television cable is being dragged behind them: he sneaks forward, lifts it up, and in this manner follows Z.D.F. German Television into the bowels of the well guarded fortress, sheepishly carrying the end of a cable.

The television crew position themselves behind one of the goals, a metre behind the line. He sits down on the grass, watches the first half attentively and reflects on the work of the Uruguayan goalkeeper. Time after time the burly German players come thundering like buffalo towards him; recalling his own goalkeeping efforts in Bureå I.F., and how much of a coward he was when the opposition advanced, he feels deeply sympathetic. From this perspective, and not that of the *elevated press box*, which is also the television viewer's, the logic of the game is transformed. Spatial awareness is reduced, empty spaces blur and disappear. He is full of admiration for the players, who, despite their horizontal perspective still have an overview of the whole field, performing with the same range of vision as the high tribunes. But here, from his position a few feet away, all likeness to "a chess-game on a green pitch" fades away; later, to test his observation, he tries to play chess with the board on the same level as his eye, he loses quickly, and judges his observation to be confirmed.

At half-time he walks beside the pitch to stretch his legs. Inside this Mexican Berlin wall there is no security at all. Midway down the length of the pitch he suddenly takes it into his head to look for a toilet and he enters the tunnel where the players disappeared. He is bound to find one.

The corridors are almost completely deserted.

He turns left and walks about thirty metres; no security men. He sees an open door and goes through it, finding himself in the German changing room, where the players are sitting on the benches in complete silence. In the middle of the room stands Franz Beckenbauer, the coach, dressed in a smart suit and looking at ease; turning his head, he says nothing, but his expression is quizzical, or possibly politely critical of the intruder. Without losing his composure, he utters a brief *Entschuldigung!* and retraces his steps along the empty corridor. He finds his way to the press box, where he watches the second half.

What impressions does all of this give the Investigator? Almost none, other than recollection of his dangerous and less than successful experience in goal for Bureå I.F.

The world holds its breath as, through countless television cameras, it watches a balcony in the Olympic village, where a masked terrorist appears from time to time. Meanwhile he is walking through the underground corridors in the direction of the Canadian squad's parking garage, next to the Israeli one.

When he asks a policeman, "Can you show me the way to the Canadian team's toilets?" he is answered with a hesitant and anxious shake of the head. Clearly leaving a vague sense of guilt. Not to have acted in the friendly and helpful manner according to the principle of *Heiterkeit* decreed for these Olympic Games.

He realises the doves have not had time for second thoughts; the hawks have flown in with a mighty beating of wings and hold them captive in their claws.

The basement is poorly lit, the garages half empty. As he walks further in he sees that preparations are under way for a rescue bid: here and there a policeman running, shadows, armed civilians, officials sprinting. As so many of the policemen are in plain clothes, so as not to attract attention, he attracts no attention either.

He finally reaches the basement directly beneath the Israeli block. He does not need to ask. This is it. A rescue bid is imminent. A group of policemen and explosives experts are pointing upwards, speaking in low voices. On the ceiling there is a lump of something that looks like plastic padding, presumably the explosive, supported on props. He can instantly see what their plan is. They intend to blast their way into the Israeli camp through the floor.

They are discussing the thickness of the floor. Someone has a technical drawing.

He stands beside them and after a while he asks if they intend to coordinate the explosion with an attack from outside. He implies that *it is an important question*. They stare at him and ask him who he is.

In proper fashion he shows them his pass, hidden under his shirt. Immediately and courteously they throw him out.

What insights does this give him?

There are many. Amongst them, how the grand and rather moving German dream of *Heiterkeit* has been destroyed: their dream of enjoyment and openness cancelling out thirteen years of history.

This was a turning point in history, it was true, but not in the way they had dreamt.

Twelve hours later he stood on the open square in front of the Israeli block with his face, like everyone else's, turned towards the sky, watching the helicopter lift off.

That it held a cargo of corpses, no-one knew.

From that day on he has not been able to look at a helicopter of that sort without remembering Munich '72. The terrorists and the hostages, according to the demands, would be flown by helicopter to an airport, and from there they would fly to Cairo. Further negotiations would take place there.

Meanwhile, it is clear to all, there could be no further competition.

Sudden realisation: the rescue has to happen now, or the Munich Olympic Games will have to be stopped.

The logic of these Games calls for an immediate rescue operation. At any price.

That night they wrote. Lången Olsson, Janne Mosander, Stig Bodin, Lennart Ericsson and he all worked in silence, in a strange state of calm, very quietly and very efficiently. They delivered seventeen pages that night, and somewhere in Stockholm others were at work on the typesetting, the page layout and the printing. He had never worked for a newspaper in this way before, he had only written articles for the culture section.

He would always remember that night for its calm and for the fact that they liked one another.

They were a team. It was possible to be like that.

*

The Pit was never empty that night.

In the early hours – when usually only about twenty of the hardiest and most inebriated would sprawl over the sofas and fall asleep – the crowd grew. The helicopter had landed somewhere, not at Riem, perhaps Fürstenfeldbruck, yes, that was later, a military airfield. More and more cameras were set up, and instead of the normal groggy atmosphere, there was a noticeably more nervous and aggressive feeling in the air as the small hours passed.

A press conference was called for four o'clock in the morning, but half an hour earlier he had learned the truth from an Israeli journalist he had met as a young student in Jerusalem. Standing in the middle of this room, the journalist now told him with an unnatural and detached calm: "Yes, they've shot them all." Uncomprehending, he asked: "What do you mean, all?" And with the same uncanny, ice-cold calm, he answered: "They've killed all the Israelis, it's true, all of them." Unable to grasp what has been said he asked: "What do you mean, they? Who did the shooting?" With barely concealed irony he replied: "All the hostages are dead, all shot, no-one knows who shot them, Germans or Arabs presumably." He tried again: "Is it true?" And in the same controlled voice: "Hell yes, they're all dead, it's true."

At one end of the Pit the spotlights were turned on.

It was time finally to explain that the rescue bid had failed. That all the Israeli sportsmen had been killed, as well as five Arabs and one policeman. After the massacre a total of fifteen bodies lay scattered over the runway at Fürstenfeldbruck, the airport no-one had ever heard of before. All dead. *Hell yes, they're all dead, it's true.* That night five poorly equipped German marksmen from the rescue force, in the semi-dark and shooting from a long distance, had tried to free the Israelis from their captors and had failed. Hand grenades exploded, the helicopters burst into flames. Afterwards no-one could say who killed whom.

But the chase was over.

There had been no time for tiredness that night, but after the press conference – *Alle sind tot!* – the anticlimax was immense. People stayed in the Pit drinking. They slumped on sofas, chairs and floor in this huge,

225

stale-smelling, smoke-filled room, permeated in the bleak morning light by an overwhelming sense of bewilderment and emptiness. It was as if leftover wine, overturned ashtrays and broken glasses had been spewed all over the Pit and covered everything in an indescribable atmosphere of defeat and catastrophic decay. Many people slept, collapsed over tables and chairs, their mouths gaping, shirts ripped open at the neck, where their so dearly loved and cherished accreditation cards were hanging; they slept off their dejection and drunkenness.

He sat amongst them.

Writing was abandoned. The night was over and whatever happened next – and no-one knew – the 1972 Munich Olympics were also over. Next the memorial service would take place, *Trauerfeier*, which would bring to an end the twentieth Olympiad in modern times, and he would be a witness to that too.

Trauerfeier: so strange a word. To celebrate mourning.

What had he witnessed in fact? Perhaps a turning point in history, not only the victory of terrorism over enjoyment as a dream, but also an object lesson in the transition of modern warfare from a battle between armies to terror against civilians, from the theories of the great military strategist Clausewitz on the use of troops, to intifada, Nine-eleven, Iraq, and the raiding of suburban kitchens in a quest for the enemy. If it was to happen, and later he would be even more convinced of this, there was good reason for a *Trauerfeier* to mark this pivotal moment in history.

He also witnessed the closing of the Games.

It was muted, as if there had been an attempt to tone everything down in the Olympic stadium, an effort to muster an appropriate level of hopefulness, a subdued cry of joy or a loud whisper. The Games had continued for three more days. They could not give in. Carry on, but without *Heiterkeit*. Play on with sorrow. He suffered with the Games, strangely identified with this city. The intentions had been so good, and it turned out so badly.

When it had all begun so well, how could it turn out so badly?

It was hard to watch the composure of grief, especially during the *Trauerfeier*. He was there with all the others in the packed stadium, in solidarity. A line from what he later would always think of as T. S. Eliot's *Munich poem, The Waste Land*, went round and round in his head: "*My friend, what have we given? The awful daring of a moment's surrender.*" And now this surrender to the dream of man, the player, was just a wasteland.

Yet wasn't the daring worth a try?

The orchestra played "My Sweet Lord" as the competitors slowly left the centre of the arena and a few tried to run in an improvised circuit, as was the custom in Olympic closing ceremonies, before these Games were touched by sorrow. *My Sweet Lord*. He sat with the other 50,000 people, hunched up in their raincoats, swinging little lanterns on sticks that were meant to be a symbol of fellowship and rejoicing. He would always remember "My Sweet Lord" and the threatening black clouds rolling in from the west over Munich, and the sudden downpour of rain, like a merciless signal that it was all over.

He went home.

Home really did mean home: he spent ten days in his mother's kitchen in her retirement flat in Bureå. The window looked out on the church; he put his typewriter on the kitchen table and laid out in front of him all the articles, notes, sketches and diary entries he had made during his time in Munich. And he wrote a book called *The Cathedral in Munich*.

The kitchen was the right place. In the same way that West Berlin had been the right place for the story about Christian Engnestam-Lindner, his cheating father, sport, the G.D.R., and what it was like at the centre of European madness, so this kitchen in his mother's retirement flat was the right pace for the book about Munich.

When after ten days he has finished writing, his reads through his manuscript. Isn't this, he thinks, the best commentary on sport written in the Swedish language? He lifts his gaze from his mother's kitchen table, sees Bureå church and all that it signifies, remembers the humility so arduously learned and thinks about the things the *Norra Västerbotten*'s sports reporter Mr Kuri used to write about Hjoggböle's home games.

What would Merrkuri have said? "*In the role of a pine tree Enquist makes a sterling contribution*"?

Soon? No, not yet.

CHAPTER 10

AUTUMN ON BROADWAY

He went to the Dead Cats' Grotto on the 23 May 1990, his first visit after Iceland.

Bensberget was still there, the forest too, and the grotto, the setting for Eeva-Lisa's resurrection in *Captain Nemo's Library*. But it was different now. Travelling back to the airport, he noted briefly: "Everything has changed."

The grotto was smaller, seemed cramped somehow. The hill was lower. There was nothing to discover in the grotto, not even the once completely clean skeleton of a cat.

Everything shrinks. In the end there may be nothing left at all. You need to hurry before it all withers away. It needs to be pieced together.

In December 1972 he arrives, with wife and two children, at U.C.L.A. in Los Angeles as visiting professor.

Life is comfortable. He thinks he will be able to write, but he cannot. In the second week he visits the house where Brecht lived. There is a tree that overshadows the house now, as it did then. In this shadow are Brecht and Thomas Mann. Brecht must have written there; was it "Mahagony"?

In any event he himself cannot write.

He raises his arm; it does not fall on to the keys. He tries to force his unwilling hand down. But no. In California it is easy to give in to mysteriously faint signals from a world that is seductive, and not ascetic, not demanding. Running on the beach. The Californian light. "Killing

Me Softly" on the car radio. Just be carried along. *Marie, Marie, hold on tight.*

It is the most intensive phase of the Vietnam War, the Christmas bombings of Hanoi; for the last five years he has lived as part of the European debate. Some of his friends find it curious that he is spending a year in the land of American aggressors. Should he not boycott them? He does not know what to say in reply. Finally he decides that being here is the right thing.

Has he not also spent considerable time in the Soviet Union or the G.D.R., for example?

The first Vietnam demonstrations he witnessed were in Times Square in New York, in the spring of 1966. Fifty young people with placards walking round and round, being yelled at. Then the Civil Rights march in the southern states that changed his life. If his life has been so continually changed, shouldn't there be more evidence? To show what has become of him?

What happened, has happened. Should he be here at U.C.L.A.? *To retreat inside the belly of the whale*, who wrote that? Was it H. G. Wells? It was an idea at any rate, to escape inside an event. Or bury one's head?

Every morning he wakes at six and turns on the television for the Watergate hearings.

It is brilliant East Coast entertainment, top-notch political theatre. He is teaching "Contemporary Scandinavian Literature" and giving an "advanced course" on Strindberg, but he extends the subject, which feels narrow. The students are wonderful: amusing, gifted and appallingly ignorant of everything beyond the U.S.A.'s own borders. In one class he discovers that it is a shocking revelation for many that the Soviet Union was on the same side as the U.S. in the Second World War. Allies? Their smiles are friendly, but doubtful: can that really be true? *The communists*?

Concerned by this, he writes on the blackboard a summary of world history: *The Soviet Union saved us from Nazism; the U.S.A. saved us from communism.*

At least it is short.

At parties, to which he is always invited, his students smoke marijuana, and what can he say? Scandinavian literature is of little interest to them, but Ingmar Bergman is worshipped; like dervishes they bow their foreheads to the earth at the very name. He capitulates and orders from the Film Institute in Sweden a batch of Bergman films, arranges a Bergman Week with the nice boys in the university film club: young enthusiasts who in time are certain to become world-renowned figures such as Steven Spielberg or George Lucas. He scarcely remembers them, apart from their enthusiasm for Bergman's commercials from 1953, made to provide him with an income during a ban on filming in Sweden. They are on one of the rolls sent from the Film Institute and are a colossal success. The auditorium is absolutely packed that evening; they all describe them as masterly, brilliant in their own way, only are somewhat vague about what that way is.

In the Stomatol toothpaste film a very young Bibi Andersson is utterly captivating in the role of an afflicted tooth, or bacteria, he has forgotten which. Or is it the Breeze soap commercial? In any case, she is very good. She makes a sterling contribution. He still has and always will have an overgrown teenager's explosive susceptibility for beauty. His second wife looked like Kim Novak. That was his first impression, a young Kim Novak. He keeps this susceptibility to himself, plays his cards close to his chest, or is ashamed. Bibi is very young in the Breeze commercial.

Stomatol? No, it must have been Breeze.

He plays handball for the university team, scores lots of goals in the beginning, feels young again, but has a finger broken by a Swedish actor called Bo Svensson. A six-foot buffalo. So his handball career comes to an end too, and he feels a twinge of regret, once again. How much of his life has he wasted like this?

More and more to drink. Santa Monica Beach is wonderful. Everything is very peaceful, disconnected from the rest of the world and he feels transported back to the sports tour in Israel ten years previously:

beach life, sleep, a hippie existence with no responsibility, fears or demands. Play your way through the weeks.

If this is inherited, who is it from? The Fellow Traveller is almost completely absent, or at least silent. Perhaps he is ashamed? Or the opposite. At last no problem defending the extravagant motorcycle and sidecar.

It is just over two years since his time in Berlin, and only six months since he stood in the basement beneath the kidnapped Israeli sportsmen and saw the police putting explosive on the ceiling, but here in Los Angeles it is as though he is on another planet. It cannot be the same century. Here it is permissible to be irresponsible and ignorant. He is *homo ludens* once more, man, the player, and the mild Californian sun is bewitching. It is almost laudable just to drift along. After a while he decides *not even to attempt* to write. Better simply to let life coast along in a kind of sleepy drunkenness.

The university is famous for sport, its basketball team the best in the U.S.A. The academic pressure is not overwhelming, and yet he likes the atmosphere. One week a feminist seminar *rages*; he squeezes himself in, wide-eyed. Since childhood he has innocently grown used to viewing man as subject to organic oppression by strong women. It is the norm in Västerbotten. Now he listens in astonishment to Shulamith Firestone, Betty Friedan and Kate Millett in front of packed auditoria.

The latter presented a highly acclaimed comic sketch with her little finger *as a tiny earthworm*, representing the male battering ram. He stole it, shamelessly, for his first play, *The Night of the Tribades*.

Everything he had previously considered important, including keen intellectual debate on core subjects, which had existed in Berlin, was not to be found here in Los Angeles. But all the rest was.

And he discovers that the rest is of value too.

He devotes a double period to the analysis of Strindberg's one-act play *The Stronger*.

There is *something wrong* with it. Not difficult to see if you have the author's latest biography to hand, and he has. He has spent a year reading Strindberg's collected works in fifty-six volumes, and if you follow him chronologically it is easier to see when he is defending himself, and why. Strindberg has concealed something in this play, and given himself away. Seized with enthusiasm, he sets the students to work on a detective mystery: *was it the case that these two women, who were supposed to be fighting over an absent man, in fact loved each other?* He suddenly feels very fortunate, he has discovered a secret! It is like being back in history seminars, the puzzle of the Carolean letters. The monument is human, the art is to explode monumental concepts. No person is cast in one piece.

Woman is an unknown continent. Perhaps critical examination of source material will reveal her?

Maybe true works of art are hollow.

He finds it difficult to hold his private life together. He is not proud of this.

In March he travels through the Nevada desert and sees it bloom. It happens for one week every year, in Death Valley, and means that all is not without hope. He is on his own over the summer and although not used to it, he is happy to be alone. He starts writing short stories. One night on Santa Monica Beach with a woman friend from New Hampshire he sees grunions, a species of fish that wriggle up the beach to lay their eggs. This only happens once a year as well. The incredible determination to live! California is full of secret signs. Brecht's house and Thomas Mann's. They too must have known the narcotic power of this sunshine and stillness.

Perhaps they could have lived here for ever.

He comes home.

One afternoon he sits down and writes the first few pages of what he thinks is a radio play. Maybe, possibly. It concerns the same problem he discussed with his students at U.C.L.A.: the strange one-act play *The Stronger* and the question of the useless man. There are echoes in it of many things, mostly Los Angeles. Perhaps he learned something after all.

In two weeks he has finished something he calls *The Night of the Tribades*, which to his surprise is a play for the theatre, his first. In fact the play will transform his working life, will very soon be translated into over thirty languages and for a hectic decade will be the most performed Swedish play after Strindberg, with over three hundred productions.

He submits it to the Royal Dramatic Theatre and it is accepted. The shrewd director, Jan-Olof Strandberg, brings together a star cast with Ernst-Hugo Järegård, Anita Björk, Lena Nyman and Carl Billquist. It is the first time he has met Anita and from then on this miraculous actress will play nearly all his female roles. And suddenly he finds himself in a new world, the world of the theatre.

All at once theatres across Europe seem struck by the same thought, *to put on his play*, written in almost manic haste. He does not understand. It is exhilarating and he finds it hard to keep up. His mother's increasingly anxious voice on the telephone delivers warnings: he isn't getting *too big for his boots*? He skilfully reassures her. As luck would have it, he tells her, *his humility is the greatest in the land*, that phrase he has as good as borrowed from Strindberg and likes. He steels himself as well.

But clearly he is a born dramatist. There is no escaping it, he says. Where did it come from? Impossible to ascertain. The fox farmer, his mother, the scribbler, or from himself?

A mystery. The lines just slipped out.

Novels such as *The Legionnaires*, that was one thing. But *life's living, speaking characters* on a stage? The limitations are enormous, and very tempting: to have not five hundred pages to shape everything, but only people on a stage for two hours, and everything has to come out of their mouths.

He has de facto written theatre reviews since 1966 in the *Expressen*, appointed by Bo Strömstedt. Like a sort of principal critic he has struck out at most of the country's theatres. Yet, before that, his theatre experience consisted of seeing only four plays.

He sees his first play as a fourteen-year-old, sneaking into Bureå Folkets Hus despite his mother's embargo; the legendary Bullen Berglund, who had a sausage named after him, is in the lead role in an Agatha Christie. It finishes with a shot being fired. The breathless and gun-shy Bureå audience jumps, some people scream. He leaves Folkets Hus disturbed and astounded; it was reality in a way that the dialogues he wrote and presented at the Band of Hope or at the end of Sunday school could never imitate.

Especially the shot. He understands that theatre has to *move* people.

Later he sees three plays at Uppsala Stadsteater. After that he becomes a theatre critic.

Undaunted, he disguises his ignorance of a professional critic's code of practice with an astute and penetrating style, as if he were reviewing books. Inwardly smiling, he defends himself easily against his own bad conscience. He has, after all, produced a thesis on literature. That should suffice. The text is paramount. Actors, those figures hovering on stage, are fundamentally a side issue, charge hands; they are dismissed with a few encouraging words at the end. "*In the role of Hamlet, Karl Petterson made a sterling contribution.*"

Once again the dispassionate tone of the pseudonymous Mr Kuri in the *Norra Västerbotten*, on crucial matches in the Northern Counties Coastal League.

What does he know about theatre? And what does he know about actors?

He is forty-one years old and he is entering a new world. He is *bewitched*, a word he uses only too often. To write novels is to cloak oneself in isolation. In contrast, theatre is life, and people, and coming in from the cold. All at once he is writing only drama: *The Night of the Tribades, From the Lives of Rainworms, For Phaedra, The Hour of the Lynx*. It is all a game. The more his plays spread across the theatres of Europe, the more invitations he receives to spend a week or so attending rehearsals; it might be Munich or Amsterdam or Turin or Warsaw or the Théâtre de la Madeleine in Paris. Not Moscow, yet, he notes.

The Tribades has been translated into Russian, but has been banned by the Interior Minister, who gives a blank refusal to the theatres seeking permission to perform it. It is baffling; the play is hardly politically controversial. His agent endeavours to find out the reason from the relevant official, who declares that the play appears to be about two women who might be lesbian, and as such holds no interest for a Soviet audience, *as there are no lesbian women here.* The agent attempts persuasion: "But the play is being performed in the whole of the Eastern Bloc, at seven theatres in Poland alone." To which the man at the Ministry for the Interior excitedly replies: "Aha! Poland is completely different. You know the Poles; there are loads of lesbian women there!"

It is a learning process; he sees what he writes shaped by different European approaches to the theatre, applied to the same text. Gone is the isolation of the novelist. He is a travelling salesman, selling himself.

During the first week of rehearsals at the Royal Dramatic Theatre he sits at the back, silent and unobtrusive, trying to learn. In a break he sees that Lena Nyman has struck thick black lines on her script through all his stage directions, including the psychological. Disappointed, he asks her why. In surprise she replies: "Well, I need to be free of what you were thinking, of course."

Thus, with faltering steps, he enters the world of theatre.

He had always imagined that what he wrote *was his alone.*

But in the theatre nothing was his alone. Hence everything in the theatre was less solitary, but at the same time more painful.

Perhaps he was even writing drama as a child. That was his own, because it was never printed. Not even sketched out. He could call it escapism, and feel a tiny bit ashamed.

Could he be dreaming?

It did not matter that friends were thin on the ground in those days. There was just the forest and the maps and the snow and the starry firmament and Flash Gordon and the Fellow Traveller. He could act out scenes in peace, undisturbed. The pine trees could not interfere. He recklessly moved characters around in the gigantic forest setting.

The scenes were often moving and when he came home from school with tears in his eyes his mother sympathetically asked him if he had fallen over and hurt himself. The performance ended abruptly then, nothing left of what he had imagined and portrayed. The stage was empty. Bunkum! But very soon the scene for the next emotional episode: normal characters, whose soundlessly moving lips produced deep voices! Invisible, except to him catching his breath! Next time a happy ending and a radiant – and for his mother utterly incomprehensible – smile.

But he has complete control.

Now he is writing his scenes in the same way. As if he is out in the forest. But suddenly a point comes when everything changes. Written down, submitted, casting done! The text is peopled by actors. Now they are in it *together*.

He had actually dreamt of this. Now it is reality.

But the concentration of living people to be heard from the stage, and whose lips are not soundless and speak his words, is not easy to bear. There is, he discovers, a strange relationship between playwright, text and actor, and he is not mature enough to handle it. *The one who did the writing* is like a furious married man watching intercourse between *his wife, the text* and a strange actor.

And who is the director anyway? A feudal lord demanding his *droit du seigneur*?

As a writer he is someone who *is called*.

He finds he is not regarded as the master who engineered *the right tone*, but as the person who has to confirm that the actor has found it. He is, they say, the first one to permeate the text. *Permeate* is the right word. In his head, the first run-through has already happened. He does not know if they detest, fear or admire him for this. At any rate they love him if he approves.

However, between the author and the actor is an interpreter, the director. If any disputes arise during rehearsals, the director is instantly the actor's enemy. Into the fray steps *travelling salesman*, Enquist, as an ally. Maybe he holds the answer to how these characters, written down in words, *truly* think. For he has listened in on the first, deadly silent, performance.

Isn't that performance *the true one*?

The argument basically concerns the word *true*. When he wrote novels there was never any doubt. He owned sole rights to the truth.

Not any more.

With time he learns to resist his scepticism about the theatre: the idea that if he shuts his eyes the world ceases to exist. In Bratislava he sees a shattering performance of *From the Lives of Rainworms* in which he suddenly finds out who his heroine Mrs Heiberg is. It is not the only time. He also learns to avoid mistakes.

The usual mistake is that, three weeks before an opening night, he receives an invitation to sit in on rehearsals in, say, Munich. Or Krakow. And he accepts.

The production has reached quite an advanced juncture. The first superficial disagreements, essentially to do with interpretation, but projected on to absurd things, such as the wrong shoes or insensitivity on the part of the prompter, these can be overcome. The author comes and listens to a run-through. Afterwards the actress who is playing, for example, Mrs Heiberg in *From the Lives of Rainworms* says, "P.O., may I ask you something?" To which he replies, "Of course, go ahead." And when she presents her analysis of the role, he nods ingratiatingly and with an almost erotic look of hope – she is strikingly attractive – says, "Yes, that's it! I think that's absolutely right! You've understood!"

She does not know that he, in total ignorance of theatre power games, has just left Sjön, Hjoggböle, and at that point their world falls apart.

She immediately scuttles to the enemy, i.e. the director, with whom she no longer has a sexual relationship, neither clandestine nor open, and is therefore free, and says: "This is what I've said all along, all along.

And you didn't listen. But now P.O. says so. It's a good job he's here. But the theatre should have invited him in much sooner. After all, he's written the play. He says that what I thought was right. P.O., come here and tell him what you meant. You can listen to P.O. now, so I can sort this out once and for all. For God's sake, I'm just an actor and obviously don't count, I've only got my intuition, and that clearly doesn't mean a thing. No, I don't want us to break for today, and I don't want to have coffee. I want to hear what P.O. has to say. Tell us."

And so on. And so on. On one occasion the opening night is delayed by two weeks just because he praised an actress who then goes off sick.

Power games.

In the end he learns to keep his silence and only speak to the director, but like a child he has already been lured into a new role, one he enjoys a little too much. It is February 1975 when the world of the theatre opens up.

There he will remain for a long time.

In its second year his first play winds up in a place where no Swedish play in modern times has been performed, on Broadway. Real Broadway, the Helen Hayes Theater, not off, not off off. Several of his later plays are played off, but that is the Northern Counties Coastal League, this is Broadway.

It is not like anything he has learned in European theatres.

Nothing is like Broadway.

Like all Europeans he is used to state-subsidised repertory theatres; and then suddenly, after the play had its American premiere at the McCarter Theater in Princeton in the autumn of 1976 and was given a whole ecstatic page by Clive Barnes in the *New York Times*, the commercial forces storm in and four Broadway producers compete to buy this "piece of property". This item of merchandise, this commodity?

He will become acquainted with the expression "piece of property".

The sixty-page contract scares the living daylights out of him. This is business; he feels stupid and senses steely lawyers with claims for compensation behind every paragraph. One clause states that the American translator of the play owns the right to a certain percentage of all future revenue from film and subsequent theatre production or other associated rights worldwide, if the play is a success on Broadway: the explanation being that the significance of Broadway is monumental and surpasses the rest of world theatre in all respects.

Broadway is, according to this, the real reason the piece will be performed elsewhere in the world.

He *wails in protestation* that it is already being performed elsewhere in the world. It pains his newly found self-confidence and the lawyers fear a breakdown in the negotiations. Besides, he finds the idea imperialist – the Vietnam War is not long over and the European in him squeals like a stuck pig – and he does not know how he will explain it to other translators all over the world, many of whom have already finished their translations.

After ten transatlantic conversations the agent yields, furious.

He also naively thinks that the wonderful company at the McCarter Theater, whom he observed for a few weeks during rehearsals, will have their chance on Broadway. Absolutely unthinkable, stars are now required.

That winter in Uppsala he follows the hunt for stars from a distance. Jack Nicholson says he is interested, but does not want to do theatre any more, it is understood he prefers film – that way you can get drunk in the evening; you cannot do that in the theatre. It is a position he understands and with which he sympathises, but what a waste of talent. The director, Michael Kahn, goes to London to try to convince Vanessa Redgrave to play Siri von Essen, and sends him this written report: "She is delighted by the play, but is fully occupied with bringing down the British government and her work leading the Trotskyist movement in England. She revealed that as soon as she has completed this, or if there is a military coup in England, she will consider returning to Broadway. A truly remarkable woman!" Glenda Jackson would like to, but is unavailable. Maria Schell would like to, but meets opposition from the producers. It is a matter of life and strife. And Marthe Keller has been double-booked. Nevertheless, the London trip is a success, because the great English actress Eileen Atkins is caught and signs. Werner Klemperer, the much-loved television star, known best for his role as the bumbling Colonel Klink in the television series *Hogan's Heroes*, is cast in the small part of Viggo; a remarkable, shy and enormously funny actor who made a living by breaking into German in American films about evil *krauts*, he is the son of the conductor Otto Klemperer.

Eventually it is all settled. Two *great Bergman actors*, he will soon get used to the labels, in other words Max von Sydow and Bibi Anderssson, will complete the international ensemble, of whom only Klemperer is American; time will show that this has consequences for labour relations. Certain of the financiers want to change the title; *The Night of the Tribades* sounds too much like *The Day of the Triffids*, a horror film from the '50s in which the world is threatened by man-eating gherkins, something like that. He protests and the title is allowed to stand. On closer inspection the contract also includes a clause stating that the author has the right to attend rehearsals for six weeks, draw a generous allowance, and stay in the luxury suite at the Wyndham Hotel on 52nd Street.

He expresses his gratitude to his agent, Bridget Aschenberg at I.C.M., and sets off.

If P.W. could travel, so can he.

In the days before the first rehearsal he meets the producer and some – around ten – of the financiers. It is a convivial evening and it gives him a vague idea about this new world and what will happen.

The financiers are also shareholders in *Annie*. This is the musical they are now going to see, as a warm-up to an evening's drinking. For two of the investors, *Annie* is their "piece of property". *Annie* is Broadway's great new musical success about a girl who has lost her dog, leaving the audience spellbound. The highlight is when the dog enters from the left, casts a mournful and apprehensive glance at the audience, walks up to the point on the stage where he will communicate his pining for Annie (this is where he has probably been trained to receive a sausage), sits down, no Annie to the left, no Annie to the right, gets up and walks off. The house erupts in deafening applause and cheers; this is riveting, this is theatre at its best.

"*Annie* is an incredible musical," one of the financiers says in the interval. "Did you see the dog?"

The new-found American friends of and shareholders in Enquist analyse the anatomy of this success. There are children who can dance. There is a wicked old woman with redeeming features. She is a drunk and she is funny, both important elements. And a dog. And a declaration of love for New York, the most fascinating garbage heap in the world.

He does not know how much this Broadway angel has invested in *Annie*, but now, after its sensational hit, he is raking in unimaginable sums. Above all he can invest some of it in a new play that is also certain to be fabulously successful. Very original, with an extraordinarily distinguished cast, and two Bergman actors! Namely, *The Night of the Tribades*.

The Tribades has, he is led to understand, been supported by profits created by the little dog.

The première is in October.

"Aren't you worried about losing money on a project as difficult as *The Tribades*?" he asks doubtfully. But his new-found friend shakes his head, "Absolutely not." For a moment the Swedish playwright is unsure, is there something he hasn't understood? Is *The Tribades* intended to make a loss? For tax reasons? To offset profits from *Annie*? He has just seen the film *The Producers*, where *Springtime for Hitler* is intended to be a guaranteed flop. Is the sure-fire loss-making *Springtime for Strindberg* now about to be launched? But his new-found friend smiles sincerely and shakes his head, *Absolutely not!*

"P.O.," he says; he has learned how to pronounce his name correctly in just a few seconds, not like Danes, who can never do it – wrong emphasis, they stress the *O* – "P.O.," he says, "you've written a fantastic play. Quite incredible. The odds are against it, but, you know theatre is like horse racing and sometimes an outsider gets in. You've written a superb play. It has it all. Everything."

He pauses and then adds thoughtfully, almost to himself: "Apart from a dog."

The producer is called Burry Fredrik; her hair has turned a little grey in the stormy seas of Broadway, she smokes incessantly on slender cigarillos, speaks fast and intensely and always tells it *like it is*.

He likes her from the first moment.

Over lunch at Sardi's, which soon becomes his second home, the bar to be seen in for theatre people on Broadway, its walls covered in actors' portraits, she puts him in the picture.

"P.O.," she says, "I could see immediately that *The Night of the Tribades* would be a valuable Piece of Property. A very valuable asset. So I bought the rights for Broadway."

That was after the premiere in Princeton and after Clive Barnes' accolade in the *New York Times*. She had been there and watched a performance. She was not alone. Four Broadway producers had been interested after the premiere in December 1976, plus Gordon Davidson at the Mark Taper in Los Angeles, who was the worst threat, but she gained the rights in February 1977 and formed the company The Night of the Tribades Co.

The first task was to raise the core funding: 225,000 dollars was needed. There were two avenues open to them. Either to break *The Tribades* into fifty shares of 4,500 dollars each, or chase larger investments. She tried the latter first. Two of the co-producers on *Annie* immediately put up 75,000 dollars each and a third readily staked 72,000. The rest was sold in small lots. The cheapest share in Enquist was 562 dollars and 50 cents, an eighth of one unit. Most of the *small investors in Enquist* – he listens with increasing interest and feels that his understanding of the capitalist system is slowly growing, now that he is practically listed on Wall Street – laid out between 1,000 and 3,000 dollars; the list included insurance managers, housewives on Long Island and theatre-loving speculators, who maybe hoped that as a bonus they would be invited to the first-night party at Sardi's and might even get to kiss Bibi Andersson on the cheek.

Next, detailed calculations on the product's future are made. The play's break-even point is reckoned to be 48,000 dollars a week (eight performances a week, two matinees; the theatre holds just over eleven hundred people). Included in these calculations is an element for artistic operating costs. On further questioning she confirms that he is an artistic operating cost himself. Everything, almost without exception, goes on percentage. With mounting enthusiasm he discovers that he is on a rising scale. He starts at 5 per cent, after a certain amount has been earned he goes up to 7.5 per cent, and ends up at 10 per cent for a Broadway success. That would mean at least 5,000 dollars a week, a staggering sum to him in 1977. Burry smiles glumly and points out that the author's share has to be divided up. Of the basic 5 per cent, the American agency takes a tenth of the total, and then the translator takes 40 per cent of the remainder. That leaves 2.7 per cent. The Swedish theatre agency now takes its 20 per cent. Leaving 2.16 per cent.

He looks cautiously at the producer. This was at the time when Astrid Lindgren had launched her Pomperipossa campaign about marginal tax in Sweden and he is on the point of saying *and Finance Minister Sträng takes the rest*, but stops short; a Social Democrat barrier comes crashing down inside him and instead he gives a silent, satisfied nod to his friend at the lunch table in Sardi's. "P.O., my friend," she says, "the bottom line is that if it does well you'll be as rich as hell and it'll run on Broadway for years and Hollywood will make a film of the play and you'll be taken on as the ridiculously highly paid screenwriter, like Tennessee Williams, and then you'll be a wealthy and probably worse person and drink yourself to death. Or it'll do bugger all and you'll go back to being who you were."

That is precisely the question, he thinks. Not how it does. But who he was and who he will become.

To begin with they spend two days, twenty-two hours in all, examining the translation and its linguistic structure word for word.

Max is a linguistic genius and deliberates over every tone, exhausting everyone else. The union representative comes to the first rehearsal and goes through the conditions; there are rigidly strict rules and Max, Bibi and Eileen, who are foreigners and not personally concerned, look on with bored expressions. The rehearsal hall is large and the stage is marked out by tape on the floor, everything completely normal and as it would be in any European rehearsal hall. Ten or so lesser producers line the walls, buzzing like respectful and curious bees. Burry Fredrik is *the great one* and does not sit with them, knowing how to defend her territory as the main producer.

It would never occur to her. Coffee machine in the corner.

The only completely un-Swedish thing is the rehearsal times, starting at half past ten and finishing at half past six in the evening, six days a week. They often eat together at Sardi's.

And so the production is set in motion. "*Marie, Marie, hold on tight.*" As it said in *The Waste Land*.

One evening he sees *A Chorus Line*, a musical about losers. There is no reality Broadway knows better than the reality of losers.

The ones who do not get a part in the ballet, the ones who are taken out.

Each morning at 10.30 he meets a real chorus line in the corridors of the Minskoff Theater, where *The Tribades* is rehearsing. The building is colossal and is teeming with small rehearsal rooms, and in these there is constant auditioning of young actors being tested for a role in an off-Broadway or an off-off-Broadway production, or for a chance to dance in the *West Side Story* revival.

He often talks to them. Their waiting is endless, just like their hope. The union rules stipulate that auditions are open to all, but in fact the talented ones have already been handpicked. Instead the auditions are grim formalities with almost zero chance. He likes chatting with them. On one occasion he is invited to the Actors' Studio with a friend and he loves the openness and warmth and the theatre mentality.

The people waiting in the corridors of the Minskoff, however, have not got as far as the Actors' Studio.

One afternoon a girl is standing in the corridor outside rehearsal room four, crying disconsolately; when he speaks to her she says in a tremulous voice, "Are you in there with *The Tribades*?" He nods. "It's Swedish, isn't it? Isn't there a Bergman actor in it? I love *The Seventh Seal*," she adds in a very matter-of-fact way. "I wish there was more drama," she suddenly exclaims, aggressively. "*The Tribades* is drama, isn't it? How many parts are there?" He answers, "Four." Glumly, she replies, "Four. There should be more when they do drama on Broadway for once. And three foreigners!"

He realises that this is something fiercely discussed among the young actors permanently seeking work. She looks sharply at him and asks: "Do you know how many unemployed actors there are in New York?" He does know actually, but he shakes his head, he wants to hear her say the much debated figure. "Six thousand!" she says. He nods, he would have said four thousand himself, but perhaps she is right. "And this year there are only four straight plays on Broadway, the rest are just musicals."

He does not know what to say.

She looks at him and smiles. "You're one of them, aren't you?" and this time she asks him what he does. He tells her. She nods quietly and appreciatively, as if to someone who at some point in the future will write the role for her that will change her life, that is, if the imperialist forces of European theatre and capitalism's remorseless cult of stardom do not continue to exclude her and the other hopefuls waiting in their chorus line.

There is always hope – she does not intend to give up hope – but she says flatly, from her place in the corridor of the Minskoff, which for her is the chorus line for theatre work, says with a nod towards the large hall in the Minskoff Theater where *The Night of the Tribades* will shortly resume its rehearsal: "I hate them."

It is a very warm, calm New York autumn and he is in the belly of the whale. This is what he thinks, without being clear about what he means. It is a quotation from somewhere. Once, a century or two ago, it must have been 1966, he was on a pavement somewhere in the southern states, watching a protest march he had been part of, and the Black Panthers passed by on a truck, *telling a great story*, but he knew that he was in fact *standing alongside*, as an observer.

And where is he now? In the belly of the whale. The whale is Broadway.

After two weeks the understudies appear.

There is only one understudy for the two female roles; she is called Kathy McGrath, a young actress with a string of roles behind her on off-off-Broadway. But not a big box-office attraction. There is one male understudy, Bill More, who will have to stand in as either Strindberg or Viggo. It is slightly mad, but completely logical. Nothing, absolutely nothing, will be permitted to stop a performance. One cancelled performance is equivalent to a loss of ten thousand dollars *in today's terms*. So these substitutes have an obligation to learn the parts, be present at every performance in case anything should happen, be prepared to stand in *even during a performance*.

Kathy receives five hundred dollars a week for this. She is a redhead, about thirty, and smiles resignedly at him, saying she is *goddamn happy in the circumstances*. Because they wanted to save on outgoings, she was not contracted until the third week. Then she was expected to know the lines. She and Bill sit at a little table in the corner of the rehearsal hall completely silent, and when arguments flare up their silence intensifies. In fact, they are expected never, under any circumstances, to comment on the actual play. It is quite enough with the director, the regular actors, the producer, and the author.

Indeed the latter is one too many.

An understudy has to mark out the scenes, know the script and remain silent. After the first night the stage manager should, according to the contract, hold "understudy rehearsals"; these never take place. They live a shadowy existence, but Kathy tells him once that "it's lively."

They are very close, but far away. Only a catastrophe would bring them up to the surface. A fever of over 40 degrees would constitute such a catastrophe. Under that threshold, the regular actors are expected to bite the bullet and get on with it. It is a strange situation, perhaps easier for Bill, who does have one line to say: he comes on in the final scene as a photographer.

Yet they say they are happy.

They do have work, of a kind.

One evening after rehearsal he bumps into Katherine Walker, who played Marie David in the original premiere of *The Tribades* at the McCarter Theater the year before. She was the one most acclaimed by the *New York Times* and he knows she is a great actress, but she is not a *big name*. Not a star who can draw people. So she had to stand aside; he made only a half-hearted attempt to speak up for her, nothing meaningful.

He knows that, maybe she knows too; they have a beer together, and a long talk.

"What are you doing now?" he asks finally. "It's such a pity you're not here with us." She looks at him without saying a word. It was the wrong question. What cynicism. He knows it and so does she. Suddenly he sees the tears in her eyes.

They change the subject. He learns later that she is out of work, except for small advertising jobs on television. That is the way things are.

He soon begins to realise that every theatre performance is a battle-ground. Whilst sometimes it may not be very pretty, at other times it is fantastic: the rehearsal studio is magical, everything stops, the world unites around them here, in a cramped, warm space, a diving bell where every line that sounded dead and crude and impossible before suddenly takes on a strangely physical life, and it is hard to breathe and everyone knows at once that now *we're nearly there*. Nothing outside is important; but here, inside art's womb, in the moments before birth, the fantastic happens.

But the road there!

It reminds him of his own writing. Of course then he is alone. No-one to rage and rant at. To throw his coffee cup at. No point in rushing out to the toilet in tears; no point in kicking the chair over; no point in refusing to speak to a disparaging director; no point in threatening to change the stage manager or actors.

Michael Kahn is one of Broadway's most experienced directors; he is on his way up; he knows what this production means, a handicap or fillip to his career, a lever or a catapult, and now he is afraid. They have a very sensible agreement that author and director will never discuss anything together during rehearsals, but afterwards they talk for hours. Sometimes face to face, sometimes on the telephone.

Michael is concerned.

There is a great deal of money at stake. But also he feels as though he is fighting a shadow that is not quite there; when things get difficult and uncompromising, and coffee cups are thrown and so on, the threatening, ghostly figure rises up, until it really exists in Michael's now almost paranoid imagination, and it makes him angry and unsure.

"P.O., you know Bergman, and how to handle Bergman actors. What the hell does he do with them to make them so brilliant? P.O., what's a Bergman actor like? Should I come down hard on them? Or what should I do?"

Michael overestimates the Swedish author, because at that time, October 1977, he really is no Bergman expert; but he insists that a Bergman actor is only a very good actor and maybe the only explanation for the myth is that Bergman, in contrast to almost all other great film artists, uses his theatrical know-how and rehearses with them over and over again.

But for Michael Kahn the spectre of Bergman undeniably hangs over this production. Unfortunately Max and Bibi, both magnificent, bear the yoke of Bergman, despite their total dissimilarity and their different temperaments. Poles apart. Max always calm, Bibi, constantly asking and thinking, harder to handle.

Back to Michael Kahn's incessant questions.

And his own vague replies.

Afterwards he reads the concise summary in his diary.

He notes that if a problem arises in a performance, disputes usually centre around the most articulate in the company, either the problems are there, or they are not. Iron filings are attracted to someone.

His diary from September 29:

Yesterday. Arrive in the afternoon. They're doing the scene on the bed. Can see the horror on Bibi's face from the door. Obviously something has happened. Indignant comments after the actors have gone. Michael and Susan agree that Bibi blew the first act and half the second. Burry there. She thinks the second act fine, but Bibi a problem.

Burry rings in the evening. Nervous. Has had dinner with Michael. What to do? Big problem.

B.t.w. forgot to say Michael kicked the chairs. Said he hated Bibi. Tomorrow he would be Bergman.

Then: Burry – Michael – me.

On the phone with Burry: talked calmly about the problems.

Burry slightly drunk, so was I. Arranged to have breakfast at nine tomorrow morning.

Today: Burry breakfast. Are agreed on strategy. No trade-off yet. Burry will stay in the background. Big cannon.

Michael not there for morning rehearsal, teaching at the theatre academy. Meet Bibi at the door. She asks about interpretation of a phrase. I say: depends on the context. Think she should ask Michael, not me. Bibi: I'm asking you!!! Perhaps, I say, it's because we have different ideas about the Siri–Strindberg relationship. Bibi explodes, kicks a chair, throws her coffee cup. Big scene. Bibi rings agent. Rings Michael. Bibi locks herself in the john. Phone Michael, he's coming. Bibi talks to Werner. I leave. Phone Burry, tell her to come. She orders me back. Everybody in the corridor, all wave to me, ironic or encouraging, don't know which. Meeting in room 4 for Michael, Bibi and me. Bibi furious. We start to talk. Then I ask her to read the letter I wrote her the previous night.

She reads letter. Tears of woe. Situation lifts very, very slowly. Run through the first ten minutes. Fifteen. The first act. It's alive and it's bloody good!

Go up to the office. Have a glass of wine at the Howard Johnson. Up to Burry again. Rushed discussion about the music. Then up to the New York Times. They want to print the whole afterword to the play, but deliberate over certain words. Especially "used". Chicken, back down. Daren't say "capitalism".

Back to the rehearsal. Superb. Don't see Bibi afterwards. Enormous pressure on her. Wants a voice coach flown in from L.A. Suddenly crying again. Max, the father figure, comforting.
Have a drink with Max and Werner.
Boxing in the evening.

All in a day's work?

Eileen is very calm, she has a long and brilliant career behind her at the National Theatre in London and has seen most things, but one evening she tells him she is angry. She feels "under-directed". Nice girls don't get noticed.

The most extraordinary thing, however, is how much he *interferes*. Or is forced to interfere. He must be mad.

Many years later, when another of his plays, *The Magic Circle*, is being staged in Copenhagen with Fritz Helmuth in the main role, the news reaches him that it is all going very badly. Everyone is drinking, they hate each other and they are in despair. No-one knows the lines. It will have to be cancelled the week before the first night, that is the message. He goes down, spends a week in the dark rehearsal room with a delighted, eager smile playing on his wretched lips. And does not utter a word. Just shows silent, surprised enthusiasm. They all sober up, pull themselves together, and the premiere is excellent.

There he learns a different view of the function of the dramatist during the theatrical process.

It is the same as the position of the rabbit with regard to the harness horse.

A horse has become nervous and jittery when he is harnessed to the trap. Time and again he gallops off down the track. Nerves obviously frayed. A little white rabbit is placed in his stall. The neurotic horse is disconcerted at first, but the little rabbit hops calmly around, eats, sleeps and is above all quiet and unconcerned. The horse takes a sniff at him, is seized with love for his little friend, and calms down, becoming a non-galloping prizewinner once more.

The author's role is like the rabbit's.

The Night of the Tribades on Broadway is now watched intently by a curious but sceptical Market. A chamber play, four characters, but with a tremendous potential for profitability if it goes well. Perhaps this is the future?

The mounting pressure is inwardly more and more noticeable. Every slight disagreement can suddenly erupt into a huge, hopeless disaster. Everyone in the production is agreed that Max von Sydow is a wonderful man, kind, professional and fantastic in every way. Only mild demurral is heard. On one occasion when Max misses lunch at Sardi's, the girls in the company are discussing his tremendous qualities, but suddenly start to complain that he has no sexual charisma on stage. It's like bloody well kissing your old dad. How can you inject any thrill into that?

He protests indignantly in Max's absence, but is silenced, and realises that he has no authority in this area. *Max is nice and he's brilliant, but he's not sexually attractive on the stage*, is the message. And off the stage? *That has no bearing*.

He readily identifies with Max. The sheer hell of being nice. The curse of goodness. He suddenly recalls, though he does not recount this at Sardi's, the dreadful, failed, Saturday prayers of his childhood, when he had to confess a sin. Max would never pass muster with Maja Enquist, his sins are so few. So imagine everyone's surprise when the thoroughly good-hearted Max causes a fracas: in an interview in the *New York Times*, a big spread on the subject of Bergman stars on Broadway, he happens to say, "Where are the good directors on Broadway?"

Michael Kahn naturally reads the interview, is absolutely livid and goes through the roof. He rings Enquist, rages half the night, saying that he doesn't intend to take this shit. No amount of persuasion helps, and next morning he does not appear at rehearsal. Everyone is upset by the drama, Burry Fredrik orders a reconciliation lunch, the agents move into action, at one o'clock the two enemies are led to a corner table for three at Sardi's, and after a few polite, untruthful compliments he can see that calm has been restored, that it had *on no account* been his intention to compare Michael unfavourably with some distant European so-called director, forgotten his name, possibly Swedish, maybe his name is Bergman? A misunderstanding. Misquoted. Can't always rely on the *New York Times*.

They drink each other's health in dry Martini.

Much later he would understand the director's sensibility more, when he takes on the role himself.

Directing was tempting, to eliminate the glass wall between oneself and the beloved actors. In this way the loneliness of the writing desk could be traded. It can't be so hard to deal with the direction. The fear or nervousness he has felt disappears after the first time; he goes on to direct *The Tribades* himself in Copenhagen with Ghita Nørby and Fritz Helmuth, then *The Magic Circle* and *From the Lives of Rainworms* as television drama. Maybe it's not so difficult? *Doesn't he have platoon commander training in I:20*, he thinks sternly, *practically field trooper training, and experience of leading and managing troops?* He receives more and more offers, culminating in Beethoven's *Egmont* at the Royal Danish Opera House (he declines, thereby avoiding certain scandal), but does theatre instead.

Even *Miss Julie* at the Aveny Theatre with Kirsten Olesen and Ole Ernst. He savours every minute. Everything is perfect, he feels as though he is giving shape to the play for the first time with his *almost magical direction*, and breathlessly watches it unfold, as if he were the first and only spectator, not the thousandth director. The final scene, in which the angel of death beguiles the beautiful young lovers and Julie goes out to commit suicide, is magical.

Glowing reviews in the Danish press, and in *Dagens Nyheter* it is slaughtered by Bengt Jahnsson. But he recovers and assures everyone who will listen that this is the best thing he has done on a stage, amazingly enough as a director; this was the whole point of theatre, to finally attain *the heart of the matter*, and he knows he has succeeded. *August Strindberg's* Miss Julie *is on a stage for the first time!*

Wasn't it always supposed to be like this? Always?

No, he is not sinking yet. Not at the Aveny Theatre in 1985. But it is clear: the warning bells had rung during rehearsals. And he had heard them.

They rehearsed *Julie* at the Aveny, where next to the stage was a bar, and every lunch break he and Ole Ernst sat together companionably, drinking a beer. It was completely natural. This was Denmark. None of Sweden's rigorous moralising. You could relax, and they seldom drank more than one beer, and then had three hours rehearsal, and he and Ole were best friends.

Then suddenly Ole had disappeared. Two weeks before the first night.

Of course he remembered that Ole had had alcohol problems, but only now and again, with long intervals between bouts, and he knew of no actor more conscientious in his duty than Ole, one of the stars at the Royal Danish Theatre. So a beer in the middle of the day was quite acceptable. Seldom more. As director he had moral responsibility for everything, including discipline over alcohol, but they were both grown men, and it was for him to decide. Yet if he had said something, Ole would never have come up with the idea. It was inescapable.

And now he had disappeared. Everyone knew at once what had happened.

He was almost certainly somewhere on what was called death row in Copenhagen, in one of about ten bars frequented by people who had given up hope. And on the third day they found him there, still conscious, but in a bad way.

They took him home.

He and Ole, who was in despair, talked together, gently and calmly. On the fourth day they resumed rehearsals. Ole was better and his acting more compelling than ever, and no-one in the team uttered a word of criticism about *him*, about the beer every lunchtime, and *didn't he know*, and it being his responsibility!

Sitting at the director's table he knew it was entirely his fault. He had enticed Ole out on to death row. He should have listened to the alarm bells ringing.

He noticed that Ole during the final rehearsals was scratching, all over his upper body, and he asked what it was. Ole quietly explained that, "It's coming out of my body now."

"What does that feel like?" he asked.

"Like being in the middle of an anthill, sheer hell," was his reply. It was withdrawal.

Ole made a magnificent, striking Jean. That was in 1985. Now it was autumn 1977 on Broadway and he did not yet know what it could be like, to be a director, to have the responsibility, to be in the middle of an anthill. He is immersed in a day wrecked by a fight over whether there were any worthy directors on Broadway. And the entry in his diary for 2 October is: *bloody sandpit*.

Michael Kahn had asked him a question about Bergman. In the autumn of 1977 he really had no answers about Bergman and his way of handling actors.

It would be a number of years before he could answer: not until Bergman staged *From the Lives of Rainworms* at the Residenz Theatre in Munich, and later handled the first production of *The Image Makers* at the Royal Dramatic Theatre in Stockholm, subsequently making it into a film for television.

It was uncontroversial and full of trust, Bergman was amusing and loyal, with a fantastic respect for the text, a respect that was shockingly absent in other directors of lesser distinction.

Yet in hindsight he could understand Michael Kahn's almost desperate respect for the now ageing Swedish monument. As if there were *something ominous*, something slightly haunting around the notion of Bergman that made even intelligent people act irrationally.

Much later he experiences an instance of this himself.

Bergman is rehearsing the first ever staging of *The Image Makers* and the premiere is approaching. He eventually realises that the grandmaster is worried, or rather he is scared stiff. He knows that actually this is, to all intents and purposes, *normal* and has nothing to do with whether the production is running smoothly or disastrously.

Ingmar had told him about the highly confidential diary he kept about all his theatre productions in the '70s. An extremely private document. Which would never be published. Never! But in the autumn of his years when he was on Fårö, Bergman reread this record of his feelings towards theatre work and was deeply shaken.

The happy times he remembered were revealed in the diaries as a constant series of disasters. At any rate in the foreshortened perspective of his diary.

Every production filled with disputes. Nothing made sense. Went home from the theatre every day practically in tears. Not a word about the joy of working with actors, or how wonderful they were, the unshakeable and oft-repeated view he later held, only the misery. But then – every time – the unimaginable surprise at the premiere when it all came together. In fact it was bloody good.

During rehearsal, however: only misery.

Before the premiere of *The Image Makers* at the end of the '90s, his anguish was obvious. His reasons for not allowing the author to attend rehearsals were minor literary masterpieces. Each evening long conversations with the author, very constructive, but come and watch? No. An extremely plausible and imaginative diagnosis of why the following day, *most regrettably*, was not a good day to see a rehearsal or a run-through. Owing to sudden lighting problem, virus, technical breakdown, or an absolutely essential change of shoes for one of the actors.

At worst, the prompter's sprained ankle.

In the end, ten days before the first night, it is unavoidable. A resolute but very tense Bergman, in his most commanding tone, indicates the precise seat the author is to sit on. Third row, number 64. That he will sit to one side behind him, in full charge of the author's movements and facial expressions. That the auditorium is otherwise to remain empty, that it is certain to go hellishly wrong, that he needs to apologise at the outset for being so lousy, it really isn't the fault of the actors, who are amazing, that there must be no coughing, that he is pleased the author does not have a cold; and, in a voice of thunder, that finally, at last, here you are!

But a problem will arise.

Towards the end of the first act, after half an hour, there is a long monologue, lasting about twenty minutes, by the wonderful Anita Björk; her performance is raw and moving as the character she plays, Selma Lagerlöf, describes her co-dependency on her father and how his alcoholism destroyed her youth. And how she lied about her father's drinking all her life. Even in her acceptance speech when she won the Nobel Prize. And just when the mood is at its most intense, the silence at its most profound, and he knows that the next twenty minutes will be the most powerful of the play, he suddenly needs to have a pee.

This is not a normal sensation. Usually he has no problem. This is an almost seismic, erupting need that must be entirely psychological, because he knows there is no deliverance. He has never felt this fear-based respect for the monumental Ingmar Bergman before – at least not so overpoweringly – but he knows it is a fact the world over, this reverential Fear of Bergman! This mystique of the demon director! The man he has come to know as a funny, loyal friend who likes a joke – it hits him now with relentless force.

The pressure in his bladder builds up sharply, as the intensity of Anita Björk's characterisation simultaneously deepens.

All he can do is debate the alternatives in a panic, a choice between the plague and cholera. He knows his friend Ingmar Bergman sufficiently well to know that he would never, ever, forgive him if he rushed out of the auditorium. It would be recorded in Ingmar's black notebook, on the last page, where only traitors dwell, the most wicked, like the ninth circle for treachery in Dante's hell.

To leave the hall is unthinkable.

The spell would be broken. Blunt criticism from Anita Björk and Bergman himself. The need to pee a poor excuse, no-one would accept his claim for a volcanic eruption, especially not Ingmar. One alternative would be just to let it out. The Målarsalen at the Royal Dramatic Theatre has a sloping floor, it would run down, like a soundless little stream, not disturb anyone. It could be wiped up afterwards.

Or – could he last out?

The performance out front is more and more emotional. He struggles desperately, his bladder swelling uncontrollably; the physical manifestation of the respect, close to fear, in which the theatre world, beyond all borders, holds the Swedish director Ingmar Bergman.

Nothing odd about Michael's anxiety then.

He manages to hold on. Only a tiny drop seeps out.

He races out in the interval.

Afterwards he confesses all to Ingmar, who is highly delighted, confirms that he never would have forgiven him, but is fulsome in his praise for his victorious effort and resilience. He asks if Enquist prayed to God, which Enquist denies.

They then have a long talk about the problem of belief within Bergman's High Church Lutheranism and his own Moravian revivalism.

Much later he will direct plays himself, his own and those of others, and be more understanding. But he knows he loves the team spirit of a theatre rehearsal, the spirit that ultimately overcomes all conflicts.

The closeness. The silence surrounding a few people in a rehearsal room. If only there was not the dreadful premiere, reminding him of the nightmare of working for so many years on a novel, alone, day after day, year after year, finishing the manuscript, and then suddenly, one Monday morning it will be judged, torn apart, acclaimed.

The infant torn from the womb. And to go outside at six in the morning, to the letter box where the morning papers are, open the box, and there is the verdict.

To which *by common consent* one should pay no regard.

Not until the day before the preview, when the first paying audience is admitted, are the actors allowed into the Helen Hayes Theater.

The reason is simple: the theatre is in use; they are putting on the last performance of *Equus* there, at the end of its third year. The changeover has to happen like lightning. It is very tight now, and hard; the night before the first preview they rehearse until half past twelve. Michael Kahn swamps the actors with notes, sound directions, scene changes, tempo instructions.

This is Broadway, where there can also be knowledge, passion, and experience on an enormous scale. Every laugh must be planned, every inflection, every pause and rhythm. They all pack into Bibi's dressing-room and hundreds of subtle nuances are woven in while the stage-hands work next door; the lighting is dealt with separately and the night is long.

It is a small close-knit group now, and he is with them, in a tiny dressing-room. Tomorrow the merciless public will be there; and then five days to the premiere. There is no time now for bullshit and objections, Michael cuts dead all discussions in a flash and pushes on.

What is special about this premiere? He has been to quite a number already. Why the tremendous pressure everyone feels, why is Broadway so different? He does not know. But he knows that it is the case, and no matter how many rehearsals and premieres he will go through, nothing will compare to this.

Tempo. Details. Tempo. It is like a seduction; he is drawn along, goes back to his hotel in the early hours, has a glass of whisky and wonders if something has been missed, or if this perfection is the goal that everyone strives for.

No-one is demanding the sack for anyone else now. Quiet love, under the axe.

*

Everything has become so serene, almost solemn.

On the afternoon of the premiere the lights are off in the auditorium, one single light on the stage, everyone sitting in a circle reading through the play in low voices, listening to one another, almost whispering. In the small ring of light, it looks like a reading group together by an evening lamp. Afterwards a briefing by Michael. There won't be a sound from the audience, 110 critics said they are coming, they will be sitting in silence, making notes, and never laughing. Don't worry. It's sold out, fantastic advance publicity, a double-page spread in the *New York Times*, Pia Lindström did a big interview with P.O. the day before on N.B.C., great expectation on all sides. Just relax. The show is ready, straight after the curtain falls the critics will rush out, don't be concerned about that. They only have two hours to write their piece, the television critics less.

Good luck, break a leg. *Hals- und Beinbruch*.

And then, suddenly, it is all over.

In the half-darkness behind the stage they are running around in a daze, congratulating one another, decisively downing whisky out of plastic cups, Bibi is crying with exhaustion and happiness, everyone agrees it went well. It turned out to be, despite the hellishness of being the premiere, the best performance up to now, almost faultless. There need be no recriminations. So much for that. No-one had an off day.

All that remains is Sardi's, and the final judgement.

The myths surrounding Broadway include rituals: Sardi's is an important one.

It is a restaurant on a side street in the heart of the theatre district and its walls are bedecked with sketches of theatre's leading lights. Movie fame means nothing here: you need to have had a success on Broadway to go up on the wall. No, not just success; colossal success.

Sardi's is what happens on the first night. The party before the passing of judgement.

The unwritten rules require that everyone involved – one after the other, so their individual success is not confused – goes into Sardi's, now as fully paid-up members, to be met by spotlights and television and applause and cheering.

These are the brief hours between premiere and judgement. They start arriving at nine. At eleven the first reviews come through, television reviews first. At twelve they know what the *New York Times* is saying: in practice it ordains who will be the unbelievably talented winners and the tragic or comic losers. Burry expresses a degree of concern about the *N.Y.T.*: Clive Barnes had retired as chief reviewer some months before, and his love of *The Tribades*, the whole reason for the play coming to Broadway, is no longer a factor; his successor is called Richard Eder and is Irish, Catholic, with eleven children! Can that have any bearing?

Quite a lot of obscenity in *The Tribades*. Lesbian ladies. Penis size, 16 centimetres by 4, Mr Schieve!

No-one knows. But very soon it will be established. It is exactly the same as the normal artistic jungle, but much more transparent, and on a bigger scale, with dollar signs in each eye, and anxious whispering, as if there were the prospect of a flotation on the Stock Exchange, or a rumour about insider trading on nearby Wall Street.

He has difficulty hearing what people are saying. Faces are enlarged, looming close, lips moving: both floors at Sardi's are full, with at least five hundred people, but most of Broadway's angels, in other words shareholders in Enquist, seem to have gathered on the first floor. So far they are determined that this is magnificent, a fantastic hit, and they tell him so, always very close up. They are drinking, very fast, because twelve o'clock can be too late if it is a fiasco, and minutes cost. The ones who are unconvinced wear broad, mercurial smiles and avoid pronouncing a verdict.

Good is not the word! Swedish theatre's most guarded assessment exists here too.

Nothing, says Burry Fredrik with a dry smile, is harder to find in American theatre than honesty at Sardi's on a first night between nine and twelve.

Everyone seems to have some sort of connection with his play, they have to shout to make themselves heard, and, as the temperature steadily rises, they all seem confident. And want to repeat, with laughter and heartfelt embraces, that they have witnessed Broadway history and this play is going to run for five years. A woman in her sixties lifts her teenage face to his and asserts that the best friend in her life is the Swedish actor Holger Löwenadler; he hears himself say, "Well, he's been dead a long time," and smiling with the same horrible gaiety, she says, "Fantastic! Fantastic!" managing somehow, remarkably, to slide out of her own embrace. The translator, a friend from U.C.L.A., who was not responsible for the fuss about the contract, is sitting waiting, white-faced, at a table with his wife; they are still married and a colossal success will certainly strengthen his wife's love for him, otherwise divorce is imminent. He thinks: *the share price for my "piece of property" will soon be fixed and many lives depend upon it.*

Isn't that always the case? Yes, of course. But so much more obvious in this place at this time.

At eleven the television reviews start to come in.

Three are very good, one is bad, one so-so. It does not matter. Everyone is waiting for the *New York Times*. Someone goes to fetch *the first copy* hot off the press, the newspaper offices are just a few hundred metres away; everyone starts looking at the clock, any minute now the magic hour will strike – midnight and the *New York Times*. He is thinking *how strange it is* – though he has been a critic for many years, it has been in a country where reviews did not mean much – that a newspaper has such authority, transferred to a mere mortal critic, God's emissary on Broadway.

Finally Burry Fredrik arrives on the first floor at Sardi's and the hubbub subsides a little as she makes her way through the mob of enthusiasts, or the ones who are ready to gloat, or the winners-to-be, across the room to the table where he and Max are sitting, bends down and says in a steady, low voice, "P.O., it's bad."

Max lifts his face, in almost childlike amazement, and says, "Is it really bad?"

And, fighting her own disappointment, she repeats: "Yes, it's bad. We're in bad shape."

Within thirty seconds the news has reached everyone.

It is as if a fire alarm has sounded and someone has set off a foam extinguisher in the room: voices subdued, figures that had sharp outlines now fuzzy, smiles dissolving, prior engagements to attend *urgently*. There is something wrong with his focus, he realises: if he looks at a tight throng at the bar, it becomes blurred and he can suddenly see the row of bottles behind the group, even though it was impossible a moment ago, hidden as the bottles were by the people, who have now dispersed; and suddenly the restaurant is only half full. No, in a flash it has completely emptied, except for the closest mourners.

Trauerfeier! Wasn't that the right word?

A quarter of an hour later there are twenty people left, a miraculous exodus, as if they were all evacuated through previously invisible emergency exits.

Burry is still sitting at the table, he and Max on either side of her; with tears in her eyes she repeats, over and over, almost mechanically that, "Clive Barnes said on the radio it was brilliant, but that doesn't matter because he's not with the *New York Times* any more and it's bloody unfair. Unfair." He reads the *New York Times* himself, perhaps in the vain hope that Burry has misunderstood. It is a negative review, but not lethal. Well, perhaps. It is Richard Eder, he has done an honest job, but *didn't like what he saw*. Acting excellent, Max brilliant, Bibi moving, Eileen supreme. But the play!

Quite simply he does not like the play. As simple as that.

But at Sardi's the world is caving in.

Burry Fredrik keeps repeating, with a fool's obstinacy, "We've been annihilated," and he says, "But it can't be that bad," and she says again, "Yes it is, P.O., we've been annihilated."

He looks around.

Friends, enemies, vultures, hawks, they have all gone. Only the most faithful losers stay with them. The translator, his friend from U.C.L.A., is sitting in a corner completely alone; there was a chance for his marriage, but not any more. Bunkum? No, not bunkum. It is an abandoned battlefield, the sour smell of stale smoke, ash on the tables, upturned wine glasses. As if the last scene in the play they have just performed has made its mark on this final celebration. The theatrical work *The Night of the Tribades*, now finished, hangs on as if they have not quite understood that the party is over. The same *grey dawn. The night of the tribades*. He knows all the lines by heart now. *Grey dawn. The night of the tribades*. And Marie David, drunk and vomiting, and suddenly liking Strindberg very much.

The same empty glasses, the same ash spilled on the tables. And then what? Carry on?

He suddenly feels very calm, could almost laugh. *Friend! In your hour of desolation, when your soul is shrouded in darkness!* He forgets the next line of the poem. *In your hour of desolation!* So beautiful. He is now very drunk. It was still a fantastic six weeks, he thinks. "We've been annihilated," he hears her say again.

And that is exactly right. They have been annihilated, and it was fantastic, but that was all.

After nineteen performances *The Night of the Tribades* closes.

It is a full house, eleven hundred paying customers, every evening, because they sell off the tickets for next to nothing through TKTS, the discount theatre ticket agency. Only fifteen tickets were sold at full price for the third performance. Still the auditorium was full. From a financial point of view the disaster is a clear fact after only a few days.

They have been annihilated. He flies home.

CHAPTER 11

FRUIT BOWL

He returns from Broadway to something he *cannot handle*. He has not been able to handle it since the spring of 1971, and now he carries on not being able to handle it.

It is the novel about Swedish emigration to Argentina in 1910. Exile and collapse.

Perhaps there is something in the concept of *exile* that troubles him. Or the word *restlessness* scares him. He constantly and impatiently wants to be on the move, but in the act of moving, in taking that leap, he slows down and starts daydreaming. Sometimes about a little island in a marsh and the unwieldy boat and maps on greaseproof paper, or about his mother's kitchen.

The latter definitely undigested Freud.

At the same time he is terrified at the thought of writing about this, writing about the personal. Prefers Baltic legionnaires, or well-disguised hammer throwers.

Cacher is a word for disguise he has learned in the theatre world. It means hide.

Nothing bad about the kitchen. The two weeks he spent in his mother's kitchen writing about Munich were so good. She padded about quietly in the background, feeding him bits of food.

He had only to throw back his head and open his beak.

Outside the window was Bureå church, a classic Swedish church, completed in 1919, one of three ecclesiastical masterpieces in the National Romantic style, the others being Tengbom's Högalid church in Stockholm and Masthugget church in Gothenburg. It stands apart in the centre of Bureå, on a plinth of Swedish granite, the façade of hand-made brick and uncut stone, the interior limewashed in natural white; large, clean, unbelievably Swedish. They started building during the First World War, in a parish consisting of three thousand small-holders and destitute workers at Bure Bolag. Construction would cost, at current values, 445 million kronor. An unimaginable sum for this poor little parish.

The chapel in Sjön, Hjoggböle, was something else entirely. It was knocked up by volunteers and there was plenty of timber. The forest land around the village was largely untouched. P.W. brought the radiators. No, there weren't any, but the furnace!

In contrast to the chapel, the church, and the Swedishness it represented, gave expression to the rock-solid affiliation of the parish to the Church of Sweden and the bishops in Härnösand and Luleå. This was a parish in which the labour movement had not had an easy time. When the rabble-rousers arrived they were given a good thrashing by the faithful workers. In the revolutionary '70s, if one were to draw any conclusion from the angry performances by independent theatre groups, it is that the historical development of this parish was not particularly orthodox. It was almost embarrassing. The exploited and pious workers in Bureå parish were the labour movement's worst enemies.

That was certainly what had formed his own deepest roots. To be written about in private. Better to regard friends in Argentina as *riff-raff in exile*.

For many years he has known that some distant relatives emigrated to Argentina at the beginning of the century.

Though most of them came from Kiruna.

It was an emigration story, or saga, or tragedy. He decides he will go to northern Argentina for six months, to uncover the legacy of this emigration. He makes his preparations, hunts down addresses in Misiones, where the last survivors are hiding in the jungle; he thinks of it in dramatic terms, *hiding in the jungle*.

Everything is ready. Then he changes his mind, postpones his trip to South America and flies to Los Angeles. He spends eight months as visiting professor at U.C.L.A. He returns to the stacked piles of his Argentina project, hundreds of wretched pages, typed up and waiting.

He views the project with despair.

The emigrants had left after the general strike; they were unemployed and, having been blacklisted, had no hope of finding work.

There they were in their exile, and he knew roughly what had happened to them. Of the three thousand who emigrated around 1911, a thousand had returned, a thousand had died of disease and hardship in the jungle of northern Argentina, and a thousand remained where they had ended up.

Prince Wilhelm had once written a book about the emigration, *Swedes of the Red Earth*. The prince's version was quite moving, or convenient, *courageous Swedes in a struggle with unfriendly natives*. But maybe it was true. Perhaps reality was not as fair as one might hope.

Reality for the battered rabble-rousers in Bureå parish was not what it should have been either.

He finds it increasingly difficult to deal with *how it is*, as opposed to *how it ought to be*. It is the '70s after all, a time for normative thinking. It would have been more gratifying if the workers of Bureå parish had been more progressive. Or, for that matter, if his father had not bought a Chevrolet or been a member of the Knights Templar.

But reality can be quite messy. Monuments are seldom cast in one piece. This feeling *of being hoodwinked!* Even good children, like himself, whose main worry is finding a sin to confess at Saturday prayers, have a strange desire to argue, sometimes against their better judgement. The children of fundamentalism were a hard flock to handle. *Better to say it as it is, than be correct*, he writes once, and puzzles over this strange sentence before crumpling up the piece of paper.

Rarely has he found things to be as he expected. Not in the Soviet Union, or Berlin, or Munich, or Bureå parish where his noble working-class forefathers did not really behave as they should have. Year after year he delays his trip to Misiones in northern Argentina, where the emigrants stopped. Like himself, at home.

The sheaves of paper in his novel grow thicker.

Finally he goes, just to see if he can free himself.

He travels with almost no luggage at all, so that he can, unhindered, penetrate the jungle, which he assumes is there. He takes only a field rucksack, a compact military model, the one he bought during his high-jump tour in Israel in 1963.

He finds the old Swedish descendants heartbreaking.

They speak to him in an archaic biblical Swedish, unchanged for seventy years. They say they would like to *speak with him about the old country*, and in the little church in Obera they sing "Our Fathers' Church in Sweden's Land" together. It is so beautiful he could almost weep. When the Psalm Book Committee later removes this psalm he is furious, vows to leave the Church of Sweden, *history-ignorant opportunists*.

The displaced should be able to hold on to their dream.

They had come to Misiones to grow yerba, the green tea, but world prices suddenly fell and misery set in. After the Swedish government had sent over a diplomat, Counsellor Paulin, in 1913, *tidings reached the homeland* that, although it was true that the emigrant workers had been intransigent during the general strike, they should be brought back to the homeland on humanitarian grounds: they had begun to die like flies. Many of them were too proud, and only about a thousand of them gave in and came back. Most of them believed they were still blacklisted after the general strike and had very little hope. They had also died like flies. God's punishment, perhaps. The majority came from Kiruna and were not used to sand fleas.

In fact he has the whole novel ready. It is just that there is no life in it.

He knows that a young woman will be the central character in his novel, the one he thinks of as Eeva-Lisa. She was the one carrying Uncle Aron's child when she fled. There is a precedent for her, though it is not the real Eeva-Lisa, about whom he is not at liberty to speak.

Could reality be used in this way, could two lives be joined? He does not know. He knows how things were for the real young girl who was pregnant and emigrated. She got Parkinson's disease and was found dead in a village on the other side of Obera, and it was written that "in her helpless condition she was eaten alive by rats". What can he do with that? Someone took care of the child, he does not know who. The child dies in the '40s. The mother eaten alive by rats in the jungle!

No-one would believe it. A novelist's invention. He stares at the sentence that will be the last in the book, about the rats starting to eat Eeva-Lisa, *"and finally the first star glimmered on her cheek"*; it was beautiful, but only that. Nothing more.

He is diligent and the colony is loyal with its help. All their testimonies are either heroic or come from a deep sorrow, but they have no connection to him.

It was not just Swedes who fled in the years before the First World War. There was a Finnish colony that came at almost the same time, *Colonia Finlandese*, very close to the Uruguay River. The Finns were quite different, radical intellectuals who fled at the turn of the century for political reasons, from the oppression of the tsar. They behaved like intellectuals. They had never picked up an axe, still less a spade; surviving texts reveal how these Finland-Swedish freedom fighters and refugees from tsarism played the flute, slept with native women and drank themselves to death.

It is very easy to make his way, sometimes in German. Old Nazis lurking in the jungle.

He hitchhikes around in Misiones and one evening he watches Clint Eastwood in a spaghetti western, but the tapes are not in the right order and the film keeps breaking. They have to go out into the dark and have a beer and then go in again and out again, until in the end they all give up. He records his diary entries on a little tape recorder and plays them back when he returns to Sweden.

His voice sounds frightened and alone. Where is he going to go?

There is little point in falling apart.

He is filthy, washes infrequently, the Israeli army bag more and more battered, like a sack of dumplings; he often longs for a dumpling, as it happens. He sleeps badly at night in his strange shelter. He understands that these exiled mine workers from Kiruna did not have the skills required for plantation work in the jungle. *"They were not resistant to the infectious diseases prevalent there either."* A family of eight wiped out within six months; the mother transported home. Four of those to whom he speaks were born in Sweden, but have almost no memory of it and ask what the homeland is like. They have heard a rumour that employers talk to their workers and are benevolent and give everyone work with full wages and that everyone has medical care.

He agrees it is so.

The Danes, who arrived at around the same time, proved they were more sensible by settling five hundred kilometres further south at Pampas *and attained immensurable prosperity*. The Finns drank themselves into oblivion. The Swedes endured on their hard-trodden floors of clay. "Our Fathers' Church" is the most beautiful psalm. How charming to speak with you.

What is it like to live in exile? Dreams of the forsaken country are vivid, as he will soon experience.

In the end he hitchhikes northward, over the Uruguay River on a hand-operated ferry, similar to the one on the Mela stream where it flows into Hjoggböleträsket. Travels through the Rio Grande do Sul, then down along the coast. First buses and finally a flight to Rio.

The voice on the tape recorder more candid now, it notes that the choice of transport, from hitchhiking to flying, signifies apathy.

Without him noticing, expectations have begun to hang their sack of stones around his shoulders.

It is impossible to understand. He has never before been weighed down by expectations.

He was the first person in the village to take the school certificate. He was the first in his family to take the matriculation examination. Not only did he renounce becoming a primary schoolteacher, the pinnacle of the established career ladder, he *continued studying* in Uppsala. He wrote novels. There was no limit to it all. His dead father and Benefactor sat up in heaven with his mouth open, not knowing what to believe. Was it possible? How could Elof's boy do all this all on his own? Against all expectations? No-one would have believed it. From strength to strength.

He would soon be a bishop. Truly an almost biblical miracle.

And no-one could have foreseen this, still less expected it. So why this insane pressure within him? Not even sipping a delicious little glass of Bull's Blood, that unsurpassable Hungarian plonk with its inimitable aftertaste, could alleviate it.

He finds himself the Paganini of massive aborted projects.

The emigration project was not the first to run aground. Towards the end of the '60s he had buried himself in an *epic novel* about Joe Hill, but after almost a year is aware that nothing inside him connects to this story either; besides, other writers seem to have had the same idea. His need for an intrinsic connection is great. He throws out all the material he has about *this Swedish labour hero*, plus 320 typewritten pages of text. He knows that he has had never had an intrinsic connection with this exile drama about Joe Hill.

He should have learnt from his mistakes. But straight into *the Argentina project* regardless.

Finally, one winter's day in January 1976, he realises that it is not working. He looks at the folders of material and outline plots with ab-horrence, almost hatred. He has to give up. He tells himself that if he ever wants to write another novel he will have to destroy all this. And he does.

To hell with several years' work. Bunkum? No. It was bloody painful.

However, later, with rising enthusiasm, almost euphoric joy, he writes a tentative prologue to the ruined emigrant project. Suddenly much of the work he had abandoned on the situation in Bureå at he turn of the century came alive. He can do this. It is his landscape, his village, his family. He does not need to be paralysed by fear at the thought of writing about what is personal to him. He writes a novel called *The March of the Musicians*, about these people before the emigration. He destroys the emigration, but not the people. It is enjoyable, an appalling story about Grandmother Johanna Lindgren and Eeva-Lisa and Uncle Aron, who forced himself down through the ice on Burefjärden with a sack of potatoes as a weight, and Elmgren, the rabble-rouser, who *held the worm in his mouth*, thereby demonstrating to the young Nicanor the needlessness of worm cans. Inconsiderate and ruthless, he gives his family another biography, or he joins two together; it is fiction, but almost true all the same.

He is free; he can do as he wishes.

He has finished it in a year. This is the prologue, but it will never be followed by anything else. No emigration, no sand fleas, no jungle, no rats eating the paralysed girl. Just the story of a family in the Väster-botten coastland, and the birth of the labour movement in circumstances that should not have been as they were. It ends with their departure, at the railway station in Bastuträsk, and the word "signal".

In the spring of 1978 he submits the book. He is happy. He is firmly convinced that this is just the first in a series of novels, it has all been released now and he is free to write the sequel, which will be a key to the unconcealed.

How wrong he is.

Sometimes he writes a diary.

His son Mats has his eye poked out while he is playing; his diary is full of this.

Came home late and Mats still awake. The following morning he
says he wants me to collect him from school at three o'clock, refused
for reasons of principle. Now it's just a question of not accentuating
his insecurity. He's afraid of the dark. Partly natural fear about his
eye, scared the other one will disappear too, partly fear of being left
alone; he has nightmares about this. Alone in the darkness. M.
wants me to write a novel about people who are not very clever.

"Refused for reasons of principle"! What a terrifying phrase.

He takes pleasure in recording the days without a bottle of wine. He has an almost scientific control over his alcohol consumption now. The so-called IB affair has blown up in Sweden, with disclosure that a secret military organisation runs the intelligence agency, without the knowledge and control of the government, and keeps records of communists in the workplace. It is published in *Folket i Bild/Kulturfront*, a left-wing newspaper that he finds sharply reminiscent of the West German *Konkret*, apart from the fact that the German publication eventually, in response to shrinking circulation, capitulates to commercial forces and publishes photographs of naked women, who for ideological reasons, however, are skinny and have a slightly bluish tinge, to highlight the vulnerability and exploitation of these women; they also have a serial under the title "Let's Get Laid, Comrade!".

This is unthinkable, and it does not happen, in *FiB/Kulturfront*, which is governed by idealism and Jan Myrdal; several years later, when a downturn in the economy and falling circulation brings an attempt to widen the readership, a few of the Social Democrat Party faithful are added to the board as security, himself included. He understands the role he has to play, that of thin, blue-tinged nude photograph, the Social Democrat naked model led astray perhaps, but all the same he is pleased with this encouragement from the Communist Party of Sweden and accepts for the greater good.

The IB affair is painful and really not Social Democracy's finest hour.

In actual fact the affair is detestable and is badly managed by the

Social Democrat government. The IB affair is a symptom of sickness, and sick phenomena are difficult to handle; Olof Palme, who is now prime minister, survives the scandal that ends with two journalists, Peter Bratt and Jan Guillou, being sentenced to a year in prison for espionage.

It disturbs everything, including people on the periphery, such as himself. His loyalty to the party is shaken. With Lars Gustafsson he mobilises German friends in West Berlin to write in protest; he and Lars, friends from the time of the Rothvik sisters' demise, go to Magnus Enzensberger's flat in Berlin and together the three of them compose a text that is later signed by Enzensberger, Uwe Johnson, Günther Grass, Heinrich Böll and Max Frisch. In Enzensberger's cool, ironic and uncompromising prose, thorny questions are put to Palme about his responsibility for eroding faith in Swedish democracy.

Olof Palme, who is extremely jealous of his international reputation, is quite rightly furious and goes through the roof. The discreet involvement of the two Swedes is naturally not disclosed.

It is, from his safe position on the edge, a successful operation that makes him feel slightly uncomfortable. His loyalty is divided. That the extreme left delights in the IB affair is one thing, but he has no pleasure in sticking a knife into Palme's back.

Paranoia grows throughout the autumn.

There are rumours that remain unconfirmed, and after the arrests of Bratt and Guillou anything is possible. He is one of the speakers at a large public meeting in parliament; the following day Supreme Commander Stig Synnergren rings and angrily tells him that he will sue Enquist for libel.

It is a chaotic conversation. He cannot really remember what might have been libellous in what he said in parliament, but he does remember once meeting Synnergren, Sweden's highest ranking military officer, on the Kungsleden hiking trail in northern Sweden, west of the Kebnekaise mountain and south of the Singi hut, and that he looked friendly and very fit, and that they exchanged a comradely greeting. Should he mention this? But the Supreme Commander will not be interrupted and finally, as he pauses briefly for breath, Enquist sheepishly points out that he did fifteen months of military service in I:20 in Umeå, and passed out with the grade of staff sergeant, but was not offered a post in the armed forces, which he finds strange.

A short, bemused pause ensues, and then Synnergren roars that this is a serious matter and Enquist should not try to make a joke of it. Which in fact he had not tried to do. It was simply an attempt at human contact. But it leads nowhere and the Supreme Commander slams down the receiver.

The conversation does not lead to prosecution.

Is he nervous? Yes, maybe.

The atmosphere is charged and anything seems possible. One morning he receives a call from the Court of Appeals judge, Jan Gehlin, who is also chairman of the Writers' Union and has been his colleague on the committee for a number of years; he says it is rumoured that several writers will have their homes searched. Evidently Enquist is amongst them. He honestly does not know why, but he is suddenly struck by the thought that he had brought some marijuana seeds back home from his time in U.C.L.A. to number 1 Jägarvägen in Uppsala. He had placed them in a flowerpot, in which they had grown and become a handsome plant standing in the window facing the road, Jägarvägen in Uppsala. He is seized by a panic *typical of the time*, rushes home, takes a pair of scissors and cuts up the marijuana plant and flushes the beautiful leaves down the toilet.

He clearly remembers the green leaves disappearing, under the quizzical gaze of Jenny, six, and Mats, twelve. He does not answer their questions.

In his diary just a short entry with a *cryptic* account of what he has done.

Other storms of a political nature soon follow, in which he is more directly involved. Public political debate becomes a kind of drug and he cannot stop himself joining in. He is constantly angry and therefore he writes. Not books now. But articles.

And later drama.

It is after *The Night of the Tribades*; he would really like to continue writing for the theatre. He begins a collaborative work with the writer Anders Ehnmark, which, off and on, and sometimes at long intervals, will last almost his whole life.

The period is 1976 and onwards, and the IB affair is in its way the starting point for a tumultuous time. The optimistic dreams about permanent growth take a knock, New Liberalism emerges, the New Left's old criticism of the Social Democrats' lack of vision is revived, the working class is betrayed, and on this point the interests of the land of real socialism, that is the Soviet Union, and those of the left, converge. Mysterious submarines of undisclosed provenance are said to be nosing around in the archipelago; they might be Soviet, might be N.A.T.O., or might be otters and dolphins. It is the time of Palme-hating, years when it is fashionable to say that Sweden has actually become fascist and that it is going the way of the G.D.R. and that only in Albania does such oppression exist. At the same time the left, paradoxically, loses interest in politics; intellectuals are deadly serious when they say that emigration is inevitable, and not just for tax reasons.

In short, the time is ripe for satirical political writings.

He knows Ehnmark well, but not personally. He recollects that Ehnmark reviewed his second book *The Route* in the *Expressen*; with a sharpened butcher's knife, perhaps a machete, he had hacked this intelligent, technically complex, in parts *sound* but completely unreadable novel into very thin slices, with a characteristically concise sensitivity for language; and then Ehnmark had disappeared from his view.

In the press and in published books he had followed Ehnmark's progress from a distance. He seems to have been the Rome correspondent with responsibility for about half the southern hemisphere, which was quite possible in Rome, then he left the *Expressen* to work for a year on the communist daily *Norrskensflamman* in Luleå, in Sweden's most northerly province, with his wife-to-be, Annika Hagström. It was a remarkable newspaper; it had not given in to the *left's expedient hatred* for Soviet real socialism, but had managed, in its accounts of the Soviet Union, to realise the communist utopia, *though visible only from Luleå*, a utopia that was characterised in the *Flamman* by splendid medical care, well-managed kindergartens and fields full of gorgeous sunflowers.

The sunflowers are regularly displayed in pictures.

The Stockholm duo make a valiant attempt during this year to correct the picture, give the Soviet utopia a darker hue, which the decent comrades on the *Flamman* accept, because they like Ehnmark/Hagström very much. The fields of sunflowers disappear. When, after a year in Norrbotten, they leave their comrades to go and live in a lilac cottage south of Stockholm and get married, on their way through Piteå they buy the latest issue of the *Flamman* and note that the sunflowers are back.

Anders and Annika will become his friends for life.

Writing was lonely. Not writing was even worse. In actual fact, sheer hell.

Maybe with someone else?

Anders is writing a satirical novel about journalism, *Potful of Sweets*. In 1976 there is advance publication of a chapter from the novel in *Dagens Nyheter*. He reads it. It is very funny and nasty in a slightly unusual way; he rings Ehnmark and suggests they write a play together. About the media, about journalism, and power. Maybe also about financial crime and ownership interests in the Swedish newspaper market, and the consequences.

And that is how they start.

Their working method is easily explained.

In front of a typewriter they are both fundamentally afraid of other people, they hate it if someone looks over their shoulder, questions about whether *it's going well* can bring on mental breakdown, children are not allowed to snoop, wives are not allowed to look at the pages. They send letters to each other; there is a moderate distance between

Uppsala and Nykvarn, about two hundred kilometres. This is still a time when letters are dispatched and delivered. When the letter arrives with the text, the text is rewritten and sent back. The letters that end up in each of their two folders eventually reach 750 pages, their source material; the content is funny, true, obscene, highly interesting, and completely unprintable. From this a play will come.

They both find that the collaboration works. They write in totally different ways. Together they can create satire. Both suffer from the curse of a good nature, but together they can develop a darker side. Their guiding principle is absolute honesty, and that the highest offer will always be accepted, without exception, like a rural auction; he soon discovers that Ehnmark, like himself, has nothing to lose. Personal copyright to ideas or suggestions must not exist, but they are all flung into a common pot and laundered together, like the money in the financial crimes that are surfacing more and more at this time and which to a certain extent become the theme of the play they are writing.

It has the title *Chez Nous*.

The play will be the starting point for a long series of highly publicised disputes that in many ways will change both their lives. They do not know it yet, when, with frivolous exhilaration and a certain degree of brutal recklessness, they write this didactic satire about the media world they both know so well.

Chez Nous is completed in the summer of 1976.

With commendable speed it is taken up by the director at the Royal Dramatic, Jan-Olof Strandberg, who mobilises the theatre's star cast, led by Ernst-Hugo Järegård and Jan Malmsjö; it is already on the main stage by November and is a *succès de scandale*, due to Matts Carlgren's threats of libel action. He is the director of the forestry company MoDo, and therefore responsible for the closure of a sawmill in Bureå; a few unfavourable comments are made about him in the play, more specifically that a sawmill-butcher like him should not be president of the Swedish Athletics Association. This wounds the sports lover so deeply he wants to stop the play, which in its turn releases the violent forces of the media defence mechanism, so that now it is almost impossible for anything at all to stop the play; the result is that Skådebanan ticket office still has queues a kilometre long when *Chez Nous* finally has to close at the beginning of spring.

They discover for the first time, but not the last, that nothing is as viable as a thing that is close, extremely close, to being stopped. The little space between *almost* and *stopped* is the media's erogenous zone. In future the word "stopped" will accompany the three plays they write together.

Chez Nous sparks a furious year-long debate about financial crime and media responsibility; an eruption of outrage and assurances that from now on it will all be different and that no-one is guilty in the shocking way suggested in the play. After a year it all quietens down and nothing has changed, everything is as it was before, only worse. It is edifying.

He is only rattled once.

The play is being discussed in a live television confrontation on the news programme "Kvällsöppet", with the lawyer Henning Sjöström leading the MoDo troops. Once a prominent javelin thrower of seventy metres in Bureå I.F. and the national team, he is almost in tears as he pleads with his club mate Enquist and his friend to *just remove five words, which have no significance at all artistically*, and he is indeed totally right; of course they refuse, because the dispute is now a matter of honour so that retreat or even gentle common sense are utterly out of the question.

A question of principle emerges. To a certain extent in conflict with harsh reality.

The incident that shakes him, although only slightly, almost not at all, is that after the live debate a man of about fifty comes up to him and says he worked for twenty years at Bure Bolag, and they were the worst years of his life in a dirty, monotonous, badly paid job that he is now liberated from, thank God, and in his view the more sawmills or pulp mills that are closed down and replaced by people-friendly work the better, and he is wholly on the side of Matts Carlgren, for whom he has great respect as a leading sportsman.

Enquist recalls the two summers spent under the bark drum at the pulp mill and cannot but agree with him.

As luck would have it the man does not speak in the debate.

The dispute soon focuses on the function of theatre with regard to freedom of expression, and ambiguity about whose is the responsibility for publication; in short, who will go to prison if the play is brought down.

Many volunteer to take this responsibility, including obviously the authors. According to the law in force at the time, anyone who has anything at all to do with the performance can be called to account; the threat of prosecution can sweep like a searchlight over the whole company, causing great consternation over where it will come to rest. Perhaps on an actor, the one who utters the words for which the authors are morally responsible.

In the case of *Chez Nous* it will induce a run of sickness in one of the main roles. The actor who is to play the sawmill worker from Bureå and deliver the offensive lines about Carlgren's unsuitability as president of the Athletics Association is inexplicably taken ill, as is his replacement. New sawmill workers are rehearsed, but fall ill, until finally the director reads the part *from the script*, before a spellbound audience.

Meanwhile, behind the hysteria lurks a real problem, as everyone can see. The "*Chez Nous* test case" underlies the proposal for a new law for theatres that the Freedom of Speech Inquiry will later abandon, and to which, incidentally, Ehnmark was called.

You could call it the *Chez Nous* Act.

Chez Nous causes him personal conflicts as well.

The plot concerns a newspaper editorial team investigating a case of financial crime. In the first act their fact-finding uncovers a dreadful tale. Despite the beautiful background music, Mahler or Albinoni, and the elevated rhetoric, it is eventually abundantly clear to the entire audience that the activity the journalists are exposing is the porn industry. Specifically: sex in an aquarium between a poor prostitute and an eel; the latter with jaws taped together in a nod to animal protection.

But the most shocking part is something else: in the end they are investigating themselves. It is the newspaper proprietors they unmask.

If the first act is an uncovering, the second act is a cover-up; a series of increasingly brilliant intellectual deliberations over why the truth cannot be published.

If you want to lie, the best arguments are always intellectual ones. Finally they all agree that silence is imperative, as if they are fighting for freedom of speech.

The agency responsible for the uncovering and the covering-up is a newspaper. The *Expressen* feels, possibly wrongly, that the finger is pointing at them. The target might have been the intellectual hypocrisy that exists throughout the media, but is essentially a far bigger question, the freedom of journalism, proprietors' control of information, real constraints of freedom of speech, perhaps even the very lifeblood of democracy itself. Enquist, who is on the staff of the culture pages, receives an intimidating letter from Petrini, the deputy editor, asking how Enquist can "let his mouth spit while his hand takes charity and job security".

To call it *charity* is too much.

He has never considered his monthly salary in this light. Nor that his extraordinary *freedom* on the culture pages should act as a restraint, a straitjacket. He finds that he can neither write nor think under these conditions. He sends a letter of resignation to the board.

For several weeks the row is very distressing. Editor-in-chief Per Wrigstad invites him to lunch and asks him to mend his ways; in a few months he will step down and be succeeded by Bo Strömstedt, who is in despair over the situation.

But he does not want to mend his ways. That's just it. He does not really understand it himself. He likes the newspaper, and Strömstedt is his friend. But something inside him is saying: No. In many ways he finds himself breaking away, and he does not want to look back.

They write political satire and everything they do seems to result in media controversy, almost always a box-office hit.

It is not planned, but the outcry they provoke is funny at first, and then after a while not quite so funny. The number of enemies rises sharply. But he enjoys writing with Anders, who is possibly even shyer than he is, though not in the written word. Their collaboration produces almost one thousand pages of letters, a fascinating chronicle of the time, in their opinion, and of course completely unprintable.

It is thought-provoking. The unprintable side of public debate.

The next play they write is *The Man in the Street*, about the left. It is a vicious and highly informed piece; they were both absent from Sweden during the revolutionary days of 1968, but viewed the revolt from their respective European vantage points, Anders from Rome and the hub of the Red Brigade's activity, and he from Berlin and the Baader-Meinhof.

They are both agreed that the play is enormously funny and in many ways accurate, at any rate true. It portrays the type of leftist self-criticism that fifteen years later is alleged never to have existed.

The Man in the Street is performed on the Målarsalen stage at the Royal Dramatic Theatre; the national stage is now their home and the natural arena for the political drama they write. The play elicits intense debate and TV2 wants to televise it and follow the broadcast from the Målarsalen with a discussion. Although the action of the play takes place in turn of the century St Petersburg, and is a fictional account of the trial of Sasanov, the young terrorist and suicide bomber who assassinated the Interior Minister, Doctor Plehve, the witnesses called at this trial are drawn from contemporary Sweden, easily recognisable and prominent characters from the Swedish left and, to a certain extent, the German.

For this critique of elitism in the extreme left to be performed on the the Royal Dramatic Theatre's smallest stage, the Målarsalen, before an audience the size of a Soviet central committee, is one thing. One of the authors is obviously a Social Democrat, and the other is an active long-serving member of the Swedish Communists, the V.P.K. Neither of them is an enemy of the left. But to roll out this piece of leftist self-criticism, however much it may be needed, to the people – this causes consternation in the company.

Would people at home in their armchairs, who can hardly be expected to have the intellectual capacity of the higher echelons of the left, take kindly to this discussion, and would they draw the right conclusions and not leap to a hasty verdict?

If anything, the problem was: would the left take kindly to people participating in this?

That the debate among those on the left is conducted before the elite itself, in the Målarsalen, is one thing. Maybe even praiseworthy. *But the general public?*

The thing that the inexperienced Matts Carlgren failed to do, that is to say, halt a theatre production, succeeds in this case.

The outside broadcasting vans have already driven up from Malmö, but the day before transmission the play is stopped. The cast refuses to perform. The two playwrights obviously go on the offensive in the media, and are applauded by the right, but in so doing lose some honourable and intelligent friends, among them the acclaimed actor Allan Edwall. On the stage in the Målarsalen he gives an unbelievably funny portrayal of General Armfäldt, a leading figure in the fight to save elms. Unfortunately Edwall is also a central figure in the fight against the televised broadcast of *The Man in the Street*.

The play is taken off. No staging in the Målarsalen, no television broadcast.

A highly poisonous situation. A prominent left-wing friend meets Enquist on the street, grabs him by the lapels, shouting, in rage or despair, it is hard to know which, "What the fuck are you doing?"

Anders Ehnmark's wife, Annika, observes the two furious but ostensibly successful playwrights over the breakfast table and says laconically that *the end result of this dispute is effectively that you are now the sworn enemies of Allan Edwall.*

They consider this in silence. Was it worth it? Was political theatre doomed to end up as something intensely personal?

It is like a curse. Everything they do is nearly stopped, or it is stopped, or they stop it themselves.

They write a play for TV2 drama, *Speculum Principum*, about media logic steering public debate, about written and unwritten rules governing the battle for minds. It is a play about men and women of economic and political power trying to adapt to media manipulation. In short, a manual for politicians and policy-makers, like mirrors for kings, the little textbooks that taught young princes the logic of power.

The protagonists all bear their real names, which is unusual for this time. Among them is His Majesty the King, who, along with the others, has a media problem, or perhaps he has just been allotted the wrong role by the media, or quite simply has been lied to. The media machine has dictated that he will bake ginger biscuits once a year and otherwise look kind. In the play he is transformed into a brilliant intellectual of startling ability and his extensive reading astounds other rulers.

The play was recorded and the intention was to broadcast it in three parts. At a run-through the authors discovered the play had been substantially rewritten, an ambitious director having made his own interpretation of the media problem. The play that emerged was completely reworked, one character had disappeared and his lines shared between other actors, and new passages had been written. Amongst other things, the King's role had been totally changed.

He had been thoroughly remoulded.

In the original play he had been a sort of metaphor, his personality freed from the media image that determined how he was viewed. The television controllers had reacted violently to this intelligent, gifted person. It was generally acknowledged that the King was stupid, an assumption fed by the media. Therefore, in the interests of realism, the King had to be rendered stupid. Thus the King had been endowed with stupidity and his brilliant attributes conferred on others.

The lance the authors thought they had hurled at the media and publicity-mongers miraculously twists in the air and instead strikes His Majesty the King in the chest.

Thereupon the two playwrights call a halt. Writers had been known in the past to protest with different degrees of intensity about fundamental distortions of their work, but had never stopped a performance before. Still less one that had cost millions to produce. This action is taken with reference to the Copyright Act, which states that "a work may not be altered in such a way that would be prejudicial to the author's literary or artistic reputation or personality".

In consequence TV2 withdraws the three programmes and re-schedules with some repeats of English detective dramas. Unsurprisingly this draws attention. That December the tabloid headlines blare:

KING
STUPID
SAYS TV

When they visit Television House the two authors sense a certain coolness towards them, but it passes. They go on to write a detective novel together, *Dr Mabuse's New Testament*, that too a satire, about the political world in the mid '80s.

In this skirmish yet more friends have to be counted as lost. The book is a huge commercial success, but in *Månadsjournalen* an enraged critic nominates it as one of the ten worst novels ever written, along with *Finnegan's Wake* and something by Dostoyevsky. Another critic says that the book made him depressed, because "a searching piece of social criticism in literature only hits the nail on the head in a book of light fiction".

On the other hand, it was easier to withstand perpetual storms than to wait, immobilised, for nothing. And more nothing. And finally still nothing.

Satire comes from the Latin word for fruit bowl, *satura*, he learns from Anders.

A dish of mixed fruits offered to the gods; later the word was used in a figurative sense to denote unexpected meetings, contrasts, to distinguish the indistinguishable and reconcile the irreconcilable, i.e. create a surprise. For the Etruscans, a satirical play to the accompaniment of flutes was believed to drive out the plague. The supposition seems to have been that man, in the form of satire, can, by standing very close to the plague and secretly and shamefully almost liking it, delude it and make it disappear, rather like the Pied Piper of Hamelin.

It may be true. They are both very close to the media world they satirise. They are a part of it. Maybe they secretly love and admire it, at least they like observing it, this world of strange laws and ruthless subtexts.

It was like the theatre. He could never write about an evil person with credibility if he did not like him.

Perhaps he identified with him.

He continues writing for television on his own, a six-hour television series, *Strindberg: A Life*.

Its premiere is in 1981, but at that point he has already moved away. He lives in Denmark. His private life has been turned upside down. He has divorced, left his wife and two children, and is now living with his Danish wife, Lone Bastholm. That happens in 1978. They marry at the town hall along with nine Pakistani couples in a fast-moving queue. He is very happy, but feels as though he is skating on thin ice. He still has many friends who might not have been lost, but now are very far away. Sometimes he gives a shout, like an animal's cry through the ice, but he controls himself, he knows he has to take risks, he does so, and he is happy, and scared.

He will not return to Sweden until 1993, fifteen years later. This is real exile.

He will become someone else, and his life will become a different one.

PART THREE

INTO THE DARKNESS

CHAPTER 12

RAINWORM

He lives in Denmark for fifteen years.

The divorce is finalised in June 1978. He leaves his two children as well. The boy, who is called Mats, is sixteen years old and will later forgive him for this.

The girl, Jenny, is still only nine, and looks uncertainly at the gap he leaves behind.

He assumes that she too does not bear him a grudge. *Children don't understand what's happening.* Of course they have understood everything, but are helpless. He compliments his own parents on their short but intense marriage, death the only culprit, its happy legacy a child. That is his position. His current position.

For the last year the girl has seemed anxious, with strange nervous tics. They take her to a family psychotherapist, who, after two sessions, states that the problem lies with the parents, not their daughter. He believes this diagnosis to be correct. He takes the first flight to Oslo, where his Danish wife-to-be is working for two months in radio drama; they borrow a flat from a director who says his name is Stein Winge. He spends the days sitting alone in the very fine apartment, coming to a decision about whether or not he can instigate a new life.

It is a hot summer. He starts reading a number of books. He does not know if his wife-to-be is ecstatic or horror-stricken at suddenly sharing a new life with him.

There is nothing to add about his time in Oslo. He should be able to make something up, but why? he asks in his silent turmoil.

He is not sure if the fifteen years in a new land can count as actual reality, or the perceived reality of fiction.

He decides that Denmark is a province of Sweden, albeit a southerly one, and therefore he need never learn the Danish language. His wife Lone speaks Danish to him, he speaks Swedish to her. After a while he stops noticing the difference. Since general opinion in the new country is that Sweden is a land of prohibition, worthy of comparison only with Albania and the G.D.R., he is at pains to discover prohibitions in the new southern Swedish district of Denmark. Happily he finds numerous examples. His view is that a good person cannot be created by laws, but a bad person can be restrained by sanctions. Like a nasty heifer. He devotes a great deal of time and effort to observing the mandatory Swedish requirement for safety belts. His argument is economic: he does not want the hospital bills of the careless paid with his taxes. He says he does not care about life and suffering. As time goes by he finds that Denmark is not as round, humorous and good-natured as he had thought, and it makes him love his new homeland all the more. He believes himself to be living in exile, but since his new exile is self-imposed, it is not thrilling and awful, like Thomas Mann's.

He fumbles along.

His new wife becomes manager of the Royal Danish Theatre, a glorious colossus; it does not weigh him down like a burden, but fills his life. It is possible to live in the world of the theatre and be immersed; he is immersed. It has nothing to do with the world of the novel. It is another planet, with other people. The only novel he writes is a very short text of 140 pages, a love story, about a two-headed monster, Pasqual Pinon and his Maria. They live joined together, she moves her mouth but no words come forth; if anyone hurts her *she sings her pain*. It is quite soundless, but he can hear. The novel describes a completely normal marriage, it says in the book's blurb on the back cover, which he has written himself.

It is a thin book and it is a miracle it was written at all, at that time in the mid '80s. He could write for an hour or two in the mornings, when he was sober, and then nothing at all; that was the pattern.

In the afternoons, when he is drinking, the world stands still, milky white. He sleeps a lot, always dropping off with an almost happy smile; when he awakens an hour later the milky whiteness has gone and he feels cold. He slowly begins to understand he has a problem. But there are a few hours in the morning when everything is hellishly clear and sharp, like after a shower of ice-cold rain, and those are the hours he uses to work.

His marriage is blessed. They have several very happy years. Yet he observes, to begin with merely in passing, that very seldom is he able to write. It comes sometimes, suddenly, like an attack, and then it disappears. There is no explanation.

The Danish period lasts from 1978 to 1993, he owns a *ficus benjamina* that stubbornly dies, he has abandoned two children, he experiences great success as a dramatist, and he feels as though he is skating on thin ice.

It draws nearer. He tries to dodge it.

Regarding the *ficus benjamina*: the leaves kept falling off, like a warning sign, the indications of which he ignored completely and contemptuously. He had left Sweden in June 1978 and in August moved into a small two-roomed flat with his Danish wife-to-be; it was in style a rather girly apartment. He intends to start writing a novel, as yet untitled, possibly *Captain Nemo's Library*, but all that emerges is a kind of ballad in twelve verses called "Malin Häggström's Lullaby".

Nemo is *enveloped* by his fifteen years in Denmark. In a similar way he is also contained, trapped in a vessel in the volcanic cone. He cannot make a start on *Nemo*. It makes him furious but he resigns himself. Finally, fifteen years later, he writes the book. He ends the novel defiantly with the assertion: "*This is how it was, this is how it happened, and this is the whole story.*" Then it would be over. Never again would he write a novel, he declares. So stupid.

After six months he and his wife move to 25 Sortedam Dossering in Nørrebro. Not much to write home about, he used to think, a place, a new place, a kind of restlessness. His family has always lived in the same place for centuries. The same village; the only one to undertake a journey was his grandfather, to the fur exhibition in Stockholm in 1930. That was the time he and his fox travelled. But what could explain the dreadful anxiety in so many of his relatives about *where someone came from*?

People in his family *were nervous and stayed where they were*. He is nervous and moves about.

All of a sudden he wants to write a love story, because he believes he understands all about love. For the first time. It turns quite naturally into a novel about a monster. It can happen.

On the floor below lives a Mr Clausen, seventy years old, or thereabouts.

Enquist, now forty-four, is a Swede who has chosen of his own free will to live in Denmark. To the Danish public, who are usually critical of their big brother in the northeast, this is staggering but reassuring, and escape from the country in the northeast is viewed as a sign of the times.

This makes him well-nigh loved.

He writes a play about the great Danish actress Mrs Heiberg and her despised and adored Hans Christian Andersen, called *From the Lives of Rainworms*. Thanks to brilliant performances by Ghita Nørby and Jørgen Reenberg, the Swede's interpretation is accepted without the slightest hint of condescension.

All at once a new homeland. Everyone agrees it is an established fact he has found a new homeland.

He feels established, but thinks he is skating on thin ice.

Denmark is wide open like a wind-torn plain and he scarcely comprehends a thing. You can walk over a plain with your eyes shut, but not through a forest. It baffles him, makes him uncertain. There must be secrets he does not understand.

He reads *Ekstra Bladet* the whole time in an attempt to understand the country in which he is now to live. There, in this tabloid, can be found life's dregs, the filth and sleaze that will help him understand his new country – that is his vague idea. Once again he has the impression that the compass is spinning, as it does at the North Pole. He knows there might be a mistake, and it is his, and that the truth about him will soon come out. And then.

Outside the house at 25 Sortedam Dossering there is a small garden, in which to sit and drink a beer; as the years pass he learns to take his beer in a teacup, to avoid gossip.

Mr Clausen keeps him company.

In the evenings he makes a note of Mr Clausen's opinions, for he hopes to find in them the key to his new homeland. He can still write, to a limited extent; it happens during those surprisingly clear morning hours.

He is convinced that he has met his match in Mr Clausen. *Mr Clausen once had a shard of glass in his eye.*

Mr Clausen knows that the Swede is a writer and wants to teach him something about Denmark; this includes knowledge of Danish literature, especially Hans Christian Andersen. He recounts some of Andersen's fairy tales, peppered with hazy details, particularly "The Snow Queen", but some of them seem in his version to have some-how imploded, as if they had been forced inwards by some immense outer pressure, or sucked together by an inner vacuum.

Mr Clausen needs interpreting.

He regrets the loss of friends in Uppsala.

On the telephone news reaches him of great disquiet. He had a very wide circle of friends and acquaintances, all married for years, and his abrupt flight caused shock. Is it an omen? Does it herald the break-up of other marriages?

Mr Clausen likes the Swede. He likes to confide in him. He talks about Danishness. Then he disappears for a time, seems to be hiding, comes back, ashen-faced, and joins the beer-drinking Swede and his teacup. You have to make sense of it, guess at connections. It becomes more and more important to see connections.

In the evenings the Swede notes down fragments of Mr Clausen's monologues.

His life has *really not been empty and not without pain*. In confidence – because the immigrant is Swedish and has not yet mastered the Danish language and therefore cannot divulge his secrets – Clausen lets it be known that at the age of forty-eight he had a love affair with Gerda Hansen, a clerk living at that time at 14 Blaagaardsgade, Nørrebro. It lasted a year. Then his wife found out about it and it came to an end. As the Swede is a poet, his standards are doubtless more libertarian, and that is why he wants to confide in him.

Later it becomes clear to him that Gerda was Mr Clausen's sister, a piece of information that was not calculated to reach him.

The garden is small and they speak in low voices.

Mr Clausen is maybe six feet tall, weighs around 120 kilos and does not give the impression of having a poetic nature and therefore being someone who might quite naturally have lived in an incestuous relationship with his sister. As they sit in the little garden at 25 Sortedam Dossering, two men in conversation, they must have looked to passers-by like a trusting couple exchanging confidences. He with his teacup of Elephant beer, Mr Clausen with his Tuborg and his air of retired accountant.

The latter's intuition has been right. He has understood that the Swede is unbalanced, finds himself in the course of a long journey and lacking a benefactor's support.

The garden, the teacup and Mr Clausen. He himself is between forty-four and fifty-nine years old. He seems to find it more and more difficult to see where he is now, in the middle of his life. He has sought out the natural geographical location for the mid-point of his life, and that is Nørrebro. From here he can go in any direction at all.

This is the area with the highest migrant population in Scandinavia, the nucleus of riots and attacks. This is the time of organised revolutions, but the notion of "organised" has not yet reached Nørrebro, where squats and demonstrations are commonplace. Sitting in his garden, with his teacup and Mr Clausen's confessions, he is *surrounded* by Sortedammen to the south and Fælleden to the east; Fælleden is the open field where in 1772 Johann Friedrich Struensee was executed, broken on a wheel and emasculated. It is classic ground for the theatre of atrocity. But this pastoral garden is the fashionable edge of Nørrebro, the houses facing Sortedammen *the best of the worst*, they used to say to him, turned towards the idyllic expanse of water and away from the uproar and unrest.

He loves Nørrebro, because here is so close to the sordid side of life, but – at the fashionable edge – still safe. Nørrebro is the huge district in north Copenhagen that remained undeveloped until the mid-nineteenth century, actually just an expanse of clear-felled land north of Vallarna, the artillery ranges that had to be kept open in case of attack from enemies in the north. Swedes, for example.

He recalls *Soldier in the Field* and pictures shooting angles.

There are fantastic Nørrebro paintings of ethereal pastoral beauty from this period of wide-open space in the mid-eighteenth century: but suddenly a need had arisen for more housing for workers. They threw together tenement buildings in Nørrebro, built of poor-quality brick. They are constructed as a six-storey house in a square, within this is a further square house, and so on until the final house furthest in.

It was cheapest like that. They were built like boxes, one inside the other, and Copenhagen's entire working class could be crammed in. Eventually immigrants moved there, Indians, Pakistanis and Somalis, and of course he himself; though at the fashionable edge, facing Sortedammen, where it was pretty.

Knut Hamsun lived there in the 1880s. He was living on a side street called St Hans Gade when he wrote *Hunger*, in flat six, now a brothel; it was only a hundred metres from the idyllic spot where he and Mr Clausen were sitting.

A nice Pakistani small-businessman with a shop on St Hans Gade sold wine illegally. The bottles were stored behind a yellow plastic curtain. When it became difficult, and he had to have some, he went there. As he came through the door he calmly held up two fingers and his Pakistani friend silently bent down and gathered up two bottles of white wine as if nothing had happened.

He increasingly views Mr Clausen as a figure in a future novel, but he does not know how he will disguise him. Meaning hide him. He tentatively conceals this disquiet in the white wine acquired from his Pakistani friend.

Mr Clausen seems eager to hint at a great injustice.

It was distressing to be discovered by his wife, he said with an irritated laugh that was hard to interpret; he had not been living on Sortedam Dossering at that time. His understanding of what happened was that Mr Clausen and his sister were kissing in Mr Clausen's then kitchen in Frederiksberg, when his wife Bettina (née Eriksen), who was taking her usual daytime nap, awoke and heard a noise from the kitchen. *She had heard a noise from the kitchen.*

It had to be interpreted. Was that his purpose in life, to interpret, if he could no longer write? His interpretation was that Mr Clausen and his Gerda had been standing there, in broad daylight, and sister Gerda, who should have been helping prepare the evening meal, had her hands inside Mr Clausen's trousers. Mrs Bettina Clausen (née Eriksen) could see before her the familiar sight of Mr Clausen's willy, being massaged in his sister's little fist. It was Mr Clausen's willy that was familiar, as was his sister's chubby little hand, but not the two in combination. *We were just having a cuddle but my wife got the wrong idea.* Sibling love was something pure, but it could be misunderstood.

He nodded sagely. He himself had been assistant director to Vilgot Sjöman when he was shooting his film about incest, *My Sister My Love*.

With some effort he recalls that Bibi Andersson and Jarl Kulle had been the film's stars, out of reach. He talked it over with his best friend, the stills photographer Jan Halldoff, who would later direct the film based on *Chez Nous*, or *Shaynoo* as Halldoff called it. Was it in 1965 that he submitted the screenplay? He has difficulty remembering. Did it really happen? *What a lot I've been involved in!* It is shrouded in a haze, like the morning mist over the lake beyond his desk, and then the mist lifts and all that is left is the water. How is it all connected?

Mr Clausen's wife had got the wrong idea.

She shrieked like a crow and ran.

He tries to interpret the intimations that follow. *She shrieked and ran.* They caught up with her. Only an hour before dinner should have been served (it was delayed because of illness) the two lovers made an outright confession. They liked each other. Nothing more. Lingering irritation?

Mr Clausen refrained from saying how long, but it was at least a year. Full intercourse, cheating, secrets? *Gerda and I had always liked each other and it was quite natural.* To emphasise the natural, Mr Clausen asked if he had had a sister. He said he had not, but he did have a foster sister, Eeva-Lisa.

Mr Clausen asked him if he liked her; it was a trick question, he said he did, and Mr Clausen nodded in satisfaction.

It was the case that he and Gerda had deceived Bettina. She had felt crushed. But after their "exposure", Mr Clausen had had a reasoned and honest discussion with his wife and they had jointly decided not to cause a scandal. A few years earlier he had been politically active in the Frederiksberg municipality, where the taxation rates (referring only to municipal taxes) were known to be nearly 5 per cent lower than Nørrebro's (an enormous city district populated by wogs and Arabs who, according to him, due to their low or non-existent tax base, weakened the foundation for an enduring welfare state) – and husband and wife had agreed that a scandal would damage his and Frederiksberg's hitherto untarnished reputations.

Scandal? If it had been a pure unalloyed sibling love? It did not follow.

He knew he was sinking.

The windows in the flat looked out on to Sortedammen. During the day he sat at his desk staring at the water. There were swans. He noted their aggressive behaviour.

Often he would lift his arm as if to strike a key, but came to his senses.

Opposite, on the other side of the lake, he could see Copenhagen Municipal Hospital and, slightly to the right, the house with towers and pinnacles in which Johanne Luise Heiberg, the legendary actress he would later write about in *From the Lives of Rainworms*, had locked herself away. As his deranged great grandmother, Brita Margareta, had once done, *recording her life* by scratching words on the walls with a nail. There, on the other side of Sortedammen, Mrs Heiberg had confined herself for the last thirty years of her life.

That was where she wrote her memoirs, *A Life*.

If Mrs Heiberg had in her turn ventured over the lake she would have seen the place, a whorehouse with licence to serve alcohol, where she was born and where her Jewish mother, Mrs Pätges, worked. Her memoirs were examined by her friends before publication and abridged, so that none of life's obscenity should taint her memory. The deleted sections were published later in a separate volume, long and short extracts containing the forbidden. It had to be so.

He lifted his arm to press the key, but no.

He ponders over Mr Clausen's reminiscences, their connection to the deleted parts of Mrs Heiberg's life. It is harder and harder to discern what is true, and what is a veil of compassion. At the culmination of her own brilliant career, Mrs Heiberg seems to find strength in the seedy side of life.

*

One November day an autumn storm gathers in the west.

Its violent force pounds and crashes along the heaving lake; sitting at his desk, he watches the birds as they are hurled around, panic-stricken or euphoric, by blast after blast. You had to make up your mind, when you were interpreting birds or Denmark or yourself or Mr Clausen. He sees two seagulls flying past his window: they are heading westward, but the wind is so strong they are gradually, almost imperceptibly, being pushed backwards. He sees the desperation in the heavy movement of their wings as the storm *pulls them back* past him and his window. Where had they been going? Home? He sees one of the gulls turn its head towards him and he knows instantly what it is trying to tell him: *I want to do this so much, and yet I'm being forced backwards, what can I do? Help me, I wanted to do it so much and it's all going so wrong!* And slowly they are carried in the opposite direction, away from him and his window.

He also has a cat, a ginger one. The cat says nothing, but appears to be watching and waiting. He himself always wakes early and sits doing nothing, gazing out over the lake that actually might be a dam.

This is the point he has reached.

In the early morning a strange mist often hung over the water; darkness had lifted but there was still a grey blanket hovering about ten metres above the surface of the water, a kind of reflection left by the night over the glassy, quicksilver stillness. And the sleeping birds, tucked inside themselves and their dreams. It was as though he were standing on the farthest shoreline, with nothing beyond him. He could be seized by a crippling fear that life had frozen, stood still, that all movement had ceased; it was the dreadful old dream about eternity taking the form of a mountain rising out of the sea, a mile long and wide and high, and the bird that came every thousand years to sharpen its beak until the mountain had been worn away. And the fear that this was no longer a childhood dream that would vanish when he woke up, but it was reality, here in this place, at the edge of a Danish dam in central Copenhagen. But sometimes there would be a movement that would release him, deliver him: a bird taking off, soundlessly, the tips of its wings beating against the surface of the water, it was rising, free: and he saw it climb up and through the grey mist and disappear.

Eternity had come to an end, he was in total normality, there was no mountain and there was no eternity. And with any luck on these mornings he was visited by the concrete, brutal sound announcing the great Danish love story, coming from the flat below, where his secretive friend Mr Clausen lived.

The sound did not come from Mr Clausen, it came from his beloved sister.

That was what it was like in Denmark: the farthest shore with no visible horizon on the other side of the dam, birds that rose and disappeared in the morning mist, and the luring call from sister Gerda.

The fairy tale "The Snow Queen" was about a boy called Kay who got a splinter from a broken mirror in his eye and could only see ugly things. And then he went into the Snow Queen's ice palace and tried to put together a puzzle of ice pieces. Something like that. And was saved by little Gerda.

Finally he works out what happened. The pieces of the jigsaw slotted into place! He is relieved.

He might be able to start writing it down soon.

They had reached an agreement. What had happened between the three members of Mr Clausen's family had been wiped out. It had been obliterated, it never took place. No blame, no hatred, no jealousy. Naturally they never spoke about it. They continued in the same way as before. Mr Clausen's sister still came round. Her small, chubby hands could often be seen setting the table, but the only thing they closed around now was a glass. She tickled the little cat, Semiramis, with gentleness and sensitivity.

Unexpectedly she had a stroke that partially paralysed her. Mr Clausen and his wife decided then to take care of sister Gerda and look after her in their home at 25 Sortedam Dossering.

They placed her in the guest bed, supported by cushions. Gradually she started to walk again, usually in small circles in the living room. She was happiest going round and round.

Thus the caring for sister Gerda began.

The last few years had taken their toll on her somewhat plump cheeks.

Her hair was grey and quite thin, her face slightly lizard-like now she had lost weight; when you entered Mr Clausen's flat she was scarcely visible in the half-light, but if you looked carefully, her eyes seemed to swivel about. It might have been the stroke, but it was probably linked to the early stages of some form of senility. The first time he saw her, she could talk to him, quite calmly and almost intelligibly, though what she said was not entirely interesting. At the beginning of May her condition worsened in a strange respect.

Sister Gerda had started shouting.

To begin with there had been no-one else in the building, at any rate not the Swede from the flat above, who would come to understand the character of the howling noises she uttered. It did not sound as though she was in pain, more as if she had taken on the role of siren; like the ones that could be heard when there was fog in the strait. It sounded just like the foghorns from the boats beyond the Langelinie: a hoarse, lowing, raw "Mmmmmmmwwwwaaaaaaaaa", she bellowed in a strikingly deep and masculine voice, and then "OoooMMMMMM-mmwwwaaaaa," a soft moan lasting eight seconds or so and suddenly stopping. In the intervals apparently she sat quite still, staring ahead with a friendly expression. Then the cries began again.

Since he was their closest neighbour and was at home during the day, Mr Clausen confided in him. Could he hear it? Did he take offence? No, it didn't bother him. Mr Clausen said he appreciated that. The howling usually occurred in the mornings, lasted between half an hour and an hour, and then stopped. In moments of lucidity sister Gerda was dismayed and bewildered by what they told her about the noises, and said she was desperately sorry if she caused a problem.

On one occasion he went down to their flat to reassure her that it did not matter. She was pleased. He could not decide if she understood what he said, but she smiled affably. He had the impression of speaking to someone who was utterly happy, cast in one piece, and to his surprise he experienced a kind of bitter envy.

What was the difference between them? An injustice. It was her lot to moan, and his to write down minute observations, such as seagulls being forced back by the storm. The storm did not affect her.

At the end of April sister Gerda stepped out of the ice-blue cave for the first time, to take up battle with her rival and try to claim Mr Clausen back.

That was how it had to be interpreted. There was no other plausible explanation. At any rate: words came forth from the foghorn. Coherent sentences, declarations. Out in the garden, leaves were starting to appear on the little maple tree in the light spring sunshine, the swans were becoming more aggressive, stretching and twisting their necks in their courtship dance, and in Nørrebro the Pakistanis on St Hans Gade could be heard singing, accompanied by their remarkable musical instruments, their trailing melodies endlessly rising and falling like wreaths of smoke.

Mr Clausen was careful to shut the windows so that no-one could hear sister Gerda shouting. Both he and Mrs Clausen were dismayed.

Sister Gerda released her feelings of hostility against Mrs Clausen, suppressed for so long. That was the superficial interpretation. The one he preferred was that this was a song of temptation coming through the ice, and that the call contained a message for him.

"You old whore," the siren roared, her wrinkled hollow cheeks, no longer plump and alluring, grinding up and down as if she were chewing uncontrollably; her gaze was fixed on the far distance, and not on the object of her outburst of hatred and passion for truth, Mrs Clausen: "Eat your fucking shit yourself, you old whore." When Mrs Clausen gently tried to feed her: "You've always been a tart." And then the foghorn again, "MmmmmmmWWWWWWWaaaaaaaaa." Then it stopped and she began licking her lips in search of any legitimate truths that might be lurking still: "Aaaah, you old bitch, you always stank of shit and sour pisssss," and with this she found a new and much loved word, *sour-piiiiissssss*. And another pause, "You old tart." Lower now, "That's what you've always been." And then the peculiar happy smile again.

Mr Clausen did not take offence. Nor did his wife. They realised that sister Gerda now finally had to make her declaration of love and nothing would stop her. What could they have done? Mr Clausen could not put up mattresses at the window to stop the noise. And in the flat above there was only the Swedish author, and he recalled, indeed he knew, that such a man could be relied upon.

Mr Clausen seemed imbued with complete serenity. You might almost think he felt happy.

He is happy himself, though also despondent.

He loves his wife, she loves him. All at once he resumes his travels and goes to Mexico for a month for the World Cup. He convinces himself that he can still do it. *Didn't he once write about that Swedish tragedy, the extradition of the Baltic soldiers? Or the Munich Olympics?* The air in Mexico City is very thin, the heat intense, he is desperately tired and drinks copiously. He writes regular articles about the events for his newspaper. They are meaningless. He experiences it all and understands nothing. At a distance of only forty metres he sees Maradona use the hand of God and does not comprehend. He comes home, travelling up to Bureå in despair and, *in his mother's kitchen* once again, writes a book about what he has seen. He does not know what value it has. He draws together images and experiences and at the start of one chapter he writes, "This is the most important of what has been said about this game," and at the beginning of the next, "This is the worst."

Even his forced arrogance feels hollow.

It is wonderful to be in his mother's kitchen. He returns to Copenhagen. To icy mornings, the *ficus benjamina* dead and signs of life swept away.

He began to imagine what Mr Clausen was thinking.

This must be the point of what he was not doing at the moment, but ought to have done. Birds rising over the water, the mists, all this he made an effort to master, and the ice-cold mornings. But it was repetitive. It was easier with Mr Clausen's sister. He had full control over her reality and that made him happy. *It was good.* It was something he could influence and need not feel sorry if nothing happened. *Total control.* What had made them share this intense closeness? That was what he wanted to know. Then it was a matter of engaging in the process *with cheerful optimism*. No birds, no storm, no messages from gulls pushed backwards in the wind, no early mornings. He recalled the game Eeva-Lisa taught him with the dots and the elephant: you had a piece of paper with numbers on and each number had a word that meant something. No, how did it go?

In the end you traced your pencil from dot to dot and a shape emerged to give you the answer. You made it all join up. And he had been helped by Eeva-Lisa, who held her hand over his, as if guiding him. Life depends upon everything being joined up. And finally you can shout, *An elephant!* For example.

It was undoubtedly the same with Mr Clausen and his sister. So that she held her hand on his neck in the playful way only an older sister can – something, by the way, Eeva-Lisa also used to do, aside from any other comparisons, as she drew a line between the numbers, each of which had some significance. There was number three, *"the same as our telephone number!"*, and number six – *"wasn't that the Hedmans'?"* – surely this should be construed in the same way as Mr Clausen's sister whispering, "I can hear when you prop your bicycle against the wall, there's no other sound like it, because it means you'll soon be here." And then Mr Clausen would lay aside his pen and smile at her and see what the drawing represented, and she would shout, "My life!"

He notes this down and writes: *And with the very tip of her tongue she touches the shiny white edge of the rock sugar.*

If only you could have understood, just once, *how everything joined up*, it would all have been bearable.

Even the fact that Mr Clausen's sister was no longer young, and now had become ill, and bellowed, and that strange words came out of her mouth. That was the way it turned out, things like that happen, it was forgivable. Such was love. It could not be divided up, or taken back, that would have been crazy. That must be what Mr Clausen was thinking, every number had a word attached that had to be interpreted, and sometimes pictures appeared that were so alien they could not be deciphered. That was the word, *deciphered*, like the day Eeva-Lisa was driven away *and that was that*. But he himself had been visited – in that hour of great doubt and fear – by *the funny and in no way troubling memory* of a bird locked in the summer house trying in a frenzy to escape, beating its wings against the window pane, its wild eyes staring, *against the window, with its wings* – just as his mother had attracted attention with her contorted face outside the window when he was imprisoned in Bureå cottage hospital by Doctor Death – where was the good Samaritan who could release this bird from the shock and despair it was feeling?

In June no more shouts from Mr Clausen's downstairs.

Was she still alive?

He went away, and remembers clearly where he went: a seminar on documentary truth versus literary truth, a subject on which, after his novel *The Legionnaires*, he was regarded as an expert and was therefore often called upon to speak.

He came back in August. Mr Clausen had left a note in his letter box. Its tone was friendly, exuding respectful consideration: he was invited, if he so wished, to visit them in their summer cottage in Tisvilde. It had been discovered, wrote Mr Clausen, that some close friends of the Swede, Thomas and Lene Bredsdorff, owned a summer cottage in Udsholt, and if his path took him in their direction, he might perhaps continue a little further along the Danish coast, which at this time of the year possessed such unique beauty, and thereby partake, as a Swede, of the wonderful Danish countryside. And so on. Mr Clausen wrote in the same linguistic style he had used his entire working life. There was no pretence. It was fine. He was likeable, almost clever.

It was time to rouse oneself.

Mr Clausen had rented a summer cottage in Tisvilde from the middle of August, after the end of the tourist season.

It was cheaper that way. Mr Clausen had some savings put aside, but you still had to be thrifty. Husband and wife were agreed. They took a taxi out there; they had packed mattresses, food, beer and bedding from Sortedam Dossering, and sister Gerda sat in the back seat smiling and howling the whole time. The taxi driver had not objected when the couple asked him not to engage in conversation.

They had paid in silence, unloaded their belongings and were left on their own.

They had put sister Gerda on the porch while Mrs Clausen made an inspection; Gerda had blinked like a bird, as was her wont, but in her astonishment had made no noise whatsoever. "It's so quiet here," the wife had remarked, "she's going to like it." From the beach came the sound of the waves, "lapping gently". Sister Gerda rocked backwards and forwards, but remained silent. Mr Clausen had thought, *it's just that it's unfamiliar, she'll start yelling as soon as she feels at home.*

Should he visit them? He is now completely sure, utterly convinced, that for Mr Clausen and his wife love meant being useful. To be the one who was needed. Sister Gerda's shouting confirmed that he was needed. Later it began to include his wife's love for his sister as well. And Mr Clausen thought: We love one another. All three of us. Imagine if it could always have been like that.

"She'd never be happy in the hospital," Mr Clausen's wife had whispered the first evening in the summer cottage, just before they fell asleep.

*

308

He knew he was sinking.

But it was not like Uncle Aron's death in the hole in the ice on Burefjärden. Not freezing cold and quick and down into the darkest depths of the ocean.

He could at least turn to the Clausen family. He ruled over them now. In full control. The only problem was they would not be committed to paper.

In September there were no more tourists on the northeast coast of Sjælland.

Mr Clausen and his two women often sat on the deserted sand dunes watching the mist as it came slowly rolling in over the sea, as it unfurled, separated and lifted, drawing the eye far out and letting it rest on a black spot on the horizon, a cargo ship creeping homeward in its northerly direction.

Sister Gerda was shouting and wailing again.

She had grown accustomed to the summer cottage. Her cheeks had become less hollowed and wrinkled, she looked healthy and fit, had put on five kilos and could walk round the room for hours, treading with tiny steps as if intent on measuring out eternity. Sometimes they let her walk on the lawn in front of the house, with a rope round her waist and the other end secured to the front door; it had not worked very well, according to Mr Clausen, she often tied herself in knots, like a dog on a lead that is too long. It was better if she could go round in circles. As an experiment they let her walk along the shore, where she could mutter to herself rather than really shout, as if she were disoriented by the smell of seaweed and all that could be heard were indistinct accusations against someone in her puzzling life for being "an old tart" and "lecher".

No tourists.

Sister Gerda had a cord round her waist, while Mr and Mrs Clausen held on to each end of it and prevented her from sinking down into the water. Against the shrieking of birds they conversed in low voices.

Mr Clausen was once again holding his wife's hand.

At night the three of them often sat close together in bed, wrapped up in blankets; sister Gerda was nearly always the first to fall asleep. Mr Clausen and his wife were careful then not to wake her; they knew if they did that she would throw out her arm and shout, "Come here, you bloody cow!" as usual. It was as if it was all now quite normal, that with love and warmth they could watch this enigmatic cauldron boiling with the exploits of a long life, and periodically bubbles would rise to the surface containing secrets and words and sore points; that phrase, *sore points*, was something to bear in mind, it might explain something.

Sister Gerda had lived her life. No-one could expunge the sore points now.

Sometimes Mrs Clausen held sister Gerda on her knee and rocked her. The moon hung low over the water, in the mornings the grass was white and it crackled underfoot when sister Gerda measured out eternity with her tiny steps. They were pleased she had put on a little weight. Very quiet down on the shore. Had it not been for sister Gerda's shouts, it would have been almost monotonous.

Clear nights. The moon.

Mr Clausen put a pole in the middle of the lawn in front of the house, tied a rope round her waist and looped it round the pole. The rope was five metres long. Now she could walk round and round and they did not need to worry.

Sister Gerda grew stronger and stronger. She was quite sturdy now. Her cheeks glowed. Her bowel incontinence was difficult, but Mr Clausen had learned how to change her and they helped each other.

October. The three of them were completely happy.

On the morning of 21 November – someone had presumably noticed what was happening and been concerned – two officials from the social services in Gilleleje arrived. Sister Gerda was engaged in her morning walk round the post, she had worn a circular path by now, her red cheeks were shining, she had dropped a mitten and had unfortunately just filled her pants, causing the two officials mistakenly to suspect neglect. Otherwise she was in excellent spirits and was howling a song up towards the grey sky. They took the rope off her, spoke briefly to Mr Clausen, and then dragged her into the car, despite her shouts of protest. One of the officials had been scratched in the face by "the individual suffering neglect". Mr Clausen could do nothing and his wife wept incessantly.

Sister Gerda was taken to hospital. Mr Clausen was incapable of explaining why they did what they did. They had been banned from love by this intervention, it was love that had impelled them to care in this way. Perhaps he meant that he had been very close to understanding what love was, but had been prevented. From seeing at the last minute what their life had been, the instant when he could have joined it all together and understood, and the dots would have formed a picture; and he could have thrown his hands up and cried, "A different life!" There were only a few dots missing.

He never did go up to see them in their summer cottage in Tisvilde.

Mr Clausen met him on the staircase in January and told him that his sister had passed away. In the middle of his own life the Swede found the reconstruction of sister Gerda's life impossible. He placed her in the series of blighted projects. Ice had covered Sortedammen. On the other side of the now dazzling white expanse, Mrs Johanne Luise Heiberg gazed at him from the distance of 120 years. Her friends, all professors and not one of them born in a brothel, had examined her exhaustive memoirs, *A Life*, and had erased from her writings all evidence of life's impurities. Those were collected together and published in a separate volume fifty years later.

The deletions conveyed overwhelming truth.

He wrote a play entitled *From the Lives of Rainworms*. Sister Gerda now gone, her shouting, her life and the squalor of life. "Rainworm" is the Danish word for earthworm. As a child Hanne Heiberg had played on the steps of the tavern where her alcoholic father and Jewish mother lived; this inn also served as a brothel. As a seven-year-old she had been forced by her father, despite her tears, to dance on the table in the brothel, to the lasting delight of the guests, one of whom later became her protector. That was before she won her place as Denmark's foremost actress. She had dug in the earth beneath the steps and collected earthworms, which she then washed in rainwater: "When I sat on my dear stone steps I noticed that in damp weather the rainworms always wriggled out of the earth. I thought that the little worms wanted to be washed, and so to help them fulfil their wish I spent hours digging in the soil, collecting as many as I could. I washed the rainworms carefully, lovingly; I rinsed the rainworms several times, so that in the end they were completely . . . clean."

He reads this ostensibly insignificant passage, not struck out by the censors, with strange emotion. It is not possible to understand one's own life, but she had tried all the same. Sister Gerda, now completely gone from his mind, was nevertheless still present despite his determination to forget. He sees her sitting on the stage in a wheelchair, in an almost silent role: only once does she sing her dirty song from the lives of rainworms, as Mrs Heiberg's mother, or mother-in-law, or as Mrs Heiberg herself. "Can't you see, it's me," Hanne says.

Sister Gerda had burrowed inside him. Love can never be explained. Didn't he wash the leeches that lived in the stream below the green house?

He does not remember.

Unclean memories washed away. Medicinal leeches or horse leeches? He cannot recall. He is entitled to forget.

CHAPTER 13

SJÖN 3, PARIS

He is now fifty-four years old and he is sinking.

He does not know how it has happened. But he knows he is sinking.

It is the years 1986 to 1989, the Paris apartment is large, maybe seven rooms, on the fifth floor on the Champs-Elysées, there is alcohol in every cupboard, the bottles are kept for the use of the Danish embassy, and he has a ginger cat.

He is close to death. From the fantastic balcony overlooking the Champs-Elysées he can just see the Arc de Triomphe and the Eiffel Tower. The balcony is affected by dense pollution from the traffic below, but he can go out for short periods, two or three minutes, and if he has a visitor, *be enthusiastic about the view.*

He receives many visitors. He hates the apartment.

His cat, who is called August, also hates it. The cat is enormous and resplendently ginger. He has been brought from Copenhagen. He is an outdoor cat who is now an apartment cat and hence locked in. The noise of the traffic is deafening if a window is left ajar. Since it is impossible to open the doors or windows on to the street, he feels confined too. He is alone with his cat most of the day. It is no-one else's fault. His wife Lone is working at the embassy as cultural attaché, it is a state apartment he now finds himself in, with state drink. He does not know, he might owe the Danish state something. Or maybe it owes him three years. He often marches through the rooms, back and forth, in an aggrieved fashion that is ridiculous. Had it been on the stage it would have been marked "anxiety" or "unrest". Now he only means to indicate a *situation of severe distress and vulnerability*.

There are no excuses whatsoever for his apathy, he soon realises that downfall is imminent and passively submits. At that time – it is the end of the 1980s – he is fond of the expression "inescapable destruction".

He thinks in Swedish.

His French is bad, not to say pitiful. He makes a mess of it. Every day he buys the sports newspaper *L'Equipe* and reads the football reports. Once he has made his way through one match it is easier with the rest. All the articles are similar, as the same words reappear, and basically he is not interested in what actually took place.

It is the same when he writes, and so he does not write any more.

He can skim-read about matches in which he has no interest at all. He has a clear memory of words such as "skim-read" and "football report" and "cat". The cat fixes a loving gaze on him. Where will it lead? He is sinking, his thoughts growing more and more dreamlike. He imagines the Northern Counties Coastal League, Division Four, the round in northern Västerbotten when both Bureå and Hjoggböle were fighting relegation forty years earlier. This is the only thing he daydreams about, and his cat stares at him for hours, expressionless. He knows that this is the only life he will have; when it comes to an end it will be over, and this fills him with despair so deep that he seeks comfort in his cat, who stares at him steadily. He tells himself that the years he is now spending at 147 Champs-Elysées are a preparation for his death, and this does not alter the cat's unconditional love and immobility.

August is a shrewd friend, a ginger tom. In retrospect his fate, in a strange way, mimics a play he writes in Paris in 1987. The play's title is *The Hour of the Lynx* and is about a cat who died, killed by a fox, but who rose from the dead.

A resurrection tale, one of many he writes and discards during that period. Miracles seldom happen, you make your own bed and you have to lie on it and Jesus rarely has time. Did he really rise from the dead? Maybe he lay there in his rocky grave, hoping.

In an insensitive and for him surprising manner, his own benefactor, his father, has also abandoned him. Being dead, he should really have had the time, but no. Anyway, August the cat disappears one day, much later, in Copenhagen, five years after the play was written, and is found after two days badly mutilated, almost killed by one of the foxes prevalent in the suburbs of Copenhagen. His hindquarters have been practically torn off, a boy from the home for the mentally disabled has found him. What happens now is an attempt to rescue a lost cause. Most people would have killed the cat and buried it, but the boy, who is a human being after all and loves animals, thinks the cat is so beautiful, at least what remains of him is, and believes he is still alive, or should be allowed to live. The matron of the madhouse – this is what he calls it – takes pity on the animal, against her better judgement, and calls for an ambulance; a vet sews August back together.

Eventually they find out where the cat is. Lone goes to fetch him. He himself is up in Bureå where his mother is dying. August the ginger cat's tail is missing, of course, and his hindquarters mangled, but he is still alive. Killed by a fox and risen from the dead, just like the lynx and without a tail, exactly as he had written in his play five years before. He draws the humorous conclusion that God goes to the theatre, but then immediately loses his composure and weeps uncontrollably. Good Lord, for cats there is compassion.

The play about the ginger cat is the only thing he writes in Paris. They live there for three years. He rises early in the morning, and at best writes for an hour or two before he gets drunk. A play for the theatre is not very long after all. The play is about a young boy, a convict, double-murderer, imprisoned, who seems morbidly obsessed with the green house in Hjoggböle where he was born, and who is assigned the care of a cat for rehabilitative purposes. The play deals with the love story between the boy and cat.

And the possibility of resurrection, of course, but who believes in that?

He thinks: Bunkum! New initiatives required!

One dreadful morning he resolutely imposes a task upon himself: that on this new, freezing cold, foggy day he will write a line, perhaps two, about anything at all. *He will respond to a question.* It cannot be difficult. Afterwards he can enter the fog with a clear conscience.

The opening question is: *What was your first telephone number?*

He looks for a long time at what he has written down and decides to answer the question simply and honestly. So! *"My first telephone number was Sjön 3, Hjoggböle."*

The cat is lying on his desk. The cat hates France too. He refuses to look at the fantastic view over the Champs-Elysées. He often sleeps, especially after the first anguished wakefulness of the clear and icy early hours. Curled up in sleep, August once dreamed, he tells him later, that the two of them were playing football.

They are on a green field up north, maybe Östra Fahlmark, and in the dream August is a midfielder, playing for the most part a strategically defensive role, but entitled to attack if the opportunity arises. Then he sees Enquist a long way up front about to run into a new space, and when August, liberated from defensive thinking, also sees a free space across to the right, and observes his idle friend, who more often than not would be sitting silent and empty-headed at his typewriter, now moving into the same area, wide on the right, and thereby filling the gap: then August makes the pass.

It was long and accurate, he saw it reach its target, mid-step, right to his foot, *and it was a through ball.*

He liked answering the question about his telephone number. His answer corresponded to the play about the boy.

The boy sat on a chair. The boy wrote in a cell.

He told himself he was writing a play about the possibility of resurrection. He gazed at the boy, *who in turn gazed at him.* It was difficult to understand him; sometimes August the cat joined in with explanations, usually obscure, *"he guarded the frogs in his grandfather's house,"* he might say, wrinkling his brow critically, or *"in essence you've run out of juice,*" an old-fashioned kind of expression, demonstrating that he did not live in the here and now, but was making an effort to appear modern.

He is on the run, and is reverting to his childhood in order to defend the flank against a potential tank offensive. Lord, where can we hide when we're at our wits' end?

He remembers his first telephone number easily.

It was Sjön 3. *Time passes, love too, but the memory of your first telephone number will last for ever.* Such were the thoughts he had. If he wrote them down he felt a quiet despair, but he pulled himself together and in defiance carried on. Sjön 3. He felt it was something he could cling to in these dire straits, when both his benefactors, Jesus and Pappa, now did not have time. The telephone number to call was "Sjön 3"; in those days making a call was something personal, he sometimes thinks, it was reaching out like a cry of anguish in the emptiness between the villages. Or a siren call through the ice. Long-distance calls sometimes reached as far as Umeå, and then it was called a Long-Distance Call; it was something significant, something out of the ordinary, like telephoning Aunt Lilly in Brattby, where the Brattby Skolhem lunatic asylum was, and the boy with crocodile skin and other monsters he got to know. Well, soon he would be there himself. The postal address was "Sjön, Hjoggböle". That was because Sjön was part of a larger village, with the result it could not have its own name outright; it wasn't worth arguing about, most people thought.

Now he tries even harder to remember, otherwise he will go mad. Answering the question is a life-saving decision. It is a long time since he has been able to make any decision at all.

The Sjön telephone service had twelve subscribers.

He still knows most of the numbers. Hugo Renström, married to a sister of his father, had Sjön 12. The Hedmans, they were second cousins, had Sjön 6. Another of his father's sisters – he was related to everyone in the village – who lived on the other side of the valley, on the left, had the exchange. If someone rang she went to the switchboard hanging on the wall in the little room behind the kitchen, the one they called the best room, that meant the switchboard was hanging on the right as you entered, and she lifted the receiver and calmly answered "Sjön", as if nothing exceptional had happened at all. Their house was Sjön 3, almost one thousand kilometres north of Stockholm; if you were coming from Burehållet it was on the right, after the Normarks. It was high up at the edge of the forest.

The house was bright green, which was generally regarded as slightly odd, but as the village largely consisted of relatives of his father, no-one acknowledged it; there may have been one or two who mentioned it was a rather strange colour. His father *died when he was only six months old* (how comforting it was to repeat this!), so people *showed some consideration* and overlooked the colour.

It was not a stupid question about the telephone number.

That could be enlarged upon. He decides to *go over* everything, to stop himself going mad. So he concentrates on the thing he is sure about, the house. His father had built the house, by hand, as it were, with the help of his grandfather, who was the village blacksmith. Grandfather had a fox farm and was a blacksmith; when he thinks about it and about the fox that nearly killed August, it is strange he liked foxes when he was small. There was no need to. His father was a stevedore and lumberjack, but his grandfather could do anything, including build rowing boats that were generally considered spacious, unwieldy and completely seaworthy. He built one for the boy's mother too, after his father died and they moved their summer cottage to Granholmen in Hjoggböleträsket. The boat was regarded as heavy and safe. It was, after all, his grandchild's life at stake. Below the green house that was situated at the edge of the forest, there were four fields down to the stream. People said it was "half a cow-forage". That meant it would feed half a cow. Maybe it was bordering on one whole cow. But they had no cows, since his father worked on the boats. That was in the summer. In the winter he was a woodcutter. During his stay in Paris, his assessment is, and the facts are not inconsistent with this, that it must have been nearer one cow-forage, possibly more.

Exaggeration was a form of conceit, and his anguish and concern over the half or the whole cow must be seen in this light. He rises at four every morning and looks out over the freezing expanse where the Eiffel Tower shoots up like a menacing steel spike driven into the ice, as if left behind by Uncle Aron. He would like to consider himself essentially humble. His humility is often the greatest in the land. He has drunk a great deal and, wrapped in the greaseproof paper of success and love, is absolutely and completely alone.

While he writes down his reflections on the telephone number and the house, the cat is wide awake and watches him with surprise. The cat is unaccustomed to the hammering of the typewriter keys, is used to him staring straight ahead in silence, apart from the thunder of the traffic below.

Now, without hesitation, he was completing the reconstruction of Sjön 3. What else remained to be done?

The house was located at the edge of the forest.

Behind was the forest and beyond was the mountain called Bensberget, the height of which was given as 112 metres, but it was certainly significantly higher, perhaps several hundred metres. Just below the summit was the Dead Cats' Grotto, which he explored and mapped at a young age and where long ago he saved his foster sister Eeva-Lisa from freezing to death.

In front of the house were the fields with the cold-water spring and the frogs. He repeats these facts until he has calmed down. Then he is a child once more and *no-one can touch him*.

The house had two storeys, and at one end, the end with the bedroom window facing down towards the valley, there was a rowan tree. It was a lucky tree, his mother had decided. The porch was on the front, the side facing the chapel, twenty-five metres away. You entered from the direction of the chapel, in other words as if going in the direction of the Sehlstedts and the Nordmarks, and, in a wider perspective, towards

Stockholm. He had forty-two cousins. It was quite natural: for hundreds of years there were few roads between the villages and no-one managed to go very far to woo a lass, to Vallen or Lövånger at most, and there was a lot of marriage within families, and people said there was plenty of inbreeding too, resulting in one or two village idiots and an astonishing number of writers. So it was not surprising if the inbreeding made you queer in the head; and wasn't this an explanation for his incipient collapse, or at least for the alcohol that, like the sticky flytrap in the pigsty, would not let him go, and didn't this remove all blame and culpability? And weren't these circumstances mitigating, so the whole burden of guilt could be confessed away like an ordinary Saturday sin?

Yes indeed!

Then the bicycle was invented by someone in the south, towards Stockholm, young men could travel further and further from home, and there was more of a mix. Next to the porch was a veranda. In summer his mother stretched twine from the bottom to the top, so the hop plant could climb up; it was good for the bees, which did not sting as long as you did not close your hand over them and take their liberty away. They were nice and they hated being confined. They hardly ever stung, unlike the gadflies, which could drive horses crazy.

Everyone admires the seven-roomed apartment at 147 Champs-Elysées and there he comes across a series of famous faces, who intrude.

It is sometimes completely full. Some of them have no regard for August. Just as an example! One evening a number of dancers from the Copenhagen Opera arrive and bring some others along; he is married, in one way or another, to the hostess, and of course he has obligations, but it bothers him. The voices are difficult to understand. It is hard to know whether they are speaking to him. He gathers himself, but suddenly sees the dancer Nureyev sprawled on the sofa where August usually lies and he *is occupying his space*, and this Nureyev is jabbering away in his own language. He goes up to him and says, quite politely, almost, and in Swedish, *Listen, you're sitting in August's place and you could at least have asked*. But this Nureyev just looks up indifferently and carries on babbling, utterly clueless, and presumably in French. He lacks all understanding of *Swedish language and literature*.

In this manner the days pass.

There was a rosehip hedge by the green house, at the bottom, just above the cold-water spring with the frogs. The hedge was about a kilometre long, according to his earlier estimation, but later it shrank to perhaps eighty metres. It was like that with the height of Bensberget.

Every now and then a lady would come, who was not a relative, and ask if she could pick some rosehips; in paltry recompense she would leave a bucket of wild mushrooms. The morels had to be hung on threads and dried; his mother prepared them *her face darkening*, he didn't know why, but there was no-one in the village who ate morels. They had to be parboiled. In Sjön they alone ate mushrooms. Only cows ate mushrooms, but no-one told them that or criticised them for it, because his father was dead and his mother had been left on her own; there was only one person who said anything, and that was Maurits Sehlstedt, a cousin.

His father had built the house Sjön 3 himself; it had to be finished for their wedding, so the engagement dragged on. Before it was ready he planted an apple tree outside the porch as a gift for his fiancée, it was facing towards the chapel. Apple trees were unusual because they were normally killed by the frost, and later some youngsters from Västra Hjoggböle, where Pappa did not have any relatives, came and stole it. That made his mother's face darken too and she was tearful. It was the only apple tree in the village.

When the house was completed the telephone was installed and they answered "Sjön 3" as though it were the most normal thing in the world. Two more houses were built, one of them the summer cottage. Everyone in the village had to have a summer cottage, it was obligatory, and it had to be situated close to the winter dwelling, so there was not far to go between them. At most twenty metres apart. Summer cottages did not need to have double-glazing. That was the difference. Nothing strange about having two houses standing practically on top of one another. It was quite natural, no matter how little money one had; there was plenty of timber and almost any young man could build a house, that was the general opinion. For those in the green house there was not much space between the winter home and the chapel, just a winter road leading up to Bensberget and the Dead Cats' Grotto, where he saved his foster sister in an awkward and desperate situation, so his father had to squeeze the summer cottage in as best he could. It was a triangular shape, almost pointed, maybe it was pentagonal, very strange, but it fitted in. Like a boathouse, someone is supposed to have said, according to hearsay, but that did not reach his father's ears while he was still alive. It looked like a boat that had run aground with its nose on the bank, to be honest. It made you wonder about all the fuss over the French houses on the Champs-Elysées, where there was mostly repetition, no colours, at any rate not a single green house, though of course that was a matter of taste. It made you wonder about all the hoo-ha. And the uncritical adoration of Paris.

After God had called his father home, his uncles dismantled the house, the summer cottage that is, carefully marking all the timbers, and in the winter took them out over the ice to Granholmen. They re-built the summer cottage on the island, exactly as it had been before, run aground with its nose alongside the chapel. It still looked like a boathouse, slightly plough-shaped. His mother was not allowed to buy the island because of the wood, in other words the fir trees, thought to possess enormous value if felled, but she was able to rent the land. It was not freehold and she paid eighteen kronor a year in rent, which was reasonable. She was a teacher, but she did not have as high a salary as the male teacher in the school, a fact that grieved her in a way the child found exhausting. It was a manner of moaning that did not suit her, but the child soon learnt not to quarrel with her and just to listen in silence to her litanies. What is more, she had no salary in the summer; people did not in those days. He saw no problem in this, as it presented them with the good fortune of living in freedom on Granholmen in the summer. They could live on almost nothing there. During the winter months they could save. They suffered no hardship.

Grandfather built the heavy boat. The child spend all his summers on Granholmen in the company of his mother, who mostly sat on a stone gazing out over the water, but later usually gathered herself and prepared a meal. They rowed over to Koppra once a week to do the shopping.

What was she gazing at?

There were fir trees on the island with huge branches you could climb along and watch for the enemy. Sometimes they held little prayer meetings for themselves on the island. Then she would pray to Jesus Christ that the child should be spared all ills and that he should never fall into sin and especially not into alcohol.

That was the worst thing. You did not want to think about it. She sat on a stone gazing out and in her conversations with our Saviour prayed to Him that the child should not resort to alcohol.

Sometimes she wept.

What should she have said? It is not called Granholmen anymore, by the way, it seems to have been renamed Majaholmen. If only they knew. If only she knew.

He becomes almost all-seeing. Now back to the green house. Now back to the green house.

His daughter Jenny came to study at the Sorbonne and lived with them for six months. Near the beginning she asked him what he was going to do that day, and he had no answer; she only asked him at the beginning. As wise as an owl, like Selma Lagerlöf towards her ageing father, who also liked a drop of fine red wine every now and then.

But sometimes life was fun! On a return visit to Denmark he directs one of his own plays with Ghita Nørby and Fritz Helmuth, it was *The Tribades*, and now he could do what he wanted! They rehearsed in

Aalborg because Fritz and Ghita were playing *Who's Afraid of Virginia Woolf?* in the evenings. He enjoyed it. Then he returned to Paris and the fog.

Was that what he should have been, a boss, a stevedore foreman, in a different life?

Incidentally, his father built the combined privy/woodshed immediately above.

The privy had two holes for grown-ups and two on a step for children; they had obviously planned on more children before the demise of the first baby and his father. The privy was in the corner nearest the road up to the mountain with the Dead Cats' Grotto; the mountain was not as flat as it later became and the cave was deeper, presumably there had been some sort of geological disaster. If you opened the door to the privy while you were sitting there, you were practically hanging out over the valley. You could open the door and sit reading the local paper, which was the free-minded, liberal *Norran*. It had two cartoon series, one was Popeye and the other was Flash Gordon. He wiped his backside with the *Norran*, but was careful to save the pages that had Popeye and Flash Gordon. It was big step forward when they had the *Norran*, his mother always insisted; *in the old days* they used sticks that they split and kept in a box, and in spring, when they spread the shit out on the fields, it looked as though it had been raining privy sticks over the fertile earth that would soon be blooming profusely.

Then they starting wiping themselves with the *Norran*, but this did not denote any political stance.

He repeats himself constantly, is struck by an afterthought, lifts up his writing hand and looks at it with hatred.

There was a slope up to the privy and it was hard to shovel the snow in winter, but his mother was good at shovelling, and in the end it was like walking through a tunnel and no trouble at all. The cold was worse, but on the whole not a cause of misery. Over the years his mother saved enough for a modern yellow piss bucket, with a lid that had an eight-centimetre hole in the middle. The lid sloped in towards the hole. The bucket stood in the hall, so in the winter there was no need to go to the privy to piss. In the morning the piss had frozen into a thick block of yellow ice that had to be lifted out on to the slope behind the house; at the start of spring there was a pile of ice blocks, circular yellow drift ice that, in their eyes, would tempt the spring flowers out and give nourishment and strength to the plants.

The piss bucket too was a major step forward, but to begin with he had difficulty directing the stream into the hole so it did not splash. His mother was concerned and admonished him, and time and again she said that *anyone who one day is going to be able to manage his own life must learn as a child how to manage to get his piss properly into a bucket*. She was very worried about it. He has thought about it many times since. If only she had known.

Now he ought to come to the house itself.

The boy in the play *The Hour of the Lynx* – the one he wrote in the apartment at 147 Champs-Elysées in collaboration with his cat August – was driven almost insane by the house. He could think of nothing else. He was so desperately ashamed and was beside himself and *he found consolation* in the house in a wretched way. It was difficult, therefore, to write about this crazy boy. However, sometimes he would *buck up his ideas* and *think grand thoughts* and believe it was important to view the house *in its social context*, in other words the summer cottage and the privy and the hedge and the cold-water spring with the frogs.

With regard to the last of these: there was plenty of water, they fetched it from the spring at the front. You went round to the left of the rosehip hedge, except in summer when you went through a hole in the middle. It was clear spring water you should consider yourself fortunate to have. It just ran out from under the mountain. The spring was only half a metre deep and had a little wooden structure over it; he brought the water up in buckets.

In the spring there were around ten frogs that had to be protected. When he bent over he always had to guide the bucket between the frogs, which in fact might have been toads as they were quite large. When he and his mother had company – that was the right term, friends who came to visit were called company – who wanted to ingratiate themselves and attract attention, they would fetch water from the spring *so the little one didn't have to*. They always tried to scoop the frogs out, and then you had to be on your guard and save them. In a way this made him an animal-keeper. He saw it as a vocation, like a missionary or a deacon. You could be a keeper even if it was only a question of frogs. They didn't have a cat. Or a dog, for that matter.

The frogs were lovely and easy to look after. In the spring tadpoles hatched in the stream, he kept them in glass jars, and then one morning they had lost their tails and were hopping around on the kitchen floor. By pounding out the words on the typewriter, placed only ten inches or so from the back of the sleeping ginger cat, about the frogs in the cold-water spring, he goes round the problem in circles. There is nothing to be ashamed of.

He knows what he is doing. What will I do?

In March 2007 he rediscovers his answer to the question, *"What was your first telephone number?"*

He must have written it in the apartment at 147 Champs-Elysées in the winter of 1986 to 1987. There is a text of twenty-one pages, commencing with the telephone number, quite correct, and then a description of the house.

That's all.

He looks at the boy in the cell, the boy looks at him. The ginger cat curled up on the table. Endless, exhausting repetition, almost ritual, like a mass. Each room measured, the stairs to the first floor, the height of the ceilings, the quality of the bricks, radiators, as if a Västerbotten peasant architect had detailed his life's work. Everything with the utmost determination, an absurd account of beams, windows, pipes, with an objectivity from the start that only slowly dissipates: the boy calms down after a few pages, he is feeling more comfortable and breathing more evenly and shame loosens its grip; he is quite safe in his cell with the cat beside him, and in the end he finds a natural form of address for *his only remaining animal friend*.

He means the cat.

The odd thing was that there was a well in the cellar too. It didn't work. There was something wrong with it. There was iron in the water. Maybe it could have been used for washing. The stairs down to the cellar were to the right after the porch, scarcely a metre in between. There was a drain from the kitchen. There was a tub by the pantry. It must have emptied out somewhere, but not by the spring, for the frogs' sake, because they had to have clean water. In the kitchen we had a wood stove with a copper washstand, so the water warmed up when you lit the wood that I'd chopped in the woodshed that was next to the privy that was fine in summer, and in winter too actually, not like the privy at school with those thick yellow frozen circles of ice you had to prize off. The stove was a normal one, with rings. Once, while Pappa was alive, it looks as if we may have had a cat, but then he died and that was that. The explanation was that the cat shat on the stove when it was cold and Mamma was furious, that's why I couldn't ever have a cat when I was little. The cat shat on the stove! she said. The house was heated by a wood boiler in the cellar and hot-water radiators. Grandfather had stupidly laid one of the water pipes through the attic, where we kept the rock sugar I gave to Eeva-Lisa that time, and it could be minus 30 in winter up there, apart from in the little box room, where there was the pile of Allers *magazines, the one Mamma didn't buy because she was religious. Who had bought them? It could have been Pappa who bought them while he was still a bachelor and before his salvation. If you were unlucky and the boiler went out in the middle of winter and it was below minus 30, the bend in the pipe always froze, and you had to warm it up with candles to melt the blockage. Mamma was often up there in winter, wrapped in a blanket, warming the bend in the pipe with a candle, and I lay under the sheepskin in the bedroom next door and wondered why Grandfather had been so stupid he hadn't lagged it, and I knew Mamma was crying, because those times she had to warm up the bend in the blocked pipe with the candle she must have been overcome with sorrow, thinking about my father who had been taken away at such a young age and therefore couldn't warm the pipe in the attic where the rock sugar was. I was convinced this was in her mind, even though her muffled sobs didn't reach me, but I indulged in childish fantasies. She certainly used to think about Pappa, and then she maintained, when I asked, that it was so cold it was natural to cry, and if only Pappa had lived! It was as if she had a period of reflection up in the attic and was overwhelmed, you could well imagine. Pappa had been converted before he died and on his deathbed wrote a message to me. Per-Ola, become a Christian. When he owned a motorcycle with sidecar he wasn't saved, one of his brothers told me in strictest confidence, and he was more fun then. However, he never took to drink, despite being described as great fun, and on his own initiative had bought a second-hand motorbike with sidecar, this uncle whispered to me. It was important that Mamma didn't hear. After he'd been saved it might have been easier to die. That's why he wrote that message to me. Away with these thoughts about how I acted upon his advice!*

The text continues. Page after page, always about the house.

In his memoir he has in fact been thoughtless enough to leave out one other construction, a garage down by the road. This meant the green house was surrounded by two other buildings, keeping watch over his father and him: one was the chapel, and the other the garage that could accommodate a motorcycle and sidecar, before his father's salvation. Didn't he also buy a Chevrolet, maybe jointly with his younger brothers, to drive down to Bureå harbour and the boats every morning at six with the other stevedores in the village? There is nothing to substantiate this or contradict it. It was twelve kilometres and the road was sandy. The cycles had balloon tyres. Why did his father sell the motorcycle and sidecar and the second-hand Chevrolet?

During this period of great distress in the immense apartment on the fifth floor of number 147 Champs-Elysées, watched by the boy in the cell, and supported in every way throughout his suffering by the advice and guidance of August the cat, he discovered, in this account of the architecture of the green house, increasingly disturbing details about his father, his mother, himself, and about the life they led there; details that gave signals and forewarnings of what was to come.

He felt he was very close now.

In the cellar there was a square chest belonging to his aunt Elsa, who had been engaged. The engagement had been called off. When that happened, her fiancé had sent the thing back. It was like her trousseau, with sheets and pillowcases. It was in the cellar and no-one could open it. It was inauspicious. She had been almost forty, "too old really," his mother had said, whatever that meant. But it was ominous.

There was much he did not understand, bad omens, signs of fore-boding.

When she came for it, he was with her as she opened it. It was next to the wood stove, to the left of the potato cellar, where the spuds had to be stored in the dark.

That was where the chest was.

If a potato had sprouts, it meant it was alive, but when the sprouts started to grow, the potato died. It was strange: if you thought the potato was dead and wasn't sprouting, it was actually alive, but if it started to grow, it was dead. No-one could explain to him any of this life and death business, but people were always talking about it. They had to be kept in complete darkness, or they would die.

Just imagine if that was true. Just imagine.

When Aunt Elsa opened the chest, he was there; at the top there was a letter and as she read it she sniffed and seemed irritated.

"It's easy for him to say!" she said aloud. And he never found out any more.

It was the same with everything.

In front of the green house was a rowan tree his father had planted. It was a lucky tree, but for safety's sake his grandfather had built a metal staircase from the bedroom window down to the ground, in case of fire. So first there was the green house, and at the gable end the metal staircase, and in front of them the lucky rowan tree, then the rosehip hedge, then the cold-water spring with the frogs that had to be protected, then the fields, then the hill, then the main road. He does not know if his distress would be less severe if he could make a plan of the house, but the boy looks at him and he looks at the boy; if he hesitates, the cat lifts his head in a gesture of encouragement.

And he continues to write about the green house. In winter the rowan tree is full of snow and berries and birds. That's what he remembers. The telephone number is Sjön 3, Paris.

CHAPTER 14

THE FLYING SNIPE

He had known for a long time that he was sinking.

He had no illusions. He was not inclined to lie to himself or to other people. Besides, it was impossible to lie. He was a drinker.

Not that it was obvious to everyone. It wasn't.

When he was invited out to dinner he was very circumspect; he watched his blood-alcohol content with almost scientific precision, set himself certain rules, to start with whisky and then gradually switch to wine, before consoling himself after midnight with beer. To his remaining friends – his remaining friends were oddly enough almost the only ones he had ever had, they were concerned, but did not fail him – to them he would give a *brilliantly perceptive analysis* of how bad it was.

He hid nothing from his wife, but he could see from the sadness in her eyes that she had heard the analyses too many times and had seen that, in practice, nothing changed.

That his perception was utterly futile.

When he came home after these dinners or parties, he was certainly admirably lucid and charming and seemingly quite sober, but he immediately opened, and consumed, a bottle of wine. That way he did not embarrass himself in front of anyone else, apart from her of course. But she kept silent; he assumed that all she felt was sorrow.

He was sinking, but no longer slowly. He knew it, she knew it, and in the end everyone else knew it.

*

On an intellectual level he handles the problem with *startling clarity of vision*. That is partly why he is sinking.

For example, he has seen through the medical profession for a long time. When he visits a doctor in Denmark or Sweden and gives a hair-raising account of his condition, including a full and frank assessment of his alcohol consumption, no holds barred, they are sympathetic and readily focus on his depression. Usually they are of the opinion that his bouts of depression are the cause of his alcohol consumption. A perfectly obvious case.

The patient is unhappy and that is why he drinks.

They prescribe tablets of various colours and of an increasingly controversial nature, but are sure that Rohypnol in particular can solve his problem. He gradually finds that the withdrawal resulting after he has, at regular intervals, stopped taking Rohypnol, is dreadful. Possibly intensified by the fact that his alcohol consumption at the same time is constant.

The red, pink, blue or green pills prescribed by the caring, cultured doctors provide no relief at all.

They make it plain he has an artistic temperament. There is clear proof. He is practically world famous, especially as a dramatist, and especially in Denmark, where *From the Lives of Rainworms* had played to a full house on the main stage at the Royal Danish Theatre for three seasons and had been adored. The Swede has almost been converted to an honorary Dane: a nervous system of this kind is without doubt extremely sensitive. Depression is therefore natural, almost part of his constitution. It needs to be corrected and suppressed chemically. Not a single one of them says that he has been made depressed by drinking, in that order, or that his insomnia is caused by the alcohol. On the contrary, his depression is the cause of his problem. How is his marriage? Very happy, he assures them, and that is true. His relationship with his mother? And what about breastfeeding? Tired and ill-tempered, he rejects all psychoanalytical models; he would rather employ incisive arguments to demonstrate how well read he is on the subject of Freud's early relationship with Charcot, and in which he *is* an expert, in fact.

Go for analysis? He tries, but gives up of his own volition after eight sessions, partly because he feels increasingly attracted to the female analyst. So his problem has to be solved in a medically proven chemical way. To say that he should stay off the drink is far too simple, almost unscientific.

Meanwhile he sinks lower and lower.

He finds a great source of pleasure in the long analytical conversations with Scandinavian doctors, all of whom are impressed by his perspicacity and prescribe purple pills. He realises very quickly that the tablets are ineffective, apart from producing new and interesting forms of withdrawal symptoms. He also acknowledges that he cannot blame the doctors' prescriptions; the responsibility is his alone. Especially as he is lucky enough to be so very perceptive. His wide reading of international research into the harmful effects of alcoholism, and their causes, has reached an almost professional level; and since he knows that researchers *really* cannot agree, or provide unequivocal answers, he continues his experiments.

This is the only amusing element in all of this: to regard himself as a laboratory animal and to monitor what happens. He despises people who cannot see their own situation. He understands his, and he carries on drinking.

Obviously, it is recommended that he use Antabuse, a drug discovered by accident in Denmark in the '50s in tests to develop a remedy for eczema.

The people who think that Antabuse can save him underestimate the strength of his character.

He will not be beaten by this Danish tablet. He takes it in the morning, holds back for a few hours, and at around eleven has a beer. His heart rate increases, his face becomes slightly flushed, but he is not to be deterred, and at one o'clock he drinks an Elephant beer and another one two hours later. There is a violent tingling all over his body, his face is much redder, but he does not give in; this is a trial of strength he is going to win. He *will* drink his way through the Danish Tablet. His heart is thudding, but he trusts in his lumberjack genes and the strength of will inherited from his mother. He checks his pulse regularly, something he is used to from his time as an active sportsman and interval training; his pulse goes up dramatically, but it must not exceed 120 beats per minute.

His resting heart rate is normally 70.

Many years later he undergoes two heart operations, balloon angioplasty, or, the technical term, percutaneous coronary intervention. He is not worried by these operations as he knows his heart is strong. He has survived a battle with Antabuse, thus passing the test, and all will be well this time too.

By seven in the evening he has won the fight against the Danish Tablet, a difficult and dangerous feat, but the redness in his face has faded, his heart rate is down to between 80 and 85, his strength of character has been victorious, and he can start drinking wine again.

He is sinking.

When he is drunk he is never violent or aggressive, but on the contrary quite gentle and slightly absent-minded. The pace of his life is slower and more settled. He daydreams about the life that might be his, an alternative life, if everything were different. He is a normative fantasist; he drinks himself into future possibilities, falls asleep readily, wakes after an hour or so with a stabbing pain in his heart, easily rectified with a whisky tumbler of red wine; he suspects the percentage of alcohol in his bloodstream has dropped too quickly and dreams of the day he can buy equipment to test the level and create a chart. He loves drinking alone and hates to drink in the company of others; he wants to sink in and dream, preferably about the books he almost definitely will write. He can *foresee* what they will be like.

In reality he does write, occasionally, for short periods, measurable almost in minutes. He knows that he will never be able to write anything that is up to scratch with alcohol in his blood; but sometimes the cold and sober early hours bring great clarity, and he can write. During just such morning hours, in the middle of the '80s, he writes a novel called

Downfall: A Love Story, 140 pages long. These hours, or rather minutes, are not enough for any more. Strangely enough, it becomes one of his best novels. He does not seem to have lost his knack. He knows his prose is pitch-perfect, sufficient for a short novel. He knows that this may be the last.

He beholds his own downfall with humorous objectivity, because he couldn't bear it any other way. Sorrow would kill him: and why not, he sees that as an alternative, but for the time being puts his trust in gallows humour.

If only his wife and children were not so distraught. They seem to disregard entirely the cheeriness of his despair.

What is he to do?

Sjön 3 does not exist in Paris.

That he regressed to the green house and the leeches did little to help. He could not hide in a green house. In Paris almost everything else did exist, though, a wealth of culture and experiences, but he has given up, stares at the wall, sleeps. This treasure trove is outside the bubble he has wrapped around himself. He cannot take advantage of it.

They leave Paris and return to Copenhagen, his wife to a job as head of fiction on the newly launched TV2. He returns to precisely nothing, other than a raised arm with a manly and threateningly poised middle finger that still refuses to hit the keys. Now they are living in Hellerup in a beautiful house they bought when they came back.

Everything is so perfect.

His old plays are still being performed all over the world and he can live off them without any problem. He often goes away on increasingly arbitrary visits to rehearsals of his plays. He puts on weight, goes up to 106 kilos; it's not attractive, his normal weight is eighty-six.

After the brilliant premiere of *Verdunkelung* in Würzburg – was it Würzburg? Something beginning with W at any rate – there was a black hole. *Verdunkelung* was the German title for *To Phaedra*, the play that clearly tempts so many splendid older female actors, who cannot find roles compatible with their age and talent. At the party after the first night he showed great restraint, as usual, he was almost totally sober, was suitably congratulated by the accomplished actors, no hint of depression.

Afterwards. Black. Something must have happened.

Two days after the premiere – he has only a vague recollection of what happened, but *the days pass so quickly* – two days after, he wakes up in a railway siding in Hamburg, in a stationary carriage that has been uncoupled, in which he has presumably fallen asleep and been left behind. That is where he wakes up. Maybe two days later, or three? He has no idea how he managed to get into the carriage in what was probably Würzburg. Dortmund? Someone must have helped him.

Now it's time to take myself in hand, he thinks.

He dare not appeal to the Benefactor, as his response would certainly have been a sharp one, and he would have felt ashamed.

He staggers over the tracks in the siding in Hamburg and thinks, I've been *left behind*.

They all wanted to help him. It's called intervention. They wait for the moment when he is practically unconscious and thus cooperative; it's called intervention.

He was taken to department M87 at Huddinge Hospital, well-known as the only hospital in Sweden to provide treatment for alcoholism following the Minnesota Model; there were several private rehabilitation centres, but this institution came under Stockholm County Council. The department treated sixteen patients at a time and was unique; this point was frequently made by the department's management, with a threatening overtone, because treatment for alcohol-related conditions was deemed to have low priority within Swedish healthcare, or indeed neglected completely, and so M87 was unique, and for that you should feel grateful, and subordinate. As a rule of thumb, it was reckoned that about 10 per cent of the Swedish population suffered from varying degrees of alcohol problems. Huddinge Hospital's catchment area contained 160,000 people; so the same theoretical rule of thumb would suggest that 16,000 patients needed care, but there were only sixteen in M87.

They were the privileged per thousand.

The chosen few should not just be labelled as privileged, they should feel it *in their heart*; they were, in the month of January 1989, the only sixteen people in Sweden provided with treatment in the public, i.e. not private, healthcare system.

He was informed about this later. And that every patient admitted to M87 for five weeks' treatment cost the taxpayers 82,000 kronor. At then-current prices.

That is where he was taken. They all wanted to help him.

He keeps a diary during his time in M87 in Huddinge.

The content of the first few days is extremely difficult to understand; he writes with a pencil, his hand trembling, but after two days it becomes much clearer. When he was a child in the '40s, they were taught how to print the letters before they did cursive handwriting. It was a directive from the Board of Education that was later changed; the effect remained with him for life. His handwriting was so clear! Almost cringingly distinct! Is that why things happened the way they did? he thinks in one of his humorous moments.

The first page cannot have been written on the first day. But anyway, written in a shaky hand or not, the text has the following wording.

> *Sunday. Mad panic in Copenhagen. Jenny and Mats are ringing round and threatening to come down. Johan Liljenberg is talking to Lone, promising me a place if I come. I have a very vague grasp of continuity; put the plane off three times. I accuse L. of treating me like a child, robbing me of my personal choice. Catch her out with*

three flight departures. Eight o'clock in the evening in Huddinge.
Blood-alcohol level 191 milligrams. Take pills but can't sleep. Sleep
at night for two hours. Hell is burning.

Two o'clock. Must have nodded off. Wake up with the dreadful
realisation of what has happened.

After coming out of M87 he immediately writes down interpretations
of his diary in more detail.

He does not remember the journey up to Stockholm, of course.

Apparently one of his best friends, Margareta Strömstedt, meets
them at Arlanda Airport and drives Lone and him out to Huddinge. By
all accounts he was jabbering away and fractious, at times surprisingly
lucid, but slept most of the time in the car. He dimly recalls voices
talking about him and thinks, *like a child*.

Thus he was booked in and handed over.

His blood test indicates a level of 191 milligrams, whereupon the
nurse tells him that the patient who was admitted before him, last week's
intake, called Arne, had had 320 m.g., but told her he'd been unlucky to
end up in M87 and he felt perfectly fine. She seems to suggest with this
that a bad temper and a high blood-alcohol content accompanied by a
lack of self-awareness are normal attributes for inmates.

Evidently he has been brought in himself with a great hullabaloo.
After being registered and handed over, he is temporarily assigned an
examination room with a bed he swears must have been a gynaecology
chair. It would seem they are concerned he will vomit. He is sweating
profusely. Having been forced into the gynae chair without offering
much resistance, he demonstrates independence and normality by
standing up and walking around in the corridor in his pyjamas for hour
after hour.

Apparently he has been subdued but desperate, and begged im-
ploringly for tablets to help him sleep. A male nurse, who says he is
Hungarian, gives him injections of vitamin B. He tries to sleep, but wakes
"with the dreadful realisation of what has happened".

Now he starts to understand. The fall is so great, the abyss so deep.

A week earlier he had given a press conference before the premiere of *The Hour of the Lynx* at the Royal Danish Theatre, the play about the boy prisoner and his red cat.

At that time he was still living in a world of esteem and respect, but now he is very definitely locked inside a loony bin, and in the loony bin he will stay, because those around him have decided this is where he belongs. He is sweating excessively and in the early hours he feels the onset of withdrawal symptoms. It is like lying in an ants' nest. The sheets on the gynaecological bed are twisted into round wet knots, and by seven in the morning his level is down to 81 m.g.

He moans to the nurse, who still maintains he is Hungarian and gently tells him to "remember you're suffering from severe chemical poisoning," but that is no consolation.

Pathetic entry on Monday morning:

Ants crawling all over my body. All the others are in groups, but I'm not allowed. They assume I'm in withdrawal. All that's left for me is ant nests and loneliness. Out with drink. Hungarians. Social disaster.

"Loneliness." That is what it has come to. Sentimentality of the worst kind, and quite unguarded. Not like him. Bad Swedish. But he knows already that he will not be allowed to be like himself anymore.

On Monday morning, however, he becomes furiously active. The staff cannot stop him. He is determined to take part in morning assembly, which includes prayers with readings from the Big Book and A.A. texts. Unaware that he should wear civilian clothes and be dressed, he arrives in blue pyjamas, stands in the circle whilst the others sit on chairs, and listens in confusion to the ritual prayers. It is introduced with a kind of confession; he is instructed to say "Hello, my name is P.O. and I'm an alcoholic."

It is just like Holy Communion.

To take part was an act of confession, and to make a confession without believing was a mortal sin. Here you have to say honestly that you are one of the damned. True confession will be the first step to freedom from sin. He does not feel the agony of sin, just fear, and believes his heart is true but he has been thrown off balance. *For example, if he were to be deported to Norilsk, the Swedish government would intervene on his behalf! He's a well-known author after all!*

If he's not mistaken.

His clothes are wrong, everything else is wrong, he is standing like a sheep in pyjamas and his friends are staring at him in amazement, the very picture of the fall of man. I have toppled out of my normal life like a fallen angel, he thinks, but of course he's wrong.

He has fallen into the *unmistakable* hell of his normal life. The child is imprisoned and cannot talk his way out of here. Cannot beg for freedom or forgiveness; locked in.

Single words are noted down: *awakening, excuses, aggressiveness, gynaecology bed.*

Still nothing in the little notepad about the others, the fifteen friends who watch him in bewilderment and silence. And he does not know yet that they are his friends and that he will come to love them, and that he has now descended into the lowest circle of all, to which they also belong; and without them he will not survive.

The child is imprisoned.

He is ordered to the gynaecology bed to rest, but he is not sinking now, he is in free fall.

There is one thing: it is what he himself regards as his *exceptional insight*, which has for so many years helped him to interpret everything and allowed him to continue drinking with his intellectual self-respect intact. But the screaming little person down there who *still insists he's a kind of human* – what of him?

A problem for him, or rather a collision of his perceptions, now occurs when he faces the Minnesota Method of treatment. He is to be broken down until he reaches the very lowest depths of the awareness he thinks he already possesses. His perceptiveness has been the protective armour that has permitted him to carry on drinking.

But no-one has been able to teach him how to stop.

In short, the idea of the treatment is to spend four or five weeks systematically destroying and humiliating the inmates, so their lies and defence mechanisms are eliminated, until they reach their *lowest point* and then gain an understanding of their own situation, which according to the model should happen on the last day of treatment, so that when they are discharged they slowly rebuild their sense of self by attending A.A. meetings at least twice a week for the rest of their lives, combined with addiction to other chemicals.

That is the model. From a theoretical point of view he thinks he has already reached his nadir, point zero. He is in week one, has sobered up, and every cell of his body rejects annihilation, because he believes that the little that is left is *irreplaceable*. The madly screaming child will not capitulate; otherwise life will not be worth living.

Besides, he feels he is already destroyed. And given that the treatment includes the axiom that intellectual activity is one of life's deceptions and a symptom of illness, conflicts inevitably arise.

Criticism of the Method is a classic symptom of alcoholism. To *question* is fundamentally a *proof* of alcoholism. The worst kind of denial. It prevents submission. In which only defenceless emotion remains, the acceptance that the Leader's way is unconditionally the right way. And that "*only a spiritual conversion can save an alcoholic*".

Perhaps that was the case. Maybe they were right.

Perspicacity had not helped. In fact it had been the validation for continuing. But instinctively he resists. His innermost self says: I do not want to be obliterated.

After just a few days he begins almost subconsciously to view the treatment, or internment, or loony bin, in short the Minnesota Model, as a war zone where the workers are the natural enemy and the in-carcerated comrades are potential allies in *the fight against fascism*.

He does not express it as succinctly as that the first week. But it's bubbling beneath the surface.

He cannot deny his own collapse. But all of his by some chance still functioning intellectual capacity *refuses*. Quite what he is refusing is unclear, but he is intransigent. There is a great deal to distrust.

He accepts that the aim of the treatment is humiliation, but fights against surrender to a *"power greater than his own"*. On the second day he is issued with the Big Book, the text that served as the basis for the Minnesota Model of addiction treatment written in the U.S.A. in the '30s, and material about A.A. He reads. All other reading is forbidden, as are television and radio.

Suddenly he recognises himself and it is a shock. He knew, of course, that Alcoholics Anonymous grew out of the Oxford Group and Moral Rearmament, the only part of this extreme right Christian ideology he has experienced, in fact. His mother had had Bishop Giertz's *The Hammer of God* after all! And had spoken at length about the Four Absolutes of the Oxford Group: *honesty, purity, unselfishness and love*. Wasn't there something unclear about her religious roots? Revivalism or the Oxford Group?

Did it have to mean something?

Since that time several revisions of the Big Book had *cleaned it up*, both linguistically and ideologically, but the brown-tinged ideological origins can still be seen, like a shadow.

It is hard to accept the incessant assurances in the book that the Model is in no way a religious construct. The assertion that religion means nothing steadily intensifies. *"It is just a matter of being willing to believe in a power greater than myself."* Or, later: *"We made a decision to turn our will and our lives over to the care of God as we understood him."*

Perhaps God is not the God of the Bible? There is something strangely ambiguous here. The God constantly being invoked is a Director, who demands submission.

"First of all, we had to quit playing God. It didn't work. Next, we decided

that hereafter in this drama of life, God was going to be our director. He is the Principal; we are His agents. He is the Father and we are His children. Most good ideas are simple, and this concept was the keystone to the new triumphal arch through which we passed to freedom."

He reads the Big Book, the only permitted reading material, intently, and finds the passages more and more curious. *"There is a solution. We have had a deep and effective spiritual experience, which has revolutionised our whole attitude to life, to our fellows and to God."* Or the increasingly clear directive approach to treatment in the A.A. material: *"You have to make these people desperate first. Only then can you begin to use your other medicine, the ethical principles you learned from the Oxford Groups."*

He feels uneasy.

The lies of the alcoholic have to be destroyed, he understands that, but there is something that is not right. It is like being sucked into a maelstrom: the confessions, the disintegration of the patient, the humiliation, the psychological drama of the support groups, the confrontations when the sufferer is surrounded by a circle of fellow-patients and staff and is forced to listen in silence as they recount his behaviour; and everything except submission is seen as sabotage of the treatment.

He is rapidly falling apart. Part of him wants to go along with it, since he knows his intellect and arrogance have not helped him up to now. Part of him does not want to submit.

From every pore he is screaming yes, yes, and no, no. The Oxford Group, Frank Buchman, the four absolutes, and his mother's secret understanding of Bishop Giertz's high church Lutheranism. It was as if our Lord's pitiless tentacles, just like the gigantic octopus that once captured Nautilus and almost crushed Captain Nemo's submarine, had now finally captured him.

And this time the Saviour offers no redemption.

On the second day he is moved into a double room, and on the third into a dormitory with six beds. The management has decided he has to socialise and integrate with the group.

He is glad about that. The group is the only thing preventing him from going insane.

During the twenty-four hours he spends in the double room, his roommate is Jurma, the same name, he notes, as his childhood friend. Jurma is about 185 cm tall, weighs 110 kilos, at least, and speaks bad Swedish. He is admitted on the Monday, severely inebriated, and is very sad. Blood-alcohol content 225 milligrams. He has worked as a grave digger for fifteen years and now his girlfriend wants to finish with him. He is suffering dreadful withdrawal symptoms and begs his roommate to explain the emergency and his craving for alcohol. The latter goes to see the management and asks for some Librium for Jurma; he can vividly recall his own hell of two and half days earlier. It's a no. Jurma has to sweat it out, is given the Big Book and a sheaf of A.A. papers to begin reading.

The papers and the book fall on to the floor. He swears softly, not wishing to cause a disturbance.

He can't, he stutters, he can't bloody read, especially not Swedish, and definitely not the Big Book. Jurma says he is dying for a drink, preferably a strong one. He says he usually drinks moonshine. There's an awful lot of it in Södermalm in Stockholm. His girlfriend has had enough of him.

He can't understand what he's reading and says he's scared he won't be able to get through it. He couldn't read the contract he signed when he was admitted and is afraid he'll be caught out. He is sweating and tossing around in the bed. In the bed next to his, Enquist is more and more furious with the management for not giving Jurma a drink, or at least some Librium. He is almost sure Jurma has come to M87 by mistake; he does not look like the normal privileged patient, the chosen per thousand. He increasingly feels that Jurma has to be protected. He does not know what's good for him and he argues with the management: they have to help Jurma. Librium or Lithium or Rohypnol, or else Jurma will go mad, and he can't read, so what's he supposed to do with the A.A. papers?

He is informed that he should rest, not excite himself, and a psychologist comes to take his blood pressure, but not Jurma's. It is a young psychologist, who says he is twenty-three and has had a summer's experience in a psychiatric clinic. "How are feeling?" Fine. "You're not anxious?" No, I'm fine. "Don't worry about Jurma, just look after yourself, and try to relax." I am relaxed. "You seemed rather agitated back there in the office, are you nervous?" I don't think so.

His blood pressure is normal.

Why are you taking my blood pressure, he asks: is it to exercise your power? The young psychologist, whose name is Thomas, says "Of course not," but with a chilling smile. War has commenced.

On the third day Jurma absconds.

The system has flushed him away as if he were a foreign body. He is surely lost.

And so it begins.

By the end of the first week the management regard him as a cause for concern.

He makes an effort to integrate. And he does integrate. There is camaraderie among the inmates, almost love, which he believes is saving his life. He does not know much about the other fifteen yet, about their backgrounds, their loneliness, their dreams that their torment will fade away, the nights in their anthills, the hell they have been through, their shame, their despairing families and terrified children. But because he has been through all this, and knows that they know, there is an instant sense of fellowship, and with them he can be almost straight, and endure the shame.

Because he knows he is ashamed. If only there was someone in this hell who had more reason to be ashamed than he had! He would take care of that reprobate, like a Benefactor!

*

Was there a problem with the Method? Or with him?

He isn't sure. Perhaps it is mostly in him? He finds that all the inmates have made up their minds the treatment is right and good. It's strange. But because he doubts his own sanity, he decides to conform. However, when he asks them why they are like this, the reason given is that otherwise they would be sent home. Last chance. Everyone is saved. *Say yes or die.*

He is distraught. Furthermore, he suspects the management have concerns about him. He seems almost popular in the group, but he is rebellious, and it is contagious. The young psychologist, who is constantly taking his blood pressure, again asks, "Do you have the impression that you're somehow above our treatment rules?" He pulls himself together and says: No, I'm just the same as all the others. "Next week you'll have to work at fitting in." What do you mean, fitting in? "We'll have to see, but Liljenberg was not very pleased this morning."

They are concerned. The group seems to be having a good time in an alarming way.

In the support group on the morning of the fifth day, when they are all sitting in a circle, feeling scared about who is going to *reflect* first and disclose feelings and preferably burst into tears, the head nurse, who, strangely enough, resembles Nurse Ratched in *One Flew Over the Cuckoo's Nest*, seizes her moment to expose him. She observes that the line of the circle is not even, and that he is sitting very slightly outside the rest of the group.

In an extremely friendly fashion she homes in on his alienation and quite rightly nails him.

"P.O.?" Ye-e-s? "Are you feeling OK?" Great. "That's good, P.O. Can I ask you something . . . are you sitting comfortably?" Ye-e-s??? "You're sitting slightly behind the ring. Do you feel as though you want to be outside the group?" No-o-o . . . "P.O.? Don't you want to move your chair a little closer . . . to the rest of us?" Of course. "How do you feel now?" OK . . . it's just that I've got such long legs that . . . "P.O.?" Ye-e-s . . . "Do you feel you need to be defensive?" What? "Well, you're trying to defend yourself. Can you tell us how you feel now? Do you feel slightly superior to the others in the group?" No-o-o . . . but I've got such long . . . "P.O.?" Ye-e-s . . . "Tell us in your own words how it feels in here now you have joined the group and don't feel superior to it. Don't be defensive, just tell us!" But I've never felt superior to . . . "P.O.?" Ye-e-s . . . "Now you're defending yourself again and you're not opening up to your feelings. You have a problem with your denial, P.O.."

He realises in fury, and in silence, that he has lost this preliminary skirmish, and, what is worse, probably the sympathy of some of his friends.

He could have killed her. The accusation was immense. *He had been too big for his boots.*

Anything at all. Just not this.

It was Kaj who started to call her Nurse Ratched.

It gave them all a sense of self-confidence, because they had seen the film. It was not good for Nurse Ratched's authority though, that was undermined. She had once announced, when questioned, that she had not had a problem with alcohol herself, but had studied the Minnesota Model for a month in the U.S.A. If you had not been an alcoholic yourself, you didn't have any authority; that was the group's feeling.

Besides, it was hard to lie to people who had been down in the gutter.

On the Thursday Nurse Ratched had instructed them for an hour about common ways of hiding alcoholism from those around, and denying it. With a little smile they had hung on her every word and afterwards in the coffee room Kaj had summed it up:

"The mother hen has been teaching the foxes."

They laughed for a long time. These little breaches of trust! He felt in a better mood.

But Kaj was not feeling good. When they showed the film about how liver function is damaged and the liver releases fluid into the stomach so it sticks out grotesquely, Kaj turned white and began to feel ill and asked to leave the room. It was understandable. Kaj's belly was abnormally large, like a basketball, though otherwise he was thin, and he was only thirty-five. They tried to calm him down afterwards with stories of their own, but Kaj was quiet all evening. He said he was scared of dying. But they all were, him as well, even if he sometimes, increasingly, wanted to, just a bit. Though *not at the moment*, because it was war now, and he was not at all paranoid, *he said to himself emphatically*, but he would not be broken.

Better to die, in that case. But unbroken.

On the other hand, his confessions go swimmingly.

This time he actually does have something to confess. He has been collecting them, not for a week, but for several years. Not nearly as difficult as Saturday prayers when he was little and couldn't scrape together a single tiny sin.

Here it's all so easy and it's fun. He does have something to divulge, after all. At the customary point, *Five binges I would rather forget*, he relates with almost literary zeal how he wet himself at Vienna airport. They laugh, and they like him. For a moment they can forget the person in charge, just quietly like one another and tell each other about what has afflicted them. They have affliction in common.

On Saturday he is going to meet his children, who are coming on a family visit and will receive instruction about how he *will have to be treated in future*. He is looking forward to it. He needs to speak to them. They do come, but they are whisked past him into the visitors' room and spend the whole morning being told about the conditions for co-dependent family members. He waits impatiently. He can see them through the glass door and he tries to read their lips, but no sound reaches him. They are taken away; it is something he feels he has experienced before. But at about four Thomas saunters up and says, "I've sent your children home." Stunned, he asks why. Thomas says kindly that, "In our judgement you need peace and quiet and to concentrate on your work in the support group, and the management are a bit disappointed you haven't really tried to loosen up."

He is also informed that he is now completely forbidden to use the telephone and the children have been told not to try to contact him. He suddenly feels seething anger. The game to break him down has reached a new level, he believes.

He says very calmly, "You have reckoned without me."

Later in the evening he sneaks out to the payphone and tries to ring his son, who answers. But in *a voice that is far too measured*, his son appears to take the institution's side, or at least to be sympathetic to their view. And Jenny, he says, thinks the same.

He has to calm down; that is how he interprets the tone, rather than the words. He listens to his son's voice: he is talking like an adult, and the inmate is a child who is liked, but *of necessity* has been robbed of his independence.

He realises that his life is being planned. Everything will work out well, provided his life is arranged by them. His future as a child, and the rules, are being determined now. He suspects the worst. The youngsters have spoken to Lone. It is slightly vague, but they will clearly come down in shifts to Copenhagen and watch over him after he has been discharged. Tickets already booked. Something of that sort.

It has happened so fast.

Only a week ago he was a valid person, even *esteemed*, wasn't that the word? Everything he had done and written had somehow been wiped out. Where did the white elephant go? Respect? Now he has been declared incapable, practically in nappies.

Or was he like this long before?

But things will sort themselves out, as long as he is calm and *works in the support group* and *reflects* and tries to reach his *nadir*.

He has to become someone else.

The earlier version of himself has fallen apart, was wrongly constructed. He certainly wrote good books and plays, but that lifelong deception is just an escape. He is not good enough, and he has to realise that. And in this institution stop thinking and acting as if he *were still that person*, the one who has now failed. Complaints have probably been made because he doesn't quietly read the Big Book in the evenings, which is not true, he does, but not with an open heart. He is mostly chasing after remnants of fascism in it, doesn't want to *take it on board*.

A symptom of the illness.

Now all he has to do is concentrate on *disintegrating*. And not waging terrorist activities against the management.

It was a very bad conversation with his son, which soon came down to his inadequacy in the role of father many years ago; it could be true, probably is. But not just at the moment. In the end he slams down the receiver in a rage after stating that he wants no more telephone calls or contact of any kind with his children.

Now they're taking my children away as well, he thinks, and goes to sit in the kitchen.

One of the staff, Nurse Brita, is having a cup of coffee. She is in her sixties, and, in contrast to Nurse Ratched, has been in the gutter herself, but he throws a tantrum and says they are treating him like a child and taking his own children away from him, and this is fascism, they are all fascists, her included. She sits down heavily on a chair and stares down into her coffee cup in silence. He comes to his senses and apologises. She says very quietly, but he can see her lower lip is trembling, that, "It doesn't matter, it's my job to be called a fascist, I'm used to it."

He goes into the dormitory where the others are already asleep and lies on his back staring at the ceiling, thinking of nothing, but after a while it just churns round and round: *What the hell am I doing?*

On Sunday Anders and Annika come to visit and they all sit in the cafeteria.

He talks frenetically and they listen, but say little. They can see that his life is slipping through his fingers. What can they do? In the evening after Anders and Johan have fallen asleep, Annika, who is a non-con-formist, or was, as he himself once was, offers a little prayer to our Lord for his salvation. He says nothing about the *utmost shame* that has overwhelmed him since the beginning. But they might understand.

They are his best friends, and they are hoping against hope.

It is very cold outside.

He has almost forgotten it is winter, as, together with his friends, he is conveyed in a minibus to his first A.A. meeting. It is the first time he has been out of M87 and he supposes he has been hospitalised, or institutionalised, so it is quite unreal. He has no idea what happens in the world. He would have found his bearings better if he had been in prison for fifteen years and been released, but maybe the feeling is the same.

The A.A. meetings took place in the fire station basement.

There was an oblong table, with chairs. They drank coffee and they began with the usual ritual: "Hello, my name is P.O. and I'm an alco-holic," and then in unison, "Hello P.O.." There were five more from out-side, locals, so to speak. One called Hej-Ove, who was huge, not a good- looking man, a metalworker. He spoke briefly and well and led the meeting with a firm hand. They were all slightly shy at first, but the situation was defused by a small, thin friend, *the Calle Palmér of alcoholism*, he thought, who pressed on and lightened the mood. They were there for an hour.

It was impossible to describe his feelings. But he knew that he was now among people who accepted him for what he was, and they were all in the gutter, and there was no need for anyone to be ashamed. They had gathered in the basement of the fire station to support one another and say to each other *this is how it is*. And there was no-one there to direct them and they could talk together comfortably and quite jokily about how things had been since the last time. And for some it had been close, and one had suffered a relapse and felt fragile, but believed he could recover. And they nodded and told him that shit happens.

And then they read the Serenity Prayer together, the one that goes:

> God, grant me the serenity to accept the things I cannot change,
> The courage to change the things I can
> And the wisdom to know the difference.

It was actually a very fine prayer. How could this relate to his fury? Perhaps it didn't, but he didn't care. He just felt a great sense of peace. And the prayer sounded quite good now, among friends who stuck together, with no hostile presence from the management team. And slowly he was filled with tremendous peace, almost euphoria.

They all found themselves in an underclass, and they held together, and didn't look down on one another, and were not ashamed, and had seen life at its worst. And when they came out into the starry night and the blistering cold, if he had just seen the Northern Lights over Huddinge fire station, it would have been exactly as it was when he was a child and everything was possible.

And when life – back then he believed this *with complete conviction* – would most certainly go well. Not only then, under the Northern Lights, but *in the end* as well. The life you had been allotted by someone, real life, the only life; and you *certainly* would never need to be assigned or try to find a different one, when the first one had been wasted, if that were now the case.

The following day, when the telephone ban had really hit home, one of the nurses came up to him with a handwritten note and a steely, hostile smile, he thought, and gave him a message.

It was Lone who had rung from Copenhagen, with news that his play, *The Hour of the Lynx*, had had its premiere at the Royal Danish Theatre, and it had gone well. The Danish newspapers had been very positive and after the premiere, according to the message she had been unable to deliver personally, so as not to disturb his concentration, the family had had dinner. And they had, according to the messenger, thought of the absent author.

Maybe they had placed an empty chair at the table. Or something. It could have been on another planet than the one with the fire station in Huddinge.

It was the play about the crazy boy in his cell, the boy who was granted a ginger cat. The one he wrote in Paris. And the cat had died, but had risen again, which showed that miracles can happen. And the nurse in the play said a load of nonsense in his scientific way, but it had been a lesson for the female priest and she almost became a believer as a result. And resurrection was possible, and then they had eaten dinner and thought of him.

Yes, him.

If only he had had his own ginger cat, August, here with him, in this state of distress and extreme affliction.

He discovered that in fact it was the same for all the inmates.

The worst part was seeing their family members. When they attended the big confrontation sessions, it was almost unbearable. They had to be brought in, in week three, but first groomed by the management who made them feel anger towards the alcoholic in a public interrogation, in front of everyone, including other families. Then the alcoholic had to sit on a chair in the middle of the floor and his *nearest and dearest* had to face him, one after the other, and relate their worst memories of the way he had been. But, before that happened, the families had to be put through the wringer by the staff, and made to realise that if they weren't *mercilessly truthful* – that was one of the Oxford Group's four absolutes, absolute honesty – they wouldn't be helping him or her hit rock bottom.

Ragnar had entered M87 two weeks before him. As they sat together in the coffee room, he was obviously anxious. The previous week he had had a confrontation and been lambasted twice in the support group, and he had a feeling the management were unhappy with him. He also had a problem with crying. The end of his treatment was approaching and he had not broken down and wept. He thought the management regarded him as a defeat. He was also worried about his brother, whom he had not met for three years. One of the nurses had requested his brother's address, but that had made him uneasy and he had asked why. We're just going to send him some material, the nurse had replied. His brother didn't even know he had been admitted! Bloody awkward. But he had given them his address all the same. Two days later his brother had rung, very upset, having received the same questionnaire as Ragnar's ex-girlfriend, who had definitely not pulled any punches when she filled it in. It was the intimate questions regarding their sex life that were the worst. His brother hadn't filled in that part of the form, at least that was what he maintained on the phone.

But it may be that they described all the most intimate details. And then that would be used in the confrontation in front of everyone else.

The previous Saturday Ragnar had been forced to go through a confrontation session. It was his mother they had brought in. She was seventy-six. He had always had an excellent relationship with his mother; they could talk about everything, including his drinking. Afterwards she told him that the nurses had banged on for ages about how she had to be *frank and truthful*. Otherwise Ragnar would not get well. And he sat there in the middle in absolute silence, sweating. But his mother had not said anything terrible and he had pressed his lips together so he wouldn't cry.

She was so old. Wasn't used to speaking in public.

In the support group meeting the following day the staff had pounced on him. They were disappointed, not only with his mother, who, having promised she would be ruthless, had let them down, but above all with Ragnar himself. He had *frightened her into being kind* by looking angry. "Were you angry with your mother?" they kept nagging him. But he was definitely not angry; he had told her that on the day the telephone ban was lifted. He just felt so bloody sorry for her. The staff had then made an *assessment that was even less satisfactory* and made him attend a reflection session in which all the others had agreed he looked angry, almost as if he had wanted to frighten her into silence. He was hurt by this and now he wondered if he really had looked angry and very nearly scared his mother senseless.

In the end the staff had given up. Because the supervisor had been concerned, he gave him the task of explaining in a letter the reasons he blocked his emotions. If he had not done that, there would have been nothing for him to work on in the fifth week, in pure emotional terms.

But he hadn't blocked his emotions. He believed he may have looked angry, but he had just been scared. He had been so bloody scared.

He had also received an unpleasant letter from his ex-girlfriend, who said that she'd guessed this all along, and there was no way she was going to appear in person and confront him, because to her he was just a big shit-bag, and this confirmed it. He was frightened about what she had written about their sex life. If that was rammed down his throat in the support group he would go mad.

He thought he was regarded as a failure. But he did as much as he could. There were some people who had it worse.

Two of the female patients had been given the third degree in the Thing, Ragnar said; the Thing was the room with prayers and A.A. commandments on the walls. One of them, called K., had been chock-full of lies, you know, and swore that she wasn't an alcoholic, but her husband wanted to be alone for a month to have his way with that bitch she knew about, even though he denied it. Liljenberg had been tough and said she was lying, and then he read out a section from the relatives' form where her spouse said that if she didn't become teetotal he would divorce her straight off. This was such a surprise to her she started blubbing, then the following day some of the people admitted at the same time as her had criticised her and her lies, and it turned quite nasty. Then she had gone around looking depressed, but Ragnar thought she'd had no suspicion about the divorce.

Another of the female patients, someone with five children and very anxious, had been given a make-up ban as well as a telephone ban. That arose because in one of the support groups she had said that clothes boosted her self-confidence. The management thought *that was interesting* and took away her make-up so that she could break down more readily and cry.

They had compared notes in the coffee room. It was easier when you were not alone.

Ragnar supposed there might be some sense in destroying the alcoholic so he hit rock bottom. If you were annihilated in this way, you couldn't lie to yourself. But you would get out in a month. And if you were taken to pieces, and it was cold out there in the real world, at least you were *truthful and didn't lie*; but you had been *taken apart*, and what sort of a human being were you then?

Were you actually a human being?

They were all agreed that finally there was *a bloody good spirit* in the group.

But the confrontation sessions in the third week were sheer hell, when their nearest and dearest had to draw back the veil and expose the last remaining lies, if there were any. A layer of privacy survived among the inmates – in the group they had started to say inmates instead of patients, it sounded harsher, and right – that was never revealed in the internal group meetings.

In particular he remembers the typesetter called Bengt from Söder-tälje.

He was fairly taciturn and shy, in his sixties. His wife had been called in and had been put through the wringer by the staff, psyched up and made to promise to conceal nothing, for her husband's sake, and they were put on two chairs opposite one another, with the onlookers in a large circle around them. It was the first time he had witnessed relatives doing this, and it made him feel almost desperate, thinking, *how is this going to proceed in my case?* The wife had been dreadfully nervous, but also frightened that they would all be disappointed if she wasn't honest. The typesetter from Södertälje sat there, white as a sheet, as Nurse Ratched led the questions. The wife had begun rather hesitantly, her voice shaking and sometimes tearful. But her courage grew and eventually she said that as far as the erotic side of their life was concerned, it had never been good, and in the thirty years they had been married she had never had an orgasm, though she had pretended, but now she wanted to say so.

And Nurse Ratched had praised her for her honesty, and the typesetter from Södertälje, whose face was ashen, had not been allowed to say anything until the obligatory phrases at the end, that he was grateful for her honesty and that this would certainly help him be free from the chemicals that poisoned him.

That was in the morning.

Later he had seen them walking up and down the corridor, for several hours, two undersized figures, moving to and fro, close together and in absolute silence; and then she had to drive home.

Late that evening when he entered the coffee room he found Bengt, staring into his empty coffee cup, doing nothing. He seemed completely inert. And what was there to say? But just as he was about to leave, he heard him mumble something, or sing, as if he were fine-tuning a single sentence. He stopped and heard something he could almost recognise.

The same phrase. Over and over.

Flying snipes . . . seek rest . . . on soft tussocks.

It sounded almost beautiful. He sat down opposite him, but it just continued, time and again. *Flying snipes . . . seek rest . . . on soft tussocks.*

That's good, he said to Bengt, I think I recognise those lines. Is it Harry Martinson?

Bengt looked up then, as if he had only just noticed there was someone in the room, and said, "No, I was a typesetter and it's a memory chant to help me remember the order of the letters."

As if in explanation he repeated the verse that wasn't a poem, but could perhaps function as one, in an emergency, or in case of dire need:

> *Flying snipes*
> *Seek rest*
> *On soft tussocks.*

It is either denial, or defence.

He does not know, but he asks himself. It is as if there is a tiny little kernel deep inside him that holds the integrity he has gathered for fifty-five years, a kind of *self* that will not be crushed and is now desperately fighting against those who say they want to help him, and redirect his life, and change him, and first destroy and then *admonish him* to keep to the right path, kinder and meeker and above all better, and sober; and therefore not the man he was.

A different life. And a different person. With the same name. Perhaps it was the ghost boy his mother had given birth to after they carried her down the stairs and Åke Sehlstedt carried the foot-end; perhaps he would now make an entrance as him, the foetus. Force his way in. Cautioned to keep to the right path. Maybe he was now going to be transformed into the ghost boy, the good one, the nice one, who didn't drink. But first *the essence of his true self* must be destroyed.

How could he not fight to defend his true self?

He starts an admirable campaign, with modest results, to destroy the alcohol addiction treatment carried out in department M87 at Huddinge Hospital, a treatment that is all too rare.

The only one in the public sector in Sweden. He could have sought out bigger enemies, but he is now utterly determined and dangerous. Breaches of integrity are startling. The Legal Rights Foundation in 1979 established protection for the private lives of individuals. And to his delight he finds that according to chapter 5, paragraph 3 of the Penal Code "*anyone passing on information about another person's private affairs that is calculated to cause damage or suffering will be guilty of infringement of privacy and be sentenced to a fine or a prison sentence of up to six months*".

After the detainee had been registered, in his drunken state, he had signed a piece of paper. This now entitled the management to send out an intrusive questionnaire to all and sundry. When he heard that Lone had also received one but had refused to fill it in, he only just managed to hold back his tears.

The answers were then used and read out; it was an obvious case of breach of integrity. He is still furious, and unable to see what he is doing.

This power! And for what?

He defends himself. That is what he is doing. Increasingly desperately, and finally with the statute book.

But what is he defending? And why in such a frenzy?

Maybe because the treatment model he has been subjected to meant that *a new person had to be created*. And, deep down, he must have been quite fond of the old one, with his remarkable mixture of *Idrottsbladet*, Swedish Evangelical Mission and popular socialism. Now it was no longer *good enough*. It was in the Twelve Steps, rattled off five times a day, not to mention banging on about it in the group sessions. Step Four said: "*We made a searching and fearless moral inventory of ourselves*", and personal patterns of thinking were seen as *an obstacle to man's submission to a greater power*, and were thus part of the syndrome.

That was the thing about submission.

Wasn't there a touch of arrogance in his self-defence? Years on the bottle might have made his judgement a little shaky. Desperate assurances that he was good enough; ice-cold mornings without hope, and without illusions. A friend had told him sadly that he was only 70 per cent of himself, even those times he was sober; he had angrily replied that 70 per cent of him was more than 100 per cent of anyone else.

That was what he thought. Not much left now of the humility he had learned.

Or else the sick remnants of that humility had started to spread like a cancer through his lymphatic system. His teammates on M87 gazed in surprise and bewilderment at the battle he was engaging in. He knew they were on his side, but they really didn't know why, and he couldn't explain it to them, and scarcely to himself; no, he could never explain it to himself.

But in the darkness he wanted to defend his life, if indeed it was still a life worth defending.

A new world was now opening up. Maybe it was like the thermal baths and catacombs of Paris. Or was it Naples? He had strolled around Naples, in a previous life. Or was it Paris?

Come to that: he had written so much without knowing the world of catacombs.

On Friday of the second week the conflict between the management and him exploded. It began in the support group.

A very short entry in his diary.

> *They say I'm lying, try to control me, and won't give up. Got up furious, walked out. At five in the afternoon I decide to leave. Can only feel sorrow. Can't sleep at night. Sat with Eigil from four in the morning.*

Eigil was the Norwegian ski jumper who had started drinking. His dad was ambitious and imagined Olympic medals; he hated his father and began running off, and every time he was given a beating. It wasn't clear how old he was when he was so drunk he fell off a platform and a train ran over him and he lost a leg. There would be no medals.

He was ashamed about what happened. His father was ashamed as well. A cripple was nothing to be proud of.

Eigil hadn't seen his father for fuck knows how long, he explained. After he was fitted with an artificial leg he'd been sober for long periods and got a job in a private care firm, started by an electrician who wanted to diversify and called his company "Energy & Care". The county council had outsourced alcohol addiction treatment to this company "Energy & Care". The entrepreneur, who was ahead of his time, took 44,000 kronor a month of taxpayers' money, but it was Eigil who, for a miserly salary, was responsible for the care, and the profit went to "Energy & Care"; he thought it was considerable. His job, the actual care input, was to cycle around among the alcoholics in Söder, artificial leg no object, and stuff an Antabuse into them, otherwise they wouldn't receive their benefits.

Many of these alcoholics were his friends. They begged and implored him to be let off the tablet, but Eigil knew all the tricks and was hard to deceive. There were some who didn't just beg and implore, but who wept as well. To drink your way through an Antabuse was sheer hell, Eigil explained, something that wouldn't be news to his friends here on M87, he thought, and Enquist could corroborate this in any case.

But Eigil couldn't bear stuffing Antabuse into his weeping friends, and "Energy & Care" said that if he cheated, they would be pissed off and stop half his wages. In the end he had had a breakdown and started drinking again and handed in his notice. He'd had one or two bad relapses and ended up here, but when the management had wanted to send a letter to his dad and asked for the address in Oslo, Eigil had been seriously angry *for the first and last time on M87*, and he put a stop to it. He was not going to grant his dad the pleasure of knowing how things had gone.

They sat together for a long time in the coffee room on M87 in Huddinge and finally saw day break, and when their friends woke up and came out, he told them he was going to escape.

They were silent, but they could see he'd made up his mind and there was nothing they could do.

He could not abide being changed back into a child. He despised the motherly tone of the management when they told him what was best.

Was this really an assault?

It was an assault.

You have forfeited your old life and will become a child; that was the way he took it. He was frightened then. Of course he was frightened. The thought of standing before the well-meaning court of his children in the family confrontation session terrified him. He knew how he would react: he would turn to stone, and in that way lose them for ever. And they meant everything.

Better to drink himself to death.

He hated being reduced to a child. Had had enough of it. Why else would he flee?

At about eleven Anneli came up to him and told him the group had had a meeting and decided they wanted to organise a secret meeting in the Thing with him.

They wanted to give him the Last Drop.

It was actually against the rules, because he was going to quit, but it was meant as a sign that they were all on his side, even though things had turned out as they had.

No-one in the management would know.

Normally it was a ceremony held when an inmate was to be discharged after treatment. They all sat in a circle, and then they turned out the lights but kept two candles burning in the centre. The person who was about to be released sat on his chair like a link in the chain. Only inmates. No nurses and no managers. And then the one who was about to go out into the world was given a tiny piece of gold, about three millimetres in diameter. It had to be passed on by everyone in the circle, and stopped with the person who was going to leave.

She or he had to keep it as a symbol of the last drop.

As the drop was passed round the ring, A.A. prayers were said over it, or bits from the Serenity Prayer, but the most important thing was that each person holding the drop should reflect a little on what had happened and what the one being discharged should think about. And so it proceeded round the circle, and the two candles burned, and the sixteen unfortunates spent a long time in whispered accounts of how things had been, and how things ought to be from now on. And it was lovely; in actual fact it was bloody lovely.

Now he was going to receive the Drop, even though he had only been on M87 for two weeks. But his friends had considered the matter and agreed they wanted to do it anyway.

They didn't have a drop, of course, only the management had that, but otherwise they did everything the right way. Toby began, and she reflected on her experiences and hopes, and then passed on an imaginary drop, in just a slight pressure of the hand. And it went round. They'd found the two candles in the kitchen. All sixteen of them sat in the circle, and all of them had something to say to him, and finally it was his turn, the last person in the ring.

And then he said something, quite short, because he was finding it hard to speak, and thanked them for their time together, and said how much he liked them.

And that he would always, always remember them, for as long as he lived.

And it was over.

At about five in the evening he went down to the open square in front of the hospital. He went over the snow-covered square, looked back at the gigantic cubes that made up Huddinge Hospital, and that he was convinced had almost destroyed him. Either he was fleeing something that almost killed him; or he was fleeing the thing that might have saved him. He didn't know what had happened. Perhaps he would never know. Now he was running away, and giving up.

It seemed an eternity since the day he had arrived there, delivered like a package. That's what they said. A child who needed a guiding hand, maybe. But he doesn't remember. He had been given help. Now he was running away. Was in it a different life, or the same one?

The sky was pale red, lower down almost black. Winter in Sweden. No Northern Lights. He had given up. The only thing he could feel now was not anger, it was sorrow.

He had successfully defended his life, and given up.

Two months later he found himself in a hotel room in Brighton, looking out over the illustrious, disintegrating pier, and at the top of a piece of paper wrote "Captain Nemo's Library".

It looked like the title of a novel.

That was all. When he tried to write the novel, nothing happened. He knew what kind of novel it would be, but it was too soon. A book about his mother and Eeva-Lisa and himself.

It was so far away. In time, perhaps? Maybe the time would never come. He didn't know, but you can always hope.

In May he started drinking again.

CHAPTER 15

STARS OVER ICELAND

The questions were the worst thing; he couldn't answer them, not even to himself. In Paris he had started a Question Book. It was easy to begin with; for example, answering the question about the telephone number. Sjön 3, Hjoggböle.

The second question was harder: *When everything began so well, how could it turn out so badly?*

That summer of 1989, everyone was friendly and wondering. Something had happened, on M87. He talked enthusiastically about it, even if he was no longer sure what had happened, or if it had happened, which seemed to be quite tiresome for his friends, who nevertheless showed patient interest.

Everything around him was so calm. It had stopped.

He drank quietly and slowly and slept a great deal.

He hankered after a dog. He could work at times; he wrote a film script about the Åmsele murders for Jan Troell. It was a brutal triple murder; the murderer was called Juha and he decided not to write about the murders themselves, but about something he would call "Young Juha's Childhood". It would end when he was thirteen. That was when everything changed for people like Juha and himself, he imagined. You could get it into your head that all the answers lay in what had happened earlier. But it wasn't true. You could scrutinise those years of innocence, and they remained completely white.

Then he wrote a script about the murders, as expected.

His fear about something inside him dying manifested itself every morning at four o'clock. He yearned for a dog. He saw the sorrow in Lone's eyes, but it made no difference to him. The film was going to be called *Il Capitano*. He ground to a halt. Only the discipline of a sports training camp could save him and the film project now. So he drove up to Vålådalen in order to write, but took drink with him. Gunder Hägg had not done that. By the second night he couldn't sleep and in the darkness he could definitely see bats fluttering against the ceiling in the room. He knew where this was heading: when you saw animals crawling about *it was close*. All the sporting heroes of his childhood had prepared for their feats in these mountains. And he could see creatures on the ceiling. Maybe it was logical. The film's producer Göran Zetterberg came up and he worked with manic fury in the early hours so that he could write *while his lamp was still burning*. It wasn't too bad. The bats seemed to disappear.

He rose early one morning in order to banish the fear and he saw, for the first and only time in his life, a lynx up on the slalom hill. The lynx had sought him out; it stood absolutely still, he waved and said, without making a sound, so as not to frighten it away, *I've written a play about you*. It was remarkable; the lynx stood perfectly still and signalled hope, or at the very least, deep trust. It was incredible what strong signals animals could emit. Just think of August, his ginger cat. And now a lynx was standing, its head raised, observing him closely. The lynx had come down from the mountain to give him a sign.

That was in May. Almost no leaves on the trees.

He had started to make a note of the signs in nature, to see what was about to happen.

Later in the summer dragonflies seemed to be making a return. That could also be viewed as hope. The lynx did not appear very often at all. It was quite obvious it had trust in him. In June they rented a house in the archipelago and his mother came down for a week; he had to pull himself together. There's a photograph of them, they're sitting together on a wooden bench, someone took the picture, and they look really spruced up. He is tanned and she has a comical little hat on her head. The photograph is kind: he's probably drunk, but she has certainly not noticed. If she had detected the smell of drink, she would definitely have said something. Although she didn't know what it smelt like. But she would have said something like, *You haven't been drinking, have you?* She might have reminded him he was once deputy book-keeper in the Band of Hope, or some other vital memory from his youth.

He doesn't recall what they were talking about.

People looking at the two of them in the photograph would certainly have said that they could see an old woman proud of her tanned and successful son. The camera never lies, so there must have been something in that. He cannot remember them being tanned in the '40s, after their summers on Granholmen, later renamed Majaholmen.

One afternoon when he woke up on a sofa in the rented house, Lone had been sitting watching him. Her hair was wet and he asked her if she'd been swimming. "Yes, out to the island," she said. It was a distance of two hundred metres and he said, "You're mad, you could have drowned." She said she could have done, but she didn't care any more and she began to cry, and the next day he was sober. Everyone who asked thought there was a simple answer, or that someone else was responsible. But this was what made him so insanely desperate; there were no answers and nobody to blame but himself. He had directed sharp missives to the board of Huddinge Hospital and to begin with this had pleased him greatly, until he recognised there was something sick about this attempt to destroy M87. The archipelago was beautiful. Everything was perfect. His mother had returned to her home in the north after a week. His wife returned to Copenhagen and her demanding job as director of TV2.

He felt himself *acutely free.*

In late summer another rented cottage in Gryts archipelago. The youngsters rang and could detect things were not right, despite his *clarity and honesty* on the telephone. Mats and his wife Ingrid came down and drove him to Copenhagen and drove back the same night. It was 1,200 kilometres. Incredible how they all worried unnecessarily. All these people taking responsibility for him *quite needlessly*. In September someone from the Royal Danish Theatre rings and asks if he would like to direct *Egmont*. Are they completely insane? He takes a deep breath and says No thank you and at the same time is happy that almost certainly *no-one has noticed a thing*.

The summer ended.

The year 1989 was a turning point in history, but what he remembers best is the stillness, and that he slept a great deal, and that when Mats and Ingrid drove him down to Copenhagen, at the petrol station in Jönköping he saw that the dragonflies had returned; he remembers that he saw the lynx on the mountainside behind the Vålådalen hotel, and that this could be interpreted as a warning sign, like the one when his *ficus benjamina* died, and was replaced, and died, and wasn't replaced again.

That was the summer of 1989.

For a long time no annotations, no diary, no unfinished manuscripts.

Copenhagen was a wonderful city, and all his friends were wonderful, and what use was that to him? He appears to have been admitted to Gentofte Hospital for four days for detoxification, but he doesn't remember. Evidently in an ambulance, because he was found on the floor, and he was barefoot when they took him in, so they had to bring him some shoes when he was discharged. Incredible the things that happen *in haste*. To limit his consumption he now purchased white wine in five-litre boxes in Brugsen, the Danish co-op, cardboard boxes with a tap. He wanted to maintain the principles of his childhood, in other words shop at the co-op, and therefore bought wine boxes at Brugsen. Sudden periods of abstinence of five to eight days; the first twenty-four hours are the worst, as he desperately fights the tingling sensation of ants, but thanks to these recurring intervals he keeps up outward appearances. *Egmont!* What were they thinking of?

Outsiders notice nothing. He is almost completely sure of that. He is to give a speech at a fiftieth birthday party in Stockholm, but forgets the speech and the point and rescues himself elegantly, and *with his customary wit*, by singing a smutty barracks song he learned during military service. It is met with complete silence. No-one laughs. He assumes the audience, made up of the collective Swedish intelligentsia, is enthralled.

When he wakes one night as usual around four at his wife's side, everything is suddenly crystal clear and there is no going back: he thinks he has struggled and endeavoured, and nothing has helped. He sits up in bed, clasps his hands together and prays silently and reproachfully to God, saying, well, I've tried, and I've struggled, but thanks for giving me this chemical poisoning – you've given it to me, wretched God! Why are you punishing me so mercilessly, like you punished Job? And dear, kind God, the one I remember you being, can't you please take this cross from me? Because you need to know, and I'm saying this in my sharpest voice, that if you don't take this sack of potatoes from my shoulders, then I can't answer for what will happen. I'm not going to lower myself through a hole in the ice like Uncle Aron when he wanted to chisel down into Burefjärden but got stuck in the hole. No, I'll take the little Volvo and drive at full speed up to Gilleleje, where I've chosen the cliff into which I'll smash this Volvo, purchased by my wife using her diplomat's discount, but now with Swedish plates so we can park illegally wherever we like in Copenhagen, because the Danish police like Swedish immigrants, but it's a shame for Lone, who has to make do with Danish plates because she bought a new one, and has to park legally. But truly, truly, I say to you, dear God, my desperation is so great now that my patience has run out, and I cannot endure the humiliation you have imposed on me.

But then God, if he existed, spoke to him and said: "Per-Ola, have you not written a book with the title *The March of the Musicians*? Which I have on my bedside table. And have started reading. And in it I have read that the worn-out, sick and wretched animals in this tale, who are called the Town Musicians of Bremen, have begun their last march. And

369

they have said that nothing is hopeless and even the most humiliated have hope. And they have said to each other: *There is always something better than death."*

"I ask you, Per-Ola – have you or have you not written this book?

"Which you unconditionally wanted the masses to read. And in which you decreed that there is always something better than death. And now, in your delusion you are talking about crashing this almost brand-new Volvo into a cliff, with you inside it, and thereby yourself not even complying with what you command the poor book-buying reader to trust in. Are you completely mad?"

And with that God fell silent.

Then he lay down again in the bed, although the sheets were twisted in a knot and wet with perspiration. And thanks to God's injunction, or whoever He was, he was able to go back to sleep one more time.

At regular intervals he seems to be admitted for treatment, or punishment, or storage in a temporary morgue before cremation, he is not sure.

He is floating now, no longer sinking; there is nowhere further down to go. Sometimes he feels the cheerfulness you can feel when you have given up all hope and are now just waiting, yet it is a low-key kind of cheer. His friends remark in wonder that he has become so silent, even when he is in a position to speak.

If only he had had a dog.

For five days he is kept in something that is maybe called the Saint Luke's Foundation. Isn't it a Catholic hospital? It happens after something that might be a black hole. How would he know? He can make out nuns who are friendly and considerate as they change the sweaty sheets. When he asks for a shot of whisky to ease the withdrawal symptoms, an elderly veiled nun arrives with a glass and gives it to him with a radiant smile.

It is quite unbelievable. Someone who is compassionate and understands that he is still some kind of human being.

When he returns home from the nuns he is determined to compose Jean Sibelius' Eighth Symphony.

His mother, who had given a talk about this at college in Umeå, taught him that Sibelius had turned to drink as a young man. With God's help he coped incredibly well for several years. But then the demon drink gained the upper hand. And when he should have been composing his eighth symphony, it all went disastrously wrong, as if he had been driving a Chevrolet while drunk, but couldn't keep it on the road, and ended up in a ditch. And Sibelius had told everyone, including his deeply religious wife, who constantly prayed to our Lord for his salvation, that now he would write the eighth symphony, which would be his last. But Sibelius, according to his mother, had hardly managed to sit down at his composer's desk with pen in hand to write the notes, when the devil drink seized him and he was overwhelmed by a desire for the brandy bottle, and thereafter he became like the grave digger in Selma Lagerlöf's exceptional didactic book *Thy Soul Shall Bear Witness*: in other words, incapable. And year after year the poor Finn sat like a prisoner, chained by a nose ring to the devil, and lacking the ability to write a single note; he could hardly even sit on his composer's chair, but would be found sleeping under the table cradling a brandy bottle.

He could not even sit up straight. Let alone write his Eighth Symphony.

The poor Finn had struggled and struggled with the Eighth Symphony for forty years; and he promised and promised everyone who was waiting, bows at the ready, constantly assuring them that there were just a few notes left to write down, though he had done nothing and the symphony pages were blank.

That was the story of the Eighth Symphony, and Sibelius died after being pissed as a newt for forty years and without realising his life's great ambition.

When he came out after his time with the nuns, the withdrawal symptoms had lessened and he was determined.

He would write his own Eighth Symphony.

Didn't he already have a title, *Captain Nemo's Library*? It was just a question of filling in the rest. He was delighted. For several days he tried to do the filling in, but it was as if it was being erased.

Blank paper. And so he carried on drinking.

There was no justice, and no God, and punishment was eternal, like the mountain in the ocean. And he was shackled, and however hard he fought he could not free himself.

And he could see now with complete certainty that there would never be an Eighth Symphony for him.

What a remarkable year, 1989.

It was as if the world ran amok round him, and he was trapped in a glass bubble. He, who had been *brimming over with politics*, the poison from which he and Frau Meckel had prayed he would be freed. Now alcohol-fuelled sleep settled over him like a cheese dome, and he sat inside either drunk or asleep, and he didn't care. Was this what they had prayed for?

In November the Berlin Wall fell and at that time he was in Prague. He had been there many times, for rehearsals of his plays, but this time it was a theatre conference and no-one could foresee that the twentieth century would near its end that week, and nothing would be the same again. He had tried to control his consumption, and almost succeeded, but when the revolution suddenly became reality, the conference was cancelled. Or converted into a revolutionary committee, or something else. He recalls that he made a speech in a theatre auditorium in support of something. He can't remember what. But he's almost sure it had something to do with the fall of the Wall.

His memory for the most part stopped there, after the speech.

On the following night Wenceslas Square was filled with a hundred thousand people, moving like compressed shadows, *perhaps on their way in a particular direction*. Something had happened, and above all something had to happen. Just here, on this square, that he knew so well. There was a theatre right next to it; he had once followed rehearsals of one of his plays there. Wasn't it *Rainworms*? Or *The Tribades*? If this had been in his previous life, he would have said *now you're right at the centre of it, it's your duty to see*. Once he had thought his job was to move in the tidal currents of the age, and see, and then write what he saw. Like a political being, and with confidence.

But he was not that person. He was someone else.

At that moment the whole of Eastern Europe was set free. At around ten in the evening some Czech friends asked him to go with them to some kind of *secret meeting* with dissidents. But instantly he hears a familiar voice whispering within him, like a swishing sound inside his head, a voice he cannot and dare not contradict. *My friend, remember you are not free, chains hang over your body. The hundred thousand people singing and shouting around you concern you no longer. They will be set free now, but you can never be free. Their lives do not affect someone imprisoned, like you. Do not believe you are one of them. Tonight belongs to them, and above all tomorrow, but neither night nor morrow is yours.*

He stands, helpless, in the midst of the crowds on Wenceslas Square. He believes himself to be at the centre of history. But because he is in chains, he has no part in the lives of those who are about to be freed.

The relentless whispering voice offers a solution. *In your hotel room you have two bottles of wine. Go back there immediately. Let them take you prisoner. Then you can sleep.*

And thus he imprisons himself.

He felt no bitterness towards the guards, the two bottles of cheap Czech red wine, just gratitude and almost love. They had saved him from the world, from the life that had been so privileged, the life that so few others could lead. How many people had been granted the life he had had? But now it was over. He had been captured, and imprisoned, and he had to resign himself.

And actually feel gratitude.

He quietly drank himself into the prison, the place he humbly loved, like loneliness, like hotel-room sleep that soon would be his final reward. He faintly heard the din from history's turning point, November 1989 in Prague; two bottles would be exactly enough; and he loved the two guards' determination and their unrelenting devotion, which once again had saved him from the other life, the one he now had the benefit of giving up.

It didn't work out.

The fugitive from the dungeon or castle in Huddinge continued to sink. He fell and fell, and in the end everyone – not just his despairing wife and his children – could see it wasn't working out. It was not surprising that they sought desperate measures that would almost destroy him.

The second fortress was in Iceland, eighty-five kilometres north of Reykjavik. It was not a castle, nor a prison, just a treatment facility for alcoholics.

He vaguely remembers a flight; he wakes up, he doesn't know where he is going, Lone is sitting beside him, and she tells him they will soon be landing. Where? he asks with tremendous effort. Reykjavik, she replies, and he instantly falls back to sleep. In Iceland there was a treatment centre that would, by using the *unique, internationally acclaimed Minnesota Model*, this time in the private sector, save him from ultimate downfall.

Yes, indeed.

*

But it wasn't working.

They had swept together what was left of him and found a place for him at this treatment facility in Iceland. Apparently he had protested violently. Once again flights had been missed. The same morning as the flight to his detention, he broke a dental bridge, at which he was delighted, thinking he was saved. An emergency appointment destroyed his hope of rescue. The gap in his teeth was as great as the yawning abyss of his fear. Every cell in his body screams in protest at being confined, especially in a treatment facility in Iceland. You could not escape from Iceland. He assumed, in brief moments of lucidity, that that was why they had chosen Iceland.

Lone went with him, and handed him over. He did not appreciate her unbelievable perseverance. He was desperate, and drunk. In the taxi on the eighty-kilometre journey across the pitch-black Icelandic plain he spoke mechanically about absurd plans for novels and fell asleep babbling, only to wake up a few minutes later and stare out into the darkness. He was on his way to Icelandic custody.

He observed, without surprise, that now he was in hell.

It mattered little that the institution was old and worn. They could have shut him in a coal cellar. It was the first week in December, 1989, the great year of revolution was coming to a close, and he would be here for five weeks.

If he survived, he would be let out in January.

Wasn't there a smell of formaldehyde in the building? They must have wasted corpses stored in the freezer. He is informed of his blood-alcohol level on admission, but, contrary to his habit, he forgets and doesn't want to ask again. The dining room is empty; he is placed on a chair and given a sandwich and milk. Lone has left a letter she wrote on the plane. It is beautiful, full of love and optimism. His tongue rolls helplessly in the empty hole where his tooth was. A number of Icelanders pass him going left, and a nurse moves in the opposite direction. It must mean something. He folds up the letter about the bright future. A nurse asks to look at his shoes, retains them, but doesn't comment on their appearance, which baffles him until he understands. The facility is situated in the middle of a gigantic plain and accommo-dates thirty inmates; for a few short hours of daylight the horizon is wonderfully free, if you want to look at it that way. How free could a horizon be? How did a horizon that was free *feel*? The next day was another day. According to the Method, you should take one day at a time and be proud of small goals, in other words, just this one day without the devil drink.

At eleven o'clock the following day he watched, speechless, as the free horizon rolled out before him, and he understood he was imprisoned for good.

He was stuck.

Shoes vanished.

During the short hours of light in the middle of the day he could distinguish, through the small windows, a rather grubby-looking plain, partly covered in snow.

Maybe there was grass under it, or lava. The snow was dirty, and he couldn't understand why. Further away there is a chain of mountains, behind which the pleasant town of Reykjavik might lie; he vaguely remembers a previous visit to Iceland. The year after he was awarded the Nordic Council Literature Prize, he was appointed to the jury. They stay at the Saga Hotel, have lunch with the president, coffee with Laxness at his home. The director at the National Theatre, where his plays were put on, discusses continuing collaboration.

This now seems *beyond all comprehension*. Hidden somewhere in the vast Icelandic darkness maybe. He might have dreamt it; it no longer concerns him at any rate, it involved someone else, doubtless the ghost boy. How is it that he doesn't remember that time he was carried down from upstairs, not yet dead but resting in his mother's womb and Åke Sehlstedt carried the foot-end? This ghost was certainly the one who had a conversation with Vigdis. If that actually took place. A daydream most likely; anyway, he is enclosed in an Icelandic hell, and the snow is dirty, and it is without doubt due to the lava.

He is annoyed about losing the note of his blood-alcohol level. It's definitely a personal record.

He passes into the now familiar schedule of instruction designed to break him down and drive him to hit bottom, and make him see his whole life as a lie.

He is willing to concede everything at once, but it's difficult with the language barrier.

For the most part it all happens in English – he isn't sure, he isn't keeping a diary, he merely adapts, they might be speaking Scandinavian, maybe Icelandic, he doesn't recall – but he remembers keywords from M87 and his reading of the Big Book reasonably well. His fellow inmates are mostly silent. The ones who speak Icelandic play poker all the time. One of them, a bald man in his fifties with a dangerously swollen upper body and tattooed arms, has a face covered in abscesses. It looks dreadful. According to what they say, he's a junkie and has Aids and is expected to die within a year or two, but is kept here at the state's expense because there is a risk of infection.

The bald man never says anything, but stares at the newcomer. Definitely a rapist.

It's logical, at any rate. Detention amongst the damned.

He wakes obediently at seven every morning and knows that he is in hell, but that it will have to come to an end. Whether it will come quickly, or be protracted agony, he doesn't know. In the breaks he stares at the wall. He sums up his life and tries to remember if it has been a life. When he attempts to revive the Benefactor for a short while, he fails completely, and thinks he will burst into tears as a result, but not even that. What would he tell him anyway? His father doesn't need to know about Icelandic HIV-infected rapists who only sit and stare. Better spare him that.

He is described as a compliant inmate.

His passiveness mystifies the management, who have been fore-warned, but he does not have the strength for another conflict. He wraps himself up. All his raw spots will be covered now. With his new and interesting awareness, he sees that this is what you do in hell. And he conceives the main points of a theological etiquette book for lost souls who end up in hell on judgement day. Could be a bestseller. Even if hell is endless, there must still be practical advice and instructions for the damned so they can while away the time. An etiquette book for the untrained. It had helped him in Uppsala, after all.

The rules are strict, unsurprisingly. No telephone calls, no letters, no television, no newspapers, no books. Absolute ban on dropping out of the treatment. Is he really being forcibly restrained? No answer, but it seems as if he shouldn't have asked. Express a desire to get away! Where is your ambition? Besides, how could you run away from this hell, on this endless plain, in December, in Iceland?

But there is something within him that is slowly coming to life. Can he still be angry?

What does he have left of his life?

The evening of the seventh day.

He goes along the corridor, turns, walks restlessly and very slowly back and forth. Like the little couple on M87 after their marriage disintegrated. Faithful even into destruction. *Flying snipes seek rest on soft tussocks.* He goes upstairs to the upper floor and positions himself so he can look out of the window. It is pitch black. Flying snipes seek rest on soft tussocks. He wonders how things turned out for the old typesetter with his little poem. There were no statistics for how things went afterwards. More than they were willing to admit were finished. One of his friends on M87, a very well-known actress, committed suicide two months after she came out.

A shy snipe found no rest. That can happen.

Suddenly, through the window, he can see a tiny glimmer of light in the darkness. It is actually a light. It looks like a window, no, two, as if there were a house in the distance. In the far distance, several kilo-metres away, at least. Strange he hasn't seen it before. He goes down to the ground floor and looks out of the window down there. No light. Absolutely black. He goes up again and once more sees the light from the window far away.

Aha. There is a difference in level. You can only see the light from the upper floor. There is a house out there.

He sits in the coffee room, thinking hard. That night he lies staring at the ceiling for a long time. In the morning he rises at seven and drinks his coffee, vigilant. He looks at his slippers. They have taken the inmates' shoes away from them so they may not go out in the snow.

He follows the teaching with an intense and positive expression and says something perceptive in Swedish to keep them happy. His friends look questioningly at him. They can sense something. The snow is dirty. Darkness falls around two o'clock. You have to take responsibility for your own life some day.

I'll do it tonight.

A few minutes before eleven that night all was quiet. Most people were sleeping, three Icelanders were playing cards in the corridor, among them the monster, and surveillance amounted to one guard in the office.

He had no shoes, but his socks were warm and they would certainly suffice for the two kilometres or so over to the house on the other side of the plain. He did not suffer from cold feet. He went upstairs and made a mental note of the direction. Down on ground level he would hardly be able to see the light for the first kilometre, but he had to take that risk, as well as the risk that the people over there would go to bed and turn off the light. If there were any people there.

He walked slowly up to the door, which he knew was unlocked. He opened it and ran.

*

It was a long time since he had done any training, a very long time; he had done it in his previous life.

The air was cold, maybe minus four, the snow felt dry beneath his socks and he was sure they wouldn't get wet. There was obviously grass under the snow. There was maybe ten centimetres of snow. He was breathing economically, slowed his pace to a jog and after only a hundred metres the lights appeared. He had been right. But the lights seemed immeasurably far away; it might be more than two kilometres, but he had the direction now.

Why couldn't he be free of the demon drink?

He knew exactly how life should be, but he was caught up in dreams and sleep and *ye shall do nothing*. Now he was doing something; he was running. It was something. *Those buggers didn't expect this*, he thought, without making clear to himself whom he meant. He had let himself be locked up and lamented this fact, but there came a point when the moaning had to stop and he had to decide. He had done that now; he was running. It was remarkable, but he wasn't tired. It was like running along a forest path of pine needles and he felt young and light and he had taken a decision, and everything was possible.

Behind him at the facility a car's headlights came on and swung round. The beam cut through the darkness like a searchlight, but it was too late. They couldn't stop him. Flashing from the car; what did they think, that he would turn back?

He was alone in the Icelandic darkness and impossible to capture. They had deceived themselves. He would not let himself be captured.

He ran for about five minutes, and then slowly reduced his speed until he was walking. The lights in front of him were still very far away. He didn't turn round. He suddenly realised how tired he felt. This was a moment when he might have turned to the Benefactor for help, but it seemed no-one like that was available. He was completely alone with himself. It was so bloody unfair. At some time in his life he'd been caught and tied to this poison by a thin cotton thread that grew into a rope and then into an iron chain.

But when did it happen?

He could not identify that point. And if there was a God, he'd be mad at him, because at least he could have told him how his freedom would come about. Not this meaningless hell of being put to the test. And now he was of the firm belief that Job had also been livid about these futile trials, and had written it down in his text. Job was the best one in the Old Testament, he's always thought so.

But not a sound from the ruler of the universe. And he wasn't hard of hearing. But he was utterly alone. That might have been what *the tormenter was counting on*.

He walked increasingly slowly for ten more minutes. Now the lights behind him were also far away and the ones in front of him had not come any nearer. There were clearly stones under the snow, and rocks; he began to stumble and it wasn't as easy to move forward.

When he fell, he stayed on the ground. There was a clear sky that night. The stars were visible, but not the Northern Lights.

Where did they go?

He was suddenly extremely tired.

The cold air felt warm and his feet not nearly as wet as he might have expected. He rolled on to his back and looked up at the starry sky. He measured the Plough, drew a line and found the Pole Star. That was north. Hello there. In his place you might have hoped that *if it was going to happen, let it be now*. Be free, or give up. One of the two. Up above, Flash Gordon was heading for new adventures, and down where he was lying, he was waiting for a message from the stars and the celestial harp: the answer to the question, should he sleep for a while, or should he stand up and try to limp forward into a different life?

If he were not too poisoned, perhaps there would be a different life.

He could have a good rest here in the snow in the heart of Iceland. It was a peaceful way to die, to fall asleep on a plain in Iceland's interior. The finest death he knew of was that of Finn Malmgren, in his grave of ice in the Arctic. He couldn't carry on, so his Italian colleagues took off his warm clothes and dug a grave out of the ice and laid him in it. And then he died, calmly and quietly, according to what was written in the book *From Pole to Pole*. Which could be borrowed from the school library, and of course he did. And the cold water had run over his face and formed a film of ice.

That was how he imagined death. He had always thought of it in that way: frozen over, gazing up to the starry sky. It was beautiful. Not to die of something ridiculous in your stomach. Or in your mother's womb, strangled by your own cord. Maybe that was why he had come to this Icelandic hell. To escape the Model and seek out this place, right in the middle, and be able to lie here a while, for a much-needed rest, his eyes open to the starry heavens and Flash Gordon. Wasn't it the case that in the last moments of dying *you came through*, experienced the wondrous power of the Saviour, received forgiveness and salvation and divine mercy? He lay still and, closing his eyes, he tested it, but he didn't get through. Flash Gordon was in the way.

It felt so pleasant. And yet still something was wrong. It was like a little knot in his stomach that said no. No, no, no. *I've gathered up all the bits of me in order to flee, haven't I, and I've decided not to give up, and no-one will force me to stay in this hell, because they reckoned without Elof's boy, the son of the man who once owned a second-hand Chevrolet; and I'm still some kind of human being, even if all that remains of me are leftover scraps. Didn't I just make this escape because I wanted to protect my humanity up to the very end? And so I need to finish this run in a way that for me is dignified, not standing on a podium receiving a diploma, but not backing out in a dishonourable way; once you've signed up for the cross-country competition and started, it has to be completed, and you have to reach your goal; and that is not to drop out of the race and lie here in the snow and let it bury you.*

He rolled over, got up on to all fours, stood for a moment panting like an old dog and waited for strength. For a second he lost his sense of direction, thought the lights had gone out in the house he was on his way to, then he saw them again.

You are my light. That's what it's all about, none the less.

When he banged on the door he had fallen four more times and was not as presentable as he might have wished, and the man who opened the door pulled it instinctively towards him, but left a crack.

He asked if he could come in and call the police.

The Icelandic family – a teenage son came downstairs in his pyjamas after a while – spoke English. He explained briefly that he wanted to contact the police, he asked them to ring, and said that he'd been unlawfully held at the treatment centre. He was given a cup of coffee and they spoke calmly to one another. He admired their beautiful kitchen.

Evidently the police were not far away, since the institution had apparently raised the alarm. Maybe there they interpreted his breakout as the expression of a desperate desire, not for life, but for death. That was presumably the norm. After only half an hour two police cars arrived and no less than five police officers stormed into the house. He presented his case to them, spoke at length and with composure about the breach of integrity to which he considered he had been subjected, and demanded written assurance from the facility's management that he had the immediate right to return to Sweden.

It was not a slip of the tongue. He meant Sweden.

The chief of police listened in bewilderment, then turned to the father of the family and said in English, "Well, he seems very intelligent, at least."

Then he suddenly started to sob, but pulled himself quickly together. He couldn't cope with kindness. It was too much.

At two in the morning someone came as an emissary from the facility and delivered the requested assurance that he had the immediate right to cut short his treatment, provided somebody could accompany him on his journey home. Who? He sat in silence for a while.

That was the question.

The following day he contacted Göran Zetterberg, the producer of the film *Il Capitano*. He arrived on the plane from Stockholm three days later and got him out; they took a taxi to the airport. Göran had asked, "Where do you want to go now?" And he had answered, "What do you mean? I want to go home." And Göran had said, "And where's that?" And paid the taxi.

He has to thank many people for many things. He doesn't. He believes, or knows, that once he starts to thank them, he is lost.

That was the last time he was in Iceland. He had fled one night to a house with a family, and they had telephoned the police; then he had shaken the hands of the family's three now exhausted members and thanked them for the coffee.

He was driven by police escort back to the facility.

It was his second escape attempt. Had he been successful? He had protected himself. As a greeting to his friends in damnation he mumbled *flying snipes seek rest on soft tussocks* on the short journey back to the institution, where he arrived at four in the morning. The Icelandic police officers observed him in silence.

He felt excessively calm, and frozen.

He returned not to Sweden, but to Copenhagen, everything in his life clear and keenly apparent. People regarded him with astonishment, perhaps with fear. People heard about what had happened.

Where had this ferocious desire for life come from? Or had it been a desire for death?

He could no longer figure out his life or his friends. The world was full of enemies who wished him well. The words they spoke were light and beautiful and fell clanging to the ground.

On New Year's Eve only one glass of champagne, or at the most a couple.

CHAPTER 16

THE RETURN OF THE RED FOX

They came to him and said: You can't fool us. You're trying to commit suicide. You *want* to die.

But damn it, there must be nicer ways of topping yourself. Not this dirty, drawn-out, sweaty and humiliating way. To expose yourself and everyone you love to this shit, to lie in the swarming ants, crawling and stinging, the agony that never eases. The contempt. Not *hack* life off, but *scrape it off* with a rasp, slowly, as painfully as possible. You're lying in an ice hole and fighting like a beast to come up and they stand up there and say anxiously: *But you want to die.*

Actually he wanted to live. And he clawed frantically at the edge of the ice to get back up.

You want to die. Go to hell. He wanted to live.

By the middle of January 1990 it was worse than ever. He was aware of it himself and offered no resistance.

Lone, unbelievably persistent, knew a woman who was the head of a treatment centre in North Zealand. She was called Sanne. Sanne promised to find a place for him as a matter of urgency. It happened quickly. She was to collect him herself the following morning.

In the '70s Sanne had been a Danish television star and newsreader and regarded as very beautiful and talented; but when she started drinking, everything fell apart and she went up to over one hundred kilos. She had subsequently rescued herself and was now the head of Kongsdal, the treatment centre located adjacent to Fredensborg Palace, where

Struensee, the German physician, began his love affair with Caroline Mathilde, and it all ended on the scaffold.

Sanne arrived promptly at seven in the morning. She was very efficient, they got him up out of bed, dressed him and put him on a chair in the hall, and *he offered no resistance*.

He tried to put his shoes on himself, but failed.

Sanne sat on the floor and put his shoes on for him. Lone said, "He wants to have his word processor and wants to be able to ring me whenever he needs to, and I think both of these are important, or he'll only run away again." And Sanne, who was sitting on the floor and tying his laces, just said, "Well, that's completely against the rules, but I'm the boss and make the decisions, so that's what we'll do."

Lone brought his Toshiba. She put it on his lap, as if it were a puppy.

He wasn't sober – his blood-alcohol level would be a record 195 milligrams on admittance, but he would remember the moment that morning when Sanne sat on the floor and put his shoes on for him and Lone brought his word processor. Then Sanne put him in the little Citroën and fastened his safety belt and drove northwards, along Kongevejen, towards Kongsdal. It was the third attempt to save his life.

Date and time: 6 February 1990, eight o'clock in the morning.

He wanted to live. He knew that he didn't want to chisel a hole in the ice on Bjurefjärden with a sack of potatoes on his back, like Uncle Aron. But he didn't know that he was being driven into a different life.

It was the same Model, neither better nor worse, the same schedule of treatment, the same Big Book, the same visions as in M87, and probably in Iceland, if he'd understood anything there at all.

And yet everything was completely different.

There was something *Danish* about it, something warmer, as if they had breathed on the icy film and the person's face had reappeared, self-respect intact, but without the lies. It was as if Sanne's determined tone that morning when she swiftly changed the rules, put his shoes on for him, and drove him up to Kongsdal, permeated the entire time he was there.

It was a good time. Good friends. They stuck together, but not in opposition to the management. And what happened there was something other than the Method.

Some people were always finished off.

One of his friends, a woman in her forties from Hellerup, took her own life a month after she came out. He had met her husband and teenage daughters, a good, loyal family who did their bit, but she slit her wrists in the bath. It was worse for women who ended up in the gutter. Double the shame. Or so they said.

And some *could not be reached*.

At the beginning of the second week a thirty-year-old man was admitted and was instantly surrounded by rumour; it was announced that he held the Danish record of 715 milligrams. Medically impossible, but true. The friends joked about it at first; it was impossible, what a tall story, even if, as they said, he had been unconscious for three days in Copenhagen University Hospital and had three blood transfusions. But then Sanne reported that his blood-alcohol level when he was admitted to Kongsdal was in fact 515 milligrams.

And he was not unconscious.

Sanne had asked him to keep an eye on the record-holder for a few hours the first night.

It was so different now; because very little time at Kongsdal was devoted to destroying inmates, and driving them to hit bottom, there was time for them to take care of each other. The boy – he looked like a boy – lay sweating and fighting his way through the ants, burbling his opinions and recounting fragments of his life. He was a bus driver, on principle drank only sherry, and weighed just sixty-five kilos. He wanted to go home. He said he didn't intend to stay. Two days after he was admitted his parents arrived, in tears. They were a short, elderly couple who could only weep and not understand. Because he felt some kind of responsibility for the record-holder, and Sanne had asked him, he tried to tell the parents that life could be merciful, in the end, and that there was compassion. They did not appear to hold out much hope, but the father sat and held his son's right hand, as if it were still possible.

He gave advice! As if he could give them an answer when he had no answers to give himself. And yet he tried. That was the ethos at Kongsdal; after a week or two, inmates would give advice to those in the greatest distress.

After three days the record-holder could walk, albeit with faltering steps.

He was so thin. He had stopped speaking, kept quiet. In the therapy groups he was always *the silent one*. He had only spoken on that first night, in the slurring account of his life to the Swede, who stayed by him the whole night and told him that he belonged in the gutter too.

He absconded after eight days. He must have caught the bus.

He received a telephone call from his daughter, Jenny, which he took in the office. She said that she admired him, because he was trying again. And even if it didn't work this time, she still admired him *because he was trying*.

Sometimes one word can be the right word, even if it doesn't sound remarkable. His daughter admired him.

It was almost too much for him.

He replaced the receiver and said to the people in the office, who were looking at him questioningly, that it was nothing.

He had made a decision when he was lying in the snow in Iceland.

But how to do it?

He had failed so many times. He was clawing at the edge of the ice, but how long could he hold on?

On the fifth night at about ten he brought out his Toshiba before he went to bed.

They had double rooms, and he shared with a 75-year-old farmer from Jutland, who weighed about a hundred and fifty kilos, and whom they therefore called His Lordship. Each night he fell instantly to sleep and snored loudly all night, but it made no difference, the following morning he was taciturn and morose and complained, "I hardly slept a wink last night, I couldn't sleep." Maybe it was true. Who knows what dreadful dreams he dreamt?

But on the fifth night, accompanied by His Lordship's snores, he started to write *Captain Nemo's Library*. He had the title, from that week in Brighton. It stood in isolation on a page. Nothing else.

And suddenly it came so easily. He wrote and wrote, night after night, the novel about Eeva-Lisa and his mother and himself and the changeling and the ghost boy. Suddenly he could write. He had thought his drinking had destroyed his ability to write. That it had gone, for ever, but now he could feel that he was writing as he did before; it was a miracle.

And when he realised this, he suddenly knew. He had been saved.

There was no sense in it. But what sense was there in anything that had happened? During his month at Kongsdal he wrote the first third of the book. It was a book about resurrection. And when he had understood it and knew he was going to write again, he was given another life.

February 1990. Eighteen years ago.

Since then he has not drunk a drop.

What was he going to call it? A miracle?

On the last day at Kongsdal, when he was given the Last Drop by his friends and they all wept and embraced each other, he told them *what he was going to call himself*.

He was going to call himself an abstainer. It surprised them, that is, the name itself, because part of the Method was to call yourself a recovering alcoholic. But since they all loved and appreciated one another, and knew there was only a tiny unbreakable remnant of humanity inside them that could successfully cope with resurrection, and that therefore you had the right to choose your own designation, they responded to his decision with respect.

He had come up with it one night when he shut down his Toshiba, and His Lordship was snoring, and he had still not fallen asleep.

Hadn't he been admitted as a member of the junior section of the Blue Ribbon Association, the Band of Hope? A temperance society for children, in Sjön moreover, under the presidency of primary school-teacher Maja Enquist. When he was elected as an eight-year-old, hadn't he sworn a *lifelong pledge*? And after only six months he had been entrusted with his first political task, as deputy book-keeper for the section, which consisted of thirteen members. He had asked his mother if this wasn't a rather meagre task, he could be the secretary or vice president; but she had explained that as he was the teacher's son, she had to make sure there was no favouritism, or people would start talk-ing. He would have excellent opportunities to advance, she said, if he didn't break his promise.

That was where he started. To be sure, there had been a long hiatus, and to a certain extent he had broken his promise of total abstinence. But to his knowledge he had not been expelled. And there was still time to climb the ladder of trust, on the first step of which he stood.

It was not too late. And he was still a member of Sjön's Band of Hope, a total abstainer.

When *Captain Nemo's Library* came out in the autumn of 1991, he said it was the last novel he would write.

Very stupid. But he really thought it was. The circumstances were so special, from the turning point that night in the Icelandic snow, to the moment he realised he could still write, and that the book would save his life.

But after *Captain Nemo's Library* came the collection of essays, *The Cartographers*, and then the novels *The Royal Physician's Visit* and *Lewi's Journey* and *The Book about Blanche and Marie*, and the children's book

The Mountain of the Three Caves, and four plays for the theatre. It was as if something that had been sealed up for many years suddenly opened. It wouldn't stop. He just kept writing.

And then this book, which is at last finished.

Was it really the case that *Nemo* saved his life?

He was not sure what had been his real life. He touched on some of it, not all. Was it wise, anyway, to turn round, *like Lot's wife*? Should he sit, like his mother did once, for a whole summer on the beach on Granholmen and look out over the water? Or lose himself in a green house? What could he pick out as *real*, in the strange life he had lived?

And understand why he had finally been saved.

He kept on writing. His Lordship's loud snores sent him to sleep and he dreamt of a different life. Many times he fell asleep with the Toshiba on his stomach, the funny brownish-red light like a lamp in the darkness.

You are my light.

No Benefactor.

You had to stand on your own two feet, and try to walk.

Was that it, was that how it happened, was it really the whole story?

One night the elderly minor primary schoolteacher came to him again. She was the one he had once met on the forest path, before the junior athletics championships at Örjansvall, and who he decided was Jesus disguised as a minor primary schoolteacher.

His Lordship's snores were gentler now, almost human, and she came to him again. She approached him on the path below Bensberget, the one that led to the Dead Cats' Grotto, and she stopped and clapped her hands together and said, "My word, if it isn't Per-Ola! What are you doing here?" He told her he had become a writer. "My word! Isn't it difficult?" she asked, and he confirmed it was. He told her what it was like to write, how hard it was. Though it was worse not to be able to. But now he was trying to write a novel called *Captain Nemo's Library*. "A novel," she said, "you're not writing any bad words, I hope, with people swearing in it." And he assured her no bad words would appear, and the people in it wouldn't swear, because he'd promised Maja. And she asked him, "Well, what's the book about?"

This was the difficult bit. But he must not hesitate, even if it felt like boasting.

And he has to answer: "About resurrection."

Then the face of the minor primary schoolteacher, whose name he had forgotten, would brighten and she would say, "Well, I shall pray for you that it's a good novel."

About resurrection. And she would pray for him. And then he was convinced, in truth, that he would finish the book. It would be about resurrection. And have the title *Captain Nemo's Library*. The book about Eeva-Lisa and himself and his mother and the ghost boy and the Benefactor and Sjön and everything. It would tie together the last of his old life and the first of the different life he had received as a gift.

And he knew he had been saved.

PER OLOV ENQUIST was born in 1934 in a small village in Norrland, the northernmost part of Sweden. He is one of Sweden's leading contemporary writers, both as a novelist and a playwright. He has twice won the August Prize for fiction, the most prestigious Swedish literary prize, and was awarded the *Independent* Foreign Fiction Prize for *The Visit of the Royal Physician*.

DEBORAH BRAGAN-TURNER's translations include *Breathless* by Anne Swärd, *The Gravity of Love* by Sara Stridsberg and Per Olov Enquist's *The Parable Book*.

Per Olov Enquist

THE PARABLE BOOK

Translated from the Swedish by Deborah Bragan-Turner

Sweden, 1949. A boy of 15, cutting across a garden, chances upon a woman
of 51. What ensues is cataclysmic, life-altering. All the more because it cannot
be spoken of. Can it never be spoken of?

Looking back in late old age at an encounter that transformed him suddenly
yet utterly, P.O. Enquist, a titan of Swedish letters, has decided to "come out"
— but in ways entirely novel and unexpected. He has written the book that
smoldered unwritten within him his entire life. The book he had always seen
as the one he could not write.

This poignant memoir of love as a religious experience — as a modern form
of the Resurrection — is also a deeply felt reflection on the transitoriness of
friendship, the fraught nature of family relationships, and
the importance of giving voice to what cannot be forgotten.

This thoughtful book about the central difficulties of life is, in its own way, a
parable as hauntingly intense as any Bergman film.

MACLEHOSE PRESS

www.maclehosepress.com
Subscribe to our newsletter

Per Olov Enquist

THE VISIT OF THE
ROYAL PHYSICIAN

Translated from the Swedish by Tina Nunnally

It is the 1760s, the height of the Enlightenment, a time of great promise and transformation across Europe, but in the state of Denmark something is rotten. The young king, Christian VII, is a half-wit.

His queen, the English princess Caroline Mathilde, has fallen in love his most trusted advisor, the court physician, Struensee, who is engaged in a bitter ideological battle with the head of the diplomatic corps, Guldberg.

Gulberg, a cold-blooded religious fanatic, is determined too annihilate the Enlightenment ideals — which threaten to improve the lot of the peasantry and to support freedom of the press — that Struensee is introducing to Denmark.

Whoever prevails will not only control the king but the nation state. The victor will impress his legacy on the kingdom: either Struensee's free-thinking principles or the repressive proscriptions of Guldberg.

MACLEHOSE PRESS

www.maclehosepress.com

Subscribe to our newsletter